THE SEIGE OF STERNZ

Port Carin
Tarium
Lone Bay
Tarium
Sea of Kings
Bridge Sorrows
Fincastle
Sterling River
Bakea
Sternz
Broken Point
T Cedar Town
Redoak
Crixaria
Ea
Was
Roughstone
Roughstone Mountains
Xanica
Brooksville
Vetin
Helahm
Lewisburg
Schelm
Rockport
Kirnton
Hoiduhn
Malgen

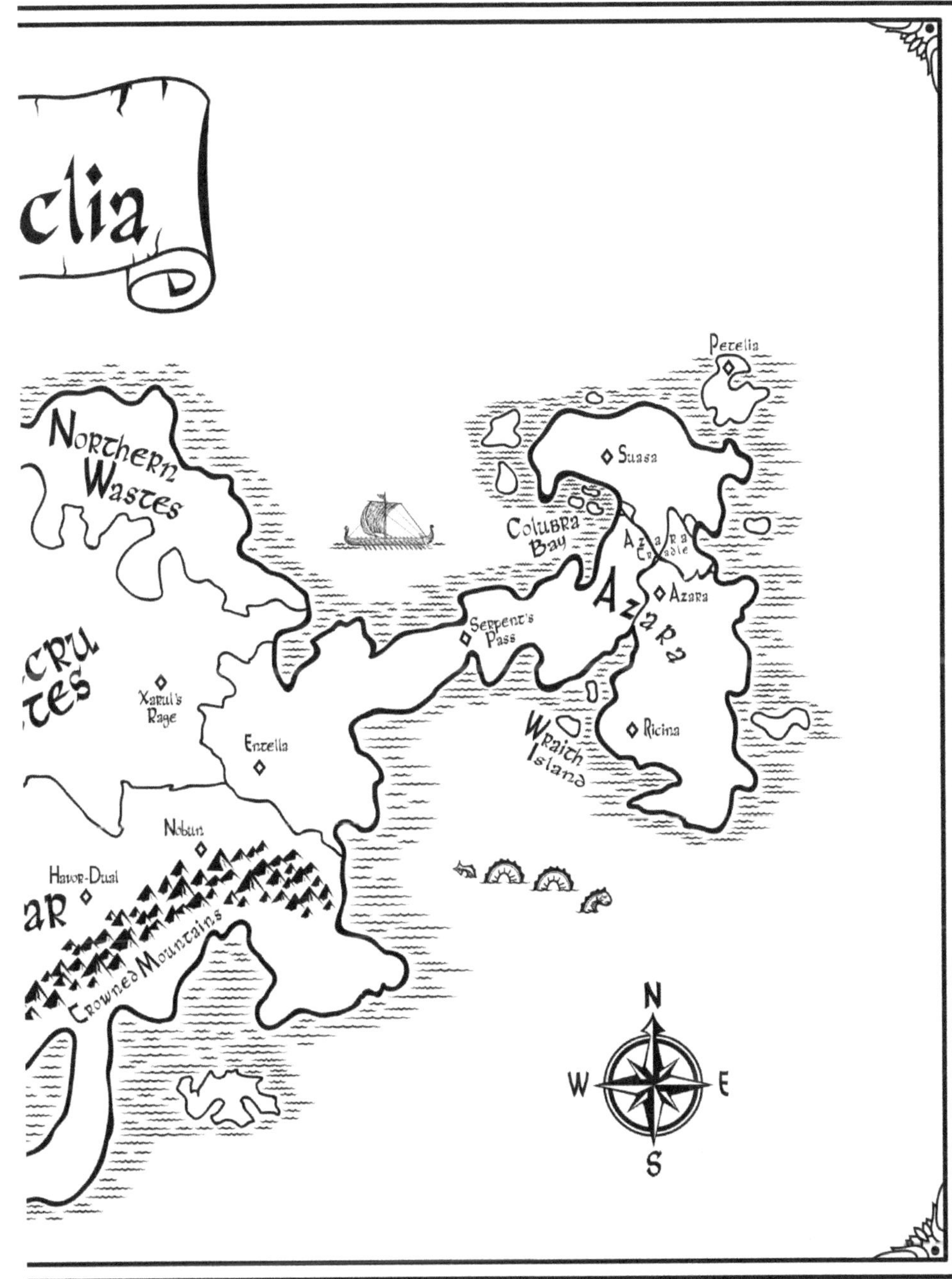
clia
Petelia
Northern Wastes
Suasa
Colubra Bay
Azara Cradle
Azara
Crutes
Azara
Xarul's Rage
Serpent's Pass
Entella
Ricina
Wraith Island
Nobun
Havor-Dual
ar
Crowned Mountains
N
W E
S

The Siege of Sternz
Copyright © 2018
Luther Salyers

Cover art by Reuben Lane
Map design by Aaron Drexler
Cover design by Jonathan Grisham for Grisham Designs

Published by WordCrafts Press
Cody, Wyoming 82414
www.wordcrafts.net

The Unbroken
Book 1

THE SIEGE OF STERNZ

Luther Salyers

WordCrafts

Day One

1

“This is suicide!” King Dylenn slammed his fist on the table.

Low burning candles provided the only light in the large stone room. Embers in the fireplace were all that remained of the once warm and comforting fire. General Izak, resplendent in his Crixarian chainmail armor and purple surcoat, winced from his position on the opposite side of the massive oak table. “I have been your general for more than 30 years,” he replied. “I know this plan sounds foolhardy, even self-destructive. But trust me. It is our best option.”

Dylenn was not convinced. “The war has raged for 15 years. We’ve always been able to hold them back. Why should we now allow them to besiege our capitol?”

Izak looked down at a map of Aclia on the table. He pointed to the Crixarian and Xanican border and responded, “My King, the new Vicar of the Isle of Tarium, Matthew Wickman, has promised to come to our aid. If we can manage to hold the Elven army here at Sternz, we have a chance of dealing the elves a blow from which they shall not recover anytime soon, allowing us to retake lost ground.”

“The Vicar could be lying! Vicar John never helped us because he didn’t want to risk losing the elves as trade partners. He was more worried about losing money than he was about helping his fellow humans.”

“True,” Izak replied. “But Vicar Matthew is different. He is personally leading his army here, and with his army's aid we can win."

"But why here; why Sternz?" Dylenn asked. "Can we not just attack the Elven army out in the field without risking the capitol of Crixaria?"

Izak allowed his finger to roam across the open field on the map and come to rest against the walls of Sternz. He blew out a resigned breath. "We are outnumbered three to one. A battle in the open field would be suicide." The old general raised his eyes to meet those of his king. "But here, at Sternz, we have the most defensible city on the continent. Its outer walls are sturdy and our inner walls have never been breached, but if the elves manage to do so, we have 75,000 battle-tested soldiers sworn to defend our walls from 225,000 elves. These are loyal troops from Crixaria and volunteers from the other three human kingdoms. The city will not fall. I promise you that. We can hold… at least until Vicar Matthew's army reaches us."

"Outnumbered three to one," The king appeared suddenly very tired. He gazed at the map, hoping, wishing some other answer would present itself. None did. He shook his head. "It's not the city they want, you know."

Izak remained silent and let Dylenn continue even though he already knew what this was about.

"Kaia. My daughter. She is still the only non-elf to be born with the ability to use magic. Her very existence is an abomination to the elves' religion. They will stop at nothing to destroy her. You know that."

Izak nodded. He *did* know that.

"Three to one," Dylenn repeated in a dull whisper. "How long can we hold out against such odds? They butchered their way through the kingdom of Xanica in less than a month. It was a massacre."

Izak's heavy eyes turned back to the map of Aclia, "They only massacred the first seven Xanican villages, and they have not massacred any of ours. Xanica fell because it had no warning. The elves just showed up and launched a surprise attack before Xanica could mount a defense. The war was over before it even began. We may have fewer in numbers, but our walls will more than make up for that disadvantage."

"They will not stop until my daughter is dead, and I don't see how trapping her inside this city will help," Dylenn's grip grew tighter on the table edges.

Izak traced his finger on the map back to Sternz. "The elves will go where Kaia is, and right now that is here. My scouts reported last night that the Elven army is closer than we had hoped. They have marched through the past two nights and have already crossed Sterling River. They could be at our eastern outer wall in a few hours." His eyes met Dylenn's, "I need your answer, Sire. Shall we defend the city and hold out until the Vicar arrives; or do you want to risk fleeing the city and being caught out in the open?"

Dylenn stared with weary eyes at Izak as he ground his teeth trying to hold back his frustration, "Why didn't you tell me? If they could be here today, why haven't you alerted the city? We should be preparing!"

Izak ignored Dylenn's question and pressed on, "Our defenses are nearly complete. We would gain nothing if we alerted the city. Our soldiers and the citizens would panic. The wasted energy would only harm us in the long run."

Dylenn paused in deep thought for a moment, noticing the countenance of his long-time friend. The war had taken its toll on Izak. His youthfulness had long since disappeared and his sense of responsibility showed on his face. Only a few years ago he had a full head of black hair that complemented his ebony skin. Now that hair was gone; only a scruffy beard remained. But Dylenn trusted Izak. He had fended off the elves for this long; he could do it again. "Give the order," Dylenn said. "We will defend the city at all costs and pray to the One that the Vicar shows up in time."

Izak breathed a small sigh of relief. *Just one more time,* he thought. *Just one more battle to win and the war would be over.* He bowed his head to the king, then turned and marched to the heavy wooden door. He opened it and waited for his eyes to adjust to the sunlight before striding into to the long stone hallway. From the open arched windows, the light shone into the hallway gleaming off the armor of 20 Crixarian officers. The men and women all stood at attention as they saw Izak. "Go to your battle stations," Izak ordered. "Prepare the city for a siege. Not you Vernon," he pointed to a handsome, well-built man with short black hair, brown eyes and a scruffy tan face. "You come with me to the King."

Vernon nodded his head, then followed Izak back into the darkened room. Sweat beaded on the young officer's brow as he came face to face with King Dylenn for the first time. Vernon bowed his head fighting to control the urge to fidget. He knew what this was about. Izak had already hinted as much. But didn't know if he was ready.

Izak intoned formally, "My King, this is Vernon Regnier. He is my finest officer and I believe he should lead the new squad we discussed."

Dylenn sized Vernon up from across the room. "How old are you, Vernon?"

Vernon met Dylenn's gaze. "I am 27 years, my King."

"Have you been in the army long?"

"I joined when I was 20. Since I am of noble birth, I have been an officer since the first day I joined." Vernon's eyes never left the king's.

Dylenn began to grind his teeth again. He stroked his red beard and fixed Izak with an unconvinced glare. "You're trusting the fate of the capitol to this..." his mouth twisted, "*young* man who has been an officer for *seven years*? There are other more experienced officers. House Regnier has been a loyal noble house for centuries, but there are other houses, more noble, with greater wealth and higher status, who might look with disfavor on such a choice, don't you think?"

Izak placed his hand on Vernon's shoulder. "My King, Vernon is one of my best officers. Yes, there are wealthier and more experienced officers, but I trust this man. I would rather put this man, whom I trust, in charge of this squad, rather than someone who is just there to please others. You asked for my recommendation. I would trust Vernon with my life."

Dylenn nodded, his decision made. He beckoned Vernon to the map, and pointed to a single spot—Sternz. "Very well. Vernon, do you know exactly what your squad will do and who you want by your side?"

Vernon shot a nervous glance at Izak. He had given this plenty of thought, but he did not think they would agree with his choices.

"Yes, my King.," Vernon answered. My squad will be a small unit consisting of four members—some of Sternz's finest warriors. We are to serve as mobile support during battle, and to prepare for, shall we say, *unconventional* missions, as needed. With your permission, my team will include Konar Qal from the Eacru Wastes, Kassandra Verbeck from Vetin, and finally the warrior Liam."

Dylenn's brow creased and he stroked his beard again as he pondered the names. "Very interesting choices," he said. "I understand your choice for Kassandra, she is of a noble house from Vetin and a deadly archer from what I've heard, but your other two choices are puzzling me. Konar Qal is well-known to me, but he is an orc, and orcs do not have the best reputation for loyalty to humans. Liam may be a human, but I fear he is just as much or even more of a risk as the orc. He is formidable on the battlefield, but all my reports say he cannot be controlled, simply ignoring orders he does not wish to follow. We know nothing of his house or lineage, not even his surname. And then there is the matter of his—wolf."

Izak stepped in. "With due respect my King, I trust Vernon's judgment. Let Vernon worry about his squad, and let us worry about the siege and the elves."

Dylenn moved around the table, and stood mere inches from the young officer. The strain showed in his eyes, but his voice was firm. "Izak's trust and respect are two very hard things to earn. It seems you have both. If Izak trusts you, then so do I." Dylenn poked his finger into Vernon's chest. "Don't let my city fall."

Vernon nodded, shocked at what he was hearing. "My King, I will not."

"Go now Vernon," Izak commanded. "Gather your squad. We will need you all very soon."

Vernon bowed his head, turned and left. Dylenn and Izak watched him hurry down the hallway. Dylenn muttered, "I pray for all our sakes that Vicar Matthew will arrive soon. I don't understand how four people can make that big of a difference and I do not wish for more people to die than is necessary."

Izak looked at a worried Dylenn. The war had aged him too, he was now much thicker around the middle and his red hair was thinning and streaks of grey appeared in his beard. He put his hand on his king's shoulder. "Have faith, my King. Not only in our god, the One, but also in the men and women fighting. This squad will become a group that our troops can rally behind. We can and will succeed in this endeavor."

"Thank you Izak," Dylenn replied. "You have been my most loyal friend and General for all these years. A king could not ask for anyone better to lead us during this solemn time. Now, if you will excuse me, I wish to spend time with my wife and daughters."

Izak bowed his head and said, "Yes my King, we will not fail."

Once Dylenn was out of sight, Izak turned back to the map. Alone, he rested both hands on the table and let his guard down. His hands shook and his knees began to buckle. "May the One help us," he prayed.

2

As the morning sun beamed off his chest, Vernon walked out of the main entrance of the citadel, through two imposing, ten-foot tall wooden doors. Dressed in his officer's armor ,with his longsword sheathed on his left hip and his steel kite shield in his left hand, he gazed upon the massive citadel. The implacable stone stronghold stood gleaming in the morning sun. Guards patrolled the top of the towers while the staff cleaned the many balconies that allowed a viewing of the area below.

Vernon resumed his walk down the stone road into the rich, upper district of Sternz, with its large hewn-stone buildings topped with wooden roofs. Common Crixarian soldiers dressed in heavy layered, brown cotton jackets and purple-dyed cotton pants to match the royal Allister family colors, saluted as he passed.

The beautiful yellow sunrise brought with it a warm, gentle breeze. While walking down the hill past a row of stone houses Vernon spotted a familiar elderly woman with a mobile stand and a foldable sign on each side that read, *Elsa's Bakery.* With a smile growing on his face, he approached the stand, allowing the aromas of sugary sweets to wash over him, and tickle wonderful childhood memories from his past.

The old woman with long, greying hair smiled ear to ear when she spotted him. "By the One, look who it is! The last time I saw you, you were only as tall as my shoulders. Now look at you. A grown, handsome man, and an officer in our King's army by the look of it."

"It's been too long Elsa. Your cinnamon rolls were the only reason I would travel with my parents to Sternz. Your rolls are known to be the best in all of Crixaria."

Elsa, with a witty grin, replied, "Oh, so you didn't stop here to see me; you just wanted one of my cinnamon rolls?" Still smiling, she handed him a confection of light, fluffy bread rolled around a warm, creamy center of cinnamon filling, and topped with sweet sugar icing.

He snatched the cinnamon roll from her hand and popped it into his mouth, relishing both the taste, and the pleasant memories it evoked.

"How much do I owe you?"

"For you," she replied, "it's on the house."

Vernon shook his head and licked the remaining sugar from his fingers. "Thank you, Elsa. But you push your stand up this hill every morning and back down every night. I can't let you go empty handed, especially since your cinnamon rolls have always been my favorite food."

He pulled five silver coins from his pouch and handed them to the old woman. Elsa stared as the coins for a moment, before handing them back to Vernon. "I only charge two Crixarian florins for these. This is too much, I can't accept it."

"Yes, you can," Vernon insisted, closing her hand around the coins. "I won't have it any other way. Call it a belated payment for all the rolls I pinched as a boy when you weren't looking. Now, you stay safe in the coming days Elsa."

Elsa smiled as she placed both hands on Vernon's, "Say hello to your parents for me, will you?"

"Of course I will," Vernon said. He gave her one last smile, snatched another cinnamon roll, and walked away.

Returning to his original path Vernon continued down the hill toward the large stone bridge that separated the upper and lower city. The bridge was the only point in Sternz that connected the upper and lower city over the river. A flat walkway, 300 feet long and 25 feet wide allowed travelers on foot, horseback, or wagons to pass over with ease. Vernon noticed a Crixarian officer with long, black hair pulled back in a ponytail sitting on the edge of the bridge with his legs hanging over the side throwing pebbles into the river below.

Vernon finished the last bite of his cinnamon roll and walked over to the officer. "You know," he said with a chuckle, "of all the people to be throwing rocks into the river when an Elven army could be here at any moment, you would be the one to do it, Gregory."

Gregory stopped mid-throw and snickered. Still sitting down, he retorted, "And of all the people to be eating sugary food to slow them down, it would be you!" Gregory smiled, stood, and extended his hand toward his friend.

Vernon reached out to shake his hand, but Gregory slipped past Vernon's outstretched hand and slapped him across his cheek, then stepped back laughing. "You've fallen for that for 20 years, my friend. When will you ever learn?"

Vernon shook his head and smiled at Gregory. "I suppose 20 years later I'm still hoping that one day you will grow up."

"We both know that will never happen. One of us has to remain cheery in these trying times. If I don't, well, then all of humanity will lose their souls."

Vernon nodded and turned to go, but in the next instant, thrust his hand into Gregory's chest, shoving him off the bridge. A look of shock crossed over Gregory's wide-eyed face as he fell into the clear blue water of the river below.

Everyone on the bridge who witnessed the friendly altercation burst into laughter. Soaking wet, Gregory stood up shoulder deep in water, sputtering.

Vernon called out to him, "I think you just helped a few people find their souls! You truly must be blessed by the One."

Gregory raised his arms above his head and roared with laughter, "Exactly!" He waded toward the pier where Vernon waited to meet him. Vernon extended his hand again, and Gregory hesitated a moment, noting his friend's mischievous smile, before deciding to take it.

Wringing water from his shirt, Gregory quipped, "I would accompany you to wherever you are going, but I am worried you will try to throw me under a horse-cart next."

Vernon grew serious. "King Dylenn has accepted General Izak's recommendation. I am on my way to gather my squad and prepare for the arrival of the Elven army."

"Ha! I told you that you would get the assignment," Gregory declared. "Out of all the officers in this army you are the one who has earned it. So, who did you pick to be in your little party?"

As they started to walk into the lower city, Vernon answered, "Konar Qal, Kassandra Verbeck, and Liam."

Gregory smirked and gave his friend a playful elbow to the ribs. "If I didn't know better, I would say you are trying to get Kassandra all to yourself. Good luck, she's only slept with half the army."

"It's not like that," Vernon replied. "You know just as well as I do that she is the best archer we have in the city, and on these walls an excellent archer will be perfect for picking off Elven officers."

Gregory raised his eyebrows. "Uh-huh. If you say so."

Vernon stopped walking and looked Gregory dead in the eyes, "You know I haven't been with anyone since it happened."

Gregory realized he overstepped. Raising his hands to his chest he said, "I wasn't trying to bring that up. We used to go out drinking and partying almost every night, but after that you just seemed to stop being yourself."

Vernon turned his eyes away. He didn't want to relive the pain. "I hate myself for what happened. It won't ever happen again. That was the reason I joined the army in the first place."

Gregory tried to lighten the mood by lightly slapping Vernon in the face. "From now on every time you get depressed I will slap you. Now enough talk about dark memories, why did you pick Konar? He isn't even a human."

"Konar is different from most orcs. I've known him for two years. I trust him. Just like me, he is here running from a past. He hasn't told me why. All I know is that it was bad enough for him to leave the Eacru Wastes and come here."

"Aren't you worried he will betray you? I have never known an orc to keep his word."

Vernon shook his head, "I truly think he is here to help us. He has loyally fought in General Izak's army for five years and has never done anything besides help both on and off the battlefield."

"That I can live with," Gregory nodded. "But what I don't understand is Liam. I mean, literally no one knows anything about him. Whenever I've seen him he is always by himself, or with that wolf of his."

Vernon put his hand on Gregory's shoulder, "I know it doesn't make much sense to you, but he is without a doubt the best fighter any of us have ever seen. At the skirmish at Pinewood I saw him singlehandedly cut down over 30 elven soldiers with ease. And his wolf frightens not only us, but also the elves."

"Well, just watch yourself around them and be safe in the coming days. I would miss slapping your face," he grinned.

The two continued to walk down the dirt streets of the lower city. The houses were not much more than wood, mud, and straw.

"Here we are," Vernon said as they walked in front of a rundown three-story wooden structure. The door was missing its top half and all the windows were missing shutters. Rotten wood could allowed the wind to enter unabated, and most of the roof was missing.

"Why are we at the medical building?" Gregory inquired. "I didn't slap you that hard did I?"

Vernon chuckled as he pointed to the roof. "Look up there."

Gregory spotted a dark green orc. Similar in form to a human, the creature appeared taller, stronger. Two small tusks protruded from its lower jaw. Large, even for an orc, this creature had long black dreadlocks tied in a ponytail. Dressed in black ragged clothes, it hammered a plank of wood onto the roof of the building. Sweat dripped off its goatee, and white, tribal tattoos rippled along his right arm with every swing of the hammer. The orc paused to wipe the sweat from its face, looked down, and spotted Vernon and Gregory.

"Vernon, my friend!" it shouted.

Vernon waved at the orc and yelled, "Konar, come down here for a minute please. I've got news."

Konar set down his hammer and nails and climbed down a ladder. Gregory took a small step back as the orc approached, in awe of the creature's height and thick muscles.

Vernon greeted Konar with the common orc greeting; making a fist with one hand and beat the other side of his chest twice. Konar returned the greeting.

"A beautiful day is it not?" Konar asked.

Vernon gazed at the morning sky appreciatively. "That it is, Konar. But as I said, I have news that won't wait. King Dylenn has given his approval for me to lead the squa—"

"Are you sure you want to—" Gregory interrupted.

Vernon fixed Gregory with a hard stare. "I told you that I trust him."

Gregory's gaze lingered on Vernon for a brief moment before he turned to Konar. "Accept my apologies, Konar. I'm sorry. It's just that orcs have been known to betray anyone for the right price. It's nothing personal. Now if you two will excuse me I must take my leave. I must try to do something useful before General Izak scolds me."

Gregory extended his hand toward Konar and Konar shook it vigorously. "Do not worry, I am used to it. I have been in the human kingdoms for five years. Vernon is only the second human to treat me as an equal."

Gregory nodded as he rubbed the shoulder of his arm that Konar shook and headed off down the street.

Konar looked back at Vernon, "Now, what were you saying about the squad?"

"King Dylenn has appointed me as the leader, and I want you to join it with me."

"Vernon," Konar replied pensively. "Aren't you afraid of what others will think? Won't having an orc with you cause more problems than its worth?"

Vernon rested his hand on Konar's shoulder, "Perhaps. But I've seen you fight and you are someone to truly be reckoned with. This is my first real command and I need someone I can trust beside me. That person is you."

"Why not Gregory?"

"Gregory is my oldest friend and a capable warrior, but he would question me at every step."

Konar set his left hand on Vernon's shoulder and with a small smile said, "Then if it truly is what you need, I will be beside you at every step."

"Thank you my friend. Now grab your armor. We still need to gather our other two members."

With a nod Konar turned and entered the medical center. Vernon followed inside, noting that even though Konar had been assigned to help repair the building, the other human workers still shied away from him.

Konar stopped in front of an old, dark brown, leather chest. He loosened the worn belt straps on both sides to open the chest and reveal crude, brown, metal armor. Without leather or padding to cushion the metal against his skin, Konar began to don his armor. First was the chest piece, a rugged sleeveless metal piece that looked like textured rock that had just been cut out of a mountain. Konar slid it over his head. Next, Konar strapped on his leg guards and greaves, then finally he pulled a pair of worn leather gloves. The orc reached one last time into the chest and pulled out a simple wood-handled hatchet, which he fastened with a string to the right side of his belt.

Puzzled, Vernon looked into the empty leather chest, "I know you didn't get rid of it. Where is your hammer?"

Konar grinned and moved the chest away from wall, revealing a spot in the floor that had not yet been repaired. Konar reached into the hole and pulled out a large war hammer, sheathed in a long, black fur scabbard. He pulled the hammer out of the sheath. Five feet in length, the war hammer was a true example of fine metal crafting.

"Crafted by the finest Tarian smiths," Konar said as he gave the war hammer a light swing.

"I don't think you've ever told me how you came into possession of that hammer," Vernon said.

Konar put the hammer back in the sheath. "It was given to me by Sal. It's perfectly balanced and lightweight compared to orcish hammers, so I am able to put more force behind a swing. I only hope that maybe since I will be on the same side of the wall as the humans that some of them will stop thinking that I'm a part of the elven army and stop trying to attack me."

Vernon laughed, but realized Konar was serious. He looked around the room and on one of the windows to the right he saw a torn purple curtain. Vernon walked over and ripped the curtain down from the rod. He dusted the curtain off and handed it to Konar, "Now then, with this, everyone will see you fight for King Dylenn and the rest of the Allister family."

Konar tucked it in his pants at the back, hanging down around the backside of his waist to his calves. "Did you make your final decisions regarding who else is going to be joining us?"

"That I have," Vernon replied. "Kassandra Verbeck and Liam will be our other two members, and before you disapprove of my choices I do have my reasons."

"You forget who you are talking to, my friend. Your decisions are yours. You do not need to explain your reasoning to me. Humans have a certain preconception of my race. I have learned not to do the same just on rumors and what others say. Granted once we meet them I may protest, but I'm willing to give everyone a fair chance."

Vernon nodded, "The world would be a far better place if all the races had your wisdom. There would be far less violence and hardships for everyone to deal with. Now let's go find Kassandra, she is known to frequent Bear Claw Tavern."

Vernon walked toward the door leading outside of the medical center, but Konar hesitated as he whispered to himself, "No one should have to do what I did to gain such wisdom."

Outside, the sun was climbing over the eastern wall. "Bear Claw Tavern is only a few blocks away from the inner wall. It shouldn't take us too long to reach it," Vernon said.

They walked side by side toward the tavern but Konar sensed something off about Vernon's manner and asked, "Are you feeling alright? You seem a bit anxious."

"I apologize if I seem that way," Vernon remarked. "This squad is an entirely new idea. General Izak thinks that if done correctly we could give our troops a rallying point. But he also sees us as a mobile strike force, a unit capable of accomplishing tasks that would otherwise require a far larger number of soldiers to do. I knew you were someone I could trust and that you won't let me down. But with Kassandra and Liam, I don't know them. I worry that my choices might be wrong; that the squad will let everyone down."

Konar considered for a moment, then replied, "If you second guess yourself, those around you will start to doubt your leadership. Also, are you afraid that the squad will let the city down, or are you afraid of letting the squad down?"

Vernon barked a wry laugh. "You truly do know everything, don't you?"

"Not as much as you seem to think," Konar joked.

Vernon stopped and gazed forward. "I have been to this city countless times, but I'm still amazed at that wall every time I see it."

The inner wall was a monument to human engineering. The solid stone wall stood 100 feet tall and 50 feet wide and surrounded the city of Sternz. Every 50 feet stood a square, fortified tower. Each tower stood 20 feet taller than the walls with slots for archers, a ballista on top, and a large purple flag with a ferocious golden bear insignia.

Konar jested, "The elves are going to have a field day trying to get through that."

Vernon just nodded. "General Izak's plan doesn't even involve the inner wall. The Vicar should arrive in two days' time and the plan is to keep the elves busy at the outer wall until then."

"Do you think that is a realistic goal?"

"I think so," Vernon replied. "The elves have been in a 150 year war with the dwarves fighting over the mines. The best elven troops as well as their best officers are dealing with that war, so the elves have been sending their recruits to fight us so far. This is a fight that we can win, and maybe even reclaim Xanica once the Vicar and his army arrives."

"We can only hope," Konar said.

Vernon viewed the streets ahead of them. "The tavern is not far, only a couple more blocks, and then we will have our third member."

3

King Dylenn walked alone with his head hanging down. Light from the arched windows on his left brushed against his face as he pondered all that could go wrong. The sunrise illuminated an idyllic vista, beautiful beyond description. Dylenn was too deep in thought to notice, but as he walked past one of the windows the warm sunlight caressed his face and he paused to enjoy it. With that gentle feeling, Dylenn looked out of the arched window with his tired blue eyes and gazed down at the city of Sternz.

He observed the rich upper district; smoke driftingly lazily from chimneys, servants bustling about their morning chores. At the bottom of the hill, separated by the bridge, the lower city was waking to the day. He smiled and closed his eyes, allowing the scent of fresh baked bread to tickle his senses. He caught the sounds of children laughing, and the squabbling of an old married couple. The gentle tap-tap of quick little footsteps interrupted his reverie. Dylenn opened his eyes to see a young girl with long, curly, cherry-blonde hair running as fast as she could down the hallway with a huge smile on her face.

"Papa!" she yelled. Dylenn squatted and extended his arms out as she jumped into his embrace. With a giant smile Dylenn lifted her up and spun her around, both of them laughing.

Dylenn set her down and knelt beside her, "Alyssa my girl, you grow bigger every day. Soon you will be as big as your sisters."

Alyssa crossed her arms and sneered at her father, "I hope not, getting older seems boring."

Dylenn chuckled, "And what would your mother say about that?"

Alyssa puffed as she looked down at her feet. Twirling her hair she pouted, "Mama said that I should act like a princess, that I'm too old for games and dolls." Alyssa looked up at her father, "But I'm only eight Papa. I don't want to grow up."

He pulled her toward him and gave her a kiss on the forehead as he gazed into her baby blue eyes. "How about this; we let Kaia and Bethany be the big girls, and you will just stay my little princess forever?"

Alyssa nodded and jumped forward, kissing her father on the cheek.

A woman's voice called out from the end of the hallway, "Alyssa? Alyssa where are you darling?"

"Over here Mama, I found Papa," Alyssa yelled back.

Queen Alezzia walked toward them and gave Alyssa a harsh reprimand, "Did I not tell you to get dressed before you started running around the citadel?"

Alyssa looked at her feet and whispered, "Yes Mama but-"

"But nothing," her mother interrupted. "Now go and get dressed for the day, and this time if you don't, I might have to keep you from going to Kaia's birthday party today."

Alyssa's eyes opened wide as she gasped. She then ran as fast as she could back to her room to get dressed.

Dylenn stood back up and kissed his Queen. "Alezzia my love, you look as beautiful as the day I first laid my eyes upon you. How are you feeling today?"

"If you're still worried that I'm in pain from Cormorden, stop. You have more pressing matters to focus on. I have been fully recovered from that sickness for over a year. I'm fine I promise."

She walked forward and rested her head on Dylenn's chest and allowed her gaze to wander out the window to the city below. "Can we win this?" she whispered.

Dylenn wrapped his arms around her, and pulled her closer. "It will be a difficult fight, I pray to the One that Vicar Matthew arrives on time."

"Do we know when he should arrive?" she asked.

"A dove arrived during the night from the Vicar with news that he will arrive in two days. He has been on the road for three months, so it shouldn't be much longer."

Dylenn ran his fingers through his wife's soft hair, "But enough of these dark thoughts, I do not wish to put any of this weight on your shoulders. Now, where are my other daughters? I wish to see Bethany and Kaia before today's matters become too great."

Alezzia took a deep breath, "Bethany is in her room getting ready for the party, but I let Kaia go to the wall."

"The wall? Why the wall?"

"Kaia told me all she wanted for her 23rd birthday was to be able to go to the eastern wall to watch the sunrise. Don't worry, I sent Sir Henry with her for protection."

"But she is allowed to go to the wall whenever she wants and shouldn't..." Dylenn's eyes widened. "Wait. Which wall?" He turned to look out the window.

Shocked at Dylenn's reaction, Alezzia stated, "The outer wall. I didn't see anything wrong with it. It is her birthday after all and the elven army is still a few days away."

Dylenn peered out the open window, squinting to see the outer wall, two miles away.

"What is it?" Alezzia asked.

Dylenn muttered, "The elves are not days away. They could be at the outer wall at any moment."

4

T he bear paw shaped sign above the door said, *Bear Claw Tavern.*
The shutters were closed, but the raucous sounds of people drinking,
a musician playing a lute, and the sound of breaking glass said the
tavern was open for business.

Konar saw that Vernon was hesitating about entering the tavern.
With a pat on the back Konar said, "Everything will be fine. Just
be confident and you will have their respect in no time."

"If only it were that simple." With a heavy sigh Vernon opened
the door to the tavern. Soldiers and working men sat in rough
wooden chairs around stout tables, playing cards, drinking and
socializing with one another.

The tavern's main room was open, but dimly lit by a small fire
in a dirt pit. Candles on the tables and mounted on the walls
added scant illumination. They flickered fitfully as the wind from
the open door caused air to rush inside. There were stairs on the
right side of the tavern that led to bedrooms which now quartered
soldiers. A chubby, redheaded woman served beer while a musician
in trademark bright red and blue tights played his lute.

Vernon pointed at silhouette of a person sitting alone in a shaded
booth. "There she is."

Konar's keener eyesight revealed a beautiful young woman. A
curious smile played across her lips. Her tan complexion was com-
plimented by chestnut hair pulled back in a warrior's ponytail and

inquisitive, bright blue eyes. She sat loose, but somehow seemed on the edge of action, and savored a slow drink of dark brown Crixarian ale.

She was dressed in full, close-fitting, long sleeved, brown leather armor which covered most of her body. Curiously, each piece was trimmed delicately at the ends with soft white fur. A finely-crafted recurve bow lay within easy reach, along with a black fur quiver of white feather tipped arrows and a black belt with two daggers sheathed in an X pattern.

Vernon and Konar started toward her when a shout rose from the center of the common room.

"Orc!"

A soldier leapt to this feet, spilling his drink in his lap as he fumbled for his sword. Tension filled the tavern as more than one patron shuffled for the door.

"You all can relax," Vernon commanded. "He is with me."

The musician resumed playing, and the tension eased a bit. Soldiers went back to their drinking, and the tavern keeper let out a relieved sigh. Vernon looked at the woman in the corner booth, who was calmly nursing her ale.

"Kassandra Verbeck?" he asked.

"That I am. And who might you be?"

"I am Vernon Regnier. This is Konar Qal. May we sit?"

Kassandra nodded her head. Vernon slid into the bench opposite her as Konar pulled up a third chair and sat. Konar glanced behind him to the bar and politely shouted, "I don't suppose I could get a jug of wine could I?"

The chubby, redhead looked up to see who was asking, but as soon as she saw the orc, she darted behind the bar and diligently starting washing glasses.

Disheartened, Konar turned back around and grumbled, "Never mind."

Kassandra's perpetual smile faded. She pointed to the serving girl, and snapped her fingers, "Hey wench! Make it two jugs and give us three glasses!"

Kassandra smiled sweetly at the young woman who delivered the wine with shaking hands. "See, that wasn't so hard was it?"

The barmaid shook her head, but as soon as she set the wine jugs and glasses down, she hurried back to the bar.

Surprised, Konar looked at Kassandra and said, "Thank you. I am not used to such kindness from most humans."

With a small laugh Kassandra remarked, "Who is she to come between someone and a good drink?"

Konar smiled back at her as he grabbed one of the wine jugs and chugged it down without bothering with a mug.

Vernon cleared his throat. "Ah, you are probably wondering why we are here."

Kassandra poured herself a drink, "That I am. It's not every day a girl is visited by an officer of Crixaria—and an orc."

Vernon leaned forward and rested his arms on the table, "General Izak has ordered the creation of an elite unit, one that will be able to achieve in small numbers what would normally take a major force to accomplish—one that will work as a team to complete whatever task assigned. Each member will bring their own unique set of skills to the team. I am the commander of that team. And I would like for you to join us."

"I assume this big fellow is a part of your *elite* unit?"

Konar nodded.

If Kassandra was surprised, it did not register on her face. "And why would a Crixarian officer in the Crixarian capitol want a Vetin volunteer, not to mention an orc, to join his unit? Would you not be more comfortable with a full squad of fellow Crixarians by your side?"

"To be honest, that was my first thought. But I believe having men and woman from all four of the human kingdoms, as well as an orc, might better represent unity for the entire city, and hopefully help all of us work together."

Kassandra nodded, her decision made in a moment. "Why not? So, is it just us? And if not, how many more people are joining us?"

Vernon and Konar stood. "I have one more person in mind, but I have no idea how to find him. Do you, perhaps, know where the warrior called *Liam* is?"

Kassandra cocked her head. "I've seen him from a distance, but I don't know him. I do know he has a pet wolf. We can probably find him that way. A wolf with a man is a hard thing to miss."

The door to the tavern burst open as two Crixarian officers barged into the room. The first was a man with long blond hair and the other, a woman with very short, shaggy brown hair. Both had longswords sheathed at their waists. The man cried out to the redheaded barmaid, "Girl, fetch us some wine! My friend and I need a drink."

Kassandra nodded to Vernon. "Friends of yours?"

Vernon grimaced, "No. The man is Ducan. The woman's name is Abby. They may be officers, but neither care about the troops under their command. They would rather drink than obey their orders to help prepare the city."

Kassandra watched as the pair of officers walked toward a shadowed figure seated in a back corner booth. Abby motioned with her head for the figure to get up and leave, but all the figure did was cross its arms and sit back into the booth.

Ducan clinched his fist as he stepped to the figure, "Listen friend, this is our booth. I don't know who you think you are, but if you don't move in the next three seconds, we will drag you outside and make sure that you will never be able to—"

Before he could finish his sentence, two piercing, yellow eyes opened from under the booth and began to rise. A growl accompanied those eyes out of the shadows; first a black paw emerged with a scar on the right leg, then more of the wolf's body became visible. An uneasy silence draped over the tavern as Ducan and Abby started to regret their decision and began to back up.

The growl increased in volume as the wolf's snout protruded from the shadows. Bared teeth caused even more uneasiness as everyone's attention was fixated on the large black wolf. The face of the wolf exuded pure hatred, and it appeared ready to attack Ducan and Abby at any moment. As the wolf's full body stepped into the light, even Konar was taken back by its sheer size. Its shoulders would reach a grown man's waist, and its thick black fur added to its size.

From the silhouette in the booth came a relaxed voice. "This is Blaster. Blaster isn't in a good mood when people threaten me. If I were you, I would leave before he decides to rip your throats out."

Trembling in fear, Ducan stuttered, "We ma-ma-meant n-no offense." The pair stumbled over each other as they backed out of the tavern.

As soon as Ducan and Abby were gone, Blaster's stance went from one of aggression to playful with his tongue hanging out. Wagging his tail as he turned around, he jumped up in the booth with the man and began to lick his face.

The man laughed and rubbed Blaster's head. "That might be the quickest you've ever scared anyone. I think the blond-haired man even pissed himself."

Kassandra said, "Well it doesn't look like we will have to go very far to find Liam."

As soon as the man heard his name, he stopped petting Blaster and questioned, "What do you want?"

Vernon hesitated a moment before he walked toward the booth, eyes on Blaster the entire time, and said, "I wish to ask a question. Nothing more, nothing less. No threats of any kind, that's for sure."

The figure leaned forward into the light, revealing his face.

A small smile crossed Kassandra's face as she whispered to Konar, "He is a lot cuter that I expected. He can't be much older than I am."

Konar raised an eyebrow. "How old is that?"

"Twenty-three."

Liam was a tan young man with brown eyes and short brown hair. His clean-shaven face showed no signs of scars. He nodded for Vernon to sit across from him. Seeing that Vernon still wasn't taking his eyes off Blaster, he smiled. "As long as you are not making threats toward either of us, you will be fine."

Vernon sat and studied the man across the table from him. At last he said, "I've seen you fight, but only from a distance. I never knew you were this young. I expected someone with your reputation to be older."

"I may be young, but Blaster and I have killed more elves than anyone else in Sternz." He scratched Blaster's ears affectionately, then added, "You said you had a question to ask me."

Vernon motioned for Konar and Kassandra to join them. Each grabbed a chair and pulled it close to the booth as Vernon explained his mission. "If you would accept, we would welcome you, as well as Blaster, as our final members."

Liam scowled. "I take it you would be giving the orders, and I would have to follow them to the letter? Blaster and I have never been keen on following someone else. And I suppose you need my answer now because the elves could arrive at any moment?"

Vernon's gaze fixed on Liam's eyes. At last he said, "You have a reputation for not playing well with others, and for ignoring orders you disagree with. I can promise you this, I will not be looking over your shoulder. I'll tell what needs doing. How you do it will be left up to you."

Liam leaned back in the booth and crossed his arms. "What's in it for me? As far as I can tell you are the only one to gain anything if I join."

Kassandra muttered to herself, "Well maybe some friends for starters, since you seem to be lacking in that area."

Liam overheard her and allowed a wry smile to cross his lips. "Perhaps I prefer to be alone."

Kassandra started to retort, glanced at the wolf, thought better of it, and remained silent.

Konar tried to disarm the situation, "From what Vernon has told me, our squad will be in the thick of the worst fighting. And from what I have heard about you, you hate elves and are damn good at fighting them. So if you were to join, we can promise that you will be able to fight more elves than you would if you were to stay on your own. Maybe even an elven Imperator or two?"

Liam's interest is suddenly piqued. "You are going after high value elves?

Vernon closed his eyes for a moment and he let out a quick sigh of relief. "More than likely, yes."

Liam extended his hand toward Vernon. "Why didn't you say so? Blaster and I will join."

Liam rose from the booth, and for the first time they saw the rest of his body. He was smaller than Vernon, but his muscles were more defined. His chest armor was a simple, sleeveless, brown leather vest with one shoulder guard on his right shoulder that looked homemade, and he wore unadorned, brown leather bracers on his forearms. Liam reached back into the booth and grabbed his weapons— two double-edged short swords with hilts of dark wood, but steel blades that were a darker gray than Vernon had ever seen. Foregoing sheaths, Liam carried his swords in his hands.

"Are your swords made of Azaran steel?" Vernon asked. "Azaran steel is lighter and stronger than any steel you can find in a human mine, and costs the world. Not even my family can afford that kind of steel. I thought only wealthy elves and even wealthier humans could afford it."

Liam didn't even glance at Vernon, "It's a long story."

"We have time," Kassandra said sweetly. "Why don't you tell us?"

"I don't think so."

Dissatisfied with Liam's answer, Kassandra decided to press him. "Then perhaps you will at least tell us where you are from?"

"No."

Before Kassandra could retort, the door of the tavern opened and more soldiers walked into the tavern; not Crixarian soldiers, but volunteers from the Isle of Tarium. Heavily armored, these soldiers worn chainmail with steel shoulder guards, gauntlets, and full plate chest armor. Their weapons were in far better condition than the Crixarian soldiers. Their gold-colored pants were elegantly made from Tarium cotton.

Konar leaned over and asked Vernon, "Is that how the Tarium Paladins look as well?"

Vernon studied the Tarium volunteers, "No. The Paladins are even more heavily armored and far better trained than this undisciplined lot. Only the Paladins are considered the army of Tarium. These are just Tarium citizens who joined the fight against the elves."

Liam walked to the other side of Vernon, "Just citizens? That armor must cost a fortune."

Vernon explained, "With the tax the Tarians collect on all believers of the One, their country is without a doubt the wealthiest of the human kingdoms."

As the last of the Tarium volunteers walked into the tavern, their commander followed them in—a young woman with long brunette hair and dark blue eyes wearing even more armor than the Tarium volunteers.

Her leg armor was thin steel plate, rising from her feet to her upper thigh. A short, chainmail skirt draped down over her upper thighs. Her waist was covered by a steel plate armor piece that stopped beneath her breasts and her upper body was cover by a gold and white striped cotton jacket. She carried a five-foot spear of the same darkened steel that Liam's swords were made of, but the spear-tip was longer than Crixarian spears, and shaped like a bird's wing.

"She is absolutely beautiful. Who is she?" Kassandra asked.

Vernon replied, "That is Zafrinia Wethin. She is the daughter of an extremely wealthy Tarium family that fishes cono. From what I've seen she could be one of the best warriors we have. Her goal was to become the first female Paladin, but I heard they didn't accept her because she was emotionally unstable. If Liam had not agreed to join, she would have been my next choice."

Konar cast a hostile glare at Zafrinia. "If you had chosen her, I would not be here right now."

"Konar I've never seen you look at someone that way, even in the heat of battle," Vernon said. "What did she do to you?"

"It's not what she did to me. It's what she did to Sal."

Kassandra interrupted, "Who is Sal?"

Vernon muttered, "The first human that befriended Konar."

Konar continued, "What Zafrinia did to Sal is unforgivable. They were once in love. Both from Tarium, only living one village over from each other, only a short distance on horseback. Zafrinia was Sal's entire world. He would take her stargazing and they would have candlelight dinners and take long walks in the woods. He was totally devoted to her, but that wasn't good enough for her. Without warning she left with no explanation at all. She arrived at his village one afternoon and told him goodbye. Sal wrote her letters asking why and begging to know what he had done wrong, but never once received a reply. Sal was devastated. He didn't know what he had done wrong. She left and didn't tell anyone why. Sal was truly alone but believe it or not things got worse. A trusted friend informed Sal only days later that Zafrinia had left Sal for another human. It was not Sal who had committed an unforgivable act, it was Zafrinia."

Kassandra interrupted, "How do you know that Zafrinia left Sal for someone else?"

Konar's heated gaze never left Zafrinia as he continued, "When you share your heart with someone for over three years and then in just two weeks after the separation are seen with someone else, it's simple to put two and two together that there was something suspicious going on. Sal was a broken man, alone and devastated, he didn't have anyone to turn to. He spent all his money on this hammer and then left the Isle of Tarium and volunteered to help the Crixarians against the elves. When I first arrived in Crixaria not a single human would speak to me besides him. His first words to me were, "It looks as if we are both unwanted outsiders, care for a drink?" We bonded over the next year, but I could clearly see that he was a broken shell of the man he once was."

"What happened to him?" Liam asked.

Konar's voice was filled with hatred, "He died two years ago at the Battle of Black Marsh, an elven spear stabbed clear through his stomach. As he was dying in my arms all he wanted was to know why—why Zafrinia would lie and abandon him for someone else, and even though he never said it, I knew that he still loved her and wished that Zafrinia had come back to him. Sal died alone and sad that day because of what Zafrinia did to him. Zafrinia eventually realized that she had made a grave mistake when she left Sal. She went to Sal's village to try to find him, but arrived just in time for the end of his cremation. Then she tried to join the Paladins, but they didn't accept her, so I guess she ended up coming here. Lost and alone—just like Sal."

Vernon tried to regain control of the situation by putting his hand on Konar's shoulder. "You don't have to worry, she isn't a part of our unit."

Konar lowered his gaze from Zafrinia and began to relax.

Liam asked Vernon, "Now that your squad is assembled, where to next?"

Vernon, confident that Konar had returned to his level-headed self, turned to Liam and replied, "Now we go to find General Izak and receive our first orders."

5

The warm sunrise cast orange rays onto the outer wall as the morning dew steamed off of the tall green grass below. A pale young woman with fiery red hair and baby blue eyes spun with her arms extended as she looked up at the sky. She was dressed in a yellow silk dress with a purple satin cloak wrapped around her. Her slippers were of the finest black leather, threaded with white cords. She stopped spinning, she crossed her arms, and gazed toward the heavy forest with a smile on her face.

Sir Henry, a wrinkled old man in a Crixarian officer's uniform, stood behind the girl, arms ready to grab her if she fell. She climbed on top of one of the stone railings at the edge of the wall, extending her hands again. She smiled and closed her eyes, relishing the warm morning breeze that brush against her face. The old officer moved closer.

"For a 75 year old man you move like you were 30, Sir Henry."

Sir Henry watched her every step. "Princess Kaia, I watched over your father when he was a child. Never once did anything bad happen to him on my watch, and I'm not going to let my career end with the princess falling off of a wall."

Princess Kaia hopped down and turned to face Sir Henry. "As long as I can remember you've always protected me. I know you won't let anything happen to me."

Sir Henry smiled at Kaia and reached into one of his belt

pouches. "I know you said not to, but I've never been married and have no children. Your family has been my family. It's not much, but I have a birthday present for you."

Sir Henry pulled out a bracelet made of daisies. Not a stem could be seen as the bracelet was a solid row of beautiful white petals. With a big smile, Princess Kaia took the bracelet and put it over her wrist.

The smile faded as Kaia looked past Sir Henry toward the city of Sternz. Over the massive inner wall, she saw the Citadel on top of the hill and part of the upper city. Her eyes became watery when she saw thousands of purple tents scattered over the two-mile stretch between the inner wall to the outer wall, where the human army camped.

With a gentle touch, Sir Henry pulled her closer and hugged her. He looked at her with her head lowered and saw an ever growing depressed expression. He placed his right hand under her chin and raised her head. With a soft, old voice and a smile he said, "A princess should not be depressed on her birthday. Today is a happy day."

"I see all those soldiers, ready to fight in a war that they don't have any control over. It's my fault that this war has happened and has taken so many lives."

"It is not your fault child. The elves are misguided in their beliefs. Now that the Tarian Vicar has joined the war, we finally have a chance for peace. Today is your birthday, do not let such dark thoughts ruin it for you."

Kaia turned back to the railing at the wall and looked out at the forest. "I've lived my entire life in Sternz. Never once was I allowed to venture out past the outer wall and into those woods or the world beyond. All because of who I am—what I am. I'm even putting your life in danger. What if the elves were to attack right now?"

"There are 200 yards of open grassland between the outer wall and the forest," Henry stated, "We would see them approaching, and even then, we have 2,000 troops in the encampment behind us to hold them at this section of the wall until the rest of our forces can get here. You are perfectly safe."

Kaia gazed out into the depths of the forest. She took a slow, deep breath, looked up at the sun and said, "They are coming for me. They won't stop until I'm dead."

"Yesterday's officers' report placed the elves at least two days away. That gives us plenty of time to walk back to the citadel, even for an old man like me," he winked.

Kaia allowed a faint smile to cross her face as she moved to accompany her protector, then noticed the laces of her shoe had become untied. She knelt to re-tie it, but felt a small splatter of warm liquid on the back of her neck. She wiped it off with her fingers and saw them coated with thick, red blood. She looked up and saw Sir Henry, his hands at his throat, gasping for air. The shaft of an arrow with dark, blue feathers was lodged in his throat.

Sir Henry stumbled backwards, blood spilling out of his neck and mouth, and tumbled from the wall to the ground far below. Kaia let out an earsplitting scream, drawing the attention of soldiers on the wall and across the encampment. Kaia instinctively crouched below the parapet. She knew the source of arrow.

Crixarian soldiers rushed toward the wall as fast as they could as horns and bells sounded the alarm. Kaia mustered enough willpower to peek over the wall. The sight astounded her. Elven soldiers, thousands of them, were running across the open expanse toward the outer wall. At first there was no sound, but a low rumbling built into a crashing thunder as the elves drew closer. Elven banners, white rectangular flags emblazoned with a blue cobra head in the foreground, dotted the landscape. The elven troops wore tight fitting, bright white, ethereal scale armor, with dark blue shirts and pants underneath. White hoods with a scale mask protected their faces.

They brandished curved sabers with small blue hilts, and their oval shields were large enough to cover the chest and abdomen.

Small clusters of elven soldiers carried wooden ladders that appeared tall enough to scale the outer wall. In the distance, Kaia saw hundreds of elven archers marching out of the woods and forming in row upon row.

"Loose!" she heard the command as a volley of arrows whistled through the air and over the wall. To Kaia's horror they fell with deadly effect on dozens of Crixarian soldiers who were rushing to her aid.

"Loose!" Another volley flew over the wall, killing dozens more.

Loud thuds echoed off the walls as the tall elven ladders fell against them. Kaia, still huddled on the wall, was grabbed by a heavyset Crixarian officer who pulled her to her feet. With desperation in his eyes he said, "We have to get you off the wall and back into the city now!"

Hearing the clashing of steel, Kaia turned to see the first of the elven troops pouring over the wall and engaging the first defenders. The heavy-set officer pushed Kaia behind him and pulled out his sword just in time to block an elven saber.

The elf smiled, blood dripping from his sword. He tilted his head, as if the warrior in front of him was of no consequence. "I will be rewarded beyond imagination for being the one to spill your blood."

Kaia backed up, wanting to run, but knew there was no place of safety. She opened her right hand and it ignited into flames. She pushed her arm forward and out of it came a burst of flames that engulfed the elven soldier. He died screaming, the stench of burning flesh permeating the air.

The heavyset officer stared at her, half in shock and half in awe. It only took a moment for him to regain his composure. He called to a soldier. "Take the princess to the inner city, now! Do not leave her side. We will hold them here for as long as we can."

The young soldier saluted and extended his hand toward Kaia, who nodded and bolted down the stone stairs to the ground below. The officer, now confident that Kaia would find a way back to Sternz, focused all his attention on the elves. "Where are my archers?" he shouted.

A Crixarian soldier arrived breathless at the top of stairs, "They are right behind me sir." The officer looked down the stairs to see hundreds of Crixarian archers positioning themselves at the rear of the wall.

"Draw! Raise! Release!"

The archers released a volley directly into the oncoming elves.

"Again!" the officer commanded. "Draw! Raise! Release!"

The archers released their arrows again and again, forcing the elven charge to falter. They formed a shield wall 100 yards from the outer wall, just beyond arrow range, and waited. As the last of the Elven troops on the wall were struck down, the human defenders let out a triumphant roar.

Kaia looked back at the outer wall and gave a sigh of relief as hundreds of human troops now gathered at the bottom of the wall ready to rush to the top when needed. She scanned the wall hoping for a glimpse of the officer who saved her life. She discovered the heavyset officer looking back at her. He smiled, nodded once, and waved toward the city indicating that she should be on her way.

"Mages!"

"Where?" The officer demanded. "The Elven mages are supposed to be dealing with the dwarves. They shouldn't be anywhere near here!"

A female human soldier yelled, "On the ridge sir, to our left."

The officer scanned the horizon. At the foot of a hill, beneath a single oak tree, stood two elves dressed in long white robes, trimmed in a dark blue scale pattern. The robes covered their entire bodies and hoods concealed their faces.

The officer shook his head and stared at the ground as he considered how to handle this new threat. The elven foot soldiers and remained steadfast behind their shield wall. The elven archers had ceased volleying arrows. The officer looked to his archers, made a quick calculation, and gave the command.

"All archers train your arrows on that hill. "Draw! Raise! Release!"

The archers released their arrows in unison. But even as the arrows flew through the air, a sour expression came over the officer's face. He knew it was a futile gesture. The arrows fell short by at least 20 yards.

Ignoring the arrows, the elven mages moved in perfect harmony. Each stepped their left foot forward, thrust their right fist into the air, then drove their right fists into the ground with all their might. Nothing happened, and a weak cheer went up from the defenders on the wall. The two mages just fell back, exhausted.

Low at first, but gaining in both volume and intensity, there was a rumble that grew into a roar. A soldier on the wall pointed to the sky and cried out in terror, "Run!" A gigantic ball of fire was crashing down from the heavens.

It was too late. The meteor raged toward the wall with a thunderous explosion. Dirt and stone went jolting in all directions as the sheer impact of the meteor caused a forceful gust of wind and dust that knocked Kaia off her feet.

Kaia's ears were ringing as she struggled to stand. Her vision was blurred. She rubbed her eyes until her vision cleared, only to see the young soldier who was assigned to see her safe back to the citadel, laying in a ragged heap at her feet, his eyes fixed and staring. The ringing in her ears subsided, but the sounds she heard were joyful cheers from the elves on the other side of the wall. When she looked around she discovered a breach in the wall with a gaping crater in the ground where the fireball had struck. Through the hole she saw the elven foot soldiers charging.

Distress horns from all across Sternz began to sound. A lone female human soldier with long blonde hair on a white horse galloped toward her. The rider slowed the horse and reached her hand out to Kaia. "Come Princess. I must get you back to the inner wall."

Kaia reached forward and grabbed the rider's hand, and was slung onto the back of the horse. Arrows whizzed by as the horse galloped toward the human encampment and the gathering human forces.

Without warning the horse slammed into the ground head first.

The female rider was flung off the horse, her skull shattering against a rock. Kaia was flung to the unforgiving ground, momentarily stunned from the force. She struggled to her feet and shook her head to clear the cobwebs. The beautiful white horse was now covered in blood and riddled with elven arrows. Elven foot soldiers pouring through the breach in the wall spotted the disoriented princess and rushed toward her. Crixarian forces desperate to engage the elves closed in from behind her. Kaia realized the elves would arrive first.

A fleet-footed Elven foot soldier sprinted ahead of his companions and gave a victory cry as he raised his sword to strike at the helpless princess, Kaia extended right hand which ignited in flames as she shot a white-hot fireball which hit the elf square in the face. Screaming in agony, her attacker dropped to the ground, beating futilely at the flames that engulfed his head.

Two female elves ran past their now dead companion, intent on killing the princess. Kaia shot another ball of flames at the first elf, but she managed to raised her shield and deflect it. Kaia tried to remain calm but her legs started to shake as both of her hands burst in flames. She aimed one shot at the elf's face. When she raised her shield to block, Kaia shot a second burst at the elf's legs. A look of sheer terror washed over the elf's face as the flames engulfed first her legs, then her torso, her armor melting and fusing with her skin.

Undeterred, the second female elf charged forward. Kaia repeated her tactic, but this warrior learned from her companion's mistake. She blocked the first fireball and leapt over the second.

Each burst of magic took its toll on elf and princess alike. Kaia could feel her strength draining as the female elven warrior trudged forward. Close enough to engage the princess with her saber, the elf feared to lower her shield, and used it as a battering ram, forcing Kaia onto her back. The blow caused the elf to drop her saber, but she pulled a curved dagger from her belt and raised it triumphantly. Kaia managed to grab the elf's wrist with one hand and deflect the killing blow. She pressed her other hand against the elf's face and summoned all her remaining strength. She released a burst of flames, small in comparison to the fireballs she had been launching, but enough to sear the flesh from her attacker's skull.

Kaia pushed the elf's body off her and scrambled to her feet. Gasping for breath, she ran toward the oncoming human forces. This time she knew that she would reach them before any more elves could get to her.

A young female officer with black hair in a ponytail rushed to her aid. "Princess Kaia, I am Captain Tori, are you injured in anyway?"

Kaia, her entire body shaking, stared without an expression as she muttered, "I... I killed people."

Tori spotted the stump of a tree at the entrance of the encampment and set Kaia down on it to rest. She knelt in front of Kaia, grabbed the flask of water from her belt and handed it to her. "Here, you've been through a lot just now and you need to regain some strength."

Kaia grabbed the flask and guzzled it down, spilling half onto the ground. With only a little of the water left, Kaia handed the flask back to Tori and thanked her.

Tori put the flask back on her belt. "I know you probably don't want to talk about it, but we need to know what happened at the wall. We saw the large ball of flames, but we need to know where the mages went."

"You don't need to worry about the mages. Using magic drains their energy. That is why I am so tired now."

Tori nodded her head and continued,. "How long will it take before they recover?"

"It all depends on the mage. I am young and haven't used very much magic. That's why I become tired even though I don't use much energy. By the way, from what I saw they were wearing the robes of elder mages. My guess is that they will be back at full strength again within two days."

Tori nodded, then said, "You know the elves were able to identify you by your dress. Begging your pardon, Princess, but you stick out like a sore thumb. Perhaps you should change into something less—conspicuous? Perhaps a soldier's uniform."

Kaia considered her beautifully crafted garments, now torn and soiled, and nodded. She moved toward the tent Tori indicated to change.

"Captain Tori," a battle-worn Crixarian soldier who was missing his right ear and several teeth ran up to Tori, panting. "Captain Tori, a contingent of elves have taken control of the eastern outer gate. The elves are entering from both the gap and the gate."

Captain Tori scowled as she muttered, "Damn it."

The eastern gate was below a hill. All she could see were dust clouds from the elven troops marching through the gate.

Captain Tori's hands clenched into fists. "They will attempt to flank our position and advance behind us cutting off any reinforcements," she muttered as Kaia walked out of the tent dressed in a Crixarian soldier's uniform that was two sizes too big for her.

"Princess I only have 5,000 troops under my command and I doubt we will receive reinforcements before the elves get here. We need to get you to the inner wall as soon as you are able."

"I am ready now."

Captain Tori peered at the soldier with the missing ear. She grabbed him by the collar and said, "You get her to the inner wall. Do not stop for anyone or anything. Do you understand?"

The grizzled old soldier nodded. If he was awed by the princess's position or title, he didn't show it.

"Captain Tori, aren't coming with me?" Kaia asked.

Tori looked toward the elven line approaching from the gap and shook her head. "Someone has to keep the elves busy."

Kaia and the old man hurried out of the camp toward the inner wall, while Captain Tori turned and marched to the front of her troops. "Brave Crixarians. We are here today as the first line of defense for our city. We face an intimidating force, but take comfort that the elves are weak. Our very own princess is more than a match for the elves."

The Crixarian soldiers laughed at that remark.

"Now how about we show them what trained fighting men and women can do to them? To victory or death!"

A roar from the Crixarian troops erupted as Captain Tori pulled her sword from its sheath and pointed it toward the oncoming elves. With a battle cry she rushed forward, her soldiers at her heels.

Kaia glanced back in time to see the two forces collide, the sound of steel on steel echoing like thunder.

"Hurry Princess," the old soldier urged. "We still have over a mile and a half to go to get to the inner wall."

"But what about the rest of the army? Won't they arrive soon?"

The old soldier scanned his surroundings as he ran, "The rest of the army is stationed all around the wall." Under his breath he added, "They won't arrive in time to help Captain Tori."

6

General Izak stood in the middle of the bridge that connected the upper and lower parts of the city. He held a large, two-handed longsword and shouted orders to officers as he tried to regain control of the army. Soldiers and civilians were frantically running around him. "Go tell Lieutenant Qing to take his division and meet the elves head on, then tell Khaled to join him!" As the soldier ran off, Vernon and his new squad ran toward Izak from the lower city.

Vernon rushed up to Izak, "What's the situation sir?"

"Elven mages broke through the outer wall. We are trying to push them back, but they are advancing closer to the inner gate every minute. And to make matters worse, King Dylenn informed me that Princess Kaia went to the eastern outer wall this morning."

Konar stepped forward, "Is there any indication that she is alive?"

Izak shook his head, "We have no report at all, but we can assume that she is alive or the elven assault would have stopped."

Liam muttered, "They wouldn't stop attacking just because she was dead."

Vernon gave Liam an icy glare before looking back at Izak, "What are our orders General?"

Izak gazed up at the massive wall behind them. "Your first task is to locate and then escort Princess Kaia back to the city. All we know is that she was wearing a yellow dress with a purple cloak and was last seen somewhere on the eastern wall. Now go! Find her and bring her back."

Vernon nodded and turned to lead the squad back across the bridge. Kassandra started to giggle.

"What could you possibly find amusing at this moment?" Konar demanded.

Kassandra just smiled. "It's just rather cliché, don't you think? That we have to rescue a damsel in distress."

Vernon scoffed, "Enough joking. We have to hurry. Every second we waste is another second that the elves could kill the princess, and I don't know about the rest of you, but I would rather our first mission be a success."

"Do not worry my friends," Konar encouraged, "I have no doubt that we will succeed in our goal. I have faith in us."

The gate at the eastern wall was a solid iron door that towered 50 feet above the ground. Zafrinia and a few hundred Tarian volunteers stood at the base of the wall. Vernon approached the Tarian commander. "Zafrinia, have there been any sightings of Princess Kaia?"

Zafrinia sighed and rolled her eyes, "No but she is probably dead by now, so I wouldn't waste your time."

Before giving anybody else a chance to reply, Kassandra smirked and snapped back at Zafrinia, "Aw, are you upset that you aren't the center of attention?"

Konar laughed to himself, but Zafrinia forced a smile. "I'm upset that four people are in some high and mighty unit that should be following my orders because I am clearly more skilled than any of you."

Vernon confronted Zafrinia. "Now is not the time to argue with each other. If you don't have any information to share, then stay out of our way, and keep the elves out of the city."

Vernon addressed his squad, "Let's go. We've wasted enough time here." As they strode toward the gate Konar made a point to bump into Zafrinia's shoulder.

"Watch it green skin." Zafrinia slurred. If Konar heard, there was no indication. He kept walking forward.

Dust clouds from the many different engagements between the inner and outer walls rose into the air, obscuring visibility.

"Alright, listen up," Vernon commanded. "Somewhere out there in that mess is Princess Kaia, and it's our job to go get her. All we know is that she was at the eastern outer wall before the attack. We have to find her and get her back to the city before the elves get to the inner wall."

Liam, who was scratching behind one of Blaster's ears asked, "So what's the plan? Giving a speech is wasting time, let's go."

Vernon took a deep breath, "Since we don't know where she is we need to cover a lot of ground as quick as we can. Konar and I will go northeast. Liam, take Blaster and Kassandra and search southeast. Any questions?"

They shook their heads and readied their weapons. Konar examined Liam, Kassandra and Blaster and then walked closer to Vernon. "Are you sure you want the two that you don't trust yet to go off on their own?" he whispered.

Before Vernon could reply, Kassandra and Liam walked within earshot. Vernon looked back at Konar and nodded once, "Good luck everyone. Let's get the Princess home."

With this last statement they ran off in separate directions, Vernon and Konar went left toward the northeast while Liam, Kassandra, and Blaster headed to the right toward the southeast.

Blaster stayed close to Liam's side, sniffing the air with his ears perked up, listening to the sounds of war around them. They stopped at the crest of a ridge. Kassandra and Liam each took a knee, while Blaster lowered his body. They looked down the hill at a small engagement of a few dozen humans and elves. Rage welled up inside of Liam as he watched, and he started to stand up to join the battle. Kassandra latched onto his arm and whispered, "Where do you think you are going?"

Liam lowered back to one knee and shook his arm free. "There can't be more than 20 elves down there," he explained. "I could join that fight and it would be over in a matter of minutes."

"I've heard how much you hate elves," Kassandra answered. "But this fight is not our mission. We have a job to do. Besides, there are more humans down there than elves, we need to continue searching for the princess."

Grinding his teeth, Liam nodded. They continued their trek toward the outer wall. Kassandra took mental note that every time they avoided another engagement, Liam's attitude grew more aggravated.

A low growl came from Blaster. Liam and Kassandra looked at the wolf, wondering what had caused him to growl. Kassandra lowered herself and surveyed their surroundings looking for any threats, but Liam stood still, staring at an elven banner that waved placidly in the gentle breeze, several hundred yards away. The banner was a blue rectangle emblazoned with a white cobra head. A hate-filled expression settled on Liam's face as his grip tightened around his swords.

"Domatin," he muttered through his teeth.

Kassandra whipped her head to Liam, "What? Who is that?"

Without answering, Liam charged toward the banner with Blaster at his heels.

Kassandra yelled, "Hey! Where exactly are you going? We have to find the princess." But her cry fell on deaf eyes.

"No wonder you don't have any friends," Kassandra muttered to herself. She surveyed her surroundings and continued to the outer wall, searching for any sign of the princess.

Vernon and Konar found less fighting between themselves and the outer wall. The uneventful travel gave Vernon time to ponder.

"Do you think the princess is still alive?" he asked his companion. "There are thousands of elves pouring through the outer wall. Even if we do manage to find her, there's no guarantee we can get her safely back to the city."

Konar gave a small smile as he replied. "You worry too much

my friend. Just as General Izak stated, if Kaia was dead the elven assault would be over. Their entire reason for going to war with you humans is to kill her. There is always hope, you must have faith."

Vernon continued, "Liam would disagree with you. He seems to think the elves are here to wipe us all out, not just the princess."

They reached the top of a hill and surveyed the area below. There were no signs of conflict in this area. Only tall grass and pink tulips blowing in the wind.

"If the fighting hasn't reached this far north I doubt the princess would be out here," Vernon surmised. "We should move closer to the breach in the outer wall."

They jogged down the hill and hurried toward the smoke trail that marked the breach.

"And about Liam, I wouldn't worry too much about what he said," Konar added.

"Why's that?"

"I can't put my finger on it, but something about him just seems off. I know he is a skilled warrior, but I don't like his demeanor, and I feel as if he is untrustworthy and hiding something. Why else would he try to distance himself from everyone? He even has two swords made of Azaran steel. Only the wealthiest humans can afford such steel, and I seriously doubt that he is from a human noble family."

Vernon slowed to a stop. "What are you getting at Konar?"

"All I am saying is that I have a bad feeling about him, and that we should watch our backs."

Vernon nodded. "I hate to admit it, but perhaps I made a mistake with him. I don't think he is a traitor. Still it might not hurt to look for a new member once we rescue the princess."

"As long as it's not Zafrinia I'll be fine with it," Konar answered.

Konar and Vernon both dropped to their stomachs as a group of 50 elves on foot appeared in the distance. As they drew closer , Konar whispered, "Can you tell what they are saying?"

Vernon whispered back. "No, we need to get closer."

Konar looked at the height of the grass, which was at the lower thigh to a human, "I'm too big, my size would give our position away. You go ahead and if they spot you, know that you won't die alone."

Vernon glared at Konar, who is was smiling back at him, before beginning to crawl on his stomach toward the group of elves. He stopped when he could discern the elves' words.

"I told you not to kill them, and you shot both of them in the back!" one elf shouted.

"You told me to stop them and I did," the second elf argued.

The first elf slapped the other across the face, "Only to wound them. It would have been nice to know why two human soldiers were trying to avoid combat and get back to the inner wall."

The second elf rubbed his face. "They were probably just scouts."

"You better hope so," the first elf declared. "Hurry up. If they were scouts then there are probably more of them around." She then turned and started jogging toward Konar's position. Vernon laid motionless, praying to The One that none of the elves would stumble over him.

The rest of the elves followed their commander past Vernon at a fast trot. They passed even closer to Konar's hiding place, but none slowed. Vernon, still on his stomach, paused for a few more moments until he could no longer hear the sound of the elves running. He slowly raised his head and looked back at where Konar should be. Konar stood with a grin.

"How did they not see you?" Vernon demanded.

Konar, shrugged his shoulders and tapped his chest piece twice, "They probably thought I was a rock."

Vernon shook his head in disbelief and motioned for Konar to follow. "We need to hurry, they could come back."

When they reached the spot where the elves had rested, Konar discovered the corpses of two Crixarian soldiers, both lying face down in the grass with arrows in their backs. Vernon stepped over the first body—a young woman with red hair. Konar knelt the second body—an old man with his right ear missing.

Vernon breathed a small, soldier's prayer: "May the One guide your soul," as Konar closed the old man's eyes. Vernon pulled the arrow out of the woman's back, but was startled to see no blood on the arrow head. He turned over the body and placed two fingers on her neck. There was a pulse, though it was weak. "This one is still alive."

Konar noticed the woman clutched a sizable rock in her right hand, but before he could make a sound she opened her eyes and swung with all her might at Konar's head. The rock thudded against his cheekbone and knocked him to the ground. Vernon rushed to the girl and wrapped her in his big arms, calling out, "We serve Crixaria!"

Konar shook the cobwebs from his head and rose to stand in front of the young woman, who was still clutching the rock. He raised his hand to his face and wiped away a stream of blood that ran down his cheek. "Konar, how bad is it?" Vernon asked.

"I've seen worse," Konar shrugged.

"Who are you?" demanded the terrified and exhausted young woman,.

"My name is Vernon Regnier and my friend here is Konar Qal. General Izak has sent us to locate and escort Princess Kaia back to the city. Any information you have regarding her whereabouts would be greatly appreciated."

The girl dropped the rock and wrapped her arms around Vernon as tears swelled in her eyes. Vernon's hands hovered to his side as he glanced at Konar.

Konar stated, "I think we found her."

"Princess Kaia?" Vernon asked.

The girl nodded and began to weep in earnest. Konar reached out a huge hand in an attempt to sooth the girl. "It's alright child. We will get you back to the city."

Kaia sniffed an apology. "I'm sorry I hit you with that rock. I thought the elves had come back."

"He'll be fine," Vernon quipped. "He's had worse wounds in bar fight with a serving wench. But I'm curious about the arrow in your back. There was no blood on it."

Kaia nodded. "The old man with only one ear, I don't even know his name, told me to lay on my stomach. He pushed an arrow through my garment until it grazed my skin. Then the told me to lay very still, no matter what happened. Then he was struck with an arrow." Kaia's eye welled with tears again. "Everyone who has tried to protect me today has died."

"I promise that you will get back to your family." Vernon looked at Konar and continued, "We need to move. Where there is one group of elves, there is likely to be more."

Konar nodded, "True, but that means going toward the major conflicts. The princess looks exhausted. I'm not sure she will be able to keep up if we move at a steady pace."

Kaia bit her lip and shook her head. "No more should die for me. I will do my best to keep up."

Konar walked behind Kaia, put his hammer in the fur sheath on his back, and swooped her into his arms. "Problem solved," Konar said with a smile. "Now you can rest and we can move at a quicker pace."

Vernon gazed at Konar. "Don't let her come to any harm. If the elves attack, I will defend. We must keep her safe at all costs."

Vernon led them directly south of their position. The clashing of steel and the cries of dying men and women from both sides grew louder as they moved closer to the raging battle. One fact became clear to all three—there were far more dead humans than there were elves.

As they crested a ridge they spotted an enormous engagement. Thousands of Crixarian soldiers were being surrounded and over-whelmed by the elven army. The unrelenting sun rose higher into the sky with no clouds in sight.

"It's a massacre," Konar muttered. "The forces at the wall must have been taken completely by surprise."

Kaia, her attention fixated on the battle, replied, "There was no warning. One minute I was enjoying the sunrise and the next minute elven mages had crashed a ball of fire into the ground, shattering a breach in the wall, and they rushed through."

Kaia's tale was interrupted by an unearthly cry.

"Humans!"

Ten elves, weapons drawn, rushed toward them.

Vernon cast about for a way out, but the sounds of conflict rang out from every direction. He drew his sword, took a deep breath, and ran directly at the approaching elves. "Konar get the girl to the city, now! I'll hold them off as long as I can."

Konar hesitated, not wanting to abandon Vernon, but one look at Kaia, exhausted, frightened, still resting in his arms, decided the matter. With a low grunt he turned and started running up the hill.

Vernon rushed forward to engage the first elf. The elf slashed with his sword. Vernon handily deflected the blow and thrust his sword into the elf's stomach. Two more elves approached in tandem, one from his left and one from his right. The remaining elves took their time, confident their companions would easily overcome the lone human.

Vernon pulled his sword out of the dead elf and lunged to his left, bringing his shield up in a swift upward motion, catching the elf under her chin and knocking her unconscious to the ground. Vernon pivoted to his right, blocked a thrust from the third elf and stabbed him in the stomach.

The remaining formed into a single group. One shouted, "He is clearly more skilled than the other the humans we have fought. Attack as one and overwhe—" An arrow fletched with white feathers pierced his chest, and he sank to his knees before collapsing on the ground, dead. Kassandra, standing on the hilltop, already had another arrow already drawn.

Konar, carrying the princess, pressed forward toward his companion, while Vernon stoically marched, shield raised, toward the remaining six elves. One charged, but was cut down by another of

Kassandra's arrows before taking a dozen steps. Confusion reigned among the five remaining elves. With no leader, they hesitated.

Vernon did not. He bolted forward and engaged another elf, as Kassandra tore the throat out of a third victim with her unrelenting arrows. Konar reached the hilltop, lowered Kaia gently to the ground beside Kassandra, unleashed a fearful roar, pulled his hammer from its sheath on his back, and plunged headlong down the hill into the melee. He leapt into the air and raised his hammer, and slammed down on an elf's head. Blood and chunks of bone splintered in all directions.

The last two elves rushed the orc, but Konar swung his hammer, obliterating the elf it contacted. The last elf raised his sword to strike at Konar, but Konar dropped his hammer, grabbed elf's wrist, and lifted the now whimpering soldier into the air. The bloodlust upon him, Konar pulled the hatchet from his belt, and slowly and deliberately split the elf's skull.

Konar dropped the carcass to the ground, and he and Vernon trotted up the hill. As they reached the top, Kassandra quipped, "You're lucky I came along when I did."

Konar smiled. "We had it under control the entire time."

Vernon ignored them both. "Princess, this is Kassandra Verbeck. She is the third member of our team, and this is..." he looked around. "Where is Liam?"

The grin faded from Kassandra's face. "I wish I knew. We were searching farther south, then out of nowhere he muttered something and just ran off."

Vernon scowled at the report. "With or without Liam we need to head toward the inner eastern gate. Kassandra, I want you to take point, Konar watch the rear, I will stay close to the Princess."

Kassandra slung her bow over her shoulder as she shook her head, "I just came from that direction. The fighting is far worse and there are even more elves. We would essentially be running through a battlefield."

"It is a risk we have to take," Vernon countered. "We still have over a mile to go to get back to the wall and the Princess must get back to the wall's safety."

Kassandra nodded reluctantly and led the way toward the inner wall. All too soon her predictions proved right, however, as the group topped a ridge that overlooked the main battle. They took cover behind some nearby rocks and watched as the immense battle raged in front of them. Everywhere they looked, either an elf or a human was being cut down on the field drenched red with blood.

"We can't go through that," Kassandra declared, vindicated.

"Agreed," Vernon replied. "We need to find a way around."

Konar nudged Vernon and whispered, "I don't think we have time for that."

Vernon, Kaia, and Kassandra all turned around to see what Konar was talking about and spotted two elves in full white scale armor with long dark blue capes searching the area to their rear. The only skin that showed was their eyes through the slits of the white silk masks that draped over their heads. A small blue cobra head adoring the forehead was the only ornament. Both elves carried a dual-bladed weapon, with slightly curved blades extending two feet in each direction.

Vernon's grip around his sword tightened as he uttered, "This can't be right. Those are Royal Praetorians. Only members of the Elven hierarchy have such protection. Kassandra," he whispered, "If they see us you will take the Princess back to the wall. Konar and I will fight them off."

Kaia grabbed Vernon's arm and started to protest, but before she could speak Konar stood up and said, "They've spotted us."

The two Royal Praetorians were walking toward them. There were no words or quick actions—just a slow, calm walk. Vernon rose to his feet as well, looked to Kassandra and nodded once. As Vernon and Konar began to run toward the Praetorians, Kassandra grabbed Kaia's arm and they ran in the direction of the main engagement. Kassandra nocked an arrow in her bow and as they ran she told Kaia, "Stay right behind me at all times. If anyone tries to attack us I will shoot them, but under no circumstance are we going to stop running."

An elf on the edge of the battle noticed the human women but before he could raise an alarm, Kassandra released her arrow and it dug deep into the elf's jaw. She immediately readied another arrow and urged Kaia onward. "This is the quickest way and we can't lose any more time. The longer it takes us to get you back to the inner wall, the longer the inner eastern gate will stay open, giving the elves more time to kill our troops and maybe even take control of the gate."

Kaia looked behind her and saw Konar and Vernon in combat with the two Royal Praetorians, but unlike the fight at the hill, Vernon and Konar were on the defensive doing everything they could to not to beaten back. The snap of Kassandra's bow releasing another arrow drew Kaia's attention back as she realized that they were starting to run into the battle.

Kassandra pulled an arrow out of a corpse, and readied it on her bow. Kaia looked at the quiver on the back of Kassandra and only spotted two arrows in reserve. An arrow hissed past them from their right. Kassandra took one glance and spotted an Elven archer 50 yards away. In a single, swift motion, Kassandra pivoted, knelt, and released. Her arrow penetrated the chest armor of the elven archer.

Kassandra urged Kaia along as she continued up the hill, but the exhausted princess could not match her speed and started to fall behind. Kassandra reached the top of the hill before she realized Kaia was only half way up, an elf warrior brandishing a short sword hot on her heels. Kassandra released an arrow that caught the elf in the throat, sending him back down the hill.

One arrow left, she sighed to herself.

At last, out of breath, Kaia reached the top of the hill. Kassandra put her hand on Kaia's shoulder and said, "I know you're tired, but we have to keep moving. The good news is we are halfway to the wall and it should be flat ground from here on out."

"And the bad news?" the princess inquired.

"The bad news is there is more concentrated fighting between here and the wall," Kassandra acknowledged. She considered her options and without a word motioned for Kaia to follow her.

Kaia panted, "Why are we running in the direction we came from?"

"Better part of valor," Kassandra replied. "We need to find a less concentrated area of fighting where we can slip though undetected. I don't have enough arrows to fight our way through."

A female elf in their path killed the human soldier she was fighting. Kassandra drew the string back on her bow and released her arrow at the elf. The arrow connected in the elf's stomach. Before Kassandra could retrieve her arrow, the elf tumbled down the hill, taking Kassandra's last arrow with her.

Under her breath Kassandra cursed, "Damn it."

She slung her bow over her shoulder and drew out her daggers. The blades were simple steel, six inches in length, razor sharp and deadly. She set off again at a brisk trot, hoping Kaia could match her slower pace, but weariness was taking its toll on the princess. Her foot connected with the protruding rock. She crashed to the ground and let out a small cry as she rolled uncontrollably down the hill.

"Princess!" Kassandra cried out, and immediately realized her mistake. A number of elven soldiers, including four Royal Praetorians, turned from the battle and started toward them.

Kassandra sprinted down the hill, but was intercepted by three elven warriors who did not appear deterred by the daggers she brandished.

Kaia tried to regain her feet, but a sharp pain in her ankle forced to back to the ground. In pain and weary beyond belief, Kaia looked about, searching for any escape route, but found none. The Royal Praetorian in front walked toward her, ready to thrust his weapon into Kaia. Kaia bowed her head, resigned to accept her fate.

A monstrous, black wolf leaped into the air and plunged his teeth

into the Royal Praetorian's neck, ripping his throat out. After flinging the Praetorian's body to the ground, the wolf ran between Kaia
and the remaining three Praetorians, growling with bared teeth.

A young human, covered in blood and brandishing two short
swords, rushed into the fray. Rage contorted his face and his bat-
tlecry was piercing and almost inhuman. He rushed toward the
first Royal Praetorian in his path. The elf struck downwards. Liam
blocked with his left sword, and with a swift swing of his right
sword, cut the elf's left leg off at the knee. The elf collapsed onto
the ground screaming in pain. Liam ignored the impotent Praetorian, and rushed to engage the remaining two.

Kaia gaped, astounded that one young man could singlehandedly
put two Royal Praetorians on the defense. The Royal Praetorian
to his right thrust his dual sword but he easily dodged to his right
and with his left leg, stomped the left knee of the Royal Praetorian,
tearing the ligaments and cartilage holding the knee together. As
the Royal Praetorian fell to his knees, Liam moved in front of him,
crossed his swords, and slit the elf's throat.

Liam turned to the last remaining Royal Praetorian, who was
now backing up. Hatred poured off Liam like sweat. Desperate,
the Royal Praetorian swung at Liam's head. Liam rolled forward
under the blow, putting him behind the elf. Liam stabbed the elf
in the back of the thigh. As the incapacitated elf fell, Liam let out
another roar and drove his right sword through the back of the
Praetorian's head.

Kassandra, who had dispatched the three elven foot soldiers,
arrived at the bottom of the hill and went to Kaia's side. She
examined Kaia's ankle. "It's not broken, but you have a nasty sprain."
She turned to attention to Liam and in a disapproving tone said,
"And just where have you been?"

After pulling his sword out of the Praetorian's head, Liam replied
quietly, "I had to take care of something."

Kassandra indicated Kaia. "We need to go. Now."

Liam nodded, and he and Blaster hurried to the front to take point. Kaia tried to stand, but the pain in her ankle was too great. Kassandra put Kaia's arm over her shoulder and together they started back up the hill. At the top they spotted Konar and Vernon approaching from the north. Konar hustled to Kaia and picked her up in his arms again.

Vernon was surprised but pleased when he saw Liam, but realized this was not the time for reunion stories. Liam continued at point, followed by Blaster and Kassandra. They all fought minor skirmishes along the way, cutting down any elven soldiers that stood between them and the gate.

As they approached the inner gate, they saw Zafrinia engaged in battle with two Royal Praetorians. Zafrinia almost seemed to be enjoying herself. As the first Royal Praetorian swung an upward strike, Zafrinia dodged and with the blunt end of her spear, struck the Royal Praetorian's groin. Zafrinia made quick work of her stunned opponent and easily ended his life with a swift jab of her spear to his abdomen. Zafrinia jerked her spear out of the first Praetorian and thrust it into the throat of the second. As the squad passed under the gate, Zafrinia snarled, "Took you all long enough."

Vernon ignored her. Kassandra, on the other hand turned and snapped sweetly, "We stopped for tea with the princess. To bad you couldn't join us, but you're obviously not important enough to dine with royalty."

Upon entering the city Vernon spotted King Dylenn and Queen Alezzia waiting for Kaia.

Konar walked forward with Kaia in his arms and reunited her with her parents. Dylenn's eyes started to water as he lunged forward to hold his daughter. Tears started to pour from his eyes as he caressed her hair. "I thought you were dead. The reports we had been receiving were only news of the elves getting closer and closer to the wall."

Kaia leaned back and looked her father in his eyes about to speak but was interrupted by Queen Alezzia shouting at the soldiers on top of the wall at the gatehouse, "Close the gate now!"

A yell from the top of the wall replied, "My Queen, we still have thousands of troops out there. We will be condemning them to their deaths!"

With an even angrier tone the Queen shouted back, "I am your Queen and you will do as I command!"

Without a response the solid gate lowered and blocked all access in and out of Sternz, trapping over half the human army outside the inner wall.

7

With the inner gate closed, the remaining human troops outside the wall were surrounded by the overwhelming number of the elves. Across the battlefields around the city of Sternz, humans were being rounded up as captives. Two elves walked through the carnage of the battlefield. One was tall, middle-aged, with long brunette hair woven into a single braid hanging over her shoulder. Her armor identified her as one of the Royal Praetorians, but the pauldrons on her shoulders were molded into the shape of a cobra's head. She smiled while large groups of human soldiers were stripped of their weapons.

The young male elf walking beside her maintained a sour expression. His long, curly blond hair flowed unfettered in the morning wind. "Prince Domatin, are you not pleased with our success?"

"Of course not!" he snapped. We should be sacking the city right now. Why did you stop the assault to the inner gate? We could have easily reached it and been inside the city by now."

The female squared her shoulders, her calm expression belied her annoyance. "Yes, some of our soldiers could have made it into the city and a few might have made it to the gate, but we would have been stretched too thin to accomplish anything of consequence. Getting past the outer wall was our objective today, and we accomplished that purpose."

Domatin was not mollified. "Great Leontina, High Imperator of

Azara. The Dwarven Blight they call you. The finest Elven strategist in over a thousand years. Demoted to fighting lowly humans."

Leontina kept her composure. "You may see it as a demotion, but I see it as a promotion. I have been given a task to fulfill, our god Colubra's will, to destroy the abomination that is the human princess. The first and greatest commandment Colubra gave our ancestors was that as long as only elves use magic, then the world could go on in relative peace."

"Children's tales," Domatin snorted.

"Even if you don't believe in Colubra, look at this from a worldly point of view," Leontina continued. "If the humans are allowed to have magic, then Kaia Allister could soon become a threat that could lead the humans to rival us one day, especially if her children also had magic, and that is something we cannot allow to happen. Besides, you should feel honored to be here. Your mother, Empress Juliana, thought it would be an excellent idea for you to redeem yourself after what transpired after Xanica."

The Elven prince's hands clinched into fist. "That was not my fault."

Leontina laughed, "And how exactly was that *not* your fault? You're the one who led the massacres on those first few villages. As I see it, you're the reason for the aftermath. Your mother may have helped cover it up, but after seeing what happened at your banner today, I'd say it was fortunate that I sent for you before your Praetorians were dismembered. You may consider yourself the greatest of all Elven warriors, but perhaps..." she left the thought incomplete and flashed him another smile.

A young female soldier interrupted. "Imperator Leontina, Prince Domatin, I have the battle report."

Leontina gave one last glance to Domatin before turning to the young elf. "Legatus Tauriel, you may proceed."

Tauriel reported, "Our initial assault was an astounding success. We only lost approximately 15,000 troops while we estimate 35,000 human dead, and another 10,000 taken prisoner."

"Interrogate the officers. Get any information you can on the weakness of that wall."

"I have already begun the interrogation process Imperator. We chose the officer who gave us the most trouble during the assault. I will update you as soon as we get any useful information."

Tauriel bowed at her waist, turned marched toward the newly formed Elven tents. Prince Domatin walked behind Leontina and whispered, "I know she is your favorite Legatus. It would be a shame for someone as beautiful as her to be killed in battle."

Leontina, no longer calm and collected, anger flashing in her eyes, confronted Domatin. "Tauriel is my second in command and a promising young officer. If you try to get to me through her, being of the Ophidian blood line will not help you."

Domatin nodded, a foul smile playing across his lips, and walked away toward the Elven encampment. Leontina shoved him from her mind, an unpleasant annoyance—nothing more, turned back and scanned the wall for any weaknesses.

Domatin spotted a group of four Royal Praetorians and approached them. They all bowed at the waist. "Do any of you know where Legatus Tauriel is interrogating the human officer?" Domatin inquired.

Still bowed at the waist, one answered, "Yes Prince Domatin. She took the human officer into that tent," pointing to a large circular wool tent behind Domatin.

Without a word Domatin turned and entered the tent. Thick wool blocked most light plunging the interior into pitch darkness, except for a single beam of sunlight that shone through a tear in the fabric on the top of the tent. The beam was shining straight onto the Crixarian officer, who was on her knees, her feet and hands tied behind her. There was no furniture in the tent—just the dirt ground, the prisoner, Tauriel, and two Elven guards. The Crixarian officer was hunched over with her head bent down. Domatin approached Tauriel and inquired, "Has she said anything of note yet?"

Tauriel kept her eyes on the prisoner and answered, "Unfortunately no. We've beat her, cut her, burned her, and all she said is her name and rank."

Tauriel inched her way toward the prisoner and punched her square in the jaw. Tauriel then squatted down, took a deep breath and said to the prisoner, "I personally don't enjoy interrogating anyone but as you understand, it is a part of war. You can decide how long this continues. Your own people closed the gate and abandoned you out here to die. They didn't even sound a horn to tell you to fall back. Just tell us where the weak spots are and no one will know it was you."

With her head still lowered, the prisoner spat out a clump out blood, grinned and answered, "Captain Tori Wells, Crixarian Infantry."

Tauriel sighed and she shook her head. Domatin said, "Legatus, your services are no longer needed here. You and your soldiers can go."

Tauriel, taken by surprise, paused for a moment, her eyebrows raised. She took a deep breath, looked back at Tori, and then signaled for the two Elven soldiers to follow her. As she was exiting the tent, Domatin added, "Also could you tell the group of Praetorians to retrieve my basket from my tent and to join me in here?" Tauriel bowed once and exited the tent.

Domatin studied Captain Wells, how fast she was breathing, the way she shifted her weight to her left side, and even the slight twitch under her right eye. He walked over to her and grabbed the back of her hair. He raised her head up and looked her straight in the eyes. He didn't say anything at first, just stared at her in silence.

Tori, in pain from her injuries, still mustered enough strength to smile. "Too afraid to do anything without your babysitters?"

Domatin laughed under his breath, "Tori, was it? Has anyone ever told you about Colubra?"

Tori stayed silent and Domatin released her hair. "I didn't think so."

His four Praetorians entered the tent and he motioned with

his right arm to sit the basket beside him. His smile grew as he continued. "You see, Tori, Colubra is the very reason we are here at this place in time. Over 10,000 years ago, when the first Empress of Azara, Quenette Ophidian, was just a small child—not even old enough to walk—her mother took a stroll through the woods one summer night. Suddenly, she was attacked by a pack of wolves. They were starving and ready to attack anything to satisfy their hunger. After the wolves were finished with the mother, they turned their attention to the crying baby. Only one thing saved the child—not an elf or human or orc—but a single, albino cobra. One cobra stood against the wolves and fended them of, spitting venom from its fangs or striking if it had to. That cobra saved baby Quenette that night.

"The next day a group of Elven hunters passed by the carnage and found Quenette, still being guarded by the cobra. They proclaimed the snake was a deity sent to save The Chosen One who would lead our people to victory. They named the cobra, Colubra, and the snake was said never to leave Quenette's side until it died of old age. The snake did however lay eggs, and more albino cobras were born. Every member of the Ophidian blood line has always had albino cobras as guardians to watch over us."

Domatin nodded toward the Praetorians. "Hold her eyes open," he commanded. Two of the Praetorians walked behind Tori, and forced her eyes open with their fingers. Domatin knelt in front of the prisoner, removed the top from the basket, and reached inside. Tori flinched as Domatin removed his arm from the basket, with a large albino cobra wrapped around it. The cobra's head was covered by a dark blue cloth, but it swayed from side to side in a macabre, sensual dance.

"Do you know what cobra venom can do to people? The venom itself causes a slow, painful death, the result of respiratory failure. The flesh surrounding the bite rots as the venom eats the skin away. But if the venom gets it the eyes—oh, this is where it gets most interesting—the victim goes blind. I'm told the pain is excruciating."

Domatin inched the snake closer to Tori's face. Tori tried to struggle backwards, but the Praetorians held her fast.

"Now you can tell me about any weakness in the wall and live, or you can continue to be a stubborn child and risk angering Colubra. It's entirely up to you."

Tori's eyes were fixed on the covered head of the cobra. She could see its tongue flickering under the cloth. She finally whimpered, "There are no weaknesses in the wall!"

Domatin sighed, "I'm afraid that's not good enough." He pressed the cobra forward until it slithered around Tori's neck. A choked scream escaped Tori's mouth as she felt the scales of the snake crawl on her bare skin. Her terrified eyes were blood red. She nodded her head once.

Domatin leaned close to her ear, flicked a snake-like tongue against her lobe, and whispered, "Tell me. Now. I won't ask a second time."

"There is a small sewer between the eastern and northern gates. But even if you send your soldiers through, they would be funneled and slaughtered in the process. The only way to get inside the inner walls is to open one of the gates from one of the gatehouses."

Domatin stood, his smile widening, "Now that wasn't so hard, was it?" He nodded at the Praetorians. Their grip on Tori strengthened and her panic magnified.

Domatin reached for the cloth resting on the cobra's head. Tori began to struggle with all her might, but the Praetorians' hold was firm. She was helpless. Domatin pulled the cloth from cobra's head. "You see, Captain Wells, I'm a man of my word. You'll live. But you took a little bit longer to answer my questions than I would have liked."

The cobra hissed as it set its gaze on Tori. Its hood extended, its tongue flicked, agitated. The cobra opened its mouth, venom dripping from its fangs, its swaying from side to side. Entranced, Tori could not have looked away, even if the Praetorians had not held her eyes open. The cobra spat a stream of venom at the helpless victim, striking her in the face. Domatin smiled as she screamed in agony.

"I've learned what I needed to know," he said. "Leave her as she is. I have work to do. You are dismissed." The Praetorians dropped the writhing prisoner to the dirt floor, saluted, and left. Domatin still had his albino cobra wrapped around his arm and he began to gently stroke its head before replacing the hood and returning it to its basket. He smiled once more at the sobbing human captain, then walked out of the tent.

Leontina spotted Domatin exiting the tent and crossed to him. "Prince Domatin, I have assembled the army in front of the city's eastern inner gate."

"Do you intend to assault the city now?"

Leontina replied, "No. It is merely a show of strength. It will demoralize the humans. I wish to parlay with the human general in command—Izak I think his name is. Perhaps even convince him that the best course of action for the people in the city would be to just hand their princess over to us. It would save much bloodshed on both sides."

To Leontina's surprise, Domatin was not angered by her news. He nodded in agreement. "Excellent. Let me change into a uniform of a Praetorian and I will gladly go with you to meet the humans."

Leontina raised an eyebrow. "Why would you change into one of their uniforms?"

"The humans may try to capture the Prince of the Elves—if they knew I was here. You know, leverage." Domatin turned and walked with his guards further into the camp.

8

General Izak stormed to the eastern gate from the lower city, his armor covered in dirt as he passed by Vernon and his team. Izak seemed not to notice Vernon and the squad, his gaze was focused on nothing but Alezzia. Dylenn saw Izak approaching and sat Kaia down on the ground before he took a few steps toward Izak, his hand extended as he tried to stop what he knew was coming. Before Dylenn could say a word, Izak fumed past him and shouted at Alezzia, "Why did you order the gate closed without even a warning? You abandoned over half our army!"

With a steel gaze Alezzia answered, "Your Princess has been safely brought back to the city. You know as well as I do that the longer the gate was open the more opportunity it would have given the elves to get inside the city. You're the one who said we could keep them at the outer wall for two days! You bear the blame for this fiasco!"

Izak clinched his fists and his teeth. He bit back a response, bowed his head, and turned to speak to Vernon. Kaia, who was still sitting on the ground, looked past Izak at the squad, particularly at Vernon. Dylenn knelt and swooped Kaia up in his arms. As he held her close she smiled at him. "I'm alright Dad, just a few cuts and bruises."

Tears swelled in Dylenn's eyes. "All of the reports we received were of the elves continuing to advance toward the gate. I was about to run out and find you myself, but your mother kept me here. Having a child in grave danger and not being able to do anything to help is a feeling I hope you never have to experience."

Kaia looked around for her mother who was still seething over her confrontation with Izak. "How is Mom doing? I know she said she is fine, but honestly, how is she?"

A sad smile crossed Dylenn's face as he looked at his wife, "Cormorden took its toll on her, just as it does all who survive. It changes the survivors. I wouldn't wish Cormorden on any living soul."

Alezzia approached and placed her hand of Kaia's shoulder, "It's good to have you safe again sweetheart. Let's return to the citadel. I'm sure your sisters will want to see you, and I also want Benjamin to take a look at your injuries."

Dylenn signaled to some Crixarian soldiers to come to him. "I will join you momentarily. I wish to speak to General Izak first." Dylenn placed Kaia into the soldiers' care and sent them on their way.

"All in all I must say you did an excellent job today," Izak commended the squad as Dylenn approached.

"Thank you for saving my daughter," he said. "You all have my gratitude and if there is anything I can do for you, don't hesitate to ask."

Everyone, except Liam, bowed their heads to the King. Dylenn nodded at Izak and inquired, "Since the first plan to keep them at the outer wall has failed, what's next?"

"We will have to hold them here. As we speak, the elves are setting up small encampments all around the wall, but I've already sent two soldiers to the north, south, and west outer gates. Their orders are to stay hidden, but when the Vicar arrives, to open the gate for him and his army."

"Sir, how bad is the situation?" Vernon asked. "Honestly."

The old general still seethed. "Roughly 45,000 of our army were either captured or killed—perhaps three times the losses suffered by the elves. So now, thanks to Queen Alezzia's command, instead of

3-to-1 odds, which were bad enough, we face 7-to-1 odds. *That's how bad our situation is. Honestly."*

A shout from the top of the wall echoed over them," Sir! The elven army is approaching!"

Izak called back, "Do they have any siege weapons with them?"

"No sir!" the soldier replied.

Izak looked at Dylenn, "It is just a show of force my King, nothing to worry about for the moment."

Another cry from the top of the wall; "Sir! A small group is approaching the gate. From here it looks like an Imperator, a Legatus, and five elven Praetorians!"

"I wonder if they want to discuss terms?" Vernon looked at his general.

Izak scratched his beard. "Perhaps." He called to the men on top of the wall, "Open the gate! I will see what they want!" Izak turned to Vernon and the squad. "Care to join me as my protection?"

As they started toward the gate, Dylenn turned to accompany them. Izak started to protest, but Dylenn cut him off. "You're going to say it's too dangerous, that I'm the king, that you can handle this. But this is my city and I have a duty to defend it just as much as you do. Perhaps they might be willing to negotiate."

Izak nodded his assent at last and the party continued toward the gate.

The solid iron gate crawled its way up as the King and company walked out to meet the small group of elves. Vernon shook his head at the sight. *The entire elven army assembled, shining in their white scale armor, ready to give their lives to kill one girl. Madness!*

The elf at the head of the contingent stepped forward and bowed."I am Imperator Leontina, and this is Legatus Tauriel."

Dylenn matched her greeting. "I am King Dylenn Allister, and this is General Izak, commander of the Crixarian army."

Konar whispered to the rest of the squad, "Keep your guards up. They might try to kill the King."

Before anymore words could be spoken, one of the Praetorians laughed. "Well hello there, Liam."

Domatin tore off his Praetorian mask and smiled daggers at Liam. Liam took a step forward, but Konar grabbed his arm, stopping him from going any farther. Even with a firm grip Konar could feel Liam straining to get away from him. Under his breath Konar whispered, "I don't know what is going on, but if you attack, it will give them cause to attack the King."

Liam's hands tightened around his swords. His eyes filled with pure hate as he stared at Domatin. But he nodded, and remained silent.

"It's been too long my old friend," Domatin smiled. "We really should catch up sometime soon." Domatin bumped Leontina as he strolled forward and addressed the king directly. "I should introduce myself. I am Domatin Ophidian, third child to Empress Juliana of the Elven Empire. I suppose you may have guessed why we are here, but let me be blunt. You can either surrender the girl now, or we will massacre every man, woman, and child in your city."

Before Dylenn could seize Domatin by the throat, General Izak stepped forward and replied. "And I suppose *you* know, that every man, woman, and child in Sternz will fight to protect the princess."

Domatin was still smiling at Dylenn as he answered, "Oh, I do hope so. A massacre is so much more fun than a simple surrender."

Domatin chuckled, turned, and started back toward the elven army. He turned and said, "It really is good to see you again, Liam." Then he sauntered away, followed by his Praetorians. Leontina, biting the inside of her cheek to keep from screaming at the insolent prince, and Tauriel bowed at Dylenn and followed him toward their army.

Dylenn grunted and strode back through the gate toward the city. Izak and the rest of squad followed—except for Liam, who stood motionless, rage painting his face, as he watched Domatin walk cheerfully away. Kassandra returned to Liam and laid a hand softly on his shoulder. She expected the rage she saw on his face. She did not expect the pain she saw in his eyes.

"What happened, Liam? How do you know him?"

Liam didn't answer. He turned, and with Blaster and Kassandra in his wake, marched toward Sternz.

Vernon blocked Liam's path, drew his sword, and pointed it at Liam's throat. Konar and Izak flanked the rogue soldier, their weapons at the ready. Blaster growled and lowered into an attack stance, but Liam commanded. "Blaster no!"

Vernon demanded, "You disappeared today. Ran off without a word, and returned with no explanation. Now, an elven prince calls you by name. And you *knew* that the elven army would be here today—information only a handful of officers were privy to. I will have an explanation, or I will have your head."

If Liam was intimidated, it did not show on his face. "If I was working for the elves do you really think I would have the reputation that I do?" he asked. "And let's just say that was all a ruse to gain your trust; you sought me out, not the other way around. If I were an elven spy, why wouldn't I have just killed the Princess instead of saving her from three Praetorians? Or better yet, just let them kill her, and spare myself the effort."

Vernon pondered Liam's word. Trust was hard to come by, and easy to lose. "That doesn't explain how you knew that the elves would be here."

"Let's just say I know how they operate," Liam replied.

"That's not good enough," Izak thundered, his sword drawn."

Liam took a deep breath and closed his eyes. He released his grip on both of his swords, allowing them to fall to the dusty ground. Piece by piece he unstrapped his armor. Finally, Liam pulled his ragged, tan shirt off, and dropped it on the ground beside his armor and weapons. From behind him, Kassandra gasped. Liam slowly turned and allowed the others to see his back.

Three deep and wide scars ran from his left shoulder all the way down to his right waist. There was also a brand on his right shoulder in the shape of a Cobra's head.

"Elves brand their slaves with this mark. My master—was Domatin."

General Izak appeared doubtful. "I've never heard of the elves freeing one of their slaves before."

Liam peered at Izak. "They don't."

"I'm sorry for whatever happened to you," Konar's deep voice rumbled. "We didn't know."

"No. You didn't." Liam picked up his shirt, armor, and weapons. "Where are our barracks?"

"In an old school house as soon as you get off the bridge into lower Sternz," Vernon said.

Without another word, Liam started walking, with Blaster at his heel.

Vernon called after him, "Where are you going?"

If Liam heard, he did not respond. Soldiers and civilians alike scooted out of his path, and he disappeared around a bend in the road.

"We probably just brought up something he didn't want to talk about," Konar observed. "Give him a little while and he will be back."

Vernon nodded. Kassandra asked, "I wonder what happened to him. Once the meeting outside the wall was over I looked into his eyes and it looked like he had been through an enormous amount of pain."

Vernon sheathed his sword, "Physical or emotional, all wounds heal."

"Scars don't," Kassandra replied.

Konar leaned back and groaned as he stretched. "I don't know about you two, but I could use a drink."

Vernon laughed, "You can always use a drink."

Domatin, still disguised as a Praetorian, walked into the command tent at the center of the main Elven camp, followed by a livid Leontina and a worried Tauriel. While Domatin walked around a table to view a siege map of Sternz, Leontina threw open the flaps of the tent and she stormed inside. "I hope you know that you've made the situation ten times worse with your little exchange."

Domatin grinned. "I don't see how. We already knew that they wouldn't surrender their princess to us."

Leontina's face grew red with rage as her handed clinched, "Perhaps, but still we could try to save as many elven lives as possible. The longer we talked with the humans, the more time Tauriel would have had to scout their defenses."

Domatin raised an eyebrow as he remarked, "The humans needed to know who was in command."

Leontina slammed her fist onto the table as she shouted, "I am in command!"

The smile on Domatin's face disappeared. "You forget your place Imperator."

"*I* am in command of the siege of Sternz! You know just as I do what Empress Juliana said would happen if we fail. I will not allow that to happen."

Domatin looked back down at the map once more and shrugged his shoulders, "You worry too much, Leontina. These pathetic humans won't last more than three days against our assault. Besides, I've already taken measures to ensure the human princess's death."

"What *measures*?" She glared at him.

Domatin rubbed his hands together and began to pace like an eager schoolboy with a secret too delicious to keep to himself. "When I integrated the prisoner, I actually accomplished something." He directed the comment at Tauriel. "She told me of a sewer gate between the northern and eastern inner walls that could be an entrance to the city."

Leontina interrupted, "And you did not think that was important enough to tell me about before now?"

Domatin smirked. "No, not really."

Leontina placed both her hands on the table, leaned forward, closed her eyes, and took a deep breath. "Please tell me you did not order an attack there. Our troops would be funneled into a narrow killing field and slaughtered if we attempted to enter the city that way."

"Nothing of the sort," Domatin quipped. "When my mother said I was to accompany you on this crusade, I thought, *What can I bring to the campaign that might help— besides my Royal Praetorians, of course.* So, I may or may not have ordered the Wraiths of Colubra and sneak into the city."

Leontina pinched the bridge of her nose, trying to avert the headache that was building. "The Wraiths may be the deadliest assassins in the world, but we have an entire city to take, and it is still surrounded by a wall. If your Wraiths fail, we still need a plan."

"I'll leave that plan to you," Domatin said. "Do as you see fit, but know this—if I feel your plans are inadequate, I will assume command. By the way, what *are* your plans?"

Leontina ground her teeth, but managed to maintain her calm. She pointed at the map. "The walls of Sternz are the largest in all of Aclia. I doubt our two mages could bring them down even at full strength. So we break down the walls with trebuchets, or eliminate the gate with battering rams. I have already ordered the construction on siege weapons, but that will take time. In the meantime, we will assault the walls at dawn and test their defenses."

Domatin, satisfied with Leontina's plan, replied, "Excellent! I shall see you tomorrow morning."

After Domatin left the tent, Tauriel asked, "Imperator, I may be overstepping my position but, what did Empress Juliana say would happen if we fail?"

Leontina replied, "Yes, you are overstepping—but I trust you. The war with the humans has taken longer than anyone anticipated, and the Dwarves have surprisingly been on the offensive and almost retaken lost ground in Schelmar. Empress Juliana feels the humans are a distraction, while the Dwarves, being closer to our borders, is the real threat which should be dealt with first. If we fail in taking Sternz and killing the human princess, I have been ordered to—" Leontina paused, her mouth twisting as if bile had rising into her mouth, "—to make peace with the humans."

Tauriel, shocked at the news, took a step back and answered, "How could she give such a command? That goes against the commandments of Colubra!"

"I know," Leontina replied. "But the war with the Dwarves is escalating and we can't afford a war on two fronts. The longer we are at war with Crixaria, the more time we give Vetin and Tarium to join their fellow humans. That is a risk we cannot take."

9

The warmth of the sun had faded and darkness enveloped Sternz. A full moon watched over the city as Liam and Blaster stood on top of the wall between the gatehouse and a tower. They looked out toward the Elven encampment, where the dead from both sides were being cremated. Liam, his arms crossed and a disdainful look across his face, scowled. "He was right there. The best chance to end his life and yet I didn't kill him."

Blaster nipped at Liam's thigh and looked at him with his tongue sticking out and wagging his tail. Liam tried to scratch behind the wolf's ear, but Blaster jumped backwards and lowered his head, his tail wagging even faster. A smile crossed Liam's face. "Ever since you were a pup you've tried to knock me down and you constantly fail. You really think this time will be any different?"

Blaster barked once and began to pace around Liam's left. Liam smirked as he lowered himself and readied his hands in front of his body. "Alright then, let's see if you can do it this time."

Blaster juked to the left, then leapt straight at Liam. Liam ducked and spun to his right, avoiding Blaster's leap. Blaster twirled around to again leap at Liam, but before Blaster could react, Liam had already jumped toward Blaster. Liam grabbed Blaster and with the momentum from the jump, the two started to roll on the wall. Liam laughed as he wrapped his arms around Blaster's stomach. Blaster rolled to his side on top of Liam, crushing him and knocking the breath out of him. Liam's grip loosed, and Blaster sprang free. A groaning Liam said, "I think we can call that one a draw." He held his chest as he stood. Blaster barked twice and tilted his head with his ears straight up.

Liam gazed at Blaster and with a confident smile said, "I took you to the ground there, what you did was cheating."

Blaster barked once and wagged his tail. Liam knelt and scratched behind Blaster's ears. "Come on, it's getting late. We should probably get some sleep before the elves attack."

Liam picked his swords up off the ground before heading down the stairs with Blaster following him.

As Liam and Blaster strolled throughout lower Sternz, they came across Zafrinia, still in her full armor, holding her spear with the blade shaped like a wing, standing with her back to them under a lit torch in front of a wooden door. She was talking to one of the volunteers from Tarium. Liam tried to find a different way to the old school house, but the Tarium volunteer, startled by the sight of the wolf, cried out and pointed at Blaster. Zafrinia turned, and with a foul grin on her face called out, "Liam! Don't be so shy. You can come this way if you choose."

Liam attempted to walk past Zafrinia without saying a word, but she lowered the shaft of her spear in his path. Zafrinia stuck her lower lip out and said, "Not even going to say hello to me?"

Liam muttered, "I have no words to say to you." He pushed the shaft of the spear away and continued to walk through the street.

Zafrinia huffed as she followed him and replied, "Come now, surely we can be friends. I heard about what happened with your squad at the gate today and it seems that you could use a friend, someone who won't abandon you or judge you. Why don't you leave them and come fight with me?"

Liam kept walking. "No."

"Suit yourself," Zafrinia answered. "I can be quite a powerful ally if you change your mind. Anyway, since it's just us alone out here, why don't you tell me a little bit about yourself?"

"No."

"Are you sure?" Zafrinia questioned. "Your entire team kind of turned on you today."

"Not all of them."

Zafrinia shrugged and changed the subject. "Your swords are quite well made. My own spear is made of Azaran steel, but that is because my family can afford it. So my question to you is, just how exactly did a dirty, rotten, elven slave acquire such a rare commodity?"

Liam stopped in his tracks, biting his tongue to keep from speaking. With a supreme effort of will he kept his eyes fixed forward. Blaster was not as composed as he turned growling at Zafrinia.

Zafrinia smacked her lips and continued, "Aw, did I hit a nerve? Perhaps you could explain to me why you're in the squad and not me? I mean, I am clearly the best fighter in the city, perhaps even in all the human kingdoms."

Liam let out one slight laugh as he turned to face her. "Alright then," he said. "Let's have it your way."

A smile crossed Zafrinia's lips as she leaned forward and whispered, "I would hate to do it now, with no one here to see you fall. Some other time perhaps, when everyone can see how much better I am than you. You are a fake."

Liam's eyebrows raised up, "I'm a fake? I have heard about what you did to Sal. How you abandoned him without a second thought. You only care about yourself. That's why you are not in the squad."

Zafrinia let out a loud sigh of annoyance as she slouched forward, "How long will that follow me around?"

Liam lowered his swords, "Not long enough." Then he turned around and continued to walk down the street. This time Zafrinia did not follow.

Liam turned to Blaster, "We have been in every country and encountered many different kinds of people. It is people like her that cause everyone around them so much pain."

Blaster barked once and the two continued to walk toward the bridge that separated the upper and lower cities. The city of Sternz appeared calm, though Liam knew everyone was busy in their own way preparing for the siege that lay ahead of them.

Liam and Blaster finally made it to the old school house where Vernon said the squad would be billeted. The building was a simple, one-story wooden structure with a thatched straw roof. The entrance was a wooden door with unshuttered windows on each side. It was dark inside, and the only sound that could be heard was earsplitting snoring.

Liam cracked open the door to see four cots, one in each corner, as well as an open fireplace in the center of the room. In the corner to his immediate left he noticed Kassandra's bow and quiver but not Kassandra. To the right was Konar who was strung out on his back in his cot with a leg and arm hanging off and an empty jug of wine on the floor beneath. In the far-right Vernon lay on his side facing the opposite direction. Blaster silently padded to the empty corner in the far-left, and jumped onto the bed. Liam started to follow, but caught a movement to his right. He perceived Vernon trying to hide something under his pillow. Liam continued toward his cot, and lowered his weapons and armor to the floor. He nodded to Blaster, who reluctantly stepped from the cot and took up a new position on the floor. The wolf's eyes were closed as if he was already asleep. Liam smiled and rubbed the top of Blaster's head.

Liam then made his way over to Vernon and whispered, "I know I haven't given anyone much of a reason to trust me, but I wanted to thank you for—" Liam stopped mid-sentence as he observed Vernon's left hand shaking rapidly. Vernon tried to clinch it, but it was too late. Liam peered at Vernon and asked, "Are you all right?"

Vernon's eyes grew wide, and he shoved his right hand further under his pillow. He chewed feverishly on something. "What are you hiding?" Liam demanded as he reached under the pillow. His fingers found a small leather pouch and he pulled it out. Vernon struggled to pull it back, but Liam managed to open the pouch, and upon seeing its contents, threw it on the ground, spilling bits of a green root onto the floor. Vernon scooted out of bed and scrambled to put the pieces of root back in the pouch. He finished chewing the pieces that were in his mouth and swallowed them.

Liam shoved his finger into Vernon's chest and whispered, "Eacru root? Of all things to be addicted to. Why are you taking that garbage?"

Vernon whispered back, "It sooths me. The chill that goes down your body, the weightlessness sensation. Sometimes the only thing that can get me to sleep is Eacru root."

Liam leaned forward. "And what about the slowed reaction time and the impaired judgment? You may not trust me, and frankly I don't care if you do. But me keeping secrets about my past doesn't compromise our lives. Your addiction does! You could get us killed because of a bad judgment call. I will not follow a leader whose decision-making and reaction time are not what they need to be."

The door burst open and Kassandra stumbled in, holding her boots in her arms as she shuffled forward and fell face-first onto her cot. Liam pointed a finger at Vernon and uttered, "We will finish this conversation later." Liam turned back toward his cot, but paused and said, "You don't need to worry about me telling Konar and Kassandra. That is your responsibility. I hope you do it before you get one of them killed."

10

A distress horn awakened Dylenn and Alezzia. Dylenn jumped out of his bed, rushed to his balcony, and gazed out toward the inner eastern wall. The sunrise and the morning dew made the air humid and wet. Dylenn spotted hundreds of troops on the wall rushing into position. He lowered his head and sighed.

Alezzia, now dressed in a simple but elegant purple silk night gown, approached her husband and leaned on his shoulder. "You wish you were down there with them, don't you?"

"Of course I do. I am their King. I should be fighting alongside those who are going to fight and possibly die to protect our daughter, not hiding away inside the citadel like a coward."

"You are many things, my king, but a coward is not one of them," Alezzia said. "What would happen if you were killed in battle? Not only would Crixaria fall into disarray, but what about your family? Your children need you."

He turned his head kissed her gently, "I love you," he said.

Before Alezzia could reply, the large wooden double doors to their bedchambers swung open. Alyssa and Kaia hurried to the balcony beside their parents. Although she was limping, Kaia managed to keep pace with her younger sister. Kaia paused beside her mother while Alyssa rushed to the stone railing on the balcony. Alezzia peered at Kaia, "Where is your older sister?"

Kaia glanced behind them to the open doorway and replied,

"Bethany is back there—somewhere. It takes her forever to get out of bed, even if the city is under attack."

Dylenn studied Kaia. He looked at the many scratches and bruises on her arms and legs. With a slight smile he asked her, "How are your wounds today?"

Kaia winced as she shifted her weight away from her swollen ankle. With a nod and smile she answered, "I'm a little better today. My ankle is still sore, but everything else was just small cuts and bruises."

Alyssa spun around and with an excited smile said, "I took good care of you Kaia, didn't I?"

Kaia laughed, "Yes you did. Alyssa came into my room last night and crawled into bed with me. She said she was going to protect me from the mean, pointed-ear people."

"And I did!" Alyssa shouted as she rushed to hug Kaia.

Dylenn picked Alyssa up in his arms and grinned. "Alyssa my dear, Crixaria would have fallen years ago if the elves weren't so terrified of you."

"Or Bethany's bed hair," Kaia quipped.

Everyone looked back to the door to see Bethany rubbing her face. Bethany grumbled as she eyed Kaia and began to scuffling to the rest of the Allister family.

Alezzia glided toward Bethany, "By the One, child, your hair is strung about everywhere. Have you no decency?"

Bethany tilted her head at her mother and with grouchy eyes and a grouchy voice replied, "Mother, it's dawn. I just woke up, and no one important is going to see me like this."

Kaia limped to Bethany and started trying to untangle her mass of dark red hair. "You never know, perhaps a handsome suitor will arrive to try and court you, but since your head looked like a stray cat, he may run away." Both Dylenn and Alyssa laughed, but Alezzia and Bethany gave Kaia a sour look.

"Papa?" Alyssa asked.

"Yes, sweetheart?"

"Can I go play in the citadel gardens today?"

Dylenn opened his mouth to answer but Alezzia interrupted. "You most absolutely will not."

"But Mama," Alyssa pouted, "I want to go play by the statue of the Hero."

Alezzia stopped finger-combing Bethany's hair and walked to Alyssa. She stood behind her youngest daughter and started braiding her hair. "And what would we do if the elves got into the city and captured you?" Alezzia glanced at Kaia. "You and each of your sisters are going to stay inside the main citadel until the Vicar and his army arrive."

Alyssa puffed and stuck her bottom lip out. She looked at her father and asked, "Papa, will you at least tell me the story again?"

Bethany, still trying to fix her hair, groaned. "Uh! Not that same old stupid story again."

Kaia arched an eyebrow at her sister. "And what exactly is wrong with the story of the Hero of Aclia?"

Bethany grumped, "It's just so boring."

"Boring?" Kaia griped, "How could it be boring? It's the story of how all the races won their freedom, led by the greatest hero of all time."

Bethany's fingers ran through her hair as she retorted, "Stories like that are just too boring. No matter how much danger the hero is in, you know they won't die—at least not until the end of the story. I like the stories that are unpredictable, where anything can happen, and anyone could die at any moment."

Hurried footsteps echoed from the corridor outside of the room. The Allister family turned to see a sweaty Sir Gregory in the doorway. Gregory spouted, "My King, General Izak sends word of the situation on the wall."

Dylenn set Alyssa on the ground and replied, "Proceed."

"My apologies. The Elven army has amassed facing the eastern inner gate and it appears they will begin the assault very soon."

Dylenn took a step forward to reply, but Alezzia interrupted, "Thank you Sir Gregory. That will be all."

Gregory bowed his head and withdrew. Alezzia walked to Bethany's side and said, "Come child, let us go get you ready for the day and do something about your hair."

As Alezzia and Bethany strolled out of the bedchambers, Alyssa, Kaia, and Dylenn all returned to the balcony. As the morning breeze blew into their faces they gazed toward the eastern inner gate to see the human forces scramble on the wall getting ready for the inevitable attack.

Alyssa looked at her father and asked, "Papa, can you tell me the story now, please?"

Dylenn knelt down beside Alyssa, wrapped her in his arms began, "Of course I will, child. Long ago, over 15,000 years, the world was under the rule of dark, evil, horrid beings of darkness called Nezdras, immortal creatures of evil that ruled over Aclia and all the four races for as long as anyone could remember. A Nezdra named Ucidere led their armies of the undead against any rebellion and was never defeated.

"The Nezdra used dark magic that reanimated dead bodies over and over, so no matter how many were killed, their army never shrunk in size, it only grew. However, Ucidere was not in control. Another being, known only as The First, was their true leader.

All Nezdra fed off the blood of the living and would take whoever they wanted as their feeding bags. But one day things changed. The Hero of Aclia rose up and learned that fire was the weakness of the Nezdra and their undead army. She united the four races and led a final rebellion against the Nezdra, and after years of war, defeated them.

For a time, all four races lived in harmony, but differences inevitably arose and drove each race to separate regions. All the races did however keep the language of old, and that is why we all can understand each other. The church of The One also states that this is why we cremate our dead, because those many years ago our ancestors burned their dead so they would not be reanimated to be used against them."

Alyssa asked, "Papa, what happened to the Hero?"

Dylenn continued as he smiled, "It is said that many years after the war she disappeared without a trace. Many say that the Hero grew tired of politics and went out in search of a glorious death while others say that the Hero died in the night."

A deep, soothing, male voice spoke from the doorway, "Don't forget about the trials of the Hero and the statues, that's the best part."

Kaia, Dylenn, and Alyssa turned to see Benjamin, a man with a long black hair dressed in a dark satin robe. His lean, gentle face showed a few wrinkles under his brown eyes as he smiled at the group.

Alyssa shied away from the man, but Kaia greeted him, "Hello Benjamin. What brings you here this early?"

Benjamin bowed his head as he answered, "I am here to check on your wounds. Are you feeling better today?"

"My ankle feels a little better, thank you," Kaia replied.

Benjamin nodded. "I can see that I am interrupting a family moment and I do not wish to be a further inconvenience. Kaia, I will check on your ankle later in the day when it pleases you." He turned around and walked back out into the corridor.

Alyssa looked upset. "I don't like that man. He is the one who made Mama mean."

Dylenn let out a slight laugh, "No dear child; he helped your mother. Cormorden is an extremely rare, deadly, and incurable disease. Out of every 100 one who contract it, perhaps only five will live. Mister Benjamin has it himself, and he helped your mother cope with the pain after the worse had passed."

Kaia shook her head, "I don't know. Something does seem off about him."

Dylenn continued, "Cormorden changes people. The pain they go through is unbelievable—they don't call it the screaming death for nothing. Cormorden has been around as long as anyone can remember, and we still don't know how it is transmitted. But if you were coughing up blood and felt like your organs were being shredded, and your bones were trying to rip their way out of your body, perhaps it would change you as well."

Dylenn saw the horrified expression on Alyssa's face and immediately regretted his words. "Enough about Cormorden. Do you want me to finish telling you about the Hero?"

Alyssa nodded her head once and nestled closer to her father. His smile grew as he continued, "You know that statue we have of her in our garden? It is said that in random locations all across Aclia, our ancestors built statues with an inscription on each one that told of a trial the Hero went through on her way to defeating the Nezdra."

Another distress horn blew from the wall and Dylenn jolted up to look toward the wall.

Kaia asked, "What's going on?"

"It has begun," Dylenn uttered.

11

The squad ran through the lower city of Sternz to reach the inner gate after the first distress horn blew. With hundreds of other soldiers rushing to the wall the streets were heavy with traffic. Konar was lagging uncharacteristically behind. Vernon asked him, "Are you alright? You look terrible."

Konar squinted his eyes against the brilliant sun. "I believe I may have had a bit too much to drink last night."

"Perhaps you should think about cutting down on alcohol," Kassandra chimed in.

Konar gave her a sour look. "I will cut down on wine when you cut down on men."

Kassandra just grunted and they continued to press forward through the crowded streets until they reached the base of the gate where General Izak was barking out orders to a group of Crixarian officers, Zafrinia among them. Izak dismissed them with a wave and the left to carry out their instructions.

Vernon inquired, "Sir, what are our orders?"

Izak took a quick glance at Vernon, "I've got too much going on to worry about you five. I have to decide which officers and their soldiers will be on the wall and which ones will be in reserve as well as preparing our ballistae. Vernon, you have total command of your unit. Go where you think you will be most useful."

Vernon saluted, then pivoted toward his companions. "The elves are going to try to reach the gatehouse and open the gate. It is the only way their army can gain access to Sternz. The main focus of the attack will be along the wall and towers closest to the gatehouse itself. Now that we know that the elven commander is Imperator Leontina we can predict the attack. It is said that she favors a heavy assault on the defenders' right flank. Konar, I want you between the gatehouse and the first tower on the right. Liam, go between the first and second towers on the right."

Kassandra interrupted. "Wait, you are splitting us up?"

"Yes," Vernon explained. "We need to be able to assist multiple points of the wall."

Kassandra rolled her eyes and grunted to herself.

Vernon continued, "Kassandra, you will be between the first and second towers on the left. I'll be between the gatehouse and the first tower on the left. Any questions?"

Everyone stayed silent. At last Konar nodded his head. "Let's get started."

Konar and Kassandra rushed to their sides of the gate while Liam and Blaster took their time sauntering past Vernon. Liam stopped just as they brushed shoulders. With a frustrated look on his face, Liam said, "If you need help getting off of the root, all you have to do is ask."

Vernon was speechless. He managed a small nod. Liam showed a hint of a grin before turning and running up the stairs with Blaster at his heels.

Once Liam was out of sight, Vernon reached into a belt pouch and pulled out a small, green piece of Eacru root. He forced it in his mouth and started to chew. His breathing settled, and he closed his eyes. He failed to see Liam looking back to him, shaking his head. When Vernon opened his eyes, Liam was at the top of the stairs.

Konar arrived at the stretch of the wall between the gatehouse and the first tower. He saw a few Crixarian soldiers in the first tower loading the ballista and preparing for the attack. Three rows of archers were in position at the back of the wall. But the bulk of the soldiers he would be fighting alongside were no Crixarians, but volunteers from Tarium. Konar groaned when Zafrinia walked out of the gatehouse behind him. She ignored him as she passed him by, without even the slightest of glances. Konar stood motionless, scanning the perimeter. He saw familiar figures passed him by, Liam and Blaster. Konar shouted, "I don't suppose you would want to switch me spots, would you?"

Liam glanced back at Konar, then he spotted Zafrinia, spinning her spear by the edge of the wall. Liam shook his head once and shouted back, "No thanks," then he and Blaster passed through the first tower to the other side.

Once in position, Liam discovered he and Blaster were also not fighting with Crixarian or even Tarium warriors. Instead their companions were men and women in an odd combination of Crixarian and elven armor. Each one also wore a strip of green cloth wrapped around an arm or leg, or tied to a belt. A deep, masculine voice boomed out to everyone on the wall, "Well by shit. Look what we have here."

All eyes turned toward Liam and Blaster. Liam readied himself for whatever might happen next. The same voice yelled out again, "No need for that, good sir! We are all friends here."

Liam turned in the direction of the voice and discovered a young, short, stocky man dressed in brown leather armor with Elven gauntlets, carrying a simple axe and wooden circle shield walking toward him. The man had close-cropped, black hair, and a large scar ran down his right cheek. He extended his arms out from his sides. "I am Makay of Xanica."

Liam interrupted, "Xanica? I thought the elves had completely overrun Xanica."

"That they have," Makay stated as he lowered his head for a

moment. But then looked back up at Liam and smiled. "But not all of us in Xanica are ready to bend the knee to the elves. We, my friend, are part of the resistance and have come here to help safeguard your precocious princess, as well as get some much-needed payback." Many of the soldiers around Makay and Liam let out a cheer of agreement. Makay strolled to Liam's side and slung his arm around Liam's shoulders.

"Now, we all have heard of you, and well, quite frankly I think I can speak for all of us when I say we feel much safer with you beside us today. Don't get me wrong, my people are some tough bastards, but well, you have a certain reputation for being able to kill elves by just looking at them. Come then, my new friend, let us prepare to give the elves a ramming they won't soon forget!"

Kassandra reached her position on the wall, which had more archers than the rest, five rows instead of three. She tested the tension of her bow. As she tugged on the bow string, a male Crixarian officer with long blonde curly hair crossed toward her. With a smile she asked him, "So I take it you are in command here?"

The officer looked her over head to toe and smiled, "That I am," he answered. "I dared not hope that someone as beautiful, and as deadly, as Kassandra Verbeck would be stationed at my section of the wall. I am Captain Ducan."

Kassandra didn't let on that she recognized him from his encounter with Liam and Blaster at the tavern. "So Captain Ducan, what is the plan?"

Ducan inched closer to her and confided, "General Izak said that the elven commander is named Leontina, and that she always favors a heavy attack on our right flank. Since most of our archers were lost between the inner and outer walls, we are going to hold our left flank and allow the archers behind me to rain death on their right and center flanks."

Ducan paused for a moment before placing his hand on

Kassandra's arm. He leaned in close and whispered, "Now, how about tonight you stop by my barracks, and you can attack *my* flank?"

Kassandra tilted her head and grinned. "As much fun as that sounds like, I wouldn't want you to get overexcited."

A puzzled Ducan stammered, "What?"

Kassandra, even cheerier than before, responded with a smile. "You know? I would be afraid that you would piss your pants in excitement before we even got started."

Ducan let out a small, high pitched laugh. His face reddened before he stomped away. Kassandra spat, then turned and looked out over the wall at the assembled elven army. Their foot soldiers and archers were beyond bow-shot, 500 yards away. Behind them were several ballistae of their own, the wood more finely carved than those of the Crixarians. The Elven ballistae were being loaded with large steel bolts. She shrugged her shoulders and muttered to herself, "Well, this probably won't last long."

Vernon looked over the wall from his position at the elven army. His left hand shook, and he tried to conceal it by gripping his shield as hard as he could and holding it close to his body. General Izak approached and placed a hand on his shoulder. "I never got a chance to properly thank you for getting Princess Allister back. Your squad's performance yesterday was nothing less than extraordinary."

After a moment's delay, Vernon surprised at Izak's words, replied, "Thank you sir. I just wish we could have saved more of our troops instead of abandoning them outside of the wall."

Izak nodded his head. His face sunk and his fist clinched. "As do I. Unfortunately that decision was taken out of our hands."

"How do you think the elves will try and assault the wall? I don't see any kind of siege equipment besides a few ballistae, which have no chance of bringing down our walls. I don't even see any ladders."

Before Izak could reply, they heard a metallic whiz followed by a loud thud from the section of the wall to their left where Kassandra was stationed.

Izak and Vernon leaned over the edge of the wall to their left and saw a large harpoon wedged into the wall only a few inches from the top. At the base of the harpoon was a large metal chain, extending all the way down to the ground, with metal hooks pointing upwards on each side.

Izak called out to the troops on top of the gatehouse, "Sound the second horn!"

One of the troops on top of the gatehouse picked up a heavy horn and let out a long blow, sounding a loud boom that alerted Sternz that the attack has begun. As soon as the sound of the horn faded, more and more harpoons thundered into the wall along all the sections. Izak yelled out again, "Someone get those harpoons out of my wall!"

A Crixarian soldier with a heavy, two-handed hammer walked forward, tossing the hammer in his hands. The soldier reached the edge and started to bring his hammer down on the harpoon. Hundreds of arrows darted through the air toward the wall, raining down along the edge of the wall, killing the soldier with the hammer and dozens of others who were close to the edge. All across the wall every time a soldier got too close to the edge, a volley of arrows followed to push the humans back.

"Leontina, you clever elf," Izak whispered in grudging admiration. "Leontina is testing our defenses. Go to one of the towers. Order everyone to move back and let them come. Once the Elves get within 200 yards of our walls, let death rain down upon them!"

Vernon nodded and rushed to the tower, entered the stone doorway of the tower, and took the small wooden stairs to two steps at a time to the top. Once there, Vernon walked past the ballista, a death machine that worked like a giant crossbow that fired wooden spikes three feet in length.

Vernon felt a cold sweat come over him and looked to his left hand, noticing that it wasn't shaking anymore. He let out a deep breath as he sweated out the effects of the Eacru root. His senses returned, and he heard thunderous footsteps marching in unison. He gazed out toward the elven army and saw the first few rows marching forward in lockstep, their shields raised and stacked close to each other ready for the humans to release volleys of arrows at them.

Vernon looked behind him at the ballista and then again to the oncoming elven line. He ordered the three soldiers on the wall, "Once they are within 300 yards begin firing."

"300?" one soldier replied, "Our normal range, if we want to be accurate, is 200 yards."

Vernon looked into the eyes of the soldier and stated, "Yes, but we do not need to be accurate. All we need to do is to kill as many elves as we can before they reach the walls. In their tightly packed lines it will not be hard for us to thin the herd."

Vernon walked to the other side of the tower and peered down to see that they were still being pushed back by Elven arrow volleys. He spotted Ducan and yelled down to him, "Ducan! The elves are within 400 yards! You can begin to return volleys!"

Ducan nodded his head and called to his, "At the ready!" Kassandra raised her bow to shoot alongside the rest of the archers. Ducan raised his left arm, paused, then screamed as he threw his arm down, "Release!" The archers released their arrows, screaming into the air, but as the arrows flew overhead, the approaching elves raised their shields, blocking the majority of the arrows.

Vernon called to Ducan. "Hold! Don't waste your arrows until we've taken care of their shields."

Once the elven line was within 300 yards, Vernon turned to the soldiers manning the ballista. "Now it's your turn."

The three soldiers got into position, one soldier went to the back to aim, another went to the right of the ballista to pull the firing lever, and the third stood on the left to reload the wooden spikes. The soldier aiming yelled, "Launch!" and the lever was pulled and a cluster of 12 wooden spikes hurtled toward the approaching elven line. The sharpened wooden spikes penetrated through the shields. Each spike did its deadly work, pinning elves to the ground and creating chaos among those nearby. Shocked, the elves momentarily let their guard down.

"Release," Ducan shouted, and volley of arrows wreaked havoc among the ranks of the elves.

Upon seeing the lone ballista firing to great success, the rest of the ballista towers soon begin shooting their spikes at the elves as well, followed by unrelenting volleys of arrows. Hundreds of elves died as the marched dutifully toward the wall.

Something's wrong, Vernon thought. *Their not returning fire at the ballista towers.* "Don't stop shooting," he commanded the ballista crew. "I need to talk to General Izak."

Vernon hurried down the wooden stairs inside the tower and back out to the section of the wall where he spotted Izak. "General Izak, sir, why are the elves letting our ballistae kill their soldiers without any opposition?"

"Leontina is testing our defenses," Izak answered. "This isn't the main assault. It's a feint. She wants to see how quickly we can reload our ballista, perhaps see if we have any other nasty surprises waiting for her."

"And do we, sir? Have any surprises, I mean."

"Unfortunately, no," the old soldier grimaced. "All we can do is hold for as long as we can." Izak stood up straight and shouted the Crixarian battle cry, "To victory or death!"

The cry was picked up and repeated along the wall and across the towers, "To victory or death!"

Konar shifted from side to side as he stood in the middle of the volunteers from Tarium. The barrage of arrows stopped and everyone watched the wall waiting for the first sign of an elven invader. Zafrinia stepped closer to the wall. An uncomfortable smile grew on her face as she cried out, "Let them come! Let's show these elves how real warriors can fight! We are not simple farmers and merchants. We are the One's true disciples!" The line of Tarium volunteers raised their fists in the air and roared. Zafrinia grinned as she yelled the Tarium battle cry, "Death to Pagans!" To which every Tarium volunteer yelled out in unison, "Death to Pagans!"

As the cry faded, elven soldiers appeared at the top of the wall. One by one, across the entire section of the wall, they came. There were 12 points where the elves were climbing. Zafrinia and Konar rushed forward with the volunteers from Tarium to expel the elves from the wall.

As the first elven soldier at Liam's position scaled the wall, Liam and Blaster sprinted forward, Makay and the rest of the Xanican resistance following close behind. The battle raged along the entire wall. The first elf swung her sword at Liam's head but he ducked under and rammed his shoulder into her stomach, hurling her back over the wall. He could hear her screaming as she plummeted 100 feet to her death. Blaster jolted behind an elf and ripped out his Achilles tendon. Liam cut him down as the elf fell to his knees. The bloodlust upon him, Liam let out a deep roar that drove fear into the hearts of the elves.

Kassandra's section of the wall was having great success keeping the assault at bay. As soon as an elf appeared at the top of the wall, a barrage of multiple arrows was released. Kassandra was able to kill an elf as soon as she saw its head peeking above the parapet. The onslaught was a drain on ammunition, and Ducan shouted to the soldiers stationed below, "We need more arrows, now!"

The soldiers started to gather up quivers of arrows and bolted as fast as they could up the stairs, but the supply was too little, too late. Her quiver empty, Kassandra set her bow down and pulled out her daggers, again holding the hilt to where the blades were pointing behind her. Ducan ordered, "Infantry get ready!" Crixarian soldiers armed with swords and axes prepared themselves. As the last of the arrows were released the infantry let out a roar and rushed forward.

Kassandra ran straight for two elves in front of her. As she got close to the elf in front she jumped forward and wrapped her legs around the neck of the first elf. Using her momentum and weight she leaned back and twisted her entire body. The neck of the elf snapped, and the twist turned Kassandra toward the second elf, where she slit her throat. As Kassandra fell to the ground she saw an elf backing up toward her. She took the dagger in her left hand and in a single motion cut the tendons behind both knees, which allowed the Crixarian soldier the advantage he needed to kill the elf.

Kassandra heard a warning yell and turned to see an elven male with his sword raised ready to strike down at her. She threw her dagger into the elf's throat. Before the elf hit the ground she had retrieved her dagger and continued the fight.

Vernon and Izak engaged with the elves as they tried to reach the gatehouse. An elf rushed toward Vernon, but he bashed the elf in the chest with his shield. As the elf stumbled backward Vernon stabbed the elf in the gut.

Izak was near the edge of the wall observing the elven army. He realized the elves were not sending any reinforcements to the wall. The last of the elves involved in this attack were climbing the metal chains. Izak shouted over the sounds of battle, "This is it people! Just a few moments longer."

As an elf struck downward at Konar, Konar tilted his hammer sideways and blocked the strike with the shaft of his hammer. He pushed the elf's arms up in the air, then bashed the elf in the face with the shaft of his hammer. The stunned elf wobbled unsteadily. Konar took a step back, readied his hammer, and with all his strength swung up, catching the elf directly under the chin, sending him into the air and over the wall. As the elf disappeared, Konar realized there were no more elves climbing over the walls.

He saw Zafrinia engaged with an elf warrior. Zafrinia lowered her spear and swept the elf's legs, then thrust her spear into his chest. Zafrinia spotted an elf on the far side of the wall. With a smile on her face she tossed her spear in the air, caught it, and with a long stride launched the spear. It pierced the elf's armor, and pinned him to the wall.

Zafrinia cried out, "Now that's how real warriors fight!"

Konar wiped the warm blood from his face and shook his head at Zafrinia's boasts. The last of the elves were cleared from the walls. Liam and Blaster soon walked through the tower separating their sections, followed by Makay. As they walked toward Konar, Makay yelled out, "By the One that boy can fight! That son of a bitch and his wolf killed at least 50 elves! I think I'll always fight beside him."

Konar joked at Liam, "I think you've made a new friend," pointing at Makay.

Liam grumbled, "Come on, let's go find Vernon and see what's going on."

As Konar, Liam, and Blaster walked through the gatehouse they saw Vernon and Kassandra talking to Izak. Bloodied Crixarian soldiers lined the wall. Vernon spotted them approaching and asked, "How'd everything go on the other side of the gatehouse?"

Liam didn't say anything, so Konar replied, "For the most part it went well. The elves seemed determined to open the gate even when there were only a handful of them left. Other than that, I say they lost more than we did."

Kassandra looked at the piles of the dead on the wall, "Those elves had to have known that this was certain death. Yet they fought as if they had a chance."

Izak replied, "Religion came be a powerful motivation. Even if you are going to certain death having the belief that you are dying for a greater purpose, to fulfill your god's will, can be motivation enough to do what is necessary."

Liam wiped the blood of his swords. "So, what next?"

Vernon replied, "You four will go back to the barracks for the time being. General Izak and I are going to go to meet with the rest of the officers and King Dylenn and discuss what to do next."

As Liam, Konar, Kassandra, and Blaster walked down the stairs, Vernon saw a troubled look cloud Izak's face. "Everything alight sir?"

Izak took a long, deep breath. He pointed at the elven camp. "They have trebuchets."

<h1 align="center">12</h1>

Domatin stormed into the Elven command tent with fire in his eyes. Leontina and Tauriel had been studying the map of Sternz but now their attention turned to Domatin. With a dark scowl across his face Domatin demanded, "Why did you stop the attack? We had the numbers to overwhelm them. We should be inside the city by now burning it to the ground, not running away like cowards!"

Leontina clicked her tongue in annoyance, and replied as if addressing a petulant child, "Prince Domatin, that was not a real attack. I told you yesterday we were going to test their defenses at dawn, which we did. We have timed the reload speed of their ballistae, determined the range of their archers, and we discovered that there weren't any traps between our army and the walls. We accomplished all we needed without sacrificing too many lives."

"I don't care about your plans," Domatin seethed. "I want to be walking the streets of Sternz by nightfall!"

Tauriel interjected, "Prince Domatin, these things take time, especially when the walls are as massive as the walls of Sternz."

Domatin muttered through his teeth, "I was not talking to you."

Leontina saw the frustration building in Domatin's face. To pull attention away from Tauriel she cleared her throat and said, "Our trebuchets have been completed ahead of schedule. Even at full strength our two mages won't be able to bring down those walls; they are just too thick. Fifty feet wide of solid stone is quite the obstacle. Our trebuchets will not only chip away at their precious wall, but the constant pounding will lower the moral of all those inside the city. We also won't lose more elven lives trying to assault and take control of the gatehouse."

Domatin's gaze lingered on Tauriel for a moment longer before he turned his attention back to Leontina. "I don't care about elven losses. I don't care about hidden traps. And I don't care about lowering human moral," he spat. "All I care about is killing an abomination that shouldn't exist!"

Leontina allowed a small smile to form as she looked at Tauriel, "Tauriel, could you please give us a moment." Tauriel bowed and walked outside the tent. Leontina, the grin still on her face, arched an eyebrow at Domatin. "And which abomination might that be? The human princess—or the slave?"

Domatin kept a firm gaze on Leontina. His sadistic grin sent chills down her spin, but she could tell by the way Domatin's hands were shaking that she had struck a nerve. Leontina pressed her advantage, "I've known you the entire 300 years you've been alive, and I've never known you to be a particularly religious person. I think the real reason you are here is to make sure no one finds out what you did to cover up the slave's escape."

"Enough," Domatin muttered.

But that didn't stop Leontina. "How exactly does it feel to be the first elf in over 2,000 years to lose a slave? Granted, I didn't put two and two together until I saw the slave fighting and saw what happened at your banner. What you care about, my dear Prince, is killing the abomination, and by that I mean preventing anyone from finding out the truth. How much longer do you think you can keep it hidden? It will eventually come out. And when it does, it will destroy you."

"I said enough!" Domatin shouted. Leontina stopped talking but didn't wavier in her stance or gaze.

A numb silence enveloped the tent before Domatin forced a grin back onto his face. "Be careful what you say Imperator. We wouldn't want anything bad to happen to you or any of your Legati."

Leontina remained firm, motionless as she stared at Domatin. With a faint puff Domatin added, "Now, I'm going to eat breakfast before this waste of a morning passes." He pointed his finger at Leontina. "Remember, I want to be walking in the streets of Sternz by nightfall. That is not a request." He turned and stormed out of the tent.

Tauriel walked back into the tent to see Leontina massaging the back of her neck. She could sense the tension still swirling in the room. She said, "I apologize if I spoke out of turn earlier."

"Not at all. Prince Domatin is just upset. He will cool down soon."

"The prince looked even more agitated as he left," Tauriel observed. "If it's not overstepping, what was said between you? I couldn't make out much from outside, but it didn't sound pleasant."

Leontina shook her head as she rubbed her eyes, "I wish I could tell you, but it could set off a chain of events that could cause more harm than good. Let's just say that it dealt with why he is really here."

"Does it have to do with that human at the wall—Liam, I think was his name?" Tauriel inquired.

Leontina's face paled as she rushed to place a hand over Tauriel's mouth. She whispered, "For your sake do not talk about, ask anyone about, or even think about that human."

Tauriel's eyes widened as Leontina's hand slid from her mouth. She lowered her voice and asked, "If it is that bad, shouldn't everyone know? If it is something that could affect the troops or elves back home, do they not have the right to be told?"

Leontina kept her eyes on the flaps to the tent as she responded, "If not for your own sake at least for your mother's, let this go."

Tauriel took a small step backward. "My mother? What does my mother have to do with anything?"

Leontina looked Tauriel in the eyes, "I just don't want to see her become even worse. You know that I wouldn't hurt her in any way, but you've seen how Domatin acts, and we both know that if he found out you were the one who started rumors or uncovered anything he didn't want found out, he wouldn't rest until you were begging for death. Just focus on taking the wall and nothing else. I don't care what you see or hear, just focus on the wall."

Tauriel's eyes began to water as she stood firm, "My mother is sick enough without the Prince around her."

Leontina asked, "Is she getting any better?"

Tauriel's head lowered. "No. She is still bed ridden. Our doctors don't know how to fix her and I know she is miserable, just lying in bed all day."

Leontina walked around the table and held her. With a soothing voice she said, "Tauriel, you have been the best officer in my army since the first day you arrived. It's high time you have a command of your own, and I promise as soon as we have accomplished Colubra's will, I will speak to Empress Julianna myself about getting you stationed closer to home, hopefully in Azara itself."

"Thank you Imperator. I will continue to serve both you and Colubra to the best of my ability."

"I know you will," Leontina responded with a smile. "Come now, let us distract ourselves and go take a look at our trebuchets."

Leontina and Tauriel walked out of the command tent and passed through the encampment. Every step they took was met with smiling and eager faces. Moral was high as elven troops were hard at work building other siege engines, using wood from the many trees beyond the outer wall. As they arrived near the trebuchets Tauriel asked, "How many do we have now?"

"Fifty, but by nightfall we should have 200," Leontina replied.

"That many?" Tauriel said. "Couldn't we use the extra wood elsewhere?"

Leontina nodded her head, "I don't know about you, but I would like to get this done as soon as possible. The sooner we fulfill Colubra's will the sooner we can return home. And I would prefer to break down their walls without losing more elven lives than necessary."

They walked up to the first of the trebuchets—massive, wooden war machines capable of launching large rocks hundreds of feet into or over the walls of Sternz. The frame of the trebuchet was shaped in a triangle, the top of the frame had a long wooden beam that on the longer side had a sling made of wool, while the shorter had the large counter weight. As Leontina and Tauriel approached, the workers stopped and bowed. Leontina bowed in return, then asked, "Legatus Conra. When can we begin launching?"

Conra replied, "The first 50 can begin at any time Imperator. We can add the rest as they are completed throughout the day."

"Very good," Leontina said with a smile. "Begin firing at once. Aim for both sections of the wall immediately beside their gate. I don't want you to launch into the city itself. We are here to kill one abomination, not the entire city. Do I make myself clear?"

"Yes Imperator!"

The group loaded a large rock, which took four elves to move, onto the trebuchet. As the order circulated through the camp the action was repeated at the trebuchets. Each trebuchet stood ready, an elf at each one ready to pull a lever to launch. Leontina stood with a satisfied grin. She looked to Conra. "Bring their walls down."

Conra nodded, then shouted, "Pull!"

Fifty levers were pulled, and 50 massive rocks hurled into the air toward the wall.

13

Vernon and Izak stood on top of the wall as the human army recovered from the first assault. Izak gave an order to some nearby Crixarian soldiers, "Gather the dead from both sides and cremate them. Recover what weapons and armor you can, even from the elves; we will need as much as we can get in the coming days."

Vernon looked out toward the tents of the Elven encampment, watching as they rushed their own wounded into medical tents, when a commotion toward the rear caught his eyes. "General," Vernon said, "I think we need to get off the wall."

Izak glanced over just in time to see the Elven trebuchets release their projectiles. Izak yelled out, "Get down!"

Everyone on the wall scrambled as the boulders whirled through the air. The rocks slammed against the wall, each one shaking the enormous wall as they shattered and bounced off. After the last of the first wave of projectiles had hit the wall, Vernon hustled to the edge and looked down assess the damage. The rocks had made some slight scratches and knocked down a few of the elves harpoons, but nothing severe.

Vernon reported to Izak and said, "Not much damage, sir. At this rate it will take them at least two weeks to break down our wall."

Izak shook his head. "If this is all they have. But I'm sure they are building more. Come, let's go the officers meeting and brief the King on the situation." As they were leaving Izak issued orders to the soldiers on the wall, "If you can, get those harpoons out of the wall. If you can't, at least try to pull the chains up off the ground so that the elves can't climb up whenever they choose."

Vernon and Izak descended the stairs and marched through lower Sternz, constantly aware of the crashing of the rocks against the inner wall. Vernon asked, "Where is the officers meeting?"

Izak nodded to a patrol rushing past them as he replied, "Bear Claw Tavern. Everyone knows its location, even our allies from Tarium and Xanica."

"Won't it be busy there at this time of day?" Vernon asked as the sun was approaching the peak of the sky.

Izak answered, "Normally yes but I sent a few officers ahead of us to clear it out and prepare some tables for everyone."

As the two men walked through the lower city they notice that the citizens were calm—some helping the bloodied and wounded soldiers, others opening their homes as places to give aide. Children were running and laughing through the streets, almost oblivious to the sounds of crashing rocks. They felt safe with walls to protect them. Izak ground his teeth. *I wonder how long the wall will hold?*

Vernon and Izak were the last two to arrive at Bear Claw Tavern. All the worn wooden tables had been moved to circle the open fireplace. The only people in the building were Dylenn and Alezzia, Crixarian officers including Gregory, Ducan and Abby, and finally, the officers from the other kingdoms such as Zafrinia and Makay. Vernon and Izak sat down in the only remaining two chairs beside Dylenn.

Dylenn nodded to everyone gathered at the table. "Izak, what is the situation?"

Izak put both hands on the table and addressed the gathered party,. "The elves are currently using trebuchets to try and break down our walls without fighting. However, they will be nowhere near complete before Vicar Matthew arrives tomorrow. Luckily since Leontina is used to fighting dwarves and sieging Dwarven cities, where there is only one entryway, we only have to worry about protecting one side of the wall. We will still patrol the other sections of the wall but not as heavily as the eastern. Her experience is dealing with one side of a city, so I am confident she will stick to what she knows."

"Said the man who said that we could hold the elves at the outer wall until tomorrow," Alezzia interrupted with her arms crossed.

A hush draped over the room as Alezzia and Izak shared an unpleasant stare. Izak scratched his beard, "During the entirety of the war these past 15 years, the elves had never once sent mages to a battle against us. The Elven high council has only sent mages to fight the dwarves. They were not—expected."

An unflinching Alezzia continued her verbal attack, "Tell me General Izak, exactly how have we been able to hold the elves back for 15 years?"

Izak knew where Alezzia was going with the conversation. As he gritted his teeth he answered, "The elves have had a difficult time adapting to our cavalry. Azara's lush mountains as well as the neighboring ruined-filled desert of the Eacru wastes and the unforgiving jagged mountains of Schelmar meant that the elves were not used to fighting with or against cavalry."

Alezzia began to lean forward in her chair, "So tell me why you convinced my husband that it was a better idea to stay locked up in these walls rather than stick to a tactic that has worked for 15 years! Why did we not sally out and push the elves back the same way we have done in the past?"

Izak looked around the room at the equally judgmental faces of his officers. With a deep breath he answered, "We simply no longer have the numbers. Crixaria has been on its own for the past 15 years. Out of the initial 75,000 troops we had available a few days ago, before the inner gates were closed and we lost half to the elves," he pointedly added, "only around 10,000 were trained to fight on horseback. I'm sorry, but 10,000 cavalry cannot defeat an elven army 200,000 strong."

"Perhaps you should be removed from command, Izak. It is clear you no longer know the best course of action."

Dylenn slammed his fist on the table, "Silence! Past decisions have been made and no one person is to blame for any of this. We must come together in this difficult time and stand as one if we are to survive until tomorrow. Now please, Izak, continue."

Izak cleared his throat before he continued. "As I was saying, the elves are using trebuchets to try to break down our walls, but they are too few to be effective any time soon. Hopefully, they do not yet know that Vicar Matthew is on his way with his army. Unfortunately, we do not know how many soldiers he is bringing with him. When we received his message saying he was sending aid, he was raising an army and was not fully amassed yet. It could be 20,000. It could be 300,000. We just simply do not know. How many soldiers the Vicar brings will determine what strategy we will employ."

From the back of the room, an older Crixarian officer asked, "If the Vicar doesn't arrive with a large force, is there anyone we can ask to send aid? Vetin maybe, or perhaps even the dwarves?"

Zafrinia, who was slumped in her chair looking bored, let out a loud harrumph. As everyone turned their attention to her, Zafrinia shrugged. "What? It was a stupid question."

Izak ignored her and answered, "The dwarves have disliked all of humankind since we took Vetin from them 300 years ago. And Vetin, well they are a democracy—which means they can't agree on anything. Xanica's resistance has sent everyone they can spare so we won't be getting anymore help from them."

"So all we can do is wait?" asked Ducan.

Izak nodded his head and replied, "Unfortunately, yes. But when the Vicar does arrive, we should have the numbers we need to win, whether it is to defend the city or to rush out and attack the elves at their camp."

As Izak finished, a loud crashing sound was heard as the ground beneath them trembled. Dylenn jumped out of his chair and headed for the front door, with Izak and the other officers close behind. Zafrinia and Alezzia stayed in their chairs as if oblivious to the event. Dylenn saw a female soldier running past and grabbed her arm, "Soldier, what is happening?"

"My King, a trebuchet projectile came over the wall and demolished two houses."

Izak asked, "How many soldiers did we loose in those houses?"

"None sir," the soldier replied. "Only the families who lived there were inside."

Izak closed his eyes while Dylenn grimaced and raised his head in the air. A voice from within the tavern asked, "How many?"

With her head lowered the soldier responded, "Seven. An older couple with two of their three grown children, and a newlywed couple who," the soldier struggled to finish her sentence, "who were expecting their first child."

Dylenn placed his hands on the soldier's shoulders. "I want you spread the word, all civilians residing in lower Sternz are to immediately evacuate into the Upper city. We must all come together in this time of need. The citizens in the upper city are to open their doors by royal command. If there is not enough room for all, then open the Citadel to the citizens of lower Sternz. Is that clear?"

"Yes my King," and she headed off to spread the word.

Dylenn turned to the officers gathered behind him, grimacing as he said, "I think now is a good time for this meeting to end. You all know what needs to be done. Do not let our city fall, not just for me, but for the men, women, and children who are counting on you to keep them safe from an unforgiving enemy."

14

Kassandra, Liam, Konar, and Blaster arrived at the old school-house. Kassandra went first to open the door but just before her hand touched the door, she stopped. She turned around to everyone else and with a smile on her face said, "I don't know about you two," Blaster interrupted her with a whine and wagged his tail. She smiled at him, "OK you three, but I would rather not be covered in blood for the rest of the day." She then nodded at the river right next to them that separated upper and lower Sternz. "Who is up for a quick swim?"

Konar grinned as he stretched his back, "That does sound like a pretty good idea. What do you say, you two?"

Blaster let out a single bark and wagged his tale harder. Liam uttered, "I will just sit on the edge."

"Suit yourself," Kassandra replied. Then she started down the stairs to a small pier above the water where she began to remove her leather armor. Konar followed but Liam shied away from looking at Kassandra as she had stripped down to just her tight black leather under garments.

Konar noticed how Liam looked away and gazed at him rather surprised. Before Konar could ask, Blaster rushed up behind them and started to tug at the front of Liam's boots. Liam said, "You can go ahead, I may get in later."

Blaster bolted toward the end of the pier. The large black wolf lunged off the pier and into the clear water below, rinsing the blood off of him. Kassandra laughed as she jumped into the water. Konar forgot about Liam for a moment and ran full sprint into the water, armor and all. The water, which came up to Kassandra's neck, only reached Konar's chest.

Liam made his way to the end of the pier, set his swords down and took off his boots. He sat on the edge of the pier, next to Kassandra's weapons and armor, and dangled his feet into the water. Kassandra swam to the pier and rested her arms on the wood beside Liam. With a cheerful smile she said, "Come on, get in water. Don't you know how to swim?"

Liam, who was trying not to look at her, kept his eyes fixed on the water as he replied, "Perhaps later." He picked up one of his boots and started rinsing the mud off of it in the river. Kassandra studied him for a moment. He was an enigma to her. She shrugged it off and reached for her armor to wash the blood off in the river.

Konar waded toward them, and noticing the tension in the air, tried to liven up the situation. The massive orc climbed out of the water and sneaked as best he could behind Liam. But Liam saw the shadow that Konar was casting over him and stopped washing his armor. Liam sighed as he stood and turned around to see Konar with a devious grin. Liam, with a serious tone, pointed to Konar as he said, "I swear by the One if you push me in the river…"

Konar stood motionless with a smile on his face. Liam continued to stare Konar down, but he knew something was amiss. He realized too late that Kassandra was moving in the water behind him. She leapt out of the water and grabbed the back of Liam's shirt, pulling him into the water. Konar and Kassandra both erupted into laughter as Liam slowly gained his footing and stood up in the water and glared at them. Kassandra said, "See, it's not so bad. And if you had started to drown, I would have saved you."

Liam scowled at her before he waded back over to the pier. Without a word, he pulled himself out of the water, grabbed his gear and stomped off toward the old schoolhouse with Blaster behind him. Konar and Kassandra burst out laughing.

"You don't think he is that mad, do you?" Kassandra asked.

"No, I just don't think he wanted to admit that it was funny."

With a cheerful smile she answered, "You are probably right. I think we are slowly opening him up."

"Slowly but surely," Konar responded.

Konar lowered his hand to help Kassandra out of the river. They both put their armor back on. As they walked toward the stairs Kassandra wrung the water from her ponytail, twisting it side to side. They entered the barracks to see that Liam had started a fire. Liam's boots were by his bed but the rest of his clothes were drying by the fire.

"Good idea," Kassandra stated as she walked toward the fire.

Konar walked to his bed and reached for a jug of wine. Kassandra frowned at Konar and said, "It's always alcohol with you. What if the elves attack and you are drunk off your ass?"

Konar took a long swig before he snarked, "What if the elves attack and you are sleeping with a guy?"

Kassandra winked and replied, "We don't actually *sleep*."

Liam stared into the fire. Konar took another long drink, then said, "Orc, Human, Elf, or Dwarf—every single one of us do something to escape reality and the pain of life. Mine is to drink. Yours is sex. And I'm sure Liam and Vernon have their own vices."

"I don't use sex to escape from anything," Kassandra puffed.

Konar set the jug of wine down and replied, "I've been alive for 75 years. So I guess I'm about half way through my life. If the elves don't kill me. I've seen plenty of women like you, both human and orc. Whether you admit it or not, you do."

Kassandra crossed her arms beneath her breasts and scowled at Konar, but before more heated words could be spoken, Blaster rushed over to the jug of wine, bit the handle between his teeth, turned his bright yellow eyes to Konar and wagged his tail.

Konar leaned down and reached for the jug. "Here boy. Careful not to spill the wine."

Kassandra started to giggle, and even Liam cracked a faint smile. Konar looked to Liam and said, "Well, are you going to tell him to give me my wine back?"

Liam shrugged. "You helped Kassandra dunk me into the river. You're on your own."

Konar grimaced and turned his attention back to Blaster. He tried to grab the jug of wine away from the playful wolf, but Blaster was too quick for him. Before Konar could retrieve his jug, the door to the schoolhouse opened and Vernon entered the room. Liam stood and walked toward the door, making it a point to bump Vernon's shoulder on the way out. Vernon gritted his teeth as he followed Liam.

"What is your problem?" Vernon demanded.

"My problem?" Liam replied, "My problem is that I'm following the orders of someone who isn't in control of his own mind and who very well could get me killed."

Vernon took a small step back, "What are you talking about?"

"The root. All you can think about is your next chew of the root."

"That's not true, Liam," Vernon said.

"Really? Because from where I stand, it looks very much like the truth."

Vernon took a deep breath as he stared back at him, "I've tried to quit. I've tried slowly cutting down on the amount I take. It just doesn't work."

Liam looked Vernon directly in the eyes,. "That's because the only way to quit the root is to just quit."

"How do you know?" Vernon asked.

Liam looked away. In hushed tone he answered, "I was not Domatin's only slave. He wouldn't dare get me hooked on the root; I made him too much money. But he did get others addicted to it just to bask when they begged him for more. He could make any of them do practically anything he wanted just to get one more chew."

"How exactly did you make Domatin money?"

Liam fixed Vernon with a glare, then shook his head and started walking toward lower Sternz.

"Just going to leave again?" Vernon called to his back. "Like you left Kassandra in the middle of a battle. Is that what you want? To be alone? Then just leave!"

Liam looked through one of the schoolhouse windows and watched Kassandra laughing at Konar and Blaster. A small smile creased his lips. "I'm not leaving. I'm just going for a walk."

Vernon breathed a sigh of relief. "Thank you," he said.

Liam didn't reply. He simply started walking toward lower Sternz.

Vernon stood at the doorway and smiled at Konar's futile attempts to get his wine back. Eventually the orc managed to corner Blaster between two walls, but Liam let out a long, high-pitched whistle. Blaster, he threw his head in the air and howled in reply, hurling the jug of wine into the air in the process. Konar lunged for it, and caught his jug before it smashed to the floor. Unfortunately, the jug was upside down, spilling what remained of the wine. Blaster ran out of the schoolhouse while Kassandra and Vernon burst out into laughter.

"Well, you finally got your wine back," Kassandra joked.

15

King Dylenn sat in the throne room of the citadel, a large rectangular open room made of the same light grey stone as the inner and outer walls. Two large wooden doors acted as the main entrance to the room, and open archways provided access to other areas of the citadel. All along both sides of the room were huge stone pillars. Running on the ground from the two large wooden doors was a long dark purple rug that stopped at the steps leading up to the thrones.

Dylenn contemplated the day's events, trying to think of the positives to avoid thoughts of all the death. His reverie was interrupted when the doors swung opened with Alezzia storming through them. Dylenn closed his eyes and took a deep breath. He knew what Alezzia had come to rant about.

"Our house? Of all places to let them stay, you said that they can stay here, with us, where we sleep?"

"Alezzia my dear, we have plenty of extra rooms."

"I don't care about the extra rooms" she protested as she mounted the stairs to her throne. "They are peasants. Dirty, lowlife, peasants—practically cattle! And you are granting them free access to where your family sleeps?"

Dylenn scanned the room before replying. "A man is born a peasant or a king. We may live different lives, but sooner or later all men die and burn in the fire as equals. Over 300,000 citizens live in our city. Everyone who resides in Sternz are citizens of Crix-aria. As king, it is my duty to keep them safe, regardless of how uncomfortable it may be for me, or how inconvenient it is for you."

Alezzia laid her hand on Dylenn's arm. Though still seething, she tried a different approach to reason with her husband. "I know *why* you are doing it. But I'm worried about our daughters' safety. The elves are known to employ assassins who are adept at blending in. Now, with the doors into the citadel wide open, what is to prevent one of them from making an attempt on Kaia's life?"

Dylenn looked her in her soft blue eyes as he responded. "The wraiths have tried before to kill Kaia. They have failed each time. They will fail this time."

"There was never a siege going on before," Alezzia pouted. "Everyone's attention is on the elves *outside* the walls. But what if there are already some *inside* our city? Now with open access to our home, an assassin could be sleeping a few doors down from our children, waiting for the right time to strike."

"I know you are worried," he answered. "But I have to do this. If it makes you feel better I will triple the guard around our daughters."

She met his gaze for few moment, then without a word, walked down the stairs and out through one of the open archways. Dylenn leaned forward in his chair, put his hands together, closed his eyes and prayed. "The One, if you are listening, please watch over my family and my people. If it means protecting my family and the city I offer you my life in return. Please help us get through this."

Alezzia walked down a corridor of the citadel, pulling a young woman in her wake. "Jaclyn, where is Kaia?"

"Kaia is in her room my Queen," Jaclyn answered, trying to keep up. "Do you wish for me to escort you there?"

"No Jaclyn, I will be fine. Go be with the other handmaidens. I will send for you later."

Even though Alezzia was not looking at her, Jaclyn bowed with respect and turned around. Alezzia passed through several hallways until she came to the wooden door to Kaia's room, guarded by six heavily armed soldiers. Alezzia knocked on the door and said, "Kaia, it's your mother. May I come in?"

"The door is unlocked," came a muffled reply from within.

Alezzia pushed the door open and entered Kaia's room. Through the swaying purple curtains, Alezzia could see Kaia standing on the balcony.

The sun was beginning to fade behind the horizon. Kaia stood still, her eyes puffy and red, a trail of tears still on her cheeks. Alezzia wrapped her arms around Kaia as only a mother could, held her close, and whispered, "I know I've been different since Cormorden, but know that what I do, I do for you and your sisters. Not once has my love for you three ever changed. You are my daughters and I love you very much."

Kaia still gazed toward the inner wall. More tears began to flow down her cheeks. She sank to her knees.

"It's all my fault. All this death. Thousands upon thousands of people have died, all because I was born. Sir Henry, Captain Tori, and countless others are all dead because of a monster like me."

Alezzia held her daughter and replied, "Kaia Allister you are not a monster. You are a smart, beautiful, elegant, young woman whom any mother would be proud to call daughter."

"I don't want anyone else to die because of me," Kaia wept. "I hate myself. Why am I so different than any of the elves who use magic? My whole life they have tried to kill me and I've never done anything to wrong any of them."

Alezzia ran her fingers through Kaia's red hair, "People condemn what they do not understand. For as long as anyone can remember elves have been the only race to use magic. Then you were born."

Kaia sniffed her nose, "Yesterday was the first time I saw anyone die. And it was the first time I had to kill someone. I saw Sir Henry's face and I heard the screams of the elves I killed, last night when I tried to sleep. I can still smell their burning flesh, and I had never heard anyone scream the way the dying did. I couldn't sleep until Alyssa climbed into bed with me. Thousands more are going to die because of me and I hate myself for it."

Alezzia looked out toward the inner wall and said, "The thousands of men and women fighting are not only fighting just for you. They all have their own reasons to fight. Yes, you are their princess, but Sternz is their home as much as it is yours. They all fight for something, whether it is for their family, hatred of elves, or simply just to see a tomorrow. Do not think that this is your fault."

Kaia began to wipe the tears away from her eyes. "Thank you mother. I love you."

Alezzia smiled at her daughter. "I know that I am different than I used to be. But no matter what happens just remember that I do what I do because I love you and your sisters. I want the world you three inherit to be one of peace and stability. One of order."

16

Domatin paced on a hill between the inner and outer walls. Each time the Elven trebuchets launched a volley, his pace quickened. After yet again another volley shattered against the wall with no effect, Domatin stopped pacing and headed toward the elven encampment where he was met by four of his Praetorians. In a hushed, devious tone, he ordered one of the Praetorians, "I want you to rush into the command tent, where I'm guessing Leontina and Tauriel are, and tell them that I have spotted a large group of humans approaching the outer wall from the south, but do not tell her I am here in the camp."

The Praetorian bowed at the waist. "As you command, my prince." The Praetorian turned and hurried toward the command tent.

Domatin moved into the shadows near the command tent, waiting for Leontina to leave. After several long minutes Leontina rushed out, followed by Tauriel and several other Legati. Leontina spurred to her left and gathered a troop to follow her toward the outer wall to intercept the human deployment.

With Leontina and her party some distance from the camp, Domatin cracked a devious smile and walked toward the edge of the elven encampment. He told the three remaining Praetorians, "Gather some officers and bring them to me. Tell them I have something I wish to discuss with them." Without hesitation the three Praetorians turned in different directions to obey the command.

Domatin waited under a tree, and studied the inner wall. He heard foot steps behind him and turned to see his three Praetorians accompanied by five Elven Legati. He pointed at the wall, which was suffering little ill effect from the bombardment.

"As you can see, Leontina's strategy is moronic, to put it kindly. After hours of continuous barrage, the human walls are unscathed, as anyone could have assumed. So, I am relieving Leontina of her command. As of now, I assume command. We need to act now and end this today. What siege equipment do we have built at this moment?"

One of the officers answered. "Prince Domatin, all that is currently ready is a single battering ram. The siege towers will not be ready until tomorrow. Should we not wait until tomorrow when more siege engines will be ready?"

Domatin fixed the officer with a cruel stare. "First, do not question me again. Second, you could easily direct the trebuchets to aim at the gate itself could you not? Damaging it enough so the battering ram could finish the job?"

The officer started sweating and began to fidget, "Yes, we could but, I really think we should wait for Imperator Leontina to return before we attack the walls again. Even if she isn't in command, her experience—"

Domatin nodded to one of his Praetorians, who immediately thrust his dual-bladed sword into the officer's back. As the officer coughed up blood and fell face first on the ground, Domatin looked at the remaining four officers and said, "Does anyone else wish to question my authority? I am Prince Domatin Ophidian and I will be obeyed! Is that clear?"

The remaining four officers bowed. "Yes Prince Domatin."

"Good," Domatin muttered. "Prepare to launch the attack. Gather 5,000 soldiers to attack the wall. I don't care about formations or about any of that useless showmanship. You will rush forward, climb the walls, batter down the gate, and we will take this city tonight. Gather your troops and then come find me at my tent. Do not start the assault until I give the command."

The four officers bowed once, and ran toward the encampment, Domatin asked one of his Praetorians, "How many of you are left?"

The Praetorian responded, "87."

Domatin nodded. "I want a few of you to join the assault. Spread out. As soon as you are in the city I want you all to focus on finding Liam. The rest of the army can worry about the princess. You will focus on killing Liam at all costs."

Domatin started back toward the elven encampment followed by two of his Praetorians. The third left to pass Domatin's orders on to the rest of the Praetorians. Once Domatin entered his tent he told the Praetorians., "I wish to be alone. See that I am not disturbed until the troops are ready to begin the attack."

Two Praetorians saluted, then took their places standing guard at the entry way to the tent. Domatin's quarters were much more extravagant than the command tent. Thick fur rugs covered the ground and fragrant candles scented the room with a warm cinnamon aroma.

Domatin unstrapped his dark-blue, scale armor and dropped it on the ground. He walked over to his large wooden bed where his pet albino cobra slept on thick furs. He grinned as the cobra lifted its head up. Domatin extended his right arm toward the cobra and it wrapped its way up his arm. The cobra slithered across his right shoulder, passed his neck, and rested its head on Domatin's left shoulder. Domatin leaned over and kissed the head of the snake just as a Praetorian entered the tent.

"I just told you not to disturbed me."

The Praetorian bowed low. "Yes, my prince. But Imperator Leontina is walking this way. She seems very upset."

"Very well, let her pass," muttered Domatin.

Leontina stormed into the tent, the veins in her neck throbbing, followed by Tauriel. In a mad rage, Leontina confronted him. "Exactly *what* do you think you are doing?"

Domatin, the cobra still on his shoulder, sat down on his bed and with a chilling grin replied, "Something you seem incapable of doing. I am taking this city, tonight. I'm ending this war once and for all."

"What I was doing was taking the city but without needlessly wasting elven lives," Leontina screamed. "What you are doing is sending my troops to their deaths!"

Domatin stroked the back of his cobra as he answered. "Their lives are mine to waste. And considering your failed attempt this morning, I'd say they will be glad to have someone else command them."

Leontina's jaw clenched tighter as she muttered through her teeth, "The attack this morning was a test."

"Well this isn't a test," Domatin glared at her.

Leontina widened her stance. "You are out of line."

"And you are out of command." Domatin took a deep breath and continued to glare back at Leontina. "You're lucky I didn't do the other thing I wanted to do even though it's something that should have been taken care of yesterday."

"And what exactly is that?" Leontina questioned.

"Kill the human prisoners."

"Absolutely not!" Leontina yelled back. "They are valuable."

"To whom? How exactly are they of value?" Domatin asked. "The humans do not have any our soldiers as prisoners, so there is no exchange to be made We already have all the information we need, thanks to Captain Tori, who is blind and utterly useless now. Feeding these human vermin is a burden and unnecessary expense."

Leontina gritted her teeth, "Situations change, and it is always better to be ready for the unexpected."

An Elven officer stuck her head in the tent and addressed Domatin, "Prince Domatin, the assault will begin on your orders."

"Well then, by all means, start the attack," Domatin said as he grinned at Leontina.

17

Distress horns blew for the second time that day. Once again Elven harpoons slammed into the wall. Vernon, Kassandra, and Konar ran out of the school house and were joined by hundreds of troops running toward the wall.

"The sun has to be at least halfway set," Konar observed. "Why would they attack now?"

Vernon gazed toward the setting sun. "They must be trying to wear us down. They have seven times as many soldiers as we do. They can rest most of them while we constantly have to fight."

"Where are Liam and Blaster?" Kassandra asked.

"He's taking a walk," replied Vernon. "But I doubt he will miss an opportunity to fight the elves, so we can probably expect him to already be heading for the wall."

As the squad ran farther into lower Sternz they saw more of the debris of war. Clothing littered the streets, children's toys trampled underfoot, and the remnants of food. But no civilians.

"What happened here?" asked Kassandra.

Vernon answered. "A stray shot from an Elven trebuchet slammed into two houses killing the inhabitants. King Dylenn ordered all residents of lower Sternz to relocate to upper Sternz."

Liam and Blaster darted out of an alley a few streets ahead of them and Konar shouted, "Liam! Wait for us."

Vernon and Konar quickened their pace toward Liam, but

Kassandra hesitated for a moment, still shocked by the mass exodus that had just taken place. She regained her composure and hurried to catch up. They arrived below the eastern gatehouse where General Izak paced with his arms behind his back.

Vernon cleared his throat. "General? What's the situation?"

Izak didn't look at Vernon as he answered. "King Dylenn has sent word that he wishes to fight. He wants to let the troops know that he is with them and that he will stand with them until the end."

"I doubt the Queen likes that idea," Kassandra jested.

Izak stopped his pacing and fixed her with a stare. "The Queen doesn't know."

A Crixarian soldier dashed down the stairs and approached Izak, "General, the elves are not in any normal formation. They are marching without ranks. They have some infantry, a small company of archers—and a single battering ram."

"How many soldiers to you estimate?"

The solder replied, "At least twice as many as this morning sir."

"Oh, Leontina. You have grown overconfident," the old general said to himself. Izak climbed the stairs and addressed his troops who had massed, awaiting orders.

"My brothers and sisters, the elves come at us now, not to test our defenses, but as a true assault. In their overconfidence they have underestimated us. They attack without thought or plan, so sure in their victory. I say, we show them exactly what an organized fighting force can do."

Cries of encouragement started to echo from across the streets as Izak continued. "Today, your king will join you in battle. I don't see any of the elven royalty fighting beside their troops. Show the elves how we fight for our king who joins us in victory!"

All the Crixarian soldiers in the streets let out a cry of excitement. Izak continued to shout, "I want the same setup as last time. Melee in front, supported by archers in back. Reserves stay on ground level and help replenish arrows. Follow me my brothers and sisters. To victory or death!"

As Crixarian soldiers started running up the stairs behind General Izak, Vernon turned and addressed the squad, "Alright, the volunteers from Xanica and Tarium are keeping watch over the other three walls, so it will be only soldiers from Crixaria here. We are going to stay close to the King and help protect him from harm." Vernon took a moment and looked at all four of his squad mates, "It's about time we start working as one. We will be working together at the same section of the wall this time."

Kassandra and Konar smiled at the sound of this while Liam nodded his head once. Many cries of excitement swelled in the air around them as King Dylenn approached. The king was no longer dressed in purple garments. He worn the uniform of a Crixarian officer in chainmail, and carried a massive two-handed sword. The great sword was the same design as most, other than the hilt. Each of the cross-guards were gold painted steel in the shape of bear claws. Under the black leather grip, the pommel was also gold colored steel, but in the shape of a ferocious bear head.

As the King approached they could see the vigor and determination in his eyes. Every footstep he took was met with the cheers from the soldiers in the streets. Halfway up the stairs, Dylenn stopped and gazed upon his loyal army. With a firm smile he pointed up to the wall. "My people! You are the bravest group of men and women Crixaria has ever had defending her. Most of you are veterans. You have served me for years against the elves. I am honored to serve beside you. Just like this wall we will remain unbroken. Our swords and shields will remain unbroken. Our resolve will remain unbroken! We will remain unbroken!"

Cheers erupted from all across the city as the fire in the soldiers' bellies ignited as Dylenn turned and climbed to the top of the stairs.

The elven forces moved forward. Just as reported, they numbered at least twice as many as they did that morning.

"Trebuchet boulders incoming!" shouted a soldier from the wall. Everyone looked toward the Elven encampment to see hundreds of rocks hurling through the air toward the wall. This time the shots impacted the iron gate and the surrounding wall.

Another shout. "Arrows incoming!" A volley of arrows tore through the air toward the front of each section of the wall, once again preventing the humans from dislodging the harpoons from of the wall.

As everyone on the wall readied themselves for the fight, King Dylenn asked, "What are some of those chains doing on top of the wall?"

"We had some difficultly trying to pry some of the harpoons out of the wall," Izak explained. "So I ordered the troops to pull the chains up so the elves couldn't climb up."

"Fair enough," replied Dylenn. "What's the plan?"

Izak narrowed his eyes. "There is no plan. We fight. We stop them at all costs from getting inside the city."

The arrows shifted from the wall to the ballista towers. Izak's jaw tightened as he shouted, "Once they are in range, give them all you can with the ballistae. Shield bearers, go protect the ballistae."

Men and women with large rectangular wooden shields ran to the towers to obey. The thick wooden shields were as tall as a human's body. Once on the top of the ballistae towers, they lined up in a shield wall, blocking the majority of the arrows. Each time the ballistae were ready to release their wooden spikes, the shield bearers lowered their shields, allowing the ballista crew to shoot.

Elven hands reached the top of the wall, pulling up the elven soldiers the were attached to. Once again, the humans on the wall rushed forward to engage them. Fierce fighting occurred across the eastern inner wall. Both human and elven blood spilled as the dead and dying tumbled off both sides of the wall, but to the defenders' surprise, the fight appeared easier than the skirmish in the morning.

Kassandra, who was at the rear with the archers, yelled out to Vernon, "They are climbing slower than this morning, but they have greater numbers. Why?"

Vernon shoved an elf off the wall as he replied, "The elves are not in formation. There doesn't appear to be enough officers to keep order. They are not raising their shields to block our arrows. Our archers and ballista teams are punishing them far greater than they were able to this morning."

Vernon looked to see how King Dylenn was doing and smiled. The King was holding his own. Dylenn swung his great sword with strength and precision. The smile left Vernon's face as he tracked three elves approaching the king from his left while he was preoccupied with another in front of him. Vernon knew he could not get there in time and looked for Liam, but Liam was even further away, and was engaging two elves himself.

Konar rushed forward and with a mighty leap, drop kicked one of the three elves, sending him back over the wall. While in the air Konar grabbed the remaining two in headlocks and twisted, snapping their necks like twigs. He jumped to his feet beside the King, grabbed his hammer, and continued fighting.

A cry went up from the wall, "Battering ram approaching!" Izak and Vernon both looked over the wall to see the massive battering ram. Twenty feet tall, the battering ram was made of wood but the ram itself was Azaran steel, shaped as the head of a cobra. The top of the battering ram was covered in a dark straw, with some kind of liquid dripping from it. At least two dozen elves were pushing it toward the gate and dozens more were guarding it.

Archers from the rear of the wall grabbed cloth-tipped arrows out of their quivers. Then they turned to the braziers around them and ignited the cloth. With arrows raised Izak yelled out, "200 feet!" The archers adjusted their aim and released their arrows. Hundreds of flaming arrows scorched through the air toward the battering ram but, had no impact on it.

Realizing the ram wasn't catching fire, Vernon shouted, "They must have soaked it with water to keep the wood wet."

Once the battering ram got within 100 feet from the gate the barrage from the trebuchets stopped.

Vernon could see Izak's eyes darting from the battering ram to the wall. Sweat poured down his face. Vernon shoved his way past an elf as he called to Izak, "Sir, permission to take my team outside of the gate and burn the ram."

"That's suicide," Izak protested. "Hundreds of elves would swarm to the ram to protect it as soon as they saw you."

Vernon replied, "That's why you focus all of the archer's arrows on the area behind the ram. I know the archers can't see where they are aiming but hundreds of arrows around the area would make it a death trap and send the elves toward the chains to climb the wall. I know it sounds suicidal but it's our best option. The trebuchets weakened the gate and if we don't burn it, the ram *will* break through."

Izak pondered Vernon's plan for a few seconds and then said, "Very well. Do it."

Vernon nodded his head and then yelled out to Konar, Liam, Blaster, and Kassandra, "Come with me!"

Kassandra asked him, "What's going on?"

Vernon answered, "The elves have coated the ram with something to stop it from being set on fire from the top so Konar and I will go outside the gates and burn it from beneath. Archers will cover us, but they can't see us so close to the wall, so Kassandra, I need you to stand at the edge of the wall and cover us the best you can. Liam, you and Blaster make sure no elf gets near her."

Liam and Kassandra nodded and headed to the edge of the wall beside the gatehouse. Kassandra readied her bow and Liam and Blaster stood beside her, killing any elves in their way as they got into position.

Vernon and Konar hurried down the stairs as they heard the battering ram start to hit the gate. Vernon grabbed a torch from the wall as he looked at Konar. "Ready old friend?"

Konar grinned. "Wouldn't have it any other way."

The gate raised just enough for them to roll under. Vernon went to the right of the ram and Konar to the left killing all the elves around the ram. Two elves remained on the right where Vernon stood. The first swung down at Vernon who blocked it with the sword in his right hand, then he shoved the torch into the elf's face. The elf cried out in pain as he flopped to the ground. Distracted, Vernon did not noticed that the last elf on his side was dressed in a white robe trimmed in blue. The Elven mage extended both arms forwards and an icy wind streamed out of his hands toward Vernon, slamming him into the wall and extinguishing the torch. Vernon regained his feet as the mage prepare another attack. Suddenly, the mage jerked, blood stained his robes, and he slumped and fell forward, a hatchet sticking out of the back of his head.

Konar wrenched the hatchet from the dead mage's skull and asked, "Well what now? Our torch is gone."

Vernon reached into his belt pouch pulled out some flint and steel. "Looks like we have to do it the old-fashioned way."

Konar nodded, and without a word turned, walking toward the back of the battering ram.

"Where are you going?" Vernon asked.

"You start the fire. Even with our archers firing around the area some elves are bound to make it through to try and retake the ram. I will hold them off."

Vernon climbed into the battering ram, tore off some of the purple cloth from his tunic, and began to strike at it with the steel and flint.

Back on the wall, Kassandra saw Konar walk to the back of the ram and said to Liam, "Something must be wrong. Konar is standing out ready to fight any elves that try to get to the ram."

"That's why you are covering him, right?" Liam said.

Kassandra pulled an arrow from her quiver and released it toward the first elf to get through to barrage of arrows, piercing her neck. "Yes," Kassandra replied. "But I only have five arrows left in this quiver." She drew another and released it, again killing another elf. "Make that four."

On the ground Konar readied his hammer to face any

approaching elves. One rushed at him from his right but Konar swung his hammer at the elf's abdomen, collapsing his lungs. The elf slowly suffocated on the ground. Konar frowned as he noticed that more elves were getting through. *I guess Kassandra has run out of arrows*, he muttered to himself.

Kassandra cursed as she shot her last arrow. Liam asked her, "When will you get more?"

"A soldier was sent several minutes ago and should arrive soon but until then Konar is on his own." Kassandra set her bow down and drew her daggers to fight beside Liam on the wall.

Konar had little trouble dispatching any elf that made it through the barrage of arrows. Then, without warning, an arrow dug deep into the right side of Konar's chest.

Vernon glanced just in time to see the arrow hit Konar and tried to hurry, but in the process, ended up cutting his hand with his sword, causing him to drop it as he grabbed his hand. Vernon bellowed out in frustration as his hand spewed blood. He retrieved his sword and tried as fast as he could to start the fire.

Konar pulled the arrow from his chest with a roar, but before he could take another step, a second arrow carved its way into his left thigh. Konar gritted his teeth and pulled the arrow out of his leg. As warm blood trickled down his leg, he looked up and saw an elven Praetorian with a bow targeting him. Konar started to make his way to the Praetorian but stopped, realizing he would leave Vernon defenseless. A third arrow whizzed past his head as several more elven soldiers ran at him.

Konar glanced at the Praetorian just in time to see him aiming again for Konar's head. Konar raised his left arm in front of his face just in time to stop the arrow from hitting his throat. However, the arrow pierced his forearm forcing him to drop his hammer. With his right hand he pulled out his hatchet and killed the oncoming elves. Another arrow cut into him, this time in his left calf. Unable to move his left leg, Konar could only watch as the Praetorian reached for another arrow, one that would likely end his life.

Liam watched the situation unfold, and cried out to Kassandra, "We need those arrows now!"

"Don't yell at me," Kassandra fussed. "I'm not the one who is late with them."

Liam cast about, trying to find a single usable arrow for Kassandra, but found none. Liam spotted one of the pulled-up chains and muttered to himself, "This is such a bad idea."

He set the sword in his left hand down and grabbed the end of the chain. Kassandra shook her head. "What do you think you're doing?"

Liam didn't answer. He ran along the wall, pulling the chain behind him. Once the chain reached its full length, he jumped off the wall, allowing the chain to swing him to the ground.

The Praetorian drew his arrow, the fletching close to his cheek, and aimed for Konar's heart. A cruel smile creased his face, just as Liam crashed into him. The arrow flew helplessly off target as the Praetorian rolled limply, like a rag doll, on the ground. Konar gasped for breath as he yelled, "Liam! Are you OK?"

Kassandra's mouth dropped open, and her eyes widened. She shook herself from her amazement, as more elves emerged from the curtain of arrows. At last, a soldier carrying 10 quivers of arrows reached the top of the stairs. Kassandra bolted toward him and grabbed two quivers for herself. She darted back to the wall, snatched up her bow as well as Liam's sword, and clambered up to the top of the gatehouse to cover the squad better.

She released arrow after arrow at the approaching elves. An elf managed to gain the ladder behind her but Blaster ripped her throat out, and took his place guarding the ladder. Without distraction, and confident that Blaster would watch her back, Kassandra provided deadly cover for Konar and Liam.

Immense pain shot through Liam's left shoulder. He stumbled to his feet when he realized Konar was still on the ground. Elven troops were rushing toward them. Konar tried to regain his feet but the damage the arrows had done to his left leg made it impossible.

Liam reached for his sword, dropped in his collision with the Praetorian, and held it with his right hand. His left arm was useless. He stumbled forward, trying to intercept three elves that were heading for Konar. Before he could reach them, Kassandra's quick arrows dropped the elves dead to the ground. Liam looked back and saw her standing on top of the gate house covering him and Konar.

The bloodlust took over, and Liam was no longer aware of the pain in his left shoulder. He let out a loud roar and took his place between Konar and the oncoming elves. The first elf charged toward him, screaming and swinging her sword low at Liam's right shin. Liam lunged forward, shoving his sword into the mouth of the elf. Three more elves rushed toward Liam. Two fell to Kassandra's arrows. The third fell to Liam's sword.

Somewhere in the distance, it seemed he heard Vernon's voice, shouting to him. "Liam let's go! The fire is started!"

Liam fought the battle frenzy, and turned around to see Vernon sprinting toward Konar. Liam, his sword still before him, inched backward toward his comrades. Together Vernon and Liam put their shoulders under Konar's arms, and limped as fast as they could toward the gate. Konar dragged his hammer with him, refusing to loose his grip on it. Kassandra killed any elves unlucky enough to break through the arrow barrage.

Kassandra called down, "The ram is on fire, open the gate!"

The gate opened just enough to give them room to roll under. The elves, realizing their only means of entering the city was ablaze began to retreat.

Kassandra and Blaster were the first to reach the bottom of the stairs to check on her companions. Blaster rushed to Liam, covering his face with slobbery licks. Kassandra asked, "Is everyone alright?"

Konar let out a painful laugh. "Nothing that a jug of wine won't cure."

From atop the wall a few Crixarian soldiers started chanting, *"Unbroken! Unbroken! Unbroken!"*

More soldiers took up the chant; *"Unbroken! Unbroken! Unbroken!"*

"Are they talking about—us?" Vernon said, stupefied by the response.

Soon it seemed as everyone on the walls and on the ground around them was chanting; *"Unbroken! Unbroken!"*

Kassandra handed Liam his sword as Izak and Dylenn shoved through the crowd of soldiers toward them.

Dylenn clapped his hands together. "Well done my friends. Despite my initial doubts you have proved to be an excellent team. With the strategic leader, sturdy defender, agile marks-woman, relentless warrior, and even a fierce mascot, I know you will be crucial and effective in the coming days."

Vernon bowed his head and replied, "Thank you my king. We live to serve. To victory or Death!"

"You are injured," Dylenn noted. "Go to the medical building. I will send Benjamin, the Allister family doctor, to treat your wounds. Go now. And rest. I must consult with General Izak."

As Vernon helped Konar follow the King, Kassandra noticed Liam and Blaster walking in the opposite direction. "Liam, where are you going? The king's doctor is this way?"

Liam grunted, "I don't like doctors. They earn their living off of others being sick, so why would they ever want us to get better? Besides, I have always taken care of myself."

Domatin was waiting in the command tent with a very upset Leontina and Tauriel for news of the attack. "What's wrong, Imperator?" he said with mock concern. "Upset that I took the city in one assault while you failed continually? Or are you upset that a simple prince could take the city that an Imperator of 500 years couldn't?"

Leontina bit her lip. "I'm upset that you went behind my back to order an assault that was doomed from the start."

Domatin interrupted as he joked, "Careful Imperator, with that tone of voice I might start to worry for my life."

A Praetorian walked hesitantly into the command tent. Domatin stood with a smile. "Well, that took less time than I thought. Praetorian, please tell the Imperator how the humans have been slaughtered. Oh, and if you happen to have the head of the princess with you, please show us."

The Praetorian lowered his eyes and mumbled, "Prince Domatin, we—we didn't take the city. Our battering ram was set on fire and our troops are in unrestricted retreat."

The smile faded from Domatin's face, replaced first by confusion, then rage. He clenched his fists and shouted, "Cowards! I'll have their heads! They dared go against my orders and retreat?" A stray thought crossed Domatin's mind and he whispered, "And just how *exactly* did the humans manage to burn the battering ram? I thought it was coated so that wouldn't happen."

The Praetorian shifted from side to side as he replied, "A Crixarian officer and an orc, my prince. They killed our men, even the mage you sent to protect the ram. The officer set fire from beneath the ram, while the orc fought off our troops. A female human covered them with arrows from the wall. We've never seen an archer with such precision, my prince. One of our Praetorians did manage to injure the orc but before the final blow could be dealt, a human boy, with a sword made of Azaran steel, swung down from the wall and slammed into him."

Seething, Domatin ordered, "Leave us Praetorian. Go, and pray to Colubra that I do not find out you were the one to start the retreat."

As the Praetorian started to exit the tent, Leontina asked, "How many elven lives were lost?"

"Perhaps 3,000 Imperator. Perhaps more," replied the Praetorian before exiting the tent.

Leontina took a deep breath before turning back to Domatin. "Perhaps 3,000. You sent 3,000 of my troops, perhaps more, to their deaths. You lost my only battering ram. You got one of our mages killed, and worse, you made us look like fools to the humans!"

"I didn't tell the mage to go," Domatin whined. "That was his choice, not mine."

"You're done," Leontina said.

Domatin looked at her with a puzzled gaze, "Excuse me?"

Leontina stood up straight and in a firm voice repeated, "You are done. You tried it your way and accomplished nothing but a waste of soldiers, supplies, and equipment."

"You forget who I am—"

"I do not care who you are! You may be a prince, but this is my command. You can leave or you can stay, but you will obey me."

Domatin stared at her, unwilling to accept the situation, but helpless to change it. His eyes filled with hatred, he stormed out of the tent.

Leontina looked at a stunned Tauriel and said, "His meddling put the entire siege at risk. He had to be put in his place."

"I understand Imperator," Tauriel replied. "What are your orders?"

Leontina walked toward the command table. As she put a map of Sternz on the table she said, "Resume the trebuchet barrage on the wall for now. After an hour stop firing. Allow the troops manning the trebuchets get some rest. Tomorrow we will hit the humans with everything we've got."

18

Kassandra, Vernon, and Konar entered the medical building that Konar had been fixing the day before. A few candles struggled to light the room, but darkness sulked through every nook and cranny. The building was packed with hundreds of bunks and bloodied tables, littered with the wounded and dying. Blood seeped through the cracks in the wooden floor. Crixarian soldiers carried the dead out to make room for the injured, but the pace was slow and the cries of the wounded was heart-wrenching. Konar and Vernon sat on two bunks side by side in the far corner of the room, while Kassandra leaned back on the wall between them.

Benjamin had just entered the building and seemed to glide toward them, stepping over the injured as if they were of no consequence. His dark purple robes were already covered in blood. He studied Konar and Vernon, but addressed Konar first. In his dark, calm voice said, "You are very lucky that you are an orc. Otherwise that arrow to your chest would have killed you."

Konar jested, "You hear that, you two. I'm the lucky one of the group."

Kassandra let out a mocking laugh. "The only luck you have Konar, is that I was there to watch your back, and that Liam was stupid enough to swing down to save you."

Konar rolled his eyes. "I have no idea what you are talking about. I had that situation under control the entire time. I was just letting that Praetorian think he had the advantage. I had him right where I wanted him."

"Uh-huh." Kassandra muttered back with a smile.

Benjamin scowled at Konar, "Hold still please."

Vernon looked at the fresh blood on Benjamin's robes. "I am surprised to see your robes covered in blood Benjamin. You weren't fighting on the wall were you?"

"No. I will gladly allow you to do the fighting. My job is to help the wounded as they come in," Benjamin replied. "The blood on my robes is theirs, not mine."

Kassandra raised an eyebrow, "I thought you were the royal doctor? And that you even suffered from Cormorden like the queen. I've heard that all Cormorden survivors become harsh and loners."

Benjamin finished wrapping Konar's chest and arm and replied, "You are correct on all accounts. You could say that I have had Cormorden longer than most survivors. The first few years are always the harshest. Cormorden changes a person, the pain we go through is unlike anything anyone else has ever experienced, and there is no way to describe it to someone who has not experienced it. That's why I came to help the Queen. I've found that if someone who has lived with Cormorden for a while helps someone who just got it, the recovery is much easier. Trust me when I say that if I had not come to help Queen Alezzia then, she would be much colder and even more harsh than she is now."

Vernon looked at Benjamin's face and noticed only a few wrinkles. He seemed younger than his years, the way he talked and how excellent his work was made him appear much older. "You don't look a day over 30. How long have you had Cormorden?" Vernon asked him.

Konar started to fidget but Benjamin stared him down with cold eyes, stopping him in an instant. Benjamin grabbed fresh cloth and started to wrap Konar's calf. "Longer than most," he answered. "At first, I was consumed with rage, but then I found my true calling. That is why I became a doctor." As Benjamin finished treating the last of Konar's injuries he instructed the orc, "You will heal much faster than a human, but don't try to use your hammer any more than you have to tomorrow."

Konar glanced at his hammer. "I can't promise anything."

Benjamin turned his attention to Vernon's left hand. He cleaned it, then began to stitch the wound. Vernon took the moment to compliment Kassandra and Konar. "You both did an excellent job today. I mean that."

Kassandra smiled. "Well thank you, Vernon. You did a fine job as well. I'm glad the king picked you to lead us. Now, if we could just get Liam to stick with us."

"Where did he go?" Konar asked.

Kassandra shook her head. "Who knows? He just walked off, mumbling something about always taking care of himself."

Benjamin interrupted, "He is even luckier than you Konar. From what I heard, he swung off the wall and walked away from it nearly unharmed. Swinging 100 feet to the ground and slamming into a Praetorian—it should have killed him."

"I wish he would open up," Kassandra said with a frown.

Vernon flinched as the stitching hit a nerve. Trying to ignore the pain he continued, "It seems as if he has a lot of anger built up inside him. Maybe it would not be the best idea to see him vent."

Kassandra took a deep breath. "Yes he does seem angry, but there's more to it than that. He seems to be in pain as well. There's something in his eyes—pain and sadness too.."

Konar stood up and stretched his back, "Just give him some time. You have to admit he is more open than he was yesterday."

Vernon lowered his head and watched Benjamin finish stitching his hand. "Maybe some things just shouldn't be brought up. Sometimes the only way you can survive another day is to bury everything inside, to pretend that certain things never happened."

Kassandra shook her head and crossed her arms. "I don't keep anything bottled up. I don't care what people know about me or think about me. And I'm happy."

"Or so you say," Konar observed.

As Benjamin finished the last of Vernon's stitches he said, "Try not to grasp anything too hard or you will rip out your stitches."

"Thank you Benjamin," Vernon said as he tried to close his hand.

Konar limped toward the door and Kassandra asked, "Your left leg just got shot with two arrows. How are you already able to walk?"

"Orcs heal much faster than humans," he quipped. "Remember? It hurts, but after two or three days I will be back to my old self. Until then, I will either try to forget the pain and tough it out, or I might just find a jug of wine."

"Of course you will," Kassandra muttered.

Vernon hopped off the bunk. "Come on. Let's go find Liam and Blaster so we can go back to our barracks and get some rest. I doubt we will get very much the next few days."

Liam rested his back against a wall in an alley. No light from the torches on the street reached him. Even the moon was cloaked in a thick blanket of clouds. Liam could just make out the outline of Blaster's silhouette sitting beside him. His left shoulder was throbbing. Every time he moved sharp pain ignited in his arm. Clenching his teeth, he muttered, "Alright boy, let's get this over with."

Blaster barked once and then stood up and brushed against Liam's right side. Liam slowly stretched out on the ground on his back. He took three deep breaths before extending his left arm out beside him. Liam grunted as every inch he moved his arm, the worse the pain got.

"Bite," Liam said.

Blaster jumped to Liam's extended arm and grabbed it in his mouth. His teeth nestled on Liam's leather bracer. Liam took several short breathes before saying, "Pull."

Blaster took small steps backwards, bringing Liam's left arm back as if Liam was reaching for something above his head. The farther Blaster went, the more pain Liam felt. His whole body began to tense. Liam's legs began to twitch and he shut his eyes. After what seemed like an eternity, Liam's shoulder popped back into place. The sound startled Blaster and he released his hold on Liam's arm and jumped backwards.

Liam moaned and rolled onto his right side. Blaster began to lick his face. Liam let out a painful laugh and said, "I'm alright now. You did well. Better than last time."

Blaster barked twice back at Liam as his ears perked up.

Liam rotated his shoulder as the pain faded. "Last time you not only drew blood when you bit me, you also peed on me when you popped it into place."

Blaster tilted his head at Liam and wagged his tail. Liam saw Vernon, Kassandra, and Konar walk past without seeing him in the dark alley. He felt the air around Blaster's tail flow faster and he knew Blaster had also spotted the group. Liam looked back down at the big wolf and smiled. "You really like them don't you? Alright go ahead, I'll catch up."

Blaster barked once and bolted out of the alley toward the group with Liam trudging behind.

Konar turned first and with a smile on his face said, "Blaster you better have a jug of wine for me and this time you better not spill it."

As Liam sauntered out of the alley, Vernon noticed he was no longer holding his shoulder.

"Shoulder feeling better?" he asked.

Liam mumbled, "It's fine. It'll be better after some rest."

Konar stretched his back and mumbled, "I feel the same way. Who else thinks we should get some sleep?"

Before Kassandra or Vernon could reply, a familiar voice called out, "Hey! I finally found you!

Vernon, Kassandra, and Konar all turned around to see Gregory walking toward them with a skip in his step and a smile on his face.

Vernon and Konar smiled when they saw him, but Kassandra raised an eyebrow and Liam scowled.

"Who is this?" Liam whispered.

Vernon waved to Gregory as he answered, "That is Gregory. He is an old friend, but be careful if he tries to shake your hand. He normally slaps you in the face as a joke."

Liam grunted as he mumbled, "If he delays us from getting home it will be the last joke he plays."

Kassandra snapped her head back around and gave Liam a strange smile.

"What?" Liam asked.

Kassandra's grin widened, "You called it *home*."

Liam started to protest, but she looked away as Gregory reached them, smiling ear to ear. "Vernon, Konar it is good to see you two again."

Gregory reached out to shake Konar's hand, but Konar simply slapped him lightly across the face. Vernon snickered, and Gregory chuckled. "I see my reputation precedes me."

Gregory then turned his eyes to Kassandra, "My lovely Kassandra, how I have missed the sight of you."

Kassandra smirked. "Gregory, dear, not once has that ever worked on me and it won't work now."

"It works on all the other girls." Gregory boasted. "Call them lovely and they melt like ice in your palms."

Gregory peered behind Kassandra to see a scowling Liam.

"Don't mind him," Konar told him. "He doesn't much like people."

An excited smile crossed Gregory's face. "To each his own. Now I have some good news to share with all of you."

Vernon asked, "Has the Vicar arrived early?"

Gregory let out a small laugh and replied, "No, but why is everything always about the war with you. Relax, it's time to unwind. Some of my fellow officers and I are having a little victory celebration at Bear Claw Tavern. Plenty of officers, some soldiers, maybe a few civilians, if you catch my meaning. It will be quite a party.

Even General Izak sent word that he might join us later. Considering the feats of The Unbroken today with the battering ram, I'd say your presence would bolster everyone's morale even more."

"The *Unbroken*?" Liam questioned. "What is that?"

"That's you. That's what everyone is calling your group," Gregory replied as he clapped his hands. "After the king's speech and what you all did at the ram, everyone started chanting, The Unbroken. I guess it just stuck. Don't worry about the wall, we've still got hundreds of soldiers guarding it. This is just a small celebration for those of us off-duty tonight. Now follow me, let's go to Bear Claw Tavern!"

Without a second thought Kassandra said, "Sounds like fun, I'm in."

Konar also nodded his head, "I was probably going to stop there anyway for a drink anyway, so why not make it two or three."

"That's the spirit!" Gregory exclaimed. "What about you Vernon?"

Vernon was pondering, "*The Unbroken*. It fits."

Gregory coughed and Vernon smiled. "Sounds good. I'll be there."

Gregory then looked to Liam, who had remained silent. With a slight tilt of his head Gregory added, "Liam you and your wolf are welcome to come as well."

Before Liam could object Kassandra said, "Come on, just for a few minutes?"

Liam looked down at Blaster, who was smiling and wagging his tail. With a heavy sigh he replied, "Blaster could use some supper."

A surprised Gregory clapped his hands once again and said, "It's settled then! Follow me and we will have a night of celebration!"

Domatin walked like a shadow through the encampment. He was only accompanied by one Praetorian as they sneaked their way past the quiet tents full of sleeping elves. Dodging patrol after patrol they stuck to the shadows. Domatin, hunched down trying not to step on anything that my crunch and announce their presence. He whispered to the Praetorian, "Are the others ready?"

The Praetorian whispered back, "Yes, Prince Domatin. They are awaiting us as you commanded."

"Good. Leontina will have no control of this. But one day she will thank me for it."

As the two reached the edge of the north side of the camp, out of earshot of any elves, Domatin began to run. After several minutes they reached the bottom of a hill. The Praetorian said to Domatin, "Just over this hill, Prince."

At the top Domatin's eyes lit up. He saw hundreds of human prisoners, surrounded by the rest of his remaining Praetorians holding torches. The humans had been stripped of their uniforms and wore simple cotton rags.

Domatin strode down the hill. He asked his companion, "Did your fellow Praetorians remember to bring the shovels?"

"Yes, my prince."

Domatin smiled and called out, "Humans! After much thought I have finally determined a fitting use for you. Personally I would rather see you all dead, but the Imperator thinks that perhaps you could be used as bargaining tools. I think we all know that no human life is worth saving. You are eating food that should be feeding elves, but you do nothing to earn it. From here on out, if you want food you have to work for it."

"What do you expect us to do?" a female soldier cried out from the center of the group.

"I expect you to dig," Domatin giggled. "You will dig no matter how tired you get. You will dig no matter how hungry you are. You will dig no matter how miserable you. And because there are thousands of you, if you don't dig, my Praetorians will simply kill you and replace you with another human who will."

Silence fell over the humans before the same female voice cried out, "You're going to kill us anyway. Why should be dig?"

Domatin grimaced, but after a moment he called out, "I know that voice. Bring her to me!"

Two Praetorians shoved their way through the humans to grab the woman and brought her to Domatin.

"My dear Captain Tori. I though you would have learned your place by now."

Tori said nothing. Domatin let out an amused chuckle. "Cobra venom in the eyes can be, shall we say, uncomfortable. I've heard it can cause people to go blind. Since I cannot take your sight—again—I suppose I'll have find a different way of punishing you for questioning my authority. Force her on her knees and hold her still."

The two Praetorians kicked her legs from under her, forcing Tori to her knees. Domatin pulled a duel-sword from a Praetorian's hand, then grabbed a second from another. He beckoned to a third Praetorian who was holding a torch. He held the blade of one of the weapons in the fire as he explained, "You see, one of the worst things that can happen when you are torturing someone is for them to die or pass out from the pain. I may have figured out a way to stop that from happening."

Domatin brought the sword out of the fire, its red-hot steel blade steaming in the brisk night air. With a smile on his face he walked back to Tori who could now hear the sizzling of the burning sword. While her attention was on the burning sword, Domatin took the other sword and slashed open her left arm to the bone. Tori cried out in pain as blood flowed down her arm. Domatin then forced the burning hot sword onto the wound, cauterizing the blood vessels. Tori's cries pierced the sky as the burning sword closed the wound.

Domatin smiled at the humans prisoners. "You see. I no longer have to worry about people bleeding out. Consider this, all of you. If you ever pass out, I can wait until you wake up, and then we can start all over again."

Domatin cut Tori across her stomach, then seared the flesh closed with the burning sword. Tori shrieked from the unbearable pain. The stench of blood and burning flesh filled the air around them. Domatin gave her only a second of recovery before cutting her once again, this time at her upper right inner thigh. After burning the wound closed Domatin raised his foot and kicked her in her throat onto the ground.

Domatin once again addressed the captives. "Does anyone else have a problem with my orders? No? Then I suggest you start digging."

As the Praetorians threw shovels onto the ground, the human prisoners picked them up and started digging. Tori whimpered, helpless and alone on the cold ground.

19

Light from the full moon peeked between the clouds as the night sky began to illuminate the city of Sternz. The Unbroken arrived at Bear Claw Tavern with Gregory leading the way. Several soldiers stumbled out of the door as Liam commented, "Is it smart for everyone to get drunk when the elves could attack at any moment?"

Gregory looked back at him with a smile, "That is why most of us will only have a cup or two."

Konar pushed past Gregory and opened the door. "Speak for yourself. I need at least one or two *jugs*."

As they entered the tavern everyone inside let out a cheer. Gregory whispered to Vernon, "You see. I told you that it would all work out. Now all the soldiers look up to you and your group."

Vernon nodded, then saw Izak sitting alone at the bar. Vernon told Gregory, "Go ahead and order a few cups for us, I need to speak to General Izak for a few moments first."

Gregory went to the bar and ordered some drinks. The chubby tavern girl saw Konar and reached under the bar and pulled out two jugs of wine. Gregory tried to swoop in but the tavern girl smacked his hands with a wooden ladle and winked at Konar. "Why, thank you, wench," Konar jested.

The redheaded tavern girl snickered. "Keep up the good work, Unbroken, and it will always be on the house."

Gregory rubbed his stinging hand and asked the tavern girl, politely, "Why don't I ever get any wine on the house?"

The tavern girl sneered at him, "Because you haven't singlehandedly stood in front of an army of elves before."

Konar took a big gulp from one of the wine jugs and walked over to a table where several strong, well-built humans sat, and issued a challenge. "Anyone here think he can beat me in arm wrestling?" Their faces all lit up as they made a place for him and each tried to best him.

Kassandra had joined a group of men and women close to the table where Konar sat, while Liam and Blaster had returned to the booth where the squad first met them.

Vernon sat down beside Izak at the bar. Izak took a quick sip of his ale before saying, "I knew I did something right when I trusted you with making this team. You not only defended the wall, but you gave our soldiers heroes they can rally behind."

"Thank you sir, but there is something I must ask you. What will happen to my team once the siege is over?"

Izak took another drink before he responded, "Well, that all depends on how the siege ends. If King Dylenn negotiates an honorable peace, you all will more than likely be personal bodyguards for princess Kaia. There may be a promotion involved. Or you could all go home and enjoy free drinks for the rest of your lives. But if we continue this war, which will more than likely happen, your team will become high value targets for the elves. You'll find yourselves fighting wherever the need is greatest, in the most important areas of battles. Anything that normally would require dozens of soldiers to pull off, same as now. At some point, you'll likely be killed in battle."

Vernon pondered Izak's words as he poured himself a small cup of ale. "If the Vicar doesn't arrive with a large enough force, is there anyone else who can help us?"

Izak finished his glass of wine, "No."

Vernon nodded. He had not expected a different answer. He

looked behind him at Kassandra and asked, "What can you tell me about Kassandra's family?"

Izak glanced at the archer, then return to his drink.. "The Verbecks are one of the few noble families of Vetin trying to keep the government from getting worse. I've heard that the Vetin government is trying to split into three different politically parties. If they do that, then all form of reason and then the government's ability to get anything productive done will cease to exist altogether."

"But wouldn't having three different parties help to keep one side from gaining absolute power?" Vernon asked.

Izak lets out a wry snort. "It always starts out that way, but it never stays that way. Just look at the dwarves. Almost 2,000 years ago they were a democracy. Then they split into two political parties. One of two things can happen with that system—civil war or the two parties plot to control the country with an iron fist. First they try to disengage the people and make them not vote by making it all seem pointless. Then they disenfranchise their citizens since no one is ever paying attention.

"In the dwarves case, their government will massacre some of their own people and blame it on the elves or the humans, or even to the other political party, just to make their people afraid. Martial law is imposed and a military dictatorship become the law of the land.

Truthfully every kind of government has its flaws, even a monarchy such as we have. But a democracy? Thank the One that Dylenn is a kind and loving King who wishes the best for his people."

Vernon leaned forward and rested his hand on Izak's shoulder, "You always get depressing when you drink."

Izak hinted at a smile. "Sorry, but you asked. I just have a lot on my mind. If the Vicar doesn't arrive with enough soldiers we may not live to see another week pass."

A shout of anger came from Konar's table as he beat another human at arm wrestling. Konar took the final sip from his first jug and then reached for his second, almost seeming unfazed by the first jug. After taking a drink Konar yelled out, "Is there no human who can best me? I'll even wrestle with my arm that got shot with an arrow!" Konar looked around the room to see if there were any newcomers in the tavern before he saw Liam, sitting in the corner looking at Kassandra. Konar wiped the drops of wine from his mouth and groaned out of his chair. He looked back at the people sitting around the table and said, "I will be right back."

Konar scooted up a chair beside Liam. Blaster had been napping and jolted awake at the noise. He bared his teeth and snarled before recognizing Konar's scent. The wolf let out a long yawn and crawled to the other side of the booth.

"You are lucky he is tired," Liam said. "You remember what happened last time someone woke him up in this booth?"

Konar snickered. "Blaster and I understand each other."

Liam chuckled, "If you say so." He glanced back at Kassandra as she laughed at something someone at her table said.

Konar scooted his chair even closer to Liam and whispered above the noisy crowd, "I've seen the way you look at her. You are getting feelings for her aren't you?"

Liam slouched in the booth and grumbled, "You are drunk."

A wide smirk grew on Konar's face. "But I'll be sober in the morning, and you'll still be in love. You know, don't take this the wrong way, but you are actually decently attractive, for a human that is. You should tell her how you feel? When we first met you, one of the first things she said was that you were cute."

Liam looked down to his feet and began to rub his hands together.

Konar had a revelation. "Wait, wait—wait. I think I understand. You've never been with a woman before, have you?".

Liam stayed silent. Konar set his jug of wine down on the floor and continued, "Of course! No wonder you shied away from her when she got undressed. Was that the first time you'd seen a girl in her under garments? I mean, surely you have kissed a woman before, right?"

Again, Liam remained silent.

Konar let out a heavy, commiserate sigh. "Never even kissed a woman. That's sad. So—sad."

"Domatin captured me when I was a child and turned me into a prize fighter. All I did was wake up, train, fight, and go back to sleep. I never had the time or opportunity to be with a girl. Now... well, now I wouldn't know how."

Kassandra laughed again, and Liam's face softened as he looked at her.

Konar reached behind him to the sheath that held his hammer. He removed the weapon and set it on the floor beside him. Then he reached for the bottom of the sheath and pulled out a small square piece of faded cloth. A happy yet painful smile appeared on the orc's face and his eyes start to water. Konar showed the cloth to Liam—a well-done drawing of the faces of a female orc and a young orc girl.

Konar sniffed. "This is my wife and daughter. You wonder how I know you have feelings for Kassandra? Because you look at her the way I used to look at my family."

Liam's brow raised. "Used to?"

Konar gazed took on a far away look. "Don't waste time my friend. Any moment could be your last—or theirs." Konar reached for his second jug of wine and took a long drink. Konar extended the jug and said, "You need a drink? It might help you relax with Kassandra?"

Liam waved the jug away and said, "No thank you. I don't drink alcohol."

"And why is that?" Konar slouched back in his chair.

"After I escaped slavery, I came across many people from many different countries as I made my way here. I even passed through dwarf lands and even a few orc villages. In almost every case, people's worse decisions occur when they are under the influence of alcohol. I've never seen a good decision made after someone consumed the stuff. I'll stick to water."

Konar took another long drink and finished the second jug, "Suit yourself. Now if you'll excuse me, I have to go humiliate some more humans."

As Konar left he almost bumped into a minstrel who had just entered the tavern. As the minstrel began to play an upbeat melody on his lute, Konar headed to the bar and received two more jugs of wine.

Liam lifted his hand and caught the attention of the bar maid, "Could I have some meat on a bone for the wolf?" The bar maid hurried into the back and when she returned, she carried a juicy leg of chicken on a plate. She set it down beside Blaster and Liam nodded to her and said, "Thank you."

Kassandra danced over to Liam. A wide-eyed Liam looked at her as she said, "You don't seem that tired anymore. Why don't you come dance with us?"

"Dance?" Liam mumbled.

Kassandra smiled. "Yes, dance. I mean look at those drunk idiots behind me. Even if you are a terrible dancer I promise you will be better than them."

Liam stayed quiet for a moment but then grabbed his swords and hustled out of the booth, while Blaster was distracted by the chicken leg. At first Kassandra got an excited smile, but it soon faded as she saw that Liam was headed for the door. She asked, "Where do you think you are going?"

Liam pushed the door open and replied, "It's getting stuffy in here, I need a few minutes of fresh air."

Kassandra paused for a moment then muttered to herself, "Not this time," and she headed outside after him.

The clouds had disappeared from the night sky as the full moon shone down upon them. Kassandra called out to Liam, "I'm tired of you always walking away from us. You left me during the first battle, you left after the meeting with Domatin, you left after we pulled you into the water, and you left after the second battle, but it is not going to happen this time."

Liam stopped walking and sighed as he turned around. Kassandra had already walked up to him. She poked her finger on his chest and continued, "None of us have done anything wrong to you, but it's like every time we get close to opening you up, you leave and I'm tired of it."

Liam stood silent under Kassandra's heated gaze. He opened his mouth, but the words refused to come out. He looked down and then tried to back away, but Kassandra would have none of it. She blocked his path, her anger fading as she placed her hand on his face and gazed into his eyes.

"What happened to you? Whatever it was, you don't have to keep running. I just want to help."

Liam held her gaze, but a flash of movement caught his eye. He tilted his head and saw two hooded figures standing at the edge of an alley. Kassandra turned to see what he was looking at.

The two figures stood as if frozen in place, staring back at them. Their tattered hoods waved as the night wind blew. Only one of the figures had sleeves, while the other one's arms were showing.

Liam whispered to Kassandra, "Look at the ground behind them where the shadows aren't covering yet."

Kassandra focused her attention behind the two figures and saw a bloody hand and a trail of blood.

Kassandra nocked an arrow in her bow as Liam readied his swords. Kassandra shouted, "Stop! If you make one move I swear to the One I will end you."

The two figures darted back into the alley. Kassandra shot but her arrow narrowly missed one of the figures and shattered against the stone wall. "Damn they are fast," she cursed.

Liam and Kassandra both ran after the figures and as they reached the entrance of the alley, they saw the figures split up at the other side. Before Liam and Kassandra could give chase, Vernon called to them, "Hold up you two!"

Kassandra and Liam turned to see Vernon followed by Konar hurrying toward them. Konar, with a slight slur said, "Whatever you were fussing about better be good, 'cause Vernon here interrupted me from my... my fifth jug."

Liam pointed one of his swords to the dead body of a Crixarian soldier on the ground, "We saw two hooded figures. Their faces were cloaked in darkness but only one had sleeves."

Vernon's eyes widened. He scanned the rooftops and shadows. "Which way did the one with the sleeves go?" he asked.

Kassandra pointed to the alley. "He turned down the right alleyway. Who are they?"

Vernon and Konar exchanged a concerned look. "They are part of the elven assassins known as The Wraiths of Colubra. A highly secretive group that I doubt even the Imperators know very much about. Konar and I will go after the one with the sleeves, you two go after the other one, but be extremely careful. They are known to coat their weapons in cobra venom. Whatever you do, don't get cut."

Liam peered behind Konar and Vernon and asked, "Just you two came out? Where is Blaster?"

Konar chuckled, "Everyone else is busy with their drink, Vernon was the only one sober enough to think something was wrong, and Blaster was busy with a bone."

Liam mumbled, "Of course he was."

Vernon drew his sword and pointed to the alleyway, "Let's go, we can't waste any more time. But be ready, they more than likely had a plan if they let themselves be seen."

The Unbroken ran down the dark alley, and at the end Vernon and Konar turned right and Kassandra and Liam turned left.

Kassandra and Liam took several turns before they entered a small, square courtyard with two-story buildings on all four sides. Above them were ropes with clothes drying that the citizens of lower Sternz had left behind. The only exit, besides the way they came, was an alleyway on the opposite side of the courtyard, where the assassin was standing. His robe laying on the ground behind him, the assassin wore skin tight black leather armor that covered his entire body except his arms. A thin leather belt around his waist held a single sheath with a dagger in it. The hilt of the dagger had a scale pattern ending in a cobra's head. His inner thighs and the area by the ribs shone with a dark blue tint. The assassin's arms were tattooed in the same scale pattern all the way down to his fingertips. The assassin's head was obscured by a hood, and his face was covered by a mask. Only his eyes were visible.

Without making a single sound the assassin slithered back into the narrow alley until all that remained was his silhouette. Kassandra shot an arrow but the assassin bent sideways to escape it. Kassandra then released a second arrow, but again the assassin evaded it with ease. She grunted as she began to draw a third arrow, but Liam grabbed her wrist as he said, "Don't waste your arrows. I will draw him out. When you see an opening, shoot him."

Kassandra shook her head, "That alley is too constrained. You won't be able to use your swords in there, and it's so dark I won't be able to tell you two apart."

Liam dropped both his swords to the ground and walked toward the assassin. "Then shoot when I tell you to."

Liam he heard the slow draw of the dagger. A soft dripping sound meant either blood or cobra venom dripped from the dagger. *Probably venom*, Liam surmised.

Kassandra's feet started to fidget as Liam entered the shadows of the alley. She readied an arrow, took a step into the courtyard, and waited for Liam to tell her when to shoot. In the alley the battle commenced. The shadow shapes moved with lightning quickness. Kassandra was unable to differentiate between the two figures as their shapes molded together in the alley. As fierce as the battle was, all Kassandra could hear was the shuffling of feet, the dagger scrapping the walls, and an occasional solid thump, when one of the combatants landed a blow.

The shuffling of feet ceased and Liam yelled, "Shoot now!" Kassandra released her arrow and all movement stopped. The thud of a body falling to the ground was followed by the sound of a body being dragged across the ground. Liam stepped out of the alley, dragging the body of the assassin with him.

"You could have let me know I shot the right person," she chided. You didn't get cut did you?"

Liam dragged the body to her. "Not a scratch," he said. He then turned the assassin's body over onto his back showing that the arrow hit the assassin directly in his throat. "If the arrow hit him there why didn't I hear him coughing up blood or any sort of noise?"

Liam knelt and pulled the mask from the assassin's face.

"By The One, why would they do that?" Kassandra asked as she took a step back. The mouth of the assassin was sealed shut. She stepped closer to get a better look, "It doesn't look like it was sown shut either, more like they severely cut the lips so when the flesh grew back, the top and bottom lips would fuse together."

Liam replied, "They do it so that if they are captured they don't talk."

He retrieved his swords and cut away at the cloth around the neck of the assassin, revealing a hole in the neck besides the one that was caused by Kassandra's arrow.

"That must be how they eat and drink," Kassandra observed. "At least they don't have to worry about how bad some food tastes. Come on. We should help Vernon and Konar."

Vernon and Konar were moving slower and with more care than Kassandra and Liam had. Vernon was in front with his shield raised in front of him. Konar followed, but noticed that Vernon was readjusting his shield every few steps, "What's wrong with your shield?"

Vernon muttered under his breath, "My shield hand is cut and I can't hold it. I had to strap it to my arm and it's just different than what I am used to."

As they approached a turn, Vernon stopped them. He inched forward along the edge of the wooden wall and peered out toward the open market area. The assassin stood in the middle of the market, still as a statue. The market was a long open area with stands on each side of the alley that held food and other goods during the day. Vernon slid back to Konar and whispered, "The assassin is waiting for us. I want you to go back the way we came and then head for the east entrance of the market. The assassin will be visible from the entrance because he is going to use that as his exit if he can't kill us from a distance. I will draw his attention and then if you can, rush in and subdue him. I want to take him alive if we can."

Konar nodded and hurried back the way they came. Vernon took a deep breath before turning the corner. An increasing itch for Eacru root tugged at the back of his mind. He shoved it away and focused his attention on the wraith. He drew his sword and held it close, ready to attack if need be. He watched the wraith for any sign of movement and noticed a slight bulge move under the sleeve of the assassin's right arm. Keeping his eyes on that arm, he then saw the right shoulder of the assassin twitch and Vernon readied his shield. The assassin's right arm slung forward and, out of the sleeve came a black cobra. Vernon raised his shield as quick as he could to cover his eyes, and just in time heard the clang as the cobra hit his shield. As soon as Vernon saw the stunned young cobra curling on the ground he smashed its head with his boot. A deep bellow was heard as Konar bolted full speed out of the eastern hallway. Konar dropkicked the assassin in the chest and sent him flying into one of the market's stands.

Vernon ran toward Konar to help him up. "Good timing," he said.

Konar stumbled up and he rubbed the back of his head as he frowned at the assassin. "Thank you, but I think I kicked the little wraith a tad bit too hard."

Vernon turned to the destroyed stand to see the lifeless body of the assassin laying in the ruble. He walked over and placed his right hand on the chest of the assassin. "Well, he's dead. Your kick completely shattered his chest."

Kassandra and Liam rounded the corner into the market only to see that the second assassin had been dealt with. Kassandra pointed at the smashed cobra and said, "Now I know why you went this way, and personally I am glad you did. I hate snakes."

Liam asked, "How did you know about the Wraiths of Colubra?"

Vernon replied, "Every Crixarian officer is briefed about their existence, but none of us ever thought we would ever have to fight one. They have tried to kill the Princess before. We need to tell General Izak about this immediately."

They hurried back to the Tavern and as soon as they entered, another cheer was heard from everyone inside. Liam walked over to Blaster, who was still chewing on the bone, and joked, "I wonder how guilty you would feel if I had died tonight while you were busy with that bone?" Blaster began to thump his tail on the booth and he barked once before going back to his bone.

Vernon hurried to Izak's side. "General, my squad and I just engaged and killed two Wraiths of Colubra."

The cup of ale slipped out of Izak's hand and crashed on the floor. "Just two?"

Vernon replied, "Yes why?"

Izak stood and ran to the door as he said, "You and your team have done well. Now go back to your barracks and get some sleep. I must go warn the king that they are inside the city."

"Why?" Kassandra asked. "We killed them both."

Izak paused at the door. "Because they always operate in groups of six."

20

Dust flew in the air when Kaia opened a book in a dark, dusty stone room with old bookcases full of aged books about magic. The only light came from the flickering of a single candle on the table where she sat. Two guards stood watch as she read the book. The door to the room creaked opened and Dylenn stepped in. He was rubbing his wet hair as he walked in, clothed in a white shirt and pants. Kaia opened the palm of her hand and forced all her attention there. Her arm flexed as a vein in her forearms bulged and it began to twitch. A small spark ignited, and just as quickly disappeared. Kaia jumped back in her chair.

Dylenn giggled. "Did that one bite back?"

Kaia slammed the book shut and grumbled, "I'm getting better with fire, but lightening is giving me trouble. And don't even get me started on ice magic. I can't do anything in that area."

He sat on the table beside her and gave her a soft smile. She looked up at her father, suddenly bashful. "Why are you looking at me like that."

"I remember when you first learned how to control your magic. All you wanted to do was to come to this room and read all day, then in the evening go to an abandoned room in the citadel and practice."

"I remember that too. Bethany would always get mad at me for not playing with her." Kaia's smile faded as she continued, "I wish the elves never found out that I used magic."

Dylenn said, "I was surprised we were able to keep it a secret for those first seven years. As a baby you were very difficult to control."

"How so?"

Dylenn stroked his beard. "I remember one of the first times you used magic—you couldn't have been more than a year old. You were laying on my chest, falling asleep, but I fell asleep before you did. When I awoke you were sitting on my chest playing with my beard. I smiled, but then you set it on fire."

Kaia laughed as she stood up to hug her father. He let out a small grunt of pain. She stepped back and asked, "Are you OK? What happened?"

Dylenn winced, smiled, and stretched his right shoulder, "Don't tell your mother, but I fought at the wall with our troops this evening. If your mother knew—"

The door to the room crept opened and Jaclyn, the Queen's handmaid, struck her head in,."I'm sorry to interrupt my King, but Queen Alezzia is on her way here and she knows that you were in the fighting today."

Dylenn sucked in an exasperated breath and replied, "Thank you for letting me know in advance, Jaclyn."

Jaclyn bowed her head and left, closing the door behind her.

"How much is she going to yell at you?" Kaia asked.

Dylenn grinned, "Oh, I will never hear the end of this one. Before your mother got Cormorden, all I had to do was make her laugh and she would forgive me for anything. Now I have to be a bit more creative."

"Dylenn!" screamed Alezzia from the hallway.

Dylenn kissed Kaia on her head and stood. The door burst open and Alezzia stood there fuming with rage.

"Hello my love," Dylenn said as he extended his arms to her.

"I heard you were on the wall fighting the elves today. Is that true?"

Dylenn glanced back at Kaia and winked at her as he whispered, "I will be right back." He strolled toward Alezzia and closed the door behind him as they left.

Kaia could hear her mother's voice increase in volume even through the closed door. She smiled as she pictured her father, standing there with a grin while her mother fussed. She put their argument out of her mind and turned her attention back to her book.

Kaia took a long breath of the night's cool air, closed her eyes, and concentrated on the palm of her hand. The slight sound of a spark was heard but she continued to focus. Soon the crackling of lightening echoed around her. When she opened her eyes, there was a small ball of lightening in her hand, dancing in all directions. A huge smile spread over her face as she studied the jolting ball of sparks.

Then another sound pierced her consciousness. This sound sent chills down her spine. She glanced to her left and saw the shadow of a hooded figure holding a dagger. She screamed and threw herself backward. The assassin's dagger slammed into the table as she fell to the floor, the breath knocked out of her. King Dylenn burst through the door followed by six soldiers. The distracted assassin glanced at the new defenders. That was all it took for Kaia to shoot a ball of flame from her hand. The wraith ignited and thrashed about on the floor, unable to cry out in pain.

Dylenn spotted a second assassin climbing out of the window and commanded the guard to follow him. Then he saw the dead bodies of the guards on the floor, their throats slit. Alezzia had followed her husband into the room and knelt over her daughter, soothing her as best she could. Dylenn sprinted out of the room to alert the Citadel of the assassin's presence.

Soon the citadel was full of Crixarian soldiers searching room to room for the wraith. Dylenn made his way to the throne room followed by dozens of soldiers. As he passed the thrones one of the soldiers yelled out, "There! To the left."

The assassin made a dash for the main door. In the throne room's brighter light Dylenn could tell this assassin was fully robed, unlike the one Kaia had dispatched. Two guards blocked the assassin's path, but without warning, the assassin flung his left arm, releasing a cobra into the air. The cobra bit down hard on the neck of one of the guards, and startled the other. The wraith drew his dagger and drove it into the neck of the other guard, jerking it free as he sprinted for the exit.

The main door flew open as Izak entered, his sharp eyes caught the Wraith approaching him. With a swift forward movement, Izak plunged his sword through the assassin's body. The wraith's hands clung to the sword as his body shook. Izak pulled his sword out and the wraith flopped to the floor. Izak focused his attention on the cobra on the floor at his feet. It was small, but deadly. While the soldiers proceeded with caution, Dylenn, enraged, grabbed a spear, marched forward and impaled the cobra's head.

"Burn the accursed creature," he commanded, then knelt beside the young soldier who was bitten. The soldier shuddered and trembled. "I'm going to die, aren't I?"

Izak nodded to Dylenn, "I will take care of this. Go and be with your family."

As Dylenn left, Izak sat down on the floor beside the soldier, "What's your name son?"

The young soldier sniffed, "Jacob, sir."

"How old are you?" he said.

"I just turned 18 a few week ago, sir. General, be honest with me, how long do I have?"

Izak closed his eyes and rubbed his beard, "Do you want all the details?"

All color disappeared from Jacob's face as he gave a half nod. Izak opened his eyes and said, "At most you have two days, at the least a few hours. The venom will first attack you from the inside. You will have severe pain, blurred vision, and you might even become paralyzed. The longer you stay alive the longer you suffer. Cobra venom has also been known to slowly eat away at the flesh of the victim, starting at the area you were bitten. It all just depends on how much venom you have in your veins."

Tears welled up in Jacob's eyes. He struggled to control himself. "Are you scared to die, sir?"

Izak looked at a boy who had nothing but fear and terror in his eyes. "Are you religious Jacob?"

Jacob's hand began to tremble, "Yes General. I haven't ever missed a mass as long as I can remember. I pray to the One every night and follow all of the commandments."

Izak clasped the boy's shaking hands. "Then you have nothing to fear, you are going to paradise."

"But what if we are wrong?" Jacob asked. "What if the elves are right. Or what about the many gods of the orcs? What if we have just been wasting our time?"

Izak placed a hand on Jacob's cheek, "That's why it is called Faith. The One is the true god."

Jacob's eyes dropped as he asked, "General, will you help me? I don't want to die a horrible death."

Izak hesitated as he looked at Jacob, until a glimmer below caught his eye. Jacob was holding a dagger with the hilt pointed to Izak. Izak looked back up at Jacob and asked, "Are you sure about this? Don't you want to say goodbye to your loved ones?"

Tears poured from Jacob's eyes, "General, my last name is Dursk. My parents and my two brothers died earlier today in their house. I have no family, no friends, not even a girl to call my own."

Without saying a word Izak took the dagger and pulled Jacob close to him as he whispered, "Close your eyes and think of playing with your brothers as a small child. Think of how your father laughed as your mother scolded you all."

Without hesitation Izak stabbed Jacob in the heart. Jacob's grip tightened on Izak for only a split second but Izak just held him even after he breathed his last breath.

Izak laid Jacob's body on the floor, then stood and addressed the soldiers that were standing in the throne room. "Make sure these two receive proper funeral piers, and then triple the guard in the citadel. There are still two more wraiths somewhere in our city."

Izak made his way through the citadel toward the room where Kaia was attacked. The entire Allister family huddled around Kaia who repeated over and over, "I'm fine." But Izak noticed she was trying to hide her trembling.

Alyssa tugged on Kaia's dress. "Kaia you can sleep in my room tonight."

"That sounds like a good idea," Kaia said as she hugged her sister.

"Alright girls it's time for bed," Alezzia said as she pointed to the door. "Come with me and I will get you all tucked in." As Alezzia exited the room she fixed Dylenn with a scornful glance.

"I have done a lot in my days to upset the Queen," Izak said. "But I don't think I have ever received a look as bad as the one you just got."

Dylenn shook his head. "She blames me for this and I think she might be right. There are hundreds of citizens taking residence in the citadel and that is probably how the wraiths got inside. Now we have to find the other four."

"Thankfully there are only two assassins left. The Unbroken killed two earlier. That is why I came here, to warn you."

Dylenn barked a wry laugh. "Only two Wraiths remaining. Well, that's good. So that's what they are called now? The Unbroken? It fits. It brings me relief knowing that the Vicar will arrive tomorrow. Are you sure the scouts you sent to the other three outer gates are still alive?"

"They should be," Izak replied. "They will make sure not to be seen until it is time to open the outer gates."

Dylenn nodded. "How are our numbers? With the Vicar's aid will we have enough troops to win?"

"I believe so," Izak answered. "After the fighting today our odds are better. With the Vicar's added numbers we should be able to hold out, even if he only brings 50,000 Paladins."

Dylenn blew out a breath. "The earlier he gets here the better. With the elves now on both sides of the wall, I don't know how much longer our sanity can hold."

21

Liam, Blaster, Vernon, and Konar were all back at the old school-house settling in for the night. Konar stumbled to his bed with Vernon's help. As soon as Konar slopped on his bed, he fell asleep, still in his armor.

Vernon crossed to his bed and started peeling off his dusty armor, piece by piece. Sleep beckoned, though his body ached from the fighting. He saw Liam watching him, and whispered, "You may not believe this, but I am glad that you decided to stay."

Liam continued unstrapping his armor. "And you might not believe me when I say that you were a far better leader during the second battle today—when you weren't under the influence of Eacru root. You might not realize it, but it's pretty easy to see when you have chewed it."

Vernon rubbed the back of his head, "How could you tell?"

"When you haven't been chewing the root, you don't shake and your reactions are sharp. You kept us together at the beginning and even when we had to separate you made sure we each did what best suited our skills."

All Vernon could muster was, "Thank you."

Liam took one step toward him and said, "You need to quit the root. Completely."

Vernon lowered his eyes. "I know, I'm trying. Before the battle this evening it took everything I had to not take a little chew."

Liam nodded, then laid down on his bed with Blaster nestling at his feet. He asked, "On a different subject, in all honesty, how bad of a situation are we in?"

"If the Vicar arrives with enough troops tomorrow we should be fine. If not, we may not be alive much longer." With that, Vernon pulled open the door of the school house and walked out into the streets of Sternz.

Dozens of soldiers were about; some were on patrol, some sharing moments with friends, and other who were just too afraid to sleep. Vernon gazed at the full moon above him, then turned and crossed the bridge that led up the hill into upper Sternz.

The streets were busier in this part of the city, as not only soldiers but citizens were walking about. *With all the citizens from lower Sternz crammed into this half of the city, it's no wonder the wraiths can move freely,* he thought.

Strong winds had picked up throughout the city, extinguishing many of the torches that lit the streets. The shadows produced by the scant light of the others were somehow otherworldly and played on the imagination. Vernon caught movement to his left and saw a hooded figured plunging in and out of the shadows down an alley. Vernon looked about for help, but to his dismay, discovered he was alone. He reached for his sword before remembered he had left it on his bed with his armor.

Unarmed and unprotected, he realized he still had to investigate. He inched his way toward the alley, and once again caught sight of the hooded figure. But there was something different about this one. His robes were not tattered. Even from a distance, Vernon could tell they were made from a fine, dark purple cloth.

Thus far Vernon had managed to stalk the assassin without being seen. When he got within 10 feet of the figure's back, he called out in a firm, commanding voice, "Hold. I am an officer in the Crixarian army. You will turn around slowly and present yourself, or you will die."

The figure stiffened and let out a small gasp before turning with shanking hands raised above its head. Vernon commanded, "Remove your hood."

Two small hands pulled the hood back to reveal Kaia's blue eyes, filled with tears and wide with fear.

"Princess Kaia? Why are you here? The streets are no longer safe."

"Because of the assassins," the princess wailed. "They tried to kill me in the citadel. One of them was right there, in the room with me."

Vernon raised his empty hand to show there was nothing to fear from him. He took a few steps toward the frightened girl. "But why are you walking the streets? Would it not be safer under the protection of the Citadel guards?"

Her lower lip began to tremble, "Maybe safer for me; but not for them."

"Princess, everything will be OK. If worse does come to worse, I promise you that every soldier in Crixaria would rather die than see the elves harm you."

Tears flowed down Kaia's face, "That's what I'm afraid of. I don't want anyone else to die for me. I never really thought of all the death that was happening—all because of me. Until now; now when death is so close to our walls. That's why I'm going to surrender myself to the elves. If I am to die, so be it. What is my death compared to the thousands that have and will die if this pointless war continued?"

Vernon took the final step toward her and wrapped her in his arms. "I don't know if this is permitted, but—" before he could finish Kaia sprang to him and wrapped her arms around his waist as she rested the side of her head on his chest. Sobs wracked her chest. "Why do they hate me so much? I never did anything to any of them. If it's because of my magic, I would gladly give it up if I could."

Vernon leaned back and looked into her soft eyes, "You shouldn't hate yourself for being different. I know it has to be scary to be in your situation. Even so, your magic isn't a curse, it's a gift. For one reason or another, the One has given you these powers for a higher purpose. Princess, your father is the best king Crixaria has had in generations. He is fair, loyal to his people, just, and loving. Trust me when I say that the men and women fighting know that he has raised you to be the same.”

“But what if the elves break through the walls before the Vicar arrives?” she argued. “I doubt faith alone will stop them from reaching me.”

A soft smile formed on Vernon’s. “Faith might not, but I will. I found you once when the outer walls fell, and if the inner walls fall, I will find you again. I will fight until my last breath to keep you safe.”

Kaia held him closer. “I will pray to the One that they don’t break through, and I will pray for your safety, Vernon.”

Vernon tilted his head. “You remember my name?”

“Of course I do,” she whispered as she rested her head on his chest.

Remembering that there could be more wraiths in the city, Vernon pulled away from Kaia’s embrace. “Come. Let’s get you back to the citadel. You need to get some rest, and I’m sure if your parents know that you have left they are worried sick about you.”

Liam laid in bed pondering the day’s events. Konar was snoring raggedly while Blaster was fast asleep. The door opened and Liam expected to see Vernon. Instead Kassandra entered, skipped to her bunk and started disrobing for the night.

“You’re home early,” Liam quipped.

“Unfortunately,” she grumbled as she dropped a boot to the floor.

Blaster raised his head and let out a long yawn, and licked his chops. Liam whispered, “Sorry boy. Didn’t mean to wake you. We will be quieter.” Blaster lowered his head and closed his eyes once more.

Kassandra undressed down to her undergarments, pulled back the blankets and crawled into her bunk. Liam turned away and asked, “Why do you do that?”

"Do what?" Kassandra nodded. "Get undressed for bed?"

"Come back here to sleep. Why do you never stay the whole night with—with whoever you are with? What about finding someone special and sharing your lives together?"

"Because people leave. Because there is no such thing as sharing, there is only taking. Love? Love doesn't exist. And if it does, it is a cruel taskmaster. Sex is a convenience. It can be had for money, or for power, or just because you need some release. And when it's finished, you can leave. No strings."

"What about couples that are together for decades? Surely there must be love in those relationships?" Liam countered.

Kassandra turned her back to Liam. "That's not love. It's fear. It's easier to stay rather than to have to start all over again. Take Zafrinia. She had a man who loved her; but as soon as someone who was more convenient showed up, she left the man that would die for her, all because the new person was more convenient for her."

Vernon walked in and both Liam and Kassandra stopped talking. Silence reigned as the leader of The Unbroken fell into bed and slept.

22

Glistening sunshine and the smell of breakfast welcomed Kassandra to the new day. She yawned, sat up and stretched, and tied her hair in a ponytail. She started putting on her leather armor while Konar cooked eggs and strips of meat over the open fire pit. He commented, "I would say good morning, but it's more like good afternoon, sleepyhead."

Vernon and Liam sat nearby, already dressed in full armor with their weapons sheathed, ready to go at a moment's notice.

"How are you feeling this morning, Kassandra?" Vernon asked.

Pulling on her boots, Kassandra mumbled, "Exhausted, but otherwise no worse for the wear. What about you?"

Vernon squeezed his hand and winced. "I probably won't be using my shield today. I can't hold it, and strapping it to my arm makes it too hard to control."

Konar put weight on his right side and declared "The wine last night dulled the pain, but today I have a raging headache."

Kassandra looked at Liam waiting for him to comment but he just sat gazing into the fire.

"Liam, how is your shoulder?"

"Fine."

"Don't mind him. He has been this way all morning," Konar whispered. "Between you and me, I think he is just hungry."

Vernon and Kassandra chuckle and even Liam cracked a grin.

Kassandra grew serious. "If it really is late in the morning, why haven't the elves attacked?"

Vernon shook his head. "I have been wondering the same thing. But that is to our advantage. The longer it takes the elves to attack, the more time it gives the Vicar to arrive."

"And more time for breakfast!" Konar spooned portions of eggs and meat onto simple wooden plates. Blaster wagged, drool forming at the corners of his mouth. He sat down in front of Konar with his ears perked up and started to whine.

"You didn't think I forgot about you, did you?" Konar reached into a bag behind him and pulled out a juicy, tender, raw leg of meat and dangled it in front of the wolf. Blaster snatched it out of Konar's hand, ran back to his spot, and started devouring it.

A squeaking of wheels sounded from outside. Vernon's face lit up. "Konar, thank you for breakfast, but dessert is on me."

Vernon flung open the door to reveal Elsa pushing her cart of cinnamon rolls toward the schoolhouse. The old woman waved to Vernon and in her elderly voice crooned, "Vernon, my boy, how are you this fine day?"

Vernon smiled back and replied, "Better now that you are here!"

Elsa looked behind Vernon. "Are those the young people you are fighting with?"

Vernon motioned for his companions to come closer. "These are my—well, these are the warriors I was chosen to lead. Everyone, this is Elsa, the best baker in all of Sternz. Elsa, this is Konar Qal, Kassandra Verbeck, Liam, and Blaster."

Elsa reached into her cart and pulled out a cinnamon roll for each of them. Konar licked his lips at the sight of the warm treat.

Vernon pulled money from his pocket, but Elsa shook her head. "Not a coin. And this time it will stay that way. I have brought a large cart today and they are all free to anyone who is risking their life to defend our city."

Vernon smiled at Elsa and grabbed his cinnamon roll.

"You will do well dear child. Be confident in yourself."

Elsa turned to Konar and said, "I can tell you have a caring but heavy heart. I know you will protect your friends."

Elsa studied Kassandra for a moment, then said, "I take it you are of noble birth? Don't resent your heritage, my dear, or forget who you are."

Elsa was silent when Liam reached for a sweet pastry. At last she whispered to him, "Don't let the past destroy you. There are brighter days ahead—if you will only allow it."

Satisfied that her work was done, Elsa pushed her cart further into lower Sternz, handing out cinnamon rolls to the soldiers who lined the streets.

Kassandra reached into a pouch on her belt, pulled out a small silver necklace, and put it around her neck. Its fine sliver chain held a medallion of a small sun with eight silver flames extending out from the center.

Liam stared after the old woman, pensive. Blaster padded up next to Liam and put one paw on his leg.

"Not this time Blaster," he said as he munched on the roll. "This one isn't for you."

Blaster laid down on his stomach, put his head between his front paws, and let out a disappointed sigh. Liam tore off a small piece of his roll. "Just a bite. But don't come whining to me when this gives you an upset stomach." Blaster gobbled down the bite and wagged his tail to show his appreciation.

As they all finished their rolls, Vernon said, "I am going to go to the wall to see if I can figure out what is going on."

Liam paused in the doorway for a moment, then followed.

"Where are you going?" Kassandra questioned.

"I need to take care of something," Liam replied over his shoulder.

Liam followed Vernon at a safe distance through the streets of lower Sternz, making sure he wasn't detected. He watched as Vernon turned into a dark alley.

With his swords in hand, Liam peeked around the corner and saw Vernon talking to a short, fat merchant. The man was dressed elegantly in red silk clothing. Vernon handed the man a small handful of coins, and the merchant passed him a root of Eacru. When Vernon exited the alley, Liam saw him put a piece of Eacru root into his mouth.

Once Vernon was out of sight, Liam slipped into the alley and approached. The fat merchant in the rich attire. "I don't think I have seen you before boy. How can I help you?"

Liam whispered, "I'm looking for some root. Do you know where I can find some?"

"Well you are in luck my boy. I am the last merchant in all of Sternz who has any Eacru root left. Which means it will cost you."

"How much root can I get for a sword made of Azara steel?" Liam pulled a sword and held it up for the merchant's inspection. The greedy merchant's eyes lit up, and he opened his chest. "For that, you can have all of my remaining stash."

Liam looked to the chest. "This is all the eacru root left in all of Sternz?"

"You are correct, my boy," the merchant confided, still eyed the sword.

"Good," Liam said. Without warning he covered the merchant's mouth and plunged his sword into the man's fat stomach. Liam stared into the eyes of the merchant and said, "I agree to your terms. You get a sword of fine Azara steel in exchange for your Eacru root. Now, you and your kind will no longer plague the streets of Sternz with your filth."

Liam pulled his sword from the dead merchant's belly, and watched as he fell to the ground. Liam turned his attention to the box of root. He pulled a single root from the box and slid it into the leather bracer on his right arm. He ripped a piece of the red silk cloth from the merchant's shirt and held it over the embers of the single torch in the alley. Once the cloth caught fire, he dropped it onto the box of Eacru root. He watched it burn for a few moments, and with the blaze was fully established, he turned and strode back toward the schoolhouse.

Kassandra was sitting on her bunk, petting Blaster's head when Liam walked through the door. Stunned, his mouth fell open.

"Why do you look as if you've seen the face of the One?" Kassandra laughed.

"This is the first time Blaster has ever let anyone else pet him."

Kassandra looked back down and smiled at a happy Blaster and said, "Looks like I'm the new favorite."

"I don't know about you three, but I say we go ahead to the wall to see what is going on," Konar interjected.

Liam and Kassandra nodded in agreement. Blaster made a quick stop at Konar's bed and grabbed something with his teeth and ran out the door. Konar saw him and yelled, "Oh no you don't! We are not doing this again."

Blaster waited outside with one of Konar's gloves in his mouth. He crouched down and wagged his tail while Konar tried to snatch it back. Every time the orc got close, Blaster darted farther away.

Kassandra and Liam walked side by side behind them. Kassandra said, "I don't think I've seen you smile like that before."

"This is the first time I've ever seen Blaster warm up to anyone as fast as this. In fact, it's the only time I've seen Blaster warm up to anyone. He normally keeps to himself. He's a lot like me, I guess. But he seems to really like you, and Konar, and even Vernon."

Kassandra watched Konar unsuccessfully dive toward Blaster. "I have heard that wolves have a heightened sense of people's intentions. If Blaster is willing to open up to us, perhaps you should too."

Liam glanced at Kassandra's necklace. "I haven't seen that before," he said, dodging her observation. "It's quite beautiful."

Kassandra held the sun medallion in her palm. "It was my mother's necklace. I try not to think about her, but then Elsa reminded me that my family has always been there for me; that I shouldn't abandon them just because of painful memories."

Liam and Kassandra walked in silence for a few moments. At

last Kassandra started to sing in a soft, gentle tone,

"My darling, My dear
Only death can keep me from thee
Though the enemy may be near
My love for you shall set me free
I will be waiting for you
Now and Forever
We will be together
Now and Forever"

"That was beautiful," Liam said, "Where did you hear that song?"

Surprised, Kassandra asked, "Have you not heard it before?"

Liam shook his head.

"It's a folk song from back in Vetin."

"I thought you didn't believe in love?"

"I don't. But I like the song, and it's the verse I know. Love may be a fairy tale, but it's a sweet and touching thought that even though the person is about to die, their love for someone gives them the courage to do what is necessary."

Liam grunted, "Nothing lasts forever. Civilizations rise and fall. People live and die. For the most part nobody remembers their names. Nothing is forever."

Kassandra began to hum the tune again, and Liam called out, "Blaster I think you've toyed with Konar enough. Let him have his glove back."

Blaster dropped the glove on the ground and a sweaty Konar picked it up. Gasping for breath, the orc said, "One of these days you won't be able to get away from me."

Blaster barked at Konar and continued to wag his tail. As the four of them drew closer to the wall, they noticed the soldiers looking and pointing at them in awe. Konar said, "Well if either of you didn't want to be famous, too bad."

"Why do you say that?" Liam asked.

"Look at them before they see us and then after they see us. Their faces brighten and their spirits sore because The Unbroken are near. I guess we really have become a symbol they can rally behind."

Kassandra laughed, "No pressure."

A single horn blown from the wall called the soldiers to battle stations. The Unbroken hurried to the gate and clambered up the stairs. The gazed out over the battlefield in stunned silence. Twenty-five siege towers were arrayed, ready to assault the walls. The towers were massive, and layered in Azara steel for added support. Atop each tower were elven archers, ready to rain death on their enemies.

Vernon walked up behind his squad. "General Izak estimates that at least 40,000 elves are gathered to assault the wall. This is no test or botched skirmish. This is the elves organized attempt to take the city. Expect no quarter.

"None asked, none given," Kassandra responded.

An eagle soared through the air above them, and in the distance foreboding storm clouds gathered to the east. "Who knows," she quipped. "Perhaps it will rain, and those siege towers will get stuck in the mud."

Leontina stood atop a hill behind the assembled elven army. She surveyed her troops and looked satisfied with her battle plan.

When Domatin walked up the hill Leontina said, "I'm surprised to see you here Domatin, I thought you would be busy staying in your tent."

"Imperator, I have ordered some of my Praetorians to assist in the assault. I hope they can be of use to you." Tauriel, surprised by how relaxed Domatin appears, immediately became suspicious and observed him carefully.

Domatin stepped closer to Leontina's side. In a quite tone Domatin asked, "So Imperator, what is your plan?"

Leontina smiled. "45,000 of our troops are going to not only take control of the wall but take the city itself. Our siege towers will allow more concentrated numbers of our soldiers to deploy on the wall while the archers on top will provide cover for them," Leontina indicated her second-in-command. "Tauriel will lead the assault on the city once the gates are open."

Domatin looked behind him at the encampment and asked, "Why not send the entire army?"

"Experience, my dear prince." A smirk appeared on Leontina's face. "Humans are known to be devious. If they have a final trick up their sleeves, they could possibly annihilate our force in one blow. I will not allow that. If we lose some to expose their tactics, we still have more in reserve to finish the job."

"Well it seems that you have everything under control here Imperator. I'm sure my advice is neither needed nor welcome. I will be back shortly to check on the assault once it has commenced." Domatin excused himself and walked back down the hill toward the encampment. Once he was out of ear shot Tauriel inquired, "Imperator, are you not worried about Prince Domatin?"

"Worried? Why would I be worried? He seemed rather calm and composed today."

"That is my point Imperator," Tauriel said. "Is it not strange that he didn't even try to undermine you? Or that he isn't whining about yesterday's failure?"

"You are over-thinking the situation. Perhaps he has finally come to terms with the fact that he just isn't qualified to take a city."

Unconvinced, Tauriel replied, "I suppose, but I still would watch my back if I were you."

"Come, let us go and prepare our soldiers for battle. Once we take the city I will keep my promise about getting you stationed closer to your mother."

"Thank you Imperator."

Once at the front of the battle lines, Leontina turned and faced her soldiers. "We are gathered here today, not just for the glory of Azara and Empress Juliana, but to fulfill the will of Colubra. The abomination that the humans dare to protect and even call *princess* will be destroyed this day. *We* are the chosen race. It was the Elves that Colubra entrusted with magic, not humans. It was not chance that you are here today. You are here because Colubra has entrusted you to achieve victory. And we will not fail!"

The elves around her let out an enthusiastic cry. Leontina turned toward to the wall and shouted out, "For the glory of Colubra!"

The Elven army marched forward toward the walls of Sternz.

23

A second distress horn sounded as the elven army approached the wall. Izak, Vernon, Liam, Kassandra, Konar, and Blaster were all at the section of the wall between the gatehouse and the first ballista tower on the right. Konar reached for his hammer on his back but grunted as he tried to lift it out of his sheath. Kassandra saw this and asked, "What's wrong, Konar?"

"My arm is still pretty tender from that arrow." Konar reached for the simple hatchet on his hip. He gave it a few light swings. "I guess this will have to do today."

Liam walked over to Vernon, who was sweating profusely, and asked, "Are you that nervous, or has the root worn off?"

"How did you know I took it today?"

"Just a lucky guess."

"I didn't chew a very big chunk of the root today," he confided. "I just needed something to take the edge off."

"I think you are better with your edge on," Liam countered, then walked back to join the rest of the group.

Once the elven army came within range of both ballistae and archers, Izak shouted the command, "Rain death upon them! Shield bearers protect your towers from the archers on top of the siege towers. Archers, target the elves on top of the towers. To Victory or Death!"

As the archers and ballistae released their volleys into the elven army, Izak realized the elves were far more organized than during the previous assault. Elven ballistae fired harpoons into the wall once again, and once again elven soldiers climbed the chains. Ten siege towers rolled toward the wall on one side of the gatehouse, and ten more moved to the other side. Five remained in reserve, outside of range of the archers.

Vernon encouraged his team with a simple question. "Everyone ready?"

"As ready as we ever will be given the circumstances," Kassandra answered.

Vernon tossed his shield to the ground. "I guess I am ready as well."

As the siege towers approached, archers at the rear of the wall grabbed arrows that had been wrapped in cloth and soaked in oil. They took turns igniting the ends in braziers. All along the wall, the archers released their flaming arrows, but many bounced off the steel plating. Those that stuck into the wood of the tower sputtered and went out, the wood treated by the elves to resist burning.

Kassandra commented to Konar, "I don't suppose you want to try and burn things from the ground up again?" Konar just shook his head.

The two towers approached the squad's position on the wall. Elven archers atop the towers began to snipe human defenders. The Elven tower tops provide little protection for the archers, and Kassandra managed to pick off three elves before they could release their arrows.

The towers rolled to within a few feet of the wall. Elven soldiers within rushed onto the top of the wall once the towers' gates lowered. Kassandra released arrow after arrow into the soldiers inside, the dead creating a barrier preventing those behind from exiting the tower. Their comrades shoved the bodies over the edge and took their place, dying from Kassandra's arrows.

The other siege towers were more successful as elven soldiers rushed out of the towers and onto the wall while elven troops climbing the harpoon chains reached the top of the wall. The fighting shifted from bow, to sword, to hand-to-hand.

Liam rushed forward to engage them, with Vernon and a company of Crixarian soldiers behind him. Liam dispatched a half-dozen elves before anyone else began to fight.

Izak realized his forces could soon be overwhelmed. He grabbed a young female officer by her shoulder. "Run as fast as you can to the west wall. Tell Zafrinia to gather her troops and bring them here now!" The officer saluted and ran, taking the stairs two at a time. As she ran toward the far side of the city, she passed a hooded figure in a dark purple robe.

Though slowed by his wounds, Konar wielded his hatchet with deadly effect. When an elf wielding a spear ran out of the tower toward him, he deftly sidestepped, grabbed the elf by the throat, slammed him to the ground, and ended him with the hatchet.

More elven arrows whizzed through the air as more elves poured onto the wall. Though Sternz' defenders fought valiantly, there was a sense that unless something remarkable happened soon, today would witness the fall of Sternz.

Leontina and Tauriel stood side by side on a hill between the encampment and the wall watching the assault take place. Twelve soldiers stood behind them, waiting for any command that Leontina might give. Domatin approached up the hill behind them to watch the battle as well. Tauriel grew nervous, but said nothing.

Leontina couldn't resist boasting. "You see Domatin, this is how you assault a city."

Domatin cringed slightly, but forced a smile back on his face. Leontina issued an order, "Send one of the reserve siege towers to right side of the gatehouse. We will concentrate our forces there and overwhelm them."

A soldier left to carry out her order, and Leontina pointed to two other soldiers. "Order the second and third reserve towers to attack at the third and fifth sections on the left side of the wall."

Leontina nodded to Tauriel. "It is time. I want you to order the last two remaining siege towers to join the assault at the fourth section of the wall on the right side. Gather 2,000 reserve soldiers from the camp. As soon as the gate is open you are to take the city."

Vernon finished killing an elf and saw that three of the five towers had begun to close in toward the wall. He turned to his left to see Izak fighting at the doorway to the gatehouse and yelled out, "General! The remaining siege towers are coming!"

The towers that reached the wall first were the two on the left side of the wall, on the opposite side of the gatehouse from where the squad was fighting. Moments later, the two towers that were attacking the same section of the wall reached their spot so that now four towers were attacking that spot.

Vernon realized that as soon as the final reserve tower reached its spot at the wall, they would be overrun and the elves would be able to open the gate. The siege tower reached the wall and began to lower its gate, just as a hooded figure clothed in the dark purple robe reached the top of the wall. Princess Kaia pushed back the hood as the elves rushed out of the tower. She raised her hands in front of her chest and shoved them forward. A massive trail of molten flames shot out toward the tower, and the cries of immolated elven soldiers pierced the sky. The tower was soon engulfed in flames, and crashed smoldering to the ground.

A cheer rose from the defenders of the wall. Kaia staggered for a moment, then took several deep breaths to steady herself, and to regain some energy. She saw Vernon staring at her slack-jawed, and smiled at him.

General Izak dispatched and elf, and ran to Kaia. "Princess, what are you doing here? It is not safe!"

"Is there any place that is safe, General?" Kaia countered. "My place is with my people. I can help."

Izak looked to Vernon, who had regained his composure. "She is your responsibility," Izak declared. "As long as she is on this wall, you and The Unbroken will protect her at all costs. Do as you see fit."

"Unbroken, rally to me!" Vernon shouted above the din of battle. A ballista bolt shattered against the gatehouse behind them, and Vernon turned to see that an area of the wall with four siege towers against it had been completely overwhelmed. Some elven soldiers had taken control of one of the ballistae and were now firing it at the humans on the wall.

"We have to take it back," said Konar as he pushed his way toward them. Vernon nodded. "I will lead the way. Kaia, stay back, and only engage if you have to. Liam and Kassandra are on their way."

Vernon and Konar rushed off as General Izak held Kaia for a moment and said, "Whatever you do, don't die."

Behind the general and the princess, a lone Praetorian whose armor was burnt black from the flames stumbled forward, and fell to the ground at Kaia's feet. Startled, Izak started to shove the smoldering soldier's body away with his foot. The Praetorian grabbed Izak's leg and twisted, sending the old soldier over the wall.

The Praetorian regained his feet and stumbled toward the princess. Kaia prepared a fireball, but the Praetorian managed to grab her wrist, causing the ball of flame to shoot into the sky.

The Praetorian pulled his duel sword from its sheath on his back and with a devastating uppercut swung at Kaia. Kaia leaned back but the sword sliced across her face from the middle of her cheek to just below her left eye. As blood flowed from her wound, the Praetorian released his grip and she fell to the ground.

The weary Praetorian hovered over Kaia and raised his sword. An arrow pierced his left shoulder, followed immediately by another in his right shoulder. Kassandra had already nocked another arrow but Liam slammed into him at a dead run before she could loose the kill shot. With a roar, Liam slit the Praetorian's throat and watched the blood drain from his body.

Vernon rushed back in time to help Kaia to her feet. He pulled a clean cloth from his belt pouch and pressed it against the wound on her face.

A faint cry of "Help!" echoed from the wall, and Konar ran to investigate. The big orc reached over the edge and pulled Izak up by the collar of his uniform.

Izak who had been hanging onto the parapet for dear life, took a few moments to catch his breath, then he pointed at a bloodied Kaia and commanded, "You are going back to the citadel now!"

Liam whistled for Blaster. "Blaster, you are going to go with the Princess."

Blaster's front paws shift side to side as he whined. Liam continued, "If the elves break through, she needs someone with her to protect her."

Blaster's right paw scratched at Liam's leg. Liam smiled. "I will be fine. Now, don't let the Princess out of your sight for any reason. Understand?" Blaster barked. Kaia started down the stairs with Blaster following close behind.

As more ballistae bolts shattered along the wall, Izak shouted, "Get control of that tower! I will deal with the elves on the other side of the gatehouse."

The female officer finally returned with Zafrinia in tow.

Zafrinia arrogantly said, "Looks like you Crixarians need to be shown how real warriors fight. I will take my troops and go aid the sections of the wall with three siege towers."

"No," Izak countered. "I need you and your people to hide in the houses along the main street heading toward the citadel. Space yourselves out to where you are in the first houses on both sides of the street, as well as the houses parallel with the wall. The elves are going to open the gate. There is no way we can prevent it. When that happens, I need you to hold them at the gate for as long as you can."

Zafrinia started to argue. "In the streets? I have the best trained troops, with the most armor, and I am a better fighter than anyone else on the wall."

"You will be wasted on the wall," Izak roared. "I need you in the streets. Now!"

Zafrinia turned and marched down the stairs, passing Crixarian reinforcements while Izak turned his attention to the gatehouse.

As Zafrinia shoved her way past Crixarians on the streets, she approached where her troops are standing. A petulant Zafrinia shouted, "Get in the buildings! If the elves open the gate it is our job to save this city since the Crixarians clearly aren't up to the challenge." The Tarian soldiers quickly moved into the two and three-story wooden buildings at the entrance of the gate, setting a deadly ambush for any elves who got through the gate.

Vernon and Liam were in front of Konar and Kassandra as they fought their way to the third tower. Liam and Vernon entered, but Konar yelled, "Kassandra, come back here, I have an idea."

Kassandra shot an attacking elf in the head before turning back toward Konar. Another elf raised her sword toward Konar, but the orc sidestepped the blow and drove the edge of his hatchet into her skull. "How does it sound to you if I were to throw you up to the top of the tower?"

Kassandra grinned and nodded her head. She readied an arrow on the bow and took several steps back. Konar turned to face her and clasped both of his hands together. Kassandra ran forward and leapt onto Konar's hands. With a mighty push Konar threw her high into the air.

While still in midair Kassandra aimed and released her arrow, catching an unsuspecting elf in the neck. Kassandra landed on the tower top, rolled, grabbed the bottom of her bow and used it as a club, smacking another elf across the face and knocking him over the edge of the wall. Kassandra pulled her daggers out and threw one at a third elf. The last remaining elf managed to regain her wits and charged at Kassandra, but she deftly sidestepped and allowed the elf's momentum to carry her over the edge.

As Liam and Vernon arrived at the top of the tower they were stunned to see Kassandra there ahead of them, retrieving her dagger from the dead elf. "Too slow," she quipped at their startled looks.

A horn sounded from the gatehouse, followed by a second, then a third.

Liam asked, "What does that mean? I thought we only blew the horns when the elves are attacking."

"That means the elves have taken the gatehouse," Vernon answered through clinched teeth. "It means the gate is opening."

A roar rose from the elven troops as the gate rose. Tauriel was the first to enter the city with her soldiers close behind. She drew her sword from the white scale sheath on her back—a long, curved, thin sword with a dark blue sapphire in the silver pommel. As several Crixarian soldiers ran forward Tauriel's troops cut them down with quick finesse.

Tauriel looked around the streets, from left to right and street level to up toward the top of the wall. The sounds of battle could still be heard, but the main street in front of her was empty. She shouted an order to her troops. "Hurry to the citadel before the humans send reinforcements!"

She led the way but after passing the first four buildings she slowed, and itching settled between her shoulders, as if someone was about to plunge a dagger there. *Something is wrong,* she muttered to herself. *This was too easy.*

Tauriel shouted, "Wait!" But it was too late. Hundreds of Tarium volunteers rushed into the streets, hacking and slashing their way through the elves. As more elves funneled into the city, more Tarians joined the fight. With no room to maneuver, the elves were being cut to pieces. Tauriel managed to kill three humans before she spotted a female human wielding a spear with the blade shaped like a wing.

Zafrinia charged toward Tauriel amidst the chaos. She hurled herself into the air and stabbed downward at Tauriel. Tauriel sidestepped and managed to dodge the initial attack, but Zafrinia quickly recovered and again jabbed her spear toward Tauriel. Tauriel took one step back and with a downward swing drove Zafrinia's spear into the ground. Before Tauriel could press her advantage, Zafrinia stepped forward and punched Tauriel in the face. Tauriel was stunned, and tried to strike Zafrinia with her sword. Zafrinia blocked the strike with her spear. Zafrinia kicked Tauriel in the gut, forcing her to the ground, then followed through lunge. Tauriel rolled out of the way and staggered back to her feet.

A smile creased Zafrinia's face. "You are better than the other elves I've killed the past few days. Don't die too soon. I need the exercise."

"No-no-no-no-no!" Leontina shouted. Domatin just stood there smirking. Leontina continued ranting, "Keep attacking the walls! Don't all just rush into the city!"

Domatin's smirk became sadistic as he watched the elven soldiers stop climbing the chains and the siege towers. All were abandoning their positions and trying to rush into the city through the open gate.

"Is that supposed to be happening?" Domatin's words dripped with arrogance. "I may not be a prestigious Imperator such as yourself, but it doesn't look like it was a very smart thing to do."

Leontina's sour gaze shifted to Domatin. "You wanted this to happen, didn't you?"

Domatin said, "I wouldn't necessarily say *wanted.* I just assumed you would fail at some point." Domatin walked down the hill, whistling to himself.

Leontina looked back to the battle and prayed, "Don't fail Tauriel, please don't fail."

Konar stood on the wall as Vernon, Kassandra, and Liam exited the tower and joined him. Vernon said, "We have to get back to the gate house and close the gate or we will lose the city."

Liam looked down and saw that more elves were trying to run

into the conflict with the Tarium volunteers in the streets. "Seems as if fewer elves are on the wall. We need to move now before they come to their senses."

"Agreed," replied Vernon. "Konar, lead the way. Liam and I will support you from behind and Kassandra will cover all of us."

Konar ran along the wall toward the gatehouse. A formation of 12 elves guarded the doorway of the gatehouse; two rows of six held their shields together forming a shield wall. Konar sped up and put all his weight on his right leg and drop-kicked the first row of the unsuspecting elves. The force of Konar's kick knocked the first row into the second.

Vernon yelled, "Liam, go!"

Liam ran toward the confused elves with his swords drawn. As they regained their composure Liam jumped over the first row and kicked one elf off the wall while his left sword sliced into the neck of another elf. He rolled to his feet at the gate house and readied himself to fight the elves inside who were tasked with making sure the gate stayed open. Liam rushed toward them, roaring as the first two approached him. The first elf swung her sword down. Liam blocked her blow with one sword he stabbed her in the stomach. He whirled and slashed the second elf across the face. He threw one of his swords at a third elf, impaling him through the chest and took a fighting stance against the remaining three. An arrow sprouted from the throat of one, and from the forehead of another. The last remaining elf tried to flee, but Liam cut him down.

Vernon and Konar rushed to the pulley holding the gate up. The heavy gate slammed to the ground, crushing all the elves beneath it, and trapping the contingent of elves who are already in the city.

A bloodied Tauriel, who was still engaged with Zafrinia, watched the gate fall. A look of pure terror cloaked her face as she realized she was cut off and trapped. Zafrinia laughed. "What are you going to do now? Not a single scratch on me and you look like you've been attacked by a wild beast."

Tauriel launched an attack, but Zafrinia easily deflected it and smacked Tauriel in the back with the blunt end of her spear. She toyed with Tauriel, taunting her. The remaining elves in the city stopped fighting and watched as Zafrinia and Tauriel continued. After several more blows, Tauriel fell to the ground and Zafrinia moved to finish her off. Zafrinia placed her right foot on Tauriel's left wrist and raised her spear in the air. Before Zafrinia could deliver the killing blow, King Dylenn walked toward them and shouted, "Hold!"

Zafrinia reluctantly lowered her spear. With a small bow she said, "King Dylenn, why are you here?"

Dylenn replied, "Once I heard the horn announcing that the elves had breached the gates, I figured I might as well meet the enemy head on, but it looks like everything is under control, thanks to you."

Dylenn then looked at the elven invaders and shouted, "Lay down your weapons and come quietly. I promise that your lives will be spared. Or fight, and you will die."

Two elven soldiers helped Tauriel to her feet. She nodded once to King Dylenn, and then to her troops. As one, they all dropped their weapons.

Soon the chant *"Unbroken! Unbroken! Unbroken!"* filled the streets as Vernon, Kassandra, Konar, and Liam walked down the stairs toward them.

Zafrinia's expression soured. "We stopped the elves from sacking the city, yet those amateurs get all the credit. There is no justice in this world."

24

Leontina stood on the hill, furious at the sight of her army returning from a failed assault on the wall. As her troops filed past her she called out, "Does anyone know where Legatus Tauriel is?"

One soldier stopped to reply, but didn't make eye contact with Leontina. With his head hanging low he said, "Legatus Tauriel was fighting inside the city when the gate closed."

As the soldier walked away, Leontina stood still looking at the wall in anguish. The sky greyed as storm clouds began to swallow the sky. Thunder echoed behind Leontina as she turned to walk back toward the encampment.

The painful screams of wounded elves echoed throughout the camp. Two Praetorians approached Leontina and in a hushed tone one of them said, "Imperator Leontina, Prince Domatin requests your presence at the command tent."

"I will speak with the prince later. I wish to be alone for now." As Leontina walked past, one of them reached out and firmly grabbed her arm, stopping her in her tracks.

The other Praetorian stated, "Prince Domatin said to tell you, it was not an actual request."

Leontina shrugged off the grip of the Praetorian and continued to walk away. Two more Praetorians cut her off and she found herself surrounded by the four Praetorians.

Leontina glared at the Praetorians. "You will burn for this."

The four Praetorians escorted Leontina through the encampment, two in front of her and two behind. When they reached the command tent Leontina noted two more Praetorians guarding its entrance. They motioned Leontina inside, where Domatin was waiting alone with his feet propped up on the command table looking down at his albino cobra which was coiled up on the ground beside him.

As Leontina took a step forward, Domatin raised his head with his sinister smile on his face and started to clap.

"Congratulations Imperator! Not only did you lose your second in command, but you sacrificed more elven lives on this one assault than we did the first two entire days combined. 40,000 dead or captured over the course of a few hours? My, that is quite an accomplishment. Fortunately we still have 155,000 left. How shall we employ them, I wonder?"

"Why was I forced to come here?" Leontina demanded.

"If I said it was because I missed you, would you believe me?"

"I assumed you had sent your Praetorian goons to assassinate me. Since I'm still alive, I presume you have a reason?" Leontina rested her right hand on the hilt of her sword sheathed at her waist.

Domatin chucked. "It was just a joke."

Leontina kept her hand on her sword as she turned back to face Domatin, who had reached down toward his albino cobra. The serpent slithered up his arm and wrap around his neck, resting its head on Domatin's shoulder. Domatin said, "I don't know what you're going to do when you get full grown. There is no way I'm carrying you around when you are a full 18 feet." He addressed Leontina. "Come with me, there is something I want to show you."

Leontina followed Domatin out of the tent into a heavy rain. Domatin dismissed his Praetorians continued to walk away from the encampment toward a hill in the distance. Leontina paused in the mud as they reached the edge of camp.

"I can assure you I don't plan on killing you. At least, that's not the plan right now."

Soaking wet, Leontina nodded and continued to follow Domatin toward the hill.

"Where are we going?" Leontina asked.

"You will see."

At the top of the hill, Leontina stood calm and waited. Domatin said, "I know you have your honor, and I have my ambition. But we both want this siege to be over as soon as possible. We just have different ways of doing things. You are organized and tactful and efficient, while I—well, I excel at tormenting people. Think what we could accomplish if we joined forces."

Leontina watched hundreds of human prisoners, digging. She asked, "How much longer before it is done?"

Domatin pondered for a moment. "Perhaps a week. But two days if we use all the human prisoners at once."

Thunder echoed above them as Leontina answered. "Do it."

Domatin's smile widened as he looked down at the humans. "And one more thing. I would like command of our trebuchets."

"Why," Leontina's eyebrow raised.

Domatin smiled and said, "I assume you will attack the walls tomorrow, just to keep the humans on their toes."

"Correct," Leontina replied.

Domatin wrapped his arm around Leontina's shoulder and said, "Give me control of our trebuchets and I promise you, I will make the humans afraid to fall asleep. I promise that they will be utterly exhausted in two days."

Leontina muttered, "Do as you will."

Domatin released Leontina and started to walk back toward the encampment before pausing again. "Oh, and one more tiny request? I will also need to use some of our oil. I am guessing that the humans will try to burn our siege towers and I'm preparing a little surprise for them."

"If we are only going to be here for two more days you can have it all."

"Excellent!"

With the heavy rain pouring over her, Leontina let out a long sigh of relief that Domatin didn't try to kill her. She watched the humans dig for several more long minutes before she also walked back to the encampment.

25

"*U*nbroken! *Unbroken! Unbroken!*" the soldiers chanted as the rain poured down all around them, rinsing the blood off of everyone's weapons and armor. The few Elven prisoners were herded together by other Crixarian soldiers. As Vernon and the rest of the squad walked toward Dylenn and Izak, all the Crixarian soldiers stared in awe at their heroes. Zafrinia, upset that she was not receiving the praise she felt she deserved, turned around and stormed off into the city, followed by some of her troops.

Dylenn sought out Vernon to congratulate him. Vernon bowed his head but Dylenn said, "No need for that good sir. From what Izak has just told me you not only rallied the troops and recovered a fallen tower but that you are the people I have to thank for closing the gate."

Vernon, humbled by Dylenn's words, replied, "Thank you, sire, but Kaia's injury was my fault. I should have stayed closer to her."

A shocked Dylenn asked, "Pardon?"

Vernon looked behind Dylenn to Izak. Dylenn turned to Izak. "Where is Kaia? Is she alright?"

"Kaia is fine. She received a cut on her face, but as soon as it happened I sent her back to the citadel. I am surprised you did not meet her on your way down here."

Dylenn looked up toward the citadel and exclaimed, "There are still two more Wraiths of Colubra in the city."

Vernon interrupted, "My King, Liam sent the wolf Blaster with her. He may be an animal but I can personally testify that he is very intelligent and will take care of your daughter. It might make you feel better to know that Blaster has even killed a Praetorian."

Izak interjected, "I know you don't want her in any danger but that siege tower that is smoking right now—she did that. If Kaia hadn't shown up when she did the gatehouse would have fallen sooner and the elves would have been able to get farther in the city before the Tarians fought them."

Dylenn's nerves calmed, but worry still permeated his voice, "Izak, you finish up here. I am going back to the citadel to make sure my daughter is safe."

As Dylenn started to jog in the mud toward the citadel, followed by seven Crixarian officers, Vernon walked said to Izak, "I apologize for bringing up Kaia. I did not know you hadn't told him."

"Don't worry, you couldn't have known."

Gregory walked up beside them, covered in blood but still full of enthusiasm. "Two of my favorite people! Vernon and the General." Then Gregory saw the rest of the Unbroken and waved to them too.

"General, I heard you got thrown off the wall today. It must have been a terrible thought to think that you wouldn't get to ever see me again."

Izak shook his head from side to side, "Gregory, you never ceases to amaze me. Now if you please, go escort the prisoners to the old warehouse at the river."

Gregory looked behind him at the small group of elves and strolled toward them. "Alright my friends. Follow me to your new accommodations." Gregory marched the elves up the hill accompanied by a troop of Crixarian soldiers keeping guard.

"Such a small number of prisoners," Konar said, "Not enough for a prisoner exchange."

Izak nodded. "Unfortunately you are right. The Tarians are known to get carried away when it comes to dealing with other races. It's a shame we were only able to capture 33 elves alive."

Kassandra looked back at the wall and asked, "Do you think the elves will try to attack again tonight?"

"I doubt it," replied Izak. "Unless they try an assault with just their harpoon chains but I don't see that happening. Especially after the losses they took today."

"General, is there any word yet on how many we lost?"

Izak looked at the soldiers around him and sighed, "Not an official count, but I estimate we lost around 10,000 today. Three days ago I had 75,000 soldiers. Now I only have perhaps 20,000. We bloodied them today, but the elves still have at least 130,000. I need the Vicar to show up with at least 50,000."

Konar gave Izak a gentle slap on the back and said, "Thankfully he should arrive today, and I don't know about any of you, but I could use a drink before he gets here."

"That does sound like a good idea," Izak continued. "Go then, you all have earned it today. When this rain stops I will order some troops to go into the siege towers and set them on fire."

The squad walked through the rainy streets of lower Sternz turning at the intersection that led to the tavern. Liam continued forward toward the old schoolhouse.

Kassandra called after him, "Liam! Aren't you coming to the tavern with us?"

Liam didn't answer, he just kept walking. Kassandra started to take off after him, but Konar stopped her, "Let him follow his own path. You do know he doesn't drink alcohol, right?"

Kassandra turned back around, confused. "He doesn't? How do you know?"

"He told me last night before the wraiths showed up," replied Konar.

Vernon said, "Come on you two. We all know Liam isn't the most sociable person."

Kaia rushed past the guards stationed at the door to her room and slammed the door to her bedchambers behind her. The trail of dried blood ran from the top of her head and onto her neck. She turned around to Blaster and said, "It doesn't look like anyone spotted us."

She approached the mirror on her dresser, and reached for a bowl of water. She dabbed a wet cloth on her neck wiping her way up to the gash on her cheek. She flinched when the damp cloth touched the area around the long cut.

Dylenn shouted from the other side of the door, "Kaia! Kaia are you in there?"

Kaia, afraid that her father would be furious with her, especially after seeing the cut on her face, tip-toed to the door and unlocked it, then backed away hoping to avoid her father's anger.

Dylenn stormed into the room, took one look as his daughter's face and rushed over to her and embraced her. Tears flowed down his cheeks. "My sweet child. I thought I had lost you."

Kaia hugged her father back and asked, "Are you not angry with me?"

Dylenn didn't release her from his arms. "There will be time enough to be angry. Right now, I'm just glad you are safe."

Blaster let out a loud bark that startled Dylenn. Kaia looked up at her father and explained, "Liam told Blaster to make sure I got back to the citadel safe."

Dylenn stared at a happy Blaster for a moment and said, "We both know that you can't keep your injury hidden from your mother, but for the love of all that is holy, do not let her know that a wolf is in the citadel."

Blaster barked and wagged his tail. Dylenn motioned for Kaia to sit on her bed while he walked to the dresser and got the bowl of bloody water. He carried it to the bed and sat down beside her, tenderly wiping the blood from her wound.

In a worried, fatherly tone he said, "I know that I cannot stop you from helping. You've always wanted to help others and from what I saw today, the city might have fallen if you hadn't destroyed that siege tower. All I ask is that you be careful and take care of yourself."

Kaia touched her father's hand and replied, "I will father, I promise."

Tiny rapid footsteps sounded from outside the door and Alyssa ran into the room, a bright smile on her face. Before either Kaia or Dylenn could say anything, Alyssa cried out, "Mama I found Kaia! And Papa too!"

"Uh-oh," Dylenn whispered.

Kaia glanced over to Blaster and said, "If you can understand me, please hide."

Blaster crawled under Kaia's bed, and Dylenn said to Alyssa, "We're going to play a little game. It's called, Don't Tell Mama About The Wolf."

Alezzia stormed into the room, her face flushed with anger at the sight of her husband in full armor. Her anger turned to alarm when she saw the cut on Kaia's face. She was ready to unleash the mother of all tongue-lashing when she realized Alyssa was still in the room. She closed her eyes, took a long deep breath, and forced a smile on her face. "Alyssa darling, will you please go find Benjamin and tell him to come to Kaia's room. After that, please go find Bethany and stay with her for a little while. Take one of the guards with you."

"Yes Mama," Alyssa replied as she skipped out of the room.

Alezzia closed the door behind Alyssa and the forced smile dropped to the ground. "Dylenn, I expect this kind of behavior from you, but Kaia? How could you?"

"I'm fine mother."

Alezzia's face turned red once again and she snapped back, "Fine? You call this fine? An inch higher and you would have lost an eye. An inch deeper and you would be dead? Kaia if you die, all this would be for nothing! And Dylenn, if you die before this siege is over, what am I supposed to do? What are our daughters supposed to do without their father helping give them a better world?"

"I know you worry, but Kaia and I are completely fine," Dylenn tried to sooth his wife, but she was having none of it.

Alezzia stood with her arms crossed beneath her breast. Dylenn knew that stance all to well. There was no arguing with that stance. "After Benjamin stitches you up, I demand that neither of you leave Upper Sternz for any reason."

Without waiting for a reply, Alezzia walked out of the room, slamming the door behind her. Dylenn chucked under his breath.

"Why are you laughing?" Kaia demanded.

"I always thought your mother was at her most beautiful when she is angry." Dylenn grew serious. "Your mother's bark is often worse than her bite. But I think she may be right. There are still wraiths somewhere in the city. It might be a good idea to remain where we can keep an eye on each other."

26

Several hours passed as the heavy rain continued to pour from the grey clouds above. Vernon and Konar had just left Bear Claw Tavern. Kassandra stayed and continued to socialize with her fellow soldiers. She was sitting at the bar surrounded by Crixarians as well as a few Tarians and resistance fighters from Xanica.

"So he just threw you up onto the top of the tower?" asked an awe-struck soldier.

Kassandra widened her smile and replied, "Yes he did. I retook the tower all by myself. Vernon and Liam arrived after I had taken care of all the elves on top of the tower."

Gregory walked in the tavern and after hearing Kassandra boast he joined in the fun, "Come now Kassandra, we both know that I am the real reason we won the battle today."

"And exactly how is that?" Kassandra questioned.

Gregory ordered a mug of ale then said, "Why, did you not see how all the elves around me died of fear? As soon as they saw that it was me they just knew their end was near."

Kassandra shook her head, "Are you sure you don't have that reversed?"

Gregory took a long drink of his ale and replied, "I most certainly do not. Did you not know that I am the legendary elf-killer, Tantabus?"

A Xanica fighter at the other end of the bar slammed his mug

194

down and declared, "If you are Tantabus then I am the left tit of the Elven Empress."

Kassandra spit out her drink and started laughing at the joke while Gregory turned and asked, "You don't think I could be the elven nightmare? And who exactly are you anyway?"

The Xanican eased out of his chair and walked over to Gregory. With a cheerful smile the man said, "You may call me Makay, good sir."

"The leader of the resistance?" Kassandra's brows rose.

Gregory laughed and said, "Not the entire resistance, just those of us that are here in Crixaria."

"Good to meet you," Kassandra held out her hand. "I am Kassandra Verbeck and this is Gregor—"

Gregory rudely interrupted, "Enough with the pleasantries. Now, why exactly don't you think I could be Tantabus?"

"Have you ever been to Azara?" asked Makay.

"No?"

"Then you cannot be Tantabus. It is said that Tantabus was some sort of elf-killer who massacred entire villages before Prince Domatin killed him."

Before Gregory could retort, Kassandra interjected, "Enough with the bedtime stories. Let's drink. We beat a full elven assault today. It's time to celebrate!"

After all three of them took a drink, Gregory said to Makay, "So, is it that I am just too handsome to be Tantabus?"

Makay laughed and shook his head. "You have as much of a chance being Tantabus as I do at being Ucidere and my fellow Xancians are all Nezdras in disguise. While I am on it, Kassandra here is the new Hero of Aclia."

"That is someone I would never want to be," Kassandra replied.

Gregory and Makay looked at her in confusion and Makay asked, "Well why not? Does saving the world, having thousands of followers, and even getting statues made in your honor spread out through the world with your trials on them not interest you?"

Kassandra took another drink as she replied, "Have you ever read one of the trials that The Hero of Aclia had to go through?"

Makay and Gregory both replied, "No."

"Well I have. On my family's estate in Vetin there was a statue of the hero of Aclia. The trial that was written on it said, 'Was once surrounded by friends, but stood alone against the darkness.' Now I don't know about either of you but I would rather not see all my friends and family die."

"Who said they have to die?" asked Gregory.

Kassandra returned the question with a question, "Have you ever heard about the Hero of Aclia's companions? Or her family?"

Makay took a long drink from his mug and said, "Alright people I think we have established that no one here is Tantabus, or Ucidere, or even the Hero of Aclia. Let us drink and be merry!"

All three of them drank from their mugs as more soldiers entered the tavern. A tall, slender, handsome man caught Kassandra's eye. "If you two will excuse me, there is something I must attend to."

Vernon and Konar walked through a rainy lower Sternz as they made their way back to the old schoolhouse. "You didn't drink as much as you normally do," Vernon observed. "Are you sick?"

Konar smiled. "Not in the slightest. It's just that it isn't after dark yet. There is still plenty of time to drink this day. Besides I would really rather take a slight break and get this armor off."

"And what would happen if the elves attacked again? Like you said, it isn't even dark yet."

Konar looked up at the storm clouds. "I doubt they will attack again today. They will need to adjust from their defeat. Besides, it will be a few hours before the rain stops and unless they try to do an all-out assault with just the chains, their siege engines will be stuck in the mud."

Thunder punctuated Konar's statement and Vernon nodded his head. Konar noticed that something else was on his friend's mind.

Vernon looked around to make sure no one was within earshot and quietly said, "There is all this talk about what will happen when the Vicar arrives but—but what if he doesn't?"

"Do you think the Vicar isn't on his way?"

"I don't know," Vernon replied. "There's just so much that could go wrong. What if he doesn't get here in time. What if he arrives, but without enough Paladins to save the city. We can't continue to sustain the losses. Another all out assault and we will lose. We simply don't have the numbers, no matter how fiercely we fight."

"In that case, I will die around friends. Come now, let us not think about such dark things. The Vicar is expected to arrive later today and we have no reason to worry."

Vernon nodded. "Perhaps you are right."

"Of course I'm right! You seem quite a bit more confident in yourself than you did two days ago."

Vernon smiled at the compliment. "Well things have gone a lot smoother in regards to our team than I thought they would."

"Both Kassandra and Liam seem to be fitting in well. We are a good team, no matter how unique we all are."

As they passed the street with the medical building they could hear the agonizing screams of dying men and women. The building was stuffed with the wounded and the streets surrounding the building were littered with the dead and dying.

Vernon sighed. "20,000 left. Of those who still live, I would guess there are at least 3,000 who are too injured to fight."

Konar snapped back. "Hey, what did I just tell you about worrying about something that hasn't happened yet?"

They continued to walk throughout the rainy streets to the old schoolhouse. Soaking wet, they entered the small building to see Liam, still wearing his armor, sitting in silence by the fire. Konar and Vernon sat down beside him and allowed the fire to leech away some of their aches. Vernon put his hand on Liam's shoulder, "Have you been here the entire time?"

Liam didn't look up. "Yes. I wasn't in the mood to be around people; especially people who seem to think I'm some kind of hero."

"Fair enough," Konar said. He looked around the room and asked, "Where is Blaster? Is he alright?"

"He is still with the Princess. I will probably let him stay with her for the night, just to help calm her nerves."

Liam turned to Vernon and asked, "The old warehouse at the river, where the elven prisoners were taken—how secure is it?"

Konar looked up from the fire. "That's an odd question."

Vernon replied, "I've heard how much you hate elves, but going to kill defenseless prisoners of war would not be the best course of action."

"That wasn't what I had in mind," Liam replied. "My concern is the Tarians. We all saw how they got carried away and killed elves even after they had surrendered. What is to stop them from finishing the job?"

"Is that empathy I hear coming from you Liam?" Konar teased.

Vernon ignored Konar and spoke to Liam, "General Izak posted Crixarian officers to guard the elves. I'm sure nothing of the kind will happen."

Liam stood, walked to his bed, and began removing his leather armor. Konar asked, "On a happier note, what are your plans after the siege?"

"Isn't it a little early to be thinking about that?" Vernon asked.

"Not at all," Konar replied.

Vernon sighed and thought about it for a few moments. "I suppose if I live through it, I will stay with the army, help rebuild the city as well as the rest of Crixaria once the Vicar helps us push the elves out. What about you Konar?"

"I will be right beside you the entire time. I have no wish to ever return to the Wastes. Crixaria is my home now, and you are my friend."

Konar knew he wouldn't get a reply from Liam but he asked anyway, "You won't tell us will you?"

Liam shook his head no.

Someone started banging on the door. Liam immediately put his right hand on the hilt of one of his swords as Vernon stood up and yelled through the door, "Who is it and what do you want?"

The door opened just a few inches as a volunteer from Tarium poked his head in the room, then entered. A tall but chubby man with short blond hair, he looked hesitant but spoke with a steady voice. "My name is Alex Vermis. Ah Liam, just the man I was looking for."

"What business do you have with me?" Liam questioned.

"Well, some of my fellow countrymen and I have something that may interest you. Nothing dangerous at all, no hidden ambush if that's what you were thinking. Think of this as a common interest."

"I'm not interested."

Unfazed, Alex continued. "Don't be so shy. I promise you will enjoy yourself."

"I will not go anywhere with you until you tell me what this is about."

Unrelenting, Alex continued, "Come on. It could be the best night you've had in quite a while."

Liam took a long deep breath as he looked at Alex. He looked like an average soldier, but one thing stuck out, the grin on his face. It was a grin Liam was all too familiar with. Nothing good ever came with a grin like that.

Liam sat in silence for a few moments as he wondered what it could be, but he knew there was only one way to find out, "Alright I'll go."

As Liam started to walk toward the door, Alex saw that Liam was still carrying his swords, "I must ask you to leave those here. I know that is a bold request but none of us will have weapons either. We don't want to get too carried away."

Liam paused, "No one will have any weapons at all?"

Alex nodded his head. Konar and Vernon watched as Liam walked back to his bed and laid his swords on the bed. Alex handed him a black fur coat and said, "Here, I figured you might not have one of your own and this rain is starting to get cold." Liam took the coat and they both walked out the door into the rainy streets.

Konar cast a worried look at Vernon. "Do you think we should follow and make sure everything is alright?"

Vernon shook his head. "Even without his swords, Liam can easily take care of a few Tarian volunteers."

"Do you think Zafrinia might try something? I think it is safe to say that she doesn't like us."

"Zafrinia is definitely the jealous type, but I do not think she would endanger the cause. Not with an army of elves on the other side of the wall."

27

Liam, cautious of what he is getting into, walked behind Alex through the streets of lower Sternz. "Liam, you have nothing to worry about," Alex tried to sooth him. "I swear that you will have a good time."

"If you don't want me to be nervous then tell me where I am going and what I will be doing when I get there."

Alex smiled. "That would ruin the surprise."

The sun had set and all that remained in the sky were thick storm clouds. They arrived at a small wooden building with no windows and a single door. Alex knocked several times before a scrawny Tarium volunteer opened the door. "Welcome back Alex," said the man at the door, "I see you found our friend."

"I sure did, but if it's not too much trouble, I'm sure Liam would rather exchange names and such inside where it isn't raining."

Liam followed Alex inside. The room was empty except for a simple rectangular table in the center laden with dozens of peppermint scented candles that filled the air with a pleasant aroma and provided a little light. Along with Alex and the scrawny volunteer, five more Tarians sat around the table. There were plenty of glasses and jugs of ale. Liam noticed a single wooden door at the back left corner of the room.

When the other Tarians saw Liam, they smiled and raised their mugs of ale at him. Just as Alex had promised, Liam didn't see a

201

single weapon anywhere in the room. Alex took off his drenched fur coat and motioned for Liam to do the same. "Liam, I would like to introduce you to some friends of mine. Everyone, you've heard of Liam."

An older Tarian stood and said, "Don't be so timid boy. Anyone who hates those elven pagans as much as we do is a welcome friend."

Alex lightly shoved Liam toward the table. He sat down beside one of the volunteers and Alex took a seat nest to him. The man sitting beside Liam asked, "Would you like some ale to settle your nerves?"

"No," Liam replied.

All eyes turned to stare at Liam, bewildered. Alex laughed, "More for me then!"

A Tarian across the table said, "So tell us Liam, where did you learn to fight the way you do? Zafrinia may boast, but I swear if you two were to ever fight, I would put my money on you."

Alex added, "Not to mention that roar of yours. It has to terrify the enemy. It scared the piss out of me the first time I heard it."

Liam fidgeted in his chair. "Just picked some stuff up earlier in life I guess."

"Oh come on, you can tell us!"

"Did the elves teach you?"

Then Alex asked, "What did they do to you? To make you hate them so much? The way you fight—it's something more, something... personal."

Before Liam could answer, the door at the back corner of the room opened and then shut. When Liam looked toward the door, he saw another Tarian leaning back and stretching. He muttered, "Oh, I needed that."

Alex hopped up and nudged Liam, "Your turn, Liam."

Liam stood and cautiously walked toward the door. Alex followed with a smile on his face. As soon as he opened the door and saw what was behind it, he stopped in his tracks and his face burned red with rage.

Inside a small muddy room, a naked Elven woman was curled

up with her back against the wall. Her mouth was gagged shut and body was covered in fresh custs and bruises. Strands of her once long elegant black hair were caked in mud. Liam looked into her deep brown eyes, and saw someone who had lost the will to live, who had given up all hope. Silent tears escaped from those eyes.

Alex gave Liam a little nudge. "I told you it would be a good surprise. It's payback time for whatever they did to you. You can do whatever you want with her, as long as you don't kill her. Some of us are ready to have a go at her for a third or fourth time."

Liam's fists clenched and he slammed his elbow into Alex's throat. He pushed him back and pinned him against the wall. The other volunteers stood up, shocked by Liam's response. Liam stared Alex straight in his eyes and demanded, "Who gave you permission to do this?"

Alex gasped for breath and Liam released a little pressure so Alex could reply. "It was Zafrinia's idea. She said that as long as we didn't kill her we could do whatever we wanted. That it was fine. We are just having a little fun. You of all people should want some payback. I thought you hated elves."

Liam returned the pressure to Alex's neck. "Since I returned to human lands two years ago, I have never once said that I hate elves. Everyone just assumes that I do."

The scrawny volunteer that had opened the door, said "If you don't like it, you can leave. We're all patriots here, and we will have our revenge."

Liam looked at the volunteers, then back to the battered Elven woman, then back at the volunteers. I'm leaving. And when I do, that elven woman is coming with me."

Three of the volunteers stepped in front of the door. "We don't think so, elf-lover."

"I share no love for their race, but I do not hate them. In my experience, all of you are worse than every elf I have ever met, with one single exception."

Two of the Tarians guarding the door reached down to their

boots and drew out small daggers. A dangerous grin crossed Liam's face. "You really want to play it that way?"

Liam felt the blood rage rising. He head-butted Alex, breaking the man's nose, then jabbed his knee into Alex's groin, doubling him over. The four volunteers who were not guarding the door rushed toward him. As Liam turned to face them, one lunged forward with a massive roundhouse swing that connected with Liam's face. Unfazed, Liam ducked under the next punch, grabbed the back of the Tarian's head and smashed it twice against the wall.

Liam leaned back on his left leg and kicked out with his right, catching one man in the stomach and sending him reeling backwards to the floor. Liam punched another in the throat, leaving him gasping for breath.

Three Tarians attempted to rush Liam at the same time, but stumbled over each other. Liam kicked one down, but the second managed to punch Liam in the stomach. While he was hunched over, the third slashed at him with a dagger, slicing him across the ribs. The two remaining Tarians closed in on a wounded Liam, assuming he would be easy prey now. Liam quick-stepped forward and snapped his head upwards, ramming his head against the bottom of the jaw of the Tarian and knocking out several teeth. The Tarian wielding the dagger tried to stab Liam again, but Liam grabbed the man's wrist with his right hand, pulled his arm until it was fully extended, and forced it down over his knee causing it to snap. The man howled in pain, his broken forearm dangling limp and useless. Liam let out a loud roar and kicked the man in the face. He dropped unconscious to the floor.

Liam stood for a moment, breathing heavily, then walked across the room to the pile of fur coats on the floor. He picked up two, then stepped over the incapacitated bodies of the Tarians as he made his way to the small room with the Elven woman. When Liam entered she started to whimper, but Liam knelt beside her and whispered, "Shh. It's OK. I'm not going to hurt you." Then he gently wrapped the coat around her body to cover her nakedness, then gently reached behind her head and untied the cloth that was gagging her.

Liam picked her up in his arms, the cut across his ribs screaming at him. When he opened the door and started to walk out into the rain, the elven woman finally spoke. "Where are you taking me?"

Liam said, "Back to the old warehouse, where your fellow elves are."

The elven woman nodded and rested her head on Liam's chest.

As the rain washed the blood and mud off of both of them, Liam asked, "What is your name?"

The woman in his arms was silent, and Liam thought she might be asleep, or to frightened to speak.

"Tauriel," she said at last. "My name is Tauriel."

"Tauriel. It's a nice name," Liam said. "My name is—"

"I know who you are," Tauriel interrupted. "You are Liam, survivor of Jonesburg."

"I thought all the elves think I am dead."

"Most do. But after what I heard you did at Domatin's banner, I figured it out."

"That doesn't explain how you know me by my human name."

Tauriel replied, "We have met before, when your king parlayed with Leontina. That was when I finally heard your human name for the first time, when Domatin revealed himself."

Tears began to form in Liam's eyes as Tauriel continued. "I watched you fight in the arena many times. I am truly sorry for all the things Domatin put you through."

Liam walked on in silence. He soon realized that Tauriel was sound asleep.

Once Liam arrived at the warehouse, he recognized Abby and Ducan who were guarding the prisoners. They both stepped out of the way, awestruck at the sight of what they were seeing. Liam walked toward the huddled group of 32 elves and gently laid Tauriel down beside them. Several of them rushed to Tauriel to care for her and one of them looked at Liam and whispered, "Thank you."

Liam nodded his head. As he exited the warehouse, he pointed at Abby and Ducan. "If you even think about letting anyone else into that building, I will find you and I can promise you that Blaster will feast on whatever is left of your bones." Liam turned and disappeared into the night.

28

When Kassandra entered the old school house, Konar and Vernon were still sitting around the fire. Kassandra closed the door and looked around and asked, "Where are Liam and Blaster?"

"I was just about to ask you the same thing," Vernon answered. "I was hoping you at least had seen Liam."

"Is Liam in trouble?" she asked.

Vernon shook his head. "Not that I know of. I just need to talk to him about something."

"Is everything alright my friend?" Konar questioned Vernon.

"Perfectly fine," Vernon replied.

Kassandra twisted her hair into a ponytail, then sat on one of the four logs around the fire, "So, what have you two been up to since you left Bear Claw Tavern?"

While Vernon looked into the fire Konar replied, "A whole lot of nothing is what. I was honestly about to go back to the tavern to get some more ale."

"More? How many jugs of wine have you had in your life?"

Konar responded, "How many men have you been with in your life?"

Before Kassandra could respond, the door of the old school house opened, and a drenched Liam stumbled in, his head hung down and his arms wrapped around his abdomen.

"Hey Liam, there is something I need to discuss with you."

Liam paused halfway through the door, then nodded his head and retreated back outside. Vernon followed him out while Konar and Kassandra continued exchanging jabs about their various vices.

Konar said, "I don't know if you are just trying to gain their approval, but you don't need to. You are a highly skilled and battle savvy warrior. You don't have to have sex with random men just to feel wanted."

Kassandra smiled sweetly at Konar's words and said, "And if you need to drink yourself into a stupor to stay entertained, I am sure I can get Liam to convince Blaster to keep stealing your belongings."

Vernon noticed Liam' ragged breathing and asked, "Everything alright?"

"What did you want to talk about?" Liam asked.

Vernon shifted uneasily side to side in the mud before saying, "I need help. I know this addiction is not healthy. I know that it is putting your lives in danger. It's just, I don't know how to stop."

After a few seconds of silence Liam said, "Stay right here, I will be right back."

Liam opened the door and stepped back into the old schoolhouse. Konar and Kassandra were laughing around the fire. Liam ignored them as he walked over to his bunk. He picked up one of his leather bracers and retrieved the Eacru root and dropped it into his right boot. As Liam crossed toward the door Kassandra saw him holding his side, blood soaking through his shirt.

"Liam what happened?"

"It's just a scratch, I will be fine."

Kassandra said, "Scratches don't bleed like that. She planted herself in front of him and pulled open his shirt. "A little scratch huh? Hold still. I need to stitch you up."

Liam shook his head. "In a minute." Then he walked out the door.

Liam approached a nervous Vernon and held up a piece of Eacru root. A confused Vernon asked, "What are you doing with root? Where did you even get this?"

"I followed you this morning and saw you with your dealer. You may not agree with what I did but I can promise you this is the last Eacru root in the entire city."

"You didn't kill him, did you?"

Liam just stared back at Vernon.

"You killed a man in cold blood?"

"He deserved it," Liam replied. "Polluting the city with this filth is not something I can forgive. I killed him and burnt his merchandise. All except this one root."

Before Vernon could protest, Liam raised the Eacru root up and broke it in half. Vernon saw that Liam's left hand was covered in blood but as he opened his mouth to say something Liam said, "We will get to the blood in a moment."

"What about the root?" Vernon asked as he looked at both pieces.

Liam extended the piece in his right hand toward Vernon and said, "We both know that the only way to quit the root is too stop completely, to not give into the temptation to take another chew. You also know that as soon as a person sticks a piece of the root into their mouth, they become an addict. So here we have two pieces, one for you and one for me. Throughout the next few days I will occasionally ask you to show me your root. If I see that you have taken some of yours, I will chew mine. We may have only known each other for a few days, but I know that you don't want anyone else to become an addict."

Vernon hesitated and then took the Eacru root out of Liam's hand and said, "How do I know that you aren't bluffing?"

Liam smiled. "I jumped off the wall to save Konar. Do you think I won't do this?"

Vernon put the Eacru root into one of the pouches on his belt and said, "Thank you."

Liam pointed to the wall behind Vernon and said, "How long do you think it will take them to burn all the way?"

Vernon turned around to see that all along the wall the wooden siege towers were being set on fire.

"As long as the rain doesn't come back, I would guess by late morning."

As the two of them watched the siege towers burn, an angry voice rang out from the bridge. "Liam!"

Vernon and Liam turned around to see Zafrinia, followed by 30 armed Tarium volunteers.

"This may have something to do with why I am bleeding," Liam said to Vernon.

Zafrinia stopped at the end of the bridge and shouted, "Vernon, I demand you let me arrest Liam!"

Vernon stepped beside Liam and called back. "What did he do to warrant such a violent reaction?"

"He has put eight of my men in the infirmary, four of them more than likely won't be able to fight ever again."

Vernon whispered to Liam, "Is this true?"

Liam nodded once. Vernon looked back at Zafrinia, then stepped in front of Liam. "I do not care if he put your entire regiment in the infirmary. He is with me. If you want to take him, you will have to fight through me."

"So be it," Zafrinia said.

Vernon shouted, "This is your last chance to stand down!"

Zafrinia and her troops continued to walk forward but stopped when the door to the old schoolhouse burst open and Konar and Kassandra ran out to see what all the commotion was about. Konar handed Vernon his sword. Kassandra had grabbed Liam's swords and handed them to him. Konar pulled out his hatchet while Kassandra drew her bow with an arrow ready to release.

Liam called out to the Tarians behind Zafrinia, "I put eight of your companions in the infirmary without my weapons. Consider your next steps very carefully. We all know this can only end badly for you."

"Elf lover!" came a cry from the rear.

Konar, Kassandra, and Vernon all look at Liam, who shrugged. "The surprise waiting for me was an elven woman taken prisoner today. Those eight men I put in the infirmary had been defiling her for sport. I put a stop to it. They told me Zafrinia gave them permission."

Vernon turned back to Zafrinia. "You ordered the defilement of a prisoner?"

"I didn't *order* it exactly. I just told them to have fun with her," Zafrinia replied.

Konar stared dumbfounded at Zafrinia. "You are a woman. What gives you the right?"

"That *female* is an elf. Who cares what happens to her?"

Kassandra aimed her arrow at Zafrinia and said, "How would you feel if that happened to you?"

Zafrinia smiled at Kassandra as she replied, "You should know, whore. I bet you would have thoroughly enjoyed it."

Tensions rose as the two groups stood ready to fight. Zafrinia's attention, as well as those of her troops, were quickly diverted to the night sky at the wall. As the squad turned around to see what was happening, they saw dozens of circular objects soaring over the wall. Some of the objects passed through the fires of the siege towers and ignited. As the objects crashed into the city, fires erupted all throughout lower Sternz. One of the objects landed between the two groups. As the object shattered, thick black liquid spilled on the ground around them. A few streets over, a large chunk of what looked to be the outer wall slammed into a building, demolishing it completely. Vernon looked at the black liquid and yelled out, "They are shooting oil into the city, and they are trying to burn it down."

Zafrinia, in an aggravated tone, said, "We will finish this later."

"Yes, we will," replied Vernon. "But right now go help out where you can. We will go to the wall and assess the situation."

As the two groups separated, more crates of oil as well as boulders and rocks slammed into the city. Fire spread as soon as they hit the ground.

The Unbroken reached the top of the wall expecting an impending attack, but were surprised to see only the Elven trebuchets were active. "I don't understand," Konar said, looked back down to the city below and said, "Are they just trying to break morale?"

They all crouched as a large boulder soared just above their heads. Vernon replied, "More than likely. But what concerns me is that they couldn't have known that we moved the civilians to upper Sternz. They no longer care who dies."

Kassandra looked out toward the Elven encampment. "There is no honor in this. I thought Imperator Leontina was known for her honor?"

With hate dripping from his lips, Liam said, "This isn't Leontina's action. This is Domatin, and he has no honor."

Vernon looked back toward the city and said, "We have to go help put out fires where we can, and help get the wounded to upper Sternz."

As they rushed down the stairs Konar asked, "What area of the city do you think is receiving the least amount of aid?"

Kassandra quipped, "My guess would be the Elven prisoners."

Vernon took her joke seriously and said, "Good idea. We need to get the prisoners to safety. They could be used later as bargaining chips."

They all followed Vernon through the burning streets. Vernon saw Elsa pushing a cart trying to escape the carnage. Vernon looked back at the wall to see a crate of tar pass though the flames of a burning siege tower. He looked back at her and shouted, "Elsa watch out!" But it was too late.

The burning crate of tar hit the roof above Elsa and the molten tar spewed all over her and her cart. Her agonizing scream was brief as the tar quickly burned her alive. As Vernon stared horrifically at her charred corpse, the rest of the squad continued to run forward. Liam turned around and yelled, "Vernon, we have to keep moving! You can grieve later." Despite his sorrow, Vernon continued on, knowing that he needed to help those who were still breathing.

They reached the old warehouse where the prisoners were being held to see that no one was guarding it. The warehouse was on fire and the flames could cause the roof to cave in at any moment.

As Konar, Liam, and Vernon looked around the street, Kassandra began to walk into the warehouse and said, "I'll go in first and make sure everyone is still alive."

Kassandra opened the door to the warehouse and saw the prisoners huddled together in the center of the room, choking on the thick smoke. "On your feet," she called. "We are getting you out of here." The elves started to follow her, there was a loud cracking sound and the roof at the front of the warehouse collapsed between them, trapping the prisoners inside.

Liam ran to the collapsed debris and tried to move it out of the way, but the burning tar caused too much heat and flames. Konar looked at both of the buildings directly beside the warehouse and then ran into the one on the left. Liam and Vernon looked at each other wondering what Konar was doing. They heard a loud crash at the wooden wall separating the two buildings and the next thing they saw was Konar inside the warehouse, helping Kassandra get the elves to safety.

Once safely outside Vernon looked at Konar and with an astonished tone said, "You ran right through the wall, didn't you?"

Konar coughed the smoke out of his lungs. "There wasn't time for anything else."

"Are you hurt," Liam asked a coughing Kassandra.

"I am fine," she coughed. "Just a lot of smoke."

Liam spotted Tauriel, still wrapped in the black fur coat. He nodded once at her, and she responded with a grateful nod.

Vernon called out, "Listen up. We are taking you to upper Sternz. Follow us and try to avoid any of the projectiles."

Vernon and Kassandra led from the front and Liam and Konar followed behind the elves. Konar joked to Liam, "You could stand by yourself in front of 100 elves and not be concerned for yourself, but let a little fire threaten Kassandra, you almost lose it. I wonder if that is the look you gave me before jumping off the wall?"

Liam gave Konar a sour look as they continued to run through a burning lower Sternz.

29

King Dylenn stood on the balcony of his bedroom. Tears rolled down his face as he watched the western area of Lower Sternz burn to the ground. Alezzia hugged him from behind. "If you are going to be out here all night at least put a shirt on," she consoled him. "You don't need to catch a cold during all this."

Dylenn's reply dripped with sarcasm, "Our soldiers are dying and the only thing I can do to help is to put a shirt on."

"We have the river," replied Alezzia. "I am sure everyone is doing their part to keep the fire contained. You must stay here. You know this. Not because I say so, but because your daughters need you to help give them a better world."

Dylenn pressed the heels of his palms against his eyes. "My city is on fire. With each passing moment more of our soldiers are dying. And there is no sign of the Vicar! Our entire defense was planned around his arrival. It will be dawn soon. I am beginning lose faith."

"What will happen if he doesn't arrive?"

Dylenn turned from the city to face his wife. "If he doesn't and the elves take lower Sternz, I want you to take our daughters and sneak out from the city. You will go to Tarium."

"What about you?"

"I will lead my army in one final defense of the city. That should buy you enough time to get away. If the elves gain control of the inner wall and our soldiers can't retake it, they will overrun the city.

With Prince Domatin in charge I doubt many civilians will be allowed to live, no matter how much Imperator Leontina objects."

Alezzia leaned forward and kissed Dylenn on his lips. Then she walked to the edge of the balcony and stared at the flames from Lower Sternz. "How long do you think we have?"

Dylenn reached for her hand and stood beside her. "Until tomorrow. If by some miracle we survive tomorrow, I doubt we will survive the fifth day."

"What if those dirty peasants you've invited into the Citadel try to take Kaia away from us?"

"Why would they do that?" he asked.

"All the elves want is Kaia. Desperate people do desperate things. If the peasants try to take Kaia, what will you do? Kill the people you fight to protect, or sacrifice the daughter you love?"

Dylenn put his arms around his wife, "No matter if it is the elves, our own citizens, the wraiths, or even Colubra herself, I promise I will do whatever it takes to keep all of you safe."

As they held each other, the door to their bed chambers burst open and an out of breath female Crixarian soldier covered in sweat and smoke panted, "Apologies, my king and queen. There has been a development between the western inner gate and outer wall at the west. One of the elven camps circling the city has come under attack."

"Soldier, do you know who they are fighting?" Dylenn asked.

"Paladins, my king. General Izak is on his way now to the western inner gate to welcome them into the city."

Dylenn's tears turned to tears of joy. "Inform Izak I will join him in a moment."

The soldier saluted and left the room. Dylenn kissed Alezzia passionately. "I knew the Vicar wouldn't abandon us."

Dylenn started to rush out of the room and head to the western inner gate, but Alezzia shouted, "Perhaps you should put a shirt on?"

Dylenn laughed, kissed her again, and reached for his shirt.

Dylenn ran toward the western inner gate followed by three Crixarian officers for protection. He spotted Izak standing below with a relieved smile on his face. A resistance fighter from Xanica on top of the wall shouted down, "They are through, sir! Shall we open the gate for them?"

Izak shouted back, "Open the gate at once! Let them in!"

The western inner gate opened. Many of the soldiers around Dylenn and Izak stood in awe at the sight of the Paladins, having never seen them before. Side by side in rows of five the Paladins walked through the gate, Knights of Tarium in shining grey plate armor from head to toe. The heavily armored Paladins entered the city with an air of determination. Their helmets covered their entire head with two thin slits in front, trimmed in gold, to provide vision. On each side of the helmet were golden wings extending straight up into the air. Under the large shoulder armor and neck guard was a golden cloth tabard, trimmed in white on the edges, extending down and coming to a point at their mid-calf, both in the front and back. In the center of the tabard at the chest area was an eagle with its wings extended side to side in white. Each Paladin carried a finely crafted grey steel flanged mace as well as grey steel kite shields with the same eagle engraved in the center.

A Paladin without a helmet walked toward Izak and Dylenn. Taller than an average man, with straight blond hair extending to his shoulders, he addressed the king formally. "King Dylenn, I am Captain John Harrison, leader of the 5th Paladin Legion of Tarium. If you wish, my friends call me Harrison."

Captain Harrison extended his hand toward Dylenn, but Dylenn brushed it aside and embraced Harrison, who was caught off-guard by this show of affection. Izak said, "I am General Izak, commanding officer here, and as you can see Captain Harrison, we are all relieved that you have arrived."

Dylenn released Harrison and asked, "Now Captain Harrison,

where is Vicar Matthew? I would speak with him and extend my gratitude to him as well."

Harrison's cool demeanor soured. "I am afraid the Vicar is not with us. In our haste to raise an army and arrive on time, we could not gather horses enough for everyone. We have been moving at a slower pace than expected. His Holiness is on his way, but it will likely be later today or possibly even tomorrow night before he arrives. My men and I volunteered to run ahead of the main army to deliver the message and to provide what aid we can until his arrival."

Izak nodded. "Thank you Harrison. How many men did you bring?"

"We are all believers of the One and should stand with each other against the pagans and bring order to the world. If it had been up to me we would have joined the war as soon as it started. I brought with me 10,000 eager Paladins. The Vicar brings an additional 75,000."

Izak and Dylenn exchanged hopeful glances as Harrison continued, "If it would please both of you, my men and I will guard the walls today, giving your soldiers some much needed rest."

"Thank you Harrison, with your help as well as the Vicar when he arrives, we will without a doubt be able to push the elves back," Izak said.

A grime covered Crixarian soldier approached. "The elves have stopped their barrage and we have contained the fires. What are your orders General Izak?"

Izak said, "Go spread the word that some Paladins have arrived, and more are coming. They will hold the walls. Tell all commanders to rest as many of their troops as they can. And soldier, are you able to carry out a mission after that?"

The Crixarian stood up straight and replied, "Yes sir, whatever is required of me."

Izak put his hand on the man's shoulder and said, "After you deliver the message, I want you to grab some food and water, find a horse and then ride out to find the Vicar and let him know the situation here. Perhaps if he knows that we are in dire need, he will proceed with greater haste."

"Of course sir," replied the soldier.

Dylenn asked, "What is your name, soldier?"

"Ethan, my King," replied the man.

Dylenn smiled at Ethan and said, "Be safe. We need every man able to fight."

Ethan bowed. "Thank you my King," he said, and took off running back toward the eastern side of Sternz.

Harrison stepped forward. "If you will excuse me King Dylenn, I will now take my Paladins and man the eastern wall. We will hold it until his Holiness arrives, I promise you that. Also two of the Vicar's Chosen volunteered to join us as well. They are more than capable of fighting on the walls, but they are at your disposal to command as you will. They should be coming through the gate soon. They will report to you. Just let them know where you want them to go."

Harrison bowed again and led the Paladins through the streets toward the eastern wall. Izak turned to Dylenn and whispered, "Vicar's Chosen—here? Why would they come here?"

A worried expression clouded Dylenn's face. "I do not know. They may be the best of the best of the Paladins, but those men do not act like humans. Their order's sole purpose is to eliminate enemies of the One, both religiously as well as militarily, by any means necessary. I have heard they achieve their goals through torture, extortion, kidnapping, even murder."

Izak and Dylenn spotted the Chosen immediately. The two figures walked toward them. Their armor was the same design as the Paladins, but of a much darker grey. Their tabard was white trimmed in gold with a gold eagle, but instead of helmets they wore a white hood, tattered around the edges. A charcoal-colored black veil was fixed into the hoods to cover their faces. The Vicar's Chosen carried the same mace and shield as the Paladins but they also carried a small crossbow on their backs.

The Chosen approached and bowed low enough for protocol, but no lower. In a deep monotone, one said, "King Dylenn. We have heard there are Wraiths of Colubra inside the walls. We are more than capable of hunting them down and expelling them from your city, should you so command."

Dylenn tried to conceal his unease. "Thank you for the offer. If you would like to help, those assassins are targeting my daughter, Kaia. If you were to protect her as bodyguards, you will probably come across them sooner or later."

The Vicar's Chose stood motionless for several long moments. The silence sent chills up Izak's spine. At last one replied, "As you wish." They turned and shambled toward the citadel as if their bodies were void of souls.

As the sun peeked over the horizon, Dylenn asked, "Now that we have some reinforcements how do you like our odds?"

Izak replied, "Paladins are better trained and better armored than most of our soldiers. As long as the elves don't have a surprise today, we should be able to hold the wall until the Vicar arrives. And with the Vicar's Chosen protecting Kaia, there is one less thing we have to worry about. I don't approve of their methods, but as long as they are with her, I doubt the wraiths will try anything."

30

Leontina yawned as she exited her tent and walked toward the command tent to prepare her forces for the day and to learn how successful Domatin's barrage was. As she walked through the camp she noticed nervous expressions on the faces of some of her officers. Leontina confronted one of them. "What is going on?"

The Elven woman met Leontina's gaze as she nervously uttered, "Imperator, there are Paladins manning the wall."

Stunned, Leontina shifted her gaze toward the wall. She rushed to the command tent, and found four Praetorians guarding the entrance. They stepped aside to allow her entrance. Domatin sat in a chair on the opposite side of the command munching on an apple. "Good morning, Imperator. Sleep well?"

Leontina ignored his greeting, "There are Paladins on the wall."

"I know," replied Domatin, taking another bite of his apple, "I knew they were here a few hours ago when they broke through one of our small guard camps by the western gate."

Leontina bit down on her bottom lip to keep from screaming. "You knew this hours ago and didn't inform me?"

"Their arrival changes nothing, sweet Leontina."

"It changes everything! For one, Tarium has now officially joined the war. Secondly, we don't know how many Paladins are in the city. And finally there could be more trying to flank us," Leontina shouted.

Domatin remained relaxed and finished eating his apple. "We knew it was a matter of time before they joined the war. And there are not that many, perhaps 10,000. There may be more coming, of course. So I sent 50,000 of our soldiers to the west to intercept any stragglers."

Leontina shook with rage. "Not only did you disrespect me by not informing me of an important development, but you've also ordered my soldiers without my permission?"

Domatin's reply dripped with arrogance, "Imperator, I think we both know that if anyone has been disrespected it is me. You have been quite rude the past few days, even though I am your prince and the best warrior Aclia has ever seen.'"

"You are not my prince."

Domatin stood and faced Leontina. "Excuse me?"

Leontina, unflinching, replied, "You heard me. You are not my prince. You are not fit to be a prince. You are an ungrateful, arrogant ass who feels entitled because his last name is Ophidian. Your brother was a true prince. Thankfully he isn't here to see the despicable prig you've become."

Domatin trembled with rage. "You will not *speak* of Tiberius."

"Tiberius was a man I would follow to death," Leontina continued. "But you? I wouldn't follow you to the latrine."

Domatin slammed his fists on the command table. "I swear to you that I will have a hand in your death. It may be tomorrow or in a hundred years, but you will die because of me."

Leontina leaned forward, acid in her voice. "You claim to be the best swordsman in all of Aclia, yet I have never once seen you fight. You've always had your slave to fight your battles for you. Now that slave is defending the walls of Sternz. Perhaps you could walk up to the gate and demand a duel with that slave. I might be compelled to follow you if you did. Or are you too much of a coward?"

Silence consumed the tent. Then Domatin simply walked out of the tent. Leontina drew a deep breath and plopped down in the chair to regain her composure.

An officer entered the tent and asked, "Imperator is everything alright? Prince Domatin seemed furious as he walked away."

"Everything is fine. Prince Domatin ate a sour apple and is a bit indisposed," Leontina replied. "We will resume the assault on the walls. How many siege towers were we able to build last night?"

"Seven. It also seems that in Prince Domatin's barrage last night, many of the human ballista towers were destroyed."

"Excellent. Send word to our last mage. The Paladins' armor is heavy plate metal. Lightening magic will do an excessive amount of damage to them. Send a siege tower to each of the three sections of the wall beside the gatehouse and the seventh on the left section beside it."

"Yes Imperator," said the officer as he exited the tent.

Leontina looked at the map of Sternz and muttered to herself, "I would like to see that pathetic snob try to kill me."

31

Covered in grime and smoke, Liam, Kassandra, Konar, and Vernon tried to dust themselves off after helping extinguish the last of the fires in lower Sternz. As Paladins walked past them on their way to the wall, Vernon took note of how many Crixarian soldiers gazed in awe at their splendid armor.

Konar smiled, "Now this is what I am talking about. With their help we will surely kick the elves all the way back to Azara."

A Paladin crossed toward them, helmet in hand, his long blond hair swaying around his shoulders. "You are The Unbroken I have heard so much about since I arrived in your city?"

"I am Vernon Regnier. The orc beside me is Konar Qal. On the other side of him is Kassandra Verbeck. And that," Vernon pointed, "is Liam."

"A pleasure to meet you all," said the Paladin. "My name is John Harrison, Captain of the 5th Legion of Paladins."

Kassandra smiled coyly, playing with her ponytail. "Well Captain Harrison, I'm sure I speak for everyone when I say that we are very glad you are here."

Harrison nodded once. "No thanks are necessary. I have often thought that Tarium should have entered this war as soon as Xanica was attacked. All followers of the One should stand together, regardless of where they live. Lucky for all of us Vicar Matthew shared my opinion. From what I hear, you four and the wolf are

223

the reason the city hasn't fallen yet. By the way, where is the wolf. Is it alright?"

"He is fine," Liam replied. "He is protecting Princess Kaia."

Harrison took note of Liam's unwelcome tone. "Pardon me, friend. Have I somehow offended you—Liam, is it? And it is customary to give your last name during an introduction. I'm afraid you have me at a disadvantage there."

Konar interrupts, "Captain Harrison, Liam didn't mean anything by it. We have been awake all night putting out the fires and, well, Liam isn't exactly the most sociable type."

"Perfectly understandable," Harrison said politely. "Now if you all will excuse me I should join my men at the wall. The Paladins will hold it today. You all should go get some rest." Harrison bowed and walked away toward the wall.

Vernon said, "I am going to go find General Izak and see if there is anything else that needs to be done."

"I shall accompany you," said Konar.

Kassandra chimed in, "So will I."

The three of them looked at Liam, who let out an exasperated sigh and said, "Fine, I will come too."

Konar and Vernon walked side by side in front while Liam and Kassandra followed a couple of paces behind.

Konar smiled at Vernon and said, "These past few days have been rough but you've done a good job."

"Do you mean that? Or are you just trying to calm my nerves?" Vernon asked.

Konar laughed, "Think about it. We saved Princess Kaia, destroyed a battering ram, took out two of the wraiths, retook the gatehouse after it fell to the elves. And we're all still alive. I call that a win."

"Thank you Konar. I suppose I just realize all the places where I've failed."

"Sometimes in life, our worries cloud reality. You are a better leader than you give yourself credit for."

Kassandra interrupted their conversation. "Wait just a minute, Harrison brought up something I hadn't thought about before."

Vernon and Konar stopped and turned around to see Kassandra staring at Liam. She asked, "Liam, what *is* your last name?"

Liam stared at the ground. Kassandra walked seductively toward him and nudged him playfully, "So, are you going to tell us, or are you going to walk away—again?"

Liam raised his head and at each of his companions. He dropped his head again and whispered, "I don't know."

Kassandra smiled at his joke. "What? You can't decide whether you would rather tell us or walk away?"

Vernon tried to stop her, "Kassandra—"

"What?" Kassandra said, confused.

Vernon nodded to Liam who was still standing there studying the ground, trying hard to hide his sorrow. Reality sunk in, and Kassandra said, "Oh."

Liam finally looked up. He shook his head and quietly replied, "I can't even remember my parents' faces, much less their names."

"Liam, I am so sorry—"

"It's fine," Liam cut her off. "Now can we please keep moving? I would like to get a little bit of rest before we have to fight again."

They walked for a while in silence through a burnt and smoky lower Sternz. Konar dropped back beside Liam and asked, "What makes you think we will have to fight again soon? Surely the Paladins can hold the wall for a day."

"The Paladins are overrated."

"Have you ever fought one?" asked Vernon.

"No, but if they are our equivalent to the elven Praetorians, warriors who claim they are better simply because their faith is stronger in their chosen god, then they are overrated."

Kassandra asked, "Are you not a believer of the One, Liam?"

"I am not," Liam stated.

Almost offended Kassandra replied, "Why not? Don't you believe in a higher power?"

"I have been in every country and met plenty of unique people with different views on religion. From the orcs in the Eacru Wastes, the elves in Azara, dwarves in Schelmar, and now here, and the only thing I can tell is that people worship whatever god their parents tell them to. Or what their culture tells them to."

Konar chimed in, "He has a point."

Kassandra looked at Konar and asked, "Are you not religious either Konar? Not even to one of the orc gods?"

Konar replied "I haven't been religious in a very long time."

Kassandra then looked over at Vernon and said, "What about you Vernon?"

Vernon replied, "I am a believer of the One, but I don't agree with everything the Tarium church does and says we should do."

"Careful no one hears you. Someone could take that for blasphemy."

Vernon laughed, "Even you have to admit that the church is corrupt. Taxing people to allow them to worship and excommunication are what should truly be considered blasphemy. People shouldn't have to pay to be saved. And as for excommunication, sinners usually already know what they are doing is wrong. They should be shown their mistake, and through fellowship be taught how it was wrong, not thrown out of the church."

Kassandra thought for a moment before looking back to Liam and Konar and asking, "Corrupt or not, don't both of you want your souls to be in Idyll with the One?"

"Idyll? What is Idyll?" Liam asked.

Vernon answered, "Idyll is the golden realm of the One. When the One's believers die, their souls go to be with the One in a place of eternal joy and peace."

"And all those that don't are sent to Stypor, an eternal nothingness. A realm of everlasting consciousness but also darkness, no light, no one to talk to, no purpose," Kassandra added.

Liam replied to Kassandra, "So you blindly follow the church in hope of not going to this Stypor?"

Kassandra smiled and said, "Not blindly. My father made sure I was well educated in the faith. And I spent time reading about other religions. I think that helped my faith. The elves worship a snake that ascended to godhood, which just doesn't make any sense. Something doesn't just turn into a god. No offense Konar ,but from what I know of the five orc gods, their commandments change depending on the person preaching. And the dwarves are atheists, so I don't think I have to explain anything there."

Vernon looked at Konar and asked, "Five orc gods? I've only heard of two."

Konar replied, "Raz Ma-dal the god of war and death, Zulga the god of fire and love, Bugak the god of earth and harvest, Sodar the god of air and wealth, and Ragas the god of water and peace. The two main orc gods are Raz Ma-dal and Zulga, the other three are not very popular."

Before anyone could respond, they realized they had reached their destination. Vernon stepped forward toward General Izak and said, "We wanted to see if you need us to do anything else before we rest for a while."

"Nothing as of now," Izak replied. "Just rest until the Vicar arrives."

Confused, Kassandra interjected, "Until he arrives? The Paladins are already here."

"Captain Harrison's volunteers are an advance force. The Vicar has been delayed and won't arrive until later today with 75,000 troops. But Harrison brought 10,000 with him. That should be sufficient to hold the wall until the Vicar arrives. You should also know that two of the Vicar's Chosen arrived as well. They have been assigned to provide additional protection for Princess Kaia."

Liam immediately raised two fingers to his lips and let out an earsplitting, high-pitched whistle.

Kassandra rubbed her ears, "Warn a girl before you do that next time, will you? And just why did you do that anyway?"

"You'll see," Liam said.

Everyone followed Liam's gaze toward the citadel, and soon saw

Blaster loping down the hill toward them. As the wolf approached, Liam held up is hand and commanded, "No. No. No. No!" then braced for impact. At full speed Blaster leaped into the air and landed on Liam, knocking him to the ground. With Liam pinned helpless beneath him, the big wolf gave him a multitude of slobbery licks all over his face.

Still laughing, but in genuine pain, Liam said, "Alright boy, that's enough."

Blaster playfully whined as he shifted his weight back and forth between his front two paws. Liam tried to push Blaster off, but Blaster playfully snapped at Liam's hands and again forced him back to the ground. Liam finally capitulated and said, "Fine! You win this time."

Blaster jumped off and sat, happily wagging his tail.

A loud horn bellowed from the wall. Izak said, "The Paladins will hold. Get some rest, but don't get too comfortable. If they falter we may need reinforcements."

32

Captain Harrison stood with some of his Paladins to the left of the gate house. As they watched the approaching elves creep forward, Harrison turned to his Paladins to give words of encouragement. "I know for some of you this will be your first real combat situation. We are no longer fighting blasphemers or putting down petty revolts. Now we will show the elves who the true god is and why the One's Paladins are the fiercest fighting force of all humanity. The elves think that because of their superior numbers that they will overrun us and open these gates. I say, not today. For every one of us they kill we will kill ten of theirs. If it comes to it, you will lay down your lives to protect the gatehouse at all costs. Death to Pagans!"

"Death to Pagans!" shouted all of the Paladins on the wall.

The siege towers reached the wall and lowered their gates. Harrison joined his men in straight line formation along the wall. The Paladins stood firm, with their shields raised, their maces at the ready. Elven soldiers rushed out of the towers toward the Paladins, colliding into the shield wall. The Paladins clubbed the elves with their maces, but more climbed over the mounting pile of dead soldiers. Still the Paladins held firm.

As suddenly as the attack began, the assault halted. The Paladins stood ready, but confused by the sudden respite. Harrison peered inside the siege tower to see elves carrying large heavy sacks climbing the final ladder up to the top where archers were normally stationed.

Realization broke through, and Harrison shouted to his men, "Watch out from above!"

Large rocks fell from top of the siege towers onto the Paladins below. Some were too heavy to be blocked by their shields and soon small gaps began to appear in the Paladins' line. The Elven soldiers took immediate advantage of the breach and rushed forward, this time breaking through the gaps in the shield wall. The once stable defense turned into an all-out brawl on the wall.

Harrison fought bravely. He thrust the top of his mace into the abdomen of an attacker, then quickly swung downward, shattering the unlucky elf's skull.

A loud clap of thunder boomed over the din of battle, shocking the Paladin captain. He scanned the morning sky but didn't see a single cloud. He dispatched another elf as a cry went up, "There is a mage on the wall!"

"A mage? Where?" Harrison demanded."

The Paladin pointed. "He came out of that siege tower on the far side of the gatehouse with both arms extended sideways. Lightning fell from a clear sky out of nowhere and killed all our men there. When our reinforcements tried to retake that section of the wall, he spewed lightning from his hands. We don't know how to fight him sir."

The ominous *clank-clank* of the gate slowly raising jarred Harrison into action. He started running, pulling a number of Paladins in his wake, toward the gatehouse. "We need to retake the gatehouse. I want you to form a barricade to keep more elves from reaching the gatehouse."

One of the Paladins argued, "If we form a shield barricade, the mage's lightening will rip us apart. We can't stand against that!"

Harrison replied, "Then remove your armor to protect yourselves from the lightning, and use dead elves for the barricade. Now go! I will take care of the mage."

Paladins fought their way into the gatehouse, while Harrison climbed the ladder to the top of the gatehouse, muttering as he climbed, "The Crixarians held this wall for three days. I'll be damned if I let it fall on the first day I am here."

Harrison could hear the shock and static of the mage's magic. He also heard the welcome sound of the gate slamming back onto the ground. *They've retaken the gatehouse*, he thought. *Now to do my part.* Harrison stood and shouted, "Reserves, to the wall!"

Paladins from all sides rushed to obey. Harrison heard the crackle and buzz of building lightening. He ran as fast as he could to the edge of the roof of the gatehouse, then launched himself toward the mage. The impact sent them both rolling across the top of the wall. The mage gained his feet, while Harrison was still on one knee. Harrison threw his shield at the mage before he could conjure more lightning, catching the elf in the stomach. The mage stumbled back toward the edge of the wall. Harrison paced toward the wheezing elf, grabbed him by the throat, and squeezed, cutting off the mage's air.

Step by step, Harrison forced the mage backward. At last Harrison dangled the whimpering elf over the edge of the wall. The elf pleaded with his eyes. Harrison simply shook his head, and released his hold. The mage appeared to float in slow motion during his long fall, before crumpling in a bloody heap when he impacted the ground.

Two elven warriors, enraged by Harrison's actions, rushed toward him. Harrison waited until the last second before deftly sidestepping the attack. One elf who was moving to fast to change direction, slammed into the edge of the wall. Harrison grabbed the stunned elf by the ankle, and tossed her off the wall. The second elf ran under more control. Harrison managed to dodge a sword thrust then he stepped forward and punched the elf in the face. The elf fell to his back and Harrison followed with a vicious kick in the throat. That elf's body joined his companions at the bottom of the wall.

As the fighting on the wall raged, Kaia sat on the bed in her room, dutifully listening to her mother yell at her.

"How did you know that wolf wasn't going to kill you?"

"Mother, I know you think that Blaster is a wild animal, but I promise you he is a very smart wolf."

"Oh, so it has a name?" Alezzia said still upset. "And just how do you know all about that boy, Liam, and his wolf?"

Kaia took a deep breath. "Three days ago when I was between the inner and outer wall running from the elves, I was trapped by four elven Praetorians. Liam and Blaster are the only reason I am here right now. They saved my life, Mother. Can you not find even a bit of gratitude in your heart for that?"

Stunned by the revelation, Alezzia said, "Why didn't you tell me?"

Kaia looked at her mother directly in the eyes as she replied, "Father didn't think you would react very well. Neither did I."

Alezzia's calm flared again into rage. "Your father knew about this?"

"Yes mother. We only wanted to keep you from worrying—"

Three slow knocks sounded from the door. Alezzia demanded, "Who is it?"

A quiet monotone replied from beyond the door, "We are here on orders from your king to protect Princess Kaia."

Alezzia opened the door to see the two Chosen standing still. Alezzia motioned them into the room. She said to Kaia, "Now this is the kind of protection you need. I'm glad your father has finally come to his senses."

Kaia watched the two men step into her room. She felt them staring at her through their masks. Unable to see their faces unnerved her.

Alezzia walked toward the door. "Now that I know you will be properly guarded, I am going to have a word with your father. We are going to have an adult conversation about keeping secrets."

Alezzia closed the door behind her, and Kaia found herself alone with the Vicar's Chosen. "What are your names?" she inquired.

"We apologize, but our names are not something you need to know."

One of the Chosen took a position in front of the door while the other then moved to the balcony.

Kaia followed him out. She rested her arms on the stone rail in front of her and gazed out toward the inner wall where the battle raged. "Do you two wish you were fighting the elves, instead of being stuck here, protecting a girl?"

Neither of the Vicar's Chosen replied.

Kaia shrugged, and allowed her attention to drift across the citadel gardens below, and settle on the statue of the Hero of Aclia.

A sly grin creased her lips. She turned back to the Vicar's Chosen and said, "If I told you I have a plan to draw out the last two Wraiths of Colubra, would you be interested?"

"Very," replied the Vicar's Chosen by the door.

33

Konar, Kassandra, and Vernon were sitting around the fire in the old school house talking, while Liam stood by the window looking toward the wall. Blaster lazed at his feet.

"Staring at the wall won't help the Paladins hold it," Kassandra quipped.

Liam replied, "I should be there."

Kassandra raised an eyebrow. "Do you have a death wish? We finally have some downtime and all you've done since we got here is stare out that damn window. At least try to take a nap or something."

Konar yawned and stretched. "A nap sounds amazing."

Kassandra pressed a question. "Liam, why do you like to fight so much?"

"What makes you think I like to fight?"

"Well for one, you're the best fighter I've ever seen. You don't get that good without a lot of practice. And two, you always seem, I don't know, exhilarated, each time we engage the elves."

Liam nodded and continued staring out the window. At last, he started talking, "For 13 years I was Domatin's slave. I wasn't a simple stone hauler or house cleaner. I didn't work the field. No, I was trained to be a gladiator. I spent every day for 13 years either training for the arena, or fighting in the arena. Defeat in the arena meant death. I didn't want to die, so I trained diligently. I killed orcs, dwarves, humans, and even a few elven criminals from time to time. Each time we engage the elves I hope to see him, so that I may end his life."

Vernon stared into the fire and nodded. "I can understand fighting for revenge."

Kassandra cast a curious glance at Vernon. "Who did what to you that you need to get revenge?"

"Not to me," Vernon's voice was tinged with sadness. "To my younger sister, Julia. Seven years ago our parents were here in Sternz on business. Gregory and I went to the neighboring village of Redoak for a hard night of drinking, and Julia went to a neighbor's house to borrow some flour to make muffins for breakfast. The next morning when Gregory and I arrived back home we found her crying in her bath holding a knife to her wrists. Before she could cut herself we grabbed the knife and I wrapped her in a towel. As I held her, she told us that on her way home the night before, a Crixarian officer jumped her and forced himself upon her. When we asked who it was she said she never saw his face due to the darkness. As soon as our parents returned home, I joined the army, hoping to one day find that man and bring him to justice. Gregory, being my loyal friend, joined me. For seven years we have found nothing useful. But I keep hoping that one day the One will give me a clue as to who it was."

Liam looked back into the room, a wry smile on his face. "So is that why you defended my actions against Zafrinia?"

Vernon continued staring into the fire. "Partially. But also because the five of us have become something of a family. And I will always protect my family."

Silence reigned for a long moment, broken by Kassandra's curiosity. "Your turn, Konar. Why are you here? Do you not have a family of your own back in the Eacru Wastes?"

Konar looked at Kassandra with a pained smile. "I used to. Not anymore."

"I am sorry. If this is something you didn't want to think about—"

"No, it is fine. Sometimes it eases the pain to talk to people you can trust. For 30 years I was married. My beautiful wife Tamar and I were childhood friends. We got married and had our baby girl Qunet. In orc culture, each tribe worships one of the five gods. We lived in a village that worshiped Zulga the orc god of fire and love. For years our village lived in peace. We weren't warriors. We prayed to find love and be blessed enough to raise a family.

One night we were attacked by Blood Mongers, orcs who are more like animals than civilized beings. They are worshipers of Raz Ma-dal, the orc god of war and death. Both my wife and my little girl were slaughtered. The next day after I burned their bodies and broke my vow of peace, I tracked the Blood Mongers to their village. I went there hoping to die, and take as many of them as I could with me. But I killed them all. Every last savage.

I couldn't return to my village. I lost my family, my community, my faith, and my purpose for living. I wondered the Wastes. I came to believe that perhaps since I failed my family, that I could redeem myself by saving another. That is how I ended up fighting for the Allisters against the elves."

Konar sniffed his nose and blinked his eyes trying not to weep. He choked a laugh and pointed a thick finger toward Kassandra. "Alright Miss Verbeck, your turn. Why are *you* here."

"Well, now, I feel a little awkward. Mine story is nowhere near as compelling as any of yours. I just simply thought it was the right thing to do."

"The right thing to do?" Vernon asked, a skeptical smirk on his face.

"Yes, the right thing to do," Kassandra defended herself. "Crixaria is the mother country of Vetin. I felt as if I should help where I could."

Konar asked, "Who taught you how to fight?"

"My father. He is a strict and overbearing father, but he means well. He paid handsomely to make sure I could defend myself." Kassandra looked at Vernon and quipped, "You should probably know that my father is extremely vindictive, so if you get me killed he will probably make sure you die in a most horrific manner."

Kassandra continued. "My mother died from Cormorden shortly after I was born. My sister Madison—one day she just disappeared. We assume she was attacked by wild animal while she was playing in the woods." Kassandra touched her necklace. "This was my mother's. It's the only one of its kind. I was always afraid to wear it, but Elsa reminded me it is important to carry their memory."

Vernon nodded. "Elsa was a remarkably wise woman. She could tell a lot about a person by just looking at them."

Blaster yawned and nudged Liam for a scratch. Kassandra said playfully, "What about you big boy? What's your story?"

Blaster whimpered and thumped his hind leg repeatedly as Liam found his itchy spot. "A few weeks after I escaped, I was wandering the southern mountains of Azara, close to the Dwarven and Elven battlefield," Liam said. "There was nothing romantic about those mountains. No jungles or cherry blossom trees, just rough, unforgiving terrain. I ducked into a cave, trying to escape the cold rain, when I heard two elves shouting from deeper inside. I slunk quietly closer, and saw a mage and a Praetorian fighting a bloodied bitch wolf protecting her last pup. The sire and four pups were already dead. The mage burned the mother on her leg and as the Praetorian moved in for the kill. That one little black wolf rushed in to protect his mother. He jumped up and bit the Praetorian on the hand. The Praetorian shook the pup off and slashed his front paw.

Something about the unfairness of it all overcame my better judgment. I rushed in and stabbed the mage in the back while the Praetorian was busy killing the mother wolf. When he turned around, I gutted him like a fish. Then the small, black wolf cub with a bloodied leg, crawled to his mother, trying to wake her up. I couldn't just leave him there. So I picked him up, nursed his wound, and carried him with me. We have been side by side ever since."

"How did you come up with the name Blaster?"

Liam laughed, "Blame the Praetorian. When the pup bit his hand, the Praetorian, he shouted "Blast her!" I thought it fit."

Kassandra, Vernon, and Konar all shared a cleansing laugh with Liam. Kassandra's eyes shone at her new-found knowledge of her companions. She fixed Liam with a compelling look and said, "Now that we're all a little more like family, why don't you tell us exactly what happened to you while you were enslaved for those 13 years?"

Liam tensed and left the window for the comfort of his bunk. Kassandra stood and followed him. "Come on Liam. You are among friends here. You can talk to us."

Liam closed his eyes. Kassandra started to press, when Vernon said, "Let it go Kassandra."

Kassandra huffed, but nodded and returned to her own bunk.

"We should all get some rest," Vernon added. "Who knows when we will have another opportunity. I will take the first watch. After a little while has passed and if nothing has happened I will wake you up and we can switch spots."

Konar nodded and was snoring within minutes. Vernon poured himself a cup of ale and took a long swig, hoping against hope that Harrison and his Paladins could hold the wall.

34

As the sun passed directly overhead, Kaia sat in the garden on a wooden bench studying an aged book of magic. Kaia looked from her book to the placid pond in front of her. Still holding the book in her right hand, she raised her left hand toward the water, focusing her attention on it. Her arm started to twitch, and her face turned red from exertion. Extreme heat blurred the atmosphere between her hand and the pond as water began to boil, then turn to steam. Kaia dropped the book and gasped for breath. The pond ceased boiling, but wisps of steam still rose from its surface.

As she regained her composure Kaia looked at the statue of the hero of Aclia. Its base was a large square slab of finely carved stone taller than Kaia. The figure of the hero was still finely detailed, despite being older than anyone can remember. The hero stood tall and straight with one fist engulfed in flames, raised in the air proudly.

Even though carved in stone Kaia could tell from the soft features of her face that the hero of Aclia was a very beautiful but very scarred woman. The hood, which covered the hero's hair and ears always made Kaia wonder what race the hero was, elf or human. Kaia read the inscription.

Here stands a monument to the savior of all races, leader of the free peoples, Hero of Aclia. Though her struggle began long ago before the rebellion when she was surrounded by a great white serpent.

Kaia smiled at the statue and then returned to her book.

At the end of the pathway behind Kaia, a pale hand, tattooed in a scale pattern, silently reached over the gate and flipped the latch, and opened the gate without making a sound. A peaceful autumn breeze gently blew through the trees. Two hooded figures crept into the pathway. One wore a sleeved garment. The other was sleeveless. The hooded figure with sleeves moved to the row of thuja trees on the left while the one without sleeves moved to the row on the right. They crouched down and crept closer to Kaia until only two trees separated them from her. The wraith on the right peered around the corner. Satisfied she was alone, the wraith slithered around the edge of tree, drew his cobra-hilted dagger, and edged silently toward Kaia.

The sleeveless wraith suddenly stopped with a faint jerk. The wraith with sleeves watched, confused, as his fellow wraith stood as still as the statue behind Kaia. When the wraith collapsed the crossbow bolt lodged in his neck became evident. The sleeved wraith panicked and flung out his right arm, releasing a black and white stripped cobra toward Kaia. An armored hand flicked out from the trees and snatched the cobra out of the air. The enraged serpent bit down hard, breaking its fangs against the steel wristguards. The Vicar's Chosen stepped around the tree, fixing the Wraith of Colubra with a hate filled glare before grasping the serpent's head with his free hand, and ripping it from its body.

The wraith stumbled backwards as he tried to escape. The first Chosen extended his crossbow in a smooth motion, aimed and released. The bolt dug into the back of the wraith's left calve sending him tumbling to the ground.

The wraith turned over and pulled a dagger from his boot, as the first Chosen forced his armored boot down hard on the wraith's neck. A second crossbow bolt pinned the assassin's hand to the ground. Even with his mouth sealed shut, the wraith moaned in agony. The second of the Vicar's Chosen joined his companion, watching the wraith struggling against the bolt in his hand. The

Chosen raised his foot and brought it down hard on the pinned hand, snapping the bolt and bones.

Kaia brought a length of rope and watched as Vicar's Chosen efficiently bound the hands and feet of the wraith.

Kaia said, "Thank you, both of you."

"No thanks are necessary. Wraiths of Colubra are our specialty."

"What will you do with him?"

In the same flat monotone, one of the Chosen said, "We will take him to the king. He will decide his fate."

Dylenn sat in the throne room, distracted from his duties for a moment by watching Alyssa chase Bethany with a tiny harmless mouse. Bethany screamed while Alyssa and Dylenn laughed. Alezzia flowed into the room followed by Benjamin, and announced, "Alyssa that is enough!"

Alyssa immediately stopped and released the mouse. As the terrified mouse scurried away, Alyssa lowered her head and pouted. "I'm sorry Mama."

"As you should be," Bethany whined.

Alezzia beckoned Alyssa to her, put her hand under Alyssa chin and raised it up so they were looking eye to eye. "Of all the trials I have had in my life, teaching you to be calm and elegant like a proper princess is proving to be the most difficult. You are too much like Kaia and your father."

Alezzia kissed Alyssa on the cheek and patted her on the back side. Bethany protested, "A kiss on the cheek? That's her punishment?"

Alezzia raised and eyebrow. "You were running for your life from a little girl and a harmless mouse? If anyone deserves punishment it is you. One day when you marry you will be queen and if a queen runs from little girls armed with mice, what will you do if the kingdom is at war?" Bethany stood still with her mouth open for a moment before storming out of the throne room.

"My love, the children were only making sport," Dylenn began, when the main door to the throne room burst open. The two Vicar's Chosen marched in, carrying the two Wraiths of Colubra, with Kaia following behind.

Alezzia turned to Benjamin and said, "Take Alyssa to her room. I would not have her see this."

Benjamin opened his hand to the young princess and said, "Come with me dear child. If you are a good girl I will tell you more about the famed Hero of Aclia." Alyssa was hesitant at first but then grabbed Benjamin's hand and they walked out of the throne room.

"What is this?" asked Dylenn.

The Vicar's Chosen dropped the wraiths, one dead and one still breathing, to the floor at the king's feet. "With Princess Kaia's help, we lured these assassins into the garden. We killed one and brought the other to you for judgment."

Alezzia, seething, took a step forward. "You used my daughter as bait?"

Kaia put herself between the Chosen and the Queen. "Mother, it was my idea."

"What if you had been killed?" Dylenn asked.

"But I wasn't," Kaia defended herself. "I'm not a child. I am a princess, the daughter of King Dylenn and Quenn Alezzia. I have a right to defend our kingdom."

Before either Alezzia or Dylenn could reply, one of the Chosen demanded in that irritating monotone, "King Dylenn, what is this man's fate?"

Dylenn pondered for a moment, then said, "Put him in the cell with the rest of the elven prisoners. We will use him when negotiating a prisoner exchange."

"As you command, King Dylenn." The Vicar's Chosen reached down to pick the wraith up when Alezzia firmly said, "No."

"No?" Dylenn said puzzled.

Alezzia glared at the wounded wraith, cool rage behind her eyes. "I doubt that the elves have even kept any of our prisoners alive, and if they have, I doubt they are in any condition to fight. This man just tried to kill our daughter. Perhaps this creature has valuable intelligence." Alezzia looked at the Vicar's Chosen and continued. "To the left of the throne room there is a hallway and at the end of that hallway is a staircase descending down to our dungeons. Take him there. Ask him any question you wish. Extract any information you can, any way you can. I don't care if you have to cut open his mouth."

Dylenn placed his hands on Alezzia's shoulders and whispered, "My love, we are not elves. I beg you, don't do this."

Alezzia's breath caught in her throat as she replied. "I have looked the other way when both you and Kaia went to the wall to fight. I stood by when you ordered citizens from lower Sternz to occupy our home. This... *Thing*... tried to kill our daughter. Do not speak to me of mercy." Dylenn backed away, as Alezzia addressed the Vicar's Chosen.

"Do it!"

As the Vicar's Chosen carried the wraith to the dungeon, the main doors once again opened and Izak and a bloodied Captain Harrison marched in.

The elves have withdrawn," Izak reported. "For now."

Dylenn then looked at Harrison and said, "Thank you Captain for aiding us this day. How bad are your casualties?"

"The are steep, Harrison confessed. "I lost 8,000 of my men. The mage's lightning was a formidable weapon. We killed perhaps 3,000 of the heathen."

"That leaves us with 17,000 battle ready troops to their 125,000. We can't survive those odds much longer."

Dylenn nodded. "Don't look so gloomy old friend. When the Vicar arrives with the rest of his army we will have enough to win. And the last of the wraiths have been dealt with."

Izak managed a faint smile. "That is good news, indeed."

Alyssa and Benjamin walked through the hallways hand in hand "Benjamin, can you tell me a story about the Hero of Aclia?"

Benjamin, nodded and in his mellifluous voice intoned, "It is said that long ago, when the Nezdra ruled Aclia, a hero was born destined to defeat the Nezdra. No one can remember what race she was but thanks to her many statues we know she was either an elf or a human. Both races claim her as their own. She was said to be the most beautiful woman of her time, but also one of the harshest. If she ever suspected that anyone was aiding the Nezdra that she would immediately kill them."

"Why would she do that?" Alyssa asked.

Benjamin continued to smile. "Well you see, the Nezdra had spies and assassins everywhere and the hero couldn't allow anything bad happen to her, or else everything would fall apart."

"How did she win?" asked Alyssa.

Benjamin continued, "She discovered that fire could kill the Nezdras. With an army of fire, not only could the hero kill Nezdras but she could also permanently kill the Nezdra's undead army."

"So now all the bad people are gone?" Alyssa asked.

Benjamin replied, "That child, all depends on who you ask. Most people assume that the hero of Aclia did rid the world of the Nezdra, others seem to think that some of them got away."

"Why?" Alyssa continued questioning.

Benjamin replied, "Well when you get older and can read better, you can read the books about the hero. In them if you pay attention you will see a name, Ucidere. He was the leader of the armies of the Nezdra. He was an extremely feared man. A powerful warrior, he killed anyone who got in his way, no mercy for anyone, not even little princesses were safe. However no mention of his name is spoken after the last battle. Many think that if he had been defeated there would be a song or tale about the person who killed him."

They reached the door to Alyssa's room and passed by the two guards at her door. Benjamin knelt down to Alyssa and asked, "What do you think?"

Alyssa smiled as she said, "I think we got them!" Then Alyssa gave Benjamin a big hug and said, "I'm sorry I was rude to you before. I thought you were why mama was mean."

Benjamin returned the hug and said, "I am used to people thinking the worst of me. Now go on in your room and play with your dolls." Alyssa ran in her room grabbing two of her dolls as Benjamin walked out and closed the door.

35

Afew flickering candles lit the corridor of the dark stone hallway as Benjamin, followed by the Queen's handmaiden Jaclyn, descended the staircase. Screams echoing from up the stairs startled Jaclyn. Benjamin heard the shuffle of her feet and turned around.

"I know you must be frightened, but I promise the wraith will not hurt you." He started to continue but stopped again. "I also promise that we will not be here very long. I only asked you to come because I may need your assistance."

Jaclyn's voice was shaky as she replied, "Assistance with what? If you don't mind me asking."

They heard another scream and Benjamin started forward again. "These Vicar's Chosen, these inquisitors, have been trying to get information from this wraith all afternoon and not once have they come to tell us of anything useful. Nothing at all, really. Sometimes you just need a different approach."

At the bottom of the stairs was a rotten wooden door that was barely attached to the hinges on the wall. Benjamin opened the door and entered into a damp, dimly lit room. The dungeon was the size of a large bedroom, but that is where the similarities ended. The walls were fixed with racks filled with instruments of torture. Ropes and chains hung from the ceiling. On the floor blood drained into a small opening. In the center of the room, the Vicar's Chosen stood on each side of the wraith, who was strapped to a wooden chair dressed only in a small black loincloth. The man bled from cuts and bruises too numerous to count.

The Vicar's Chosen looked up from his occupation. "Royal doctor? You have no business here."

Benjamin stared straight at the wraith. "The Queen ordered me to come and check on the situation, and if I see fit—to intervene." He looked at the wraith's mouth where the Chosen had cut it open. Blood flowed freely from the wounds.

Benjamin addressed the Chosen on the left and asked, "I assume the lack of a report means he hasn't said anything useful?"

"Not yet. We cut open his mouth, but the cur bit off his own tongue. We made him eat it."

The Vicar's Chosen on the right added, "We have employed all our skills without killing him. I fear he has nothing useful to tell us."

Of all the horrors in the room, it was the dispassionate, monotone voice that caused the greatest chill to run down Jaclyn's spine.

Benjamin lowered himself to gaze into the wraith's eyes and said, "Not quite everything."

Benjamin turned to a horrified Jaclyn and said, "Would you please go to the kitchen and grab a pot of honey. Then meet me and our guests near the wall where the Paladins are preparing to burn their dead."

Without a word Jaclyn turned and ran back up the stairs. Benjamin returned his icy gaze to the wraith, and with a hint of a smile whispered in his ear, "You are going to wish you had told the inquisitors something useful. You only thought you knew what pain is."

The Vicar's Chosen on the left asked, "What do you need us to do?"

Benjamin stood. "Bring him, and plenty of rope."

The Chosen pulled rope from the ceiling, then cut the wraith free from the chair. Benjamin led the way and the Chosen followed, dragging the wraith by his arms. They walked in silence through the citadel as the soldiers and civilians alike looked in horror. Once they were outside, Benjamin said, "For thousands of years, whether humans or elves, we have all been inventing new ways to inflict pain upon one another. I guarantee if you ask anyone, Cormorden is the most painful experience someone can suffer from, and I know that truth, personally. It taught me that nature can be far more cruel than anything concocted by a person."

Benjamin remained silent until they passed over the bridge and into Lower Sternz. Then he addressed the wraith. "There is no telling exactly how old you are. If you were a human, I would guess early forties, which means you are probably 500. I suspect you have seen and done some fairly disturbing things during those years. In my experience, it is not the living that inflict the most harm, but nature. Disease, wild animals, natural disasters, famine, drought, these cause far more death than even war."

They walked through the burnt streets of Lower Sternz until they arrived at an open area close to the wall. Burnt blackened wood and gray ash on the ground were all that remained of the once thriving east side of lower Sternz. Hundreds of dead Paladins laying side by side on pyres, ready to be cremated, filled the area. Two Paladins were pouring scented oil on the bodies in preparation. "You there Paladins, I crave your indulgence for a few moments." Both Paladins stopped, confused at the request, but they refrained laying their torches to the pyres.

Benjamin examined the rows of dead Paladins, observing the hundreds of flies and other carrion insects that darted through the area. He chose bodies of two Paladins who had been disemboweled, their intestines spilling out of their corpses. "Drag him through that. Make sure he gets covered in plenty of it."

The Vicar's Chosen nodded. If they were repulsed by the order, they didn't show it. They dragged the wraith through the rows of the deceased, coating his body in the congealed blood and offal of the dead. When they reached the disemboweled Paladins, the Vicar's Chosen slung the wraith down on their bodies, and forced his head into the wounds. The wraith was covered in gore and smeared in blood.

Jaclyn arrived carrying a light tan pot filled with honey. At the sight before her, she bent over wretched. Benjamin took the pot of honey from her and in his most gentle, sympathetic voice said, "Thank you Jaclyn, you may return to the citadel if you so choose."

Jaclyn threw up again, then turned and fled.

Benjamin shouted, "Enough! Bring him to me."

The Vicar's Chosen dragged the gore encrusted wraith to Benjamin, flies and biting gnats swirling around him. Benjamin indicated the rope and a couple of pieces of unburnt wood that used to be a home. "Tie each of his hands to a rope, then toss each rope over one of those pieces of wood. When you're finished, invite him to sit on the ground."

Without hesitation, the Vicar's Chosen moved to complete the task. Benjamin motioned to the Paladin with the torch, beckoning him to approach. Benjamin turned his attention back to the wraith. He set the pot of honey on the ground and shooed away the gathering insects. In his most reasonable voice, he said, "We don't have to do this. If you just give me some useful information, no more pain will come to you."

The wraith spat blood on the ground. Benjamin smiled. "I feared that would be your response." He reached out his hand and snatched the loincloth away from his groin, then he grabbed the pot of honey. He hovered over the wraith and poured the honey on top of his head, allowing it to oozed down his face, into his ears, over his neck and chest, down his back and onto his legs. When the last drop of honey was poured from the pot, he said, "Pull the ropes. Raise him up."

Benjamin turned to the Paladin with the torch, who now stood beside him, staring on in horror. "I want you to hold your torch close to his skin and harden the honey. Do not stop until every ounce of honey has latched onto his skin."

The Paladin stood motionless as he looked at the wraith dangling

249

in front of him. "Do it!" Benjamin demanded. The Paladin swallowed hard, and took one small step forward, followed by another, and another. With a shaking hand, he waved the torch over the wraith's body, causing the honey to harden and burn. The wraith screamed in agony, but the Paladin did not stop until every last part of his body was covered in hardened honey.

Benjamin said, "Thank you. Your services are no longer required. You may return to your duties. May your comrades find rest in the embrace of the One."

The Paladin lowered his head as he walked away. Benjamin addressed the wraith. "You may think the worst is over. You couldn't be farther from the true. In my years of experience I have learned that there are two ways you can attract flies; one is sugar, and the other is rotting flesh. And here we have both! All we have to do is wait—wait for the hundreds of flies to smell that warm, sweet honey and the stench of your burned flesh. You, my friend, are about to be eaten alive, piece by tiny piece."

A few flies landed on the wraith, followed by dozens, then hundreds. The wraith screamed and screamed until he was incapable of screaming. Benjamin watched, and waited. At last he walked back in front of the wraith. There was no hint of compassion in his voice. He said, "You have nothing left to fight for. You are going to die. You have no hope of rescue. Your five companions are already dead. You are alone. But you can choose to die with some dignity, rather than being eaten alive by flies. If you are praying for a rescue don't bother. You are the last of your kind in this city, the first five are already dead and the elves outside of the city are not attacking. You are alone and no one is coming to your aid."

The wraith finally nodded. The Vicar's Chosen lowered the wraith to the ground, and brushed away the flies away. With a trembling hand, the wraith wrote in the dirt;

8 not 6

Realization widened Benjamin eyes. He looked back up the hill toward the citadel, then turned back to the Vicar's Chosen who appeared oblivious to the importance of the message. "Don't just stand there. Go warn them! There are still two more Wraiths of Colubra in the city!"

A cold chill gripped Benjamin's spine and he contemplated the truth. Without the Vicar's Chosen or Blaster in the Citadel, there was no one to guard Kaia. No one even believed there was a reason to guard the princess.

Benjamin looked down at the wraith and was stunned to see him laughing. He continued laughing until the remaining Chosen separated his head from his body with his sword.

36

Kaia, Bethany, and Alyssa were all in their white night gowns sitting on a soft fur bench in the library in front of a stone fireplace with a warm glowing fire. Tall bookshelves filled with dusty old books that no one ever read lined the wall. Three open arched windows allowed a sweet breeze to blow through the room, and a simple wooden door was the only way in or out.

Bethany and Kaia read while Alyssa played with a carved wooden bear, but she quickly grew bored. Alyssa looked side to side at her sisters hoping that one of them might play with her. Bethany soon noticed Alyssa's constant fidgeting and lowered her book. "What do you want Alyssa?"

"If I go get more dolls will you play with me?"

"No."

Alyssa frowned. "But why not?"

Bethany lowered her book again, "Because for the first time in four days we are not under constant guard and I would like to read my book."

Kaia shot Bethany a chiding look and said, "Bethany, play with her. You rarely do anymore."

"You play with her if you're so concerned," Bethany shot back.

"I play with her almost every day. When was the last time you actually played with her?"

Bethany looked down at Alyssa and then back to Kaia and said,

"That's because I have more important things to do. I will be queen one day. I am quite busy preparing myself for that important task. I don't have time for playing with dolls or reading useless books."

"Useless? How exactly are my books useless?" Kaia demanded. "They teach me how to control my powers and how to cast better spells to keep us safe. What could your books possibly teach you?"

Bethany hugged her book to her chest and answered, "How to love."

Kaia shook her head in disbelief, "What?"

"This book is amazing. The main character is a lowly farmer's daughter who is torn between her love for her fiancé and childhood friend, or her love for a conquering dashing knight."

"So the heroine of your story is ungrateful?"

"Ungrateful? She is most definitely not ungrateful?"

Kaia countered, "Yes she is. She is engaged. She should remain loyal to the childhood friend who probably loves her more than life itself. She should be grateful to have someone who loves her for herself, not because she's royal or wealthy. Instead she's smitten by some fancy knight who just rode into town?"

Bethany sniffed. "You're just jealous because you have to read old books on magic."

Kaia replied, "A few days ago you said that you couldn't get interested in prophecy because there was no tension. Well, I don't get interested in books when the main character can't decide who she wants to sleep with for the night."

Bethany grunted, "You read your book, and I'll read mine."

"Kaia, can you show me some magic tricks?" Alyssa asked.

Before Kaia could reply, Bethany slammed her book shut and said, "Mother is right Alyssa, you need to grow up. Magic tricks are for babies and you are a princess."

Alyssa's lower lip began to quiver as she tried to hold back tears but Kaia pulled her close and whispered, "Don't worry about her Alyssa. She is just jealous that you act like a bigger girl than she does. For all her talk about growing up, she has yet to find a husband."

Bethany sniffed again. "It's not my fault no one has been worthy of me yet."

Kaia said, "Alright. How about I toss some fire for you?"

Alyssa clapped her tiny hands in excitement. Kaia smiled and made a fist with her right hand. She slowly raised it in front of Alyssa. With her knuckles down Kaia slowly opened her hand to reveal a small, orange flame dancing in her palm. Alyssa looked intensely at the flame. Kaia angled her palms so that they were facing each other, then tossed the flame back and forth from one hand to the other.

Kaia extinguished the flame, tousled Alyssa's hair. Alyssa lunged forward and wrapped arms around Kaia's neck, then screamed in pain. Startled Kaia and Bethany cried out, "Alyssa, what's wrong?"

Kaia stared in horror at a cobra on the floor. Two small trickles of blood dripped from Alyssa's arm, and a pair of silhouetted figures stood inside the open window to the library, the bodies of four Crixarian soldiers on the floor outside.

Amidst the chaos of Alyssa's screams and Bethany shrieks, Kaia maintained her composure. She burned the cobra to a crisp while it was still coiled on the floor, then quickly prepared another fireball for the two wraiths that rushed her sisters. She managed to contain the fire when Vernon plunged between the girls and the assassins. Liam and Blaster were on his heels and positioned themselves behind the wraiths, blocking there escape through the windows.

A snap followed by a whisking sound ended with an arrow protruding from one wraith's head, followed by Kassandra striding into the room. The last wraith glance toward the library door, but the massive form of Konar filled it.

Liam said, "I have my swords with me this time," as he walked toward the nervous wraith.

The wraith thrust his dagger at Liam, but Liam stepped under the blow, and his sword through the bottom of the wraith's jaw and out the top of his head.

Dylenn rushed into the room relieved to see the two corpses

of the wraiths. His relief lasted only a moment as he saw the fang marks on Alyssa's arm. He gathered his youngest daughter into his arms and struggled to contain the tears that welled in his eyes.

"It's okay, Papa. It doesn't hurt much." Alyssa said, trying to comfort her father.

Alezzia rushed into the room, taken back at what she saw. "What is wrong? Why is everyone crying? From what I can tell the wraiths are dead."

Alyssa, still in her father's embrace, turned her head and said, "Mama I got bit and no one is saying anything to me. I am scared mama." Alezzia stumbled backward until she was stopped by the wall, a blank look on her face.

Bethany was curled up in a ball rocking back and forth on the bench, mumbling, "It's all my fault. I should have been playing dolls with her."

Alezzia was the first to regain some composure. She shouted out the door, "If anyone can hear me, find Benjamin!"

Liam and Vernon stood in silence at the back of the bench Blaster sat beside Liam, and Kassandra snuffled against Konar.. Alezzia turned to them and asked, "How did you know to come here?"

Vernon replied, "We were on our way to the tavern for some food when Benjamin came running toward us. He told us he had discovered there were still two assassins in Sternz, and that the princess could be in danger. We came as fast as we could. Not fast enough, I fear."

Kaia's head was in her hands as she wept bitter tears. "The snake was for me. If Alyssa hadn't hugged me she would be fine."

Benjamin rushed into the room and immediately went to Alyssa. "I need to see your arm, princess."

Alyssa extended her arm toward him, and Benjamin studied the bite mark closely. After a long moment, a relieved smile creased his face. Benjamin said, "Alyssa is going to be fine."

Everyone in the room looked in stunned disbelief. Benjamin

continued, "Cobras are intelligent creatures. Kaia was its target and the cobra likely knew it. The cobra reserved its venom for Kaia. It delivered what is called a dry bite. See, there is no swelling around the bites, no necrosis. As long as the wounds don't get infected she will be perfectly fine."

The Allister family's tears of pain now turned to tears of joy as they all fell to ground around Alyssa hugging each other.

Slow footsteps shuffled through the doorway as General Izak paced into the room. Dylenn handed Alyssa to her mother and addressed his general.

"What news, Izak?"

Izak, with a stunned gaze, said, "Ethan has returned, with news of the Vicar."

Dylenn repeated, "News *of?* Not returned *with?*"

37

King Dylenn was sitting on his throne with Alezzia beside him. Izak, Kassandra, and Konar were on the left side of the stairs while Liam, Vernon, and Blaster were on the right. Ethan stood with his back to them. Even so they could tell that the news isn't good.

Kassandra whispered to Konar, "This doesn't look promising. Liam looks even more down than normal."

Dylenn nodded and then looked at Ethan, "Thank you for your hard work. Go get some food and water."

Ethan nodded and turned to leave. He passed Captain Harrison at a dead run. Harrison walked to King Dylenn and bowed. "Pardon, your majesty, but we have received word that your scout has returned. We are eager for word of the Vicar.".

Harrison soon picked up on the sober mood in the room. He politely asked again, "King Dylenn, is the Vicar here? If so, may I know where?"

Dylenn remained silent. Izak took a slow deep breath before replying, "The Vicar will not be joining us."

Konar and Kassandra spun around to General Izak as Konar questioned, "Will not be joining us...now? Or will not be joining us...at all?"

Izak took another long deep breath, then continued, "After Ethan set out, he came upon the boot prints of a large elven force, he estimated 30,000 perhaps more. He continued to ride west along the main road looking for the Vicar. What he found was the aftermath of a great battle; thousands dead, both elf and Paladin. Ethan circled around the battlefield looking for any trace of survivors. He found tracks heading west, away from us. The Vicar and his army were ambushed and either were completely obliterated, or significantly bloodied. Either way, it appears they will not be coming to our aid."

Harrison lowered his head. "I will inform my men. They need to know what lies ahead."

Izak turned to Dylenn and said, "I will do that same. We will fight the elves as long as we can tomorrow. I promise they will not reach the Citadel unscathed." Izak turned to Vernon. "At dawn tomorrow I will hold an officer's meeting here in the throne room. Join us if you wish." Izak saluted his king, walked down the stairs and out the door like a man facing his doom.

With Alezzia and Dylenn sitting in silence, Vernon began to lead the rest of the Unbroken toward the doors but Dylenn stopped them. "I don't want any of you to think that you haven't done enough. Without you this city would have fallen days ago. You have all fought valiantly. Who knows? Perhaps tomorrow you will once again be Sternz's saviors. But if not, I would say our goodbyes tonight. I fear that we may not get another chance." The Unbroken bowed as one to the king and queen, then silently walked out of throne room.

No one spoke, although they could hear sobbing from the buildings where citizens were spending their last night with their loved ones.

As the Unbroken approached the bridge, Konar slowed down to walk beside Liam. The orc leaned over and whispered, "You know tonight may be our last night. If I were you, I would tell Kassandra how you feel. You never know, she might feel the same."

Liam's gaze shifted from his feet to Kassandra several steps ahead, then returned to the ground in front of him. "There is no use. I'm not her type."

Konar patted Liam on the back and said, "You will never know if you don't talk to her. I tell you what, I will start a conversation and then you say something."

"Like what?" Liam asked.

"Whatever feels right."

Konar then yawned loudly to draw attention before saying, "I don't know about any of you, but I for could use a drink, or five."

Vernon snorted, but Kassandra surprisingly remained quiet. Vernon nudged her in the ribs and said, "Come on Kassandra, out of all of us you should be the one cracking some jokes with Konar."

"I'm not in the mood," Kassandra muttered.

As they reached the old school house, Liam walked up to Kassandra and said, "The walls haven't fallen yet, there is always hope."

Kassandra shouted back at him, "Of all people to talk about hope it's you? The disconnected loner who won't even try to open up no matter what we've all been through together?"

Konar stepped forward and said, "Kassandra calm down."

Kassandra ignored him. "I bet you wanted this didn't you? Maybe now you will get your big chance to kill Domatin, but some of us want more out of life than just to kill." Kassandra then turned to Vernon and said, "I would say I am going to the Bear Claw but it's burnt to the ground so I don't know where I am going. I will be back later." Kassandra stomped away along the river where the few buildings of lower Sternz survived.

Stunned, Konar and Vernon stood motionless as they watched Kassandra walk in one direction while Liam and Blaster walked in the other toward the old schoolhouse.

"Didn't see that coming," Vernon said, and Konar nodded.

Once inside the dark room, Liam laid down on his bunk facing the wall. Blaster jumped up at the foot of the bed and curled up at his feet.

Konar and Vernon walked into the schoolhouse. Vernon tried to encourage Liam. "We are all under a lot of stress right now, with not knowing what tomorrow may hold. I'm sure she didn't mean it."

Liam didn't respond. He just closed his eyes and tried to fall asleep. Konar and Vernon did the same but they all remained in their armor, ready to fight at a moment's notice.

Dylenn and Alezzia walked through the halls of the citadel holding hands. They reached the door to Alyssa's room to hear her, Kaia and Bethany inside. Alezzia reached to push open the door with her free hand but Dylenn gently grabbed it, pulled Alezzia toward him and held her close. Alezzia looked up at Dylenn as he placed a soft kiss on his lips.

Dylenn said, "When I first saw you many years ago I knew that I would marry you. Never once have I ever stopped loving you. You are not just my queen but you are my best friend. If tonight is truly our last night, know that I don't have a single regret. Tomorrow when the elves attack, if they get through, I want you to take our daughters and run. Go to the west gate and run as fast as you can to Tarium."

Alezzia leaned back and asked, "What about you?"

Dylenn smiled as he heard his daughters laugh. "If worse comes to worse I will remain here to rally our troops. They will need all the courage they can get."

Alezzia smiled and raised up to kiss Dylenn. Then she reached for the door and said, "Come, let us spend the night with our daughters, as a family."

As they opened the door they saw Kaia and Bethany playing dolls with Alyssa. Dylenn and Alezzia smiled at the sight of their daughters playing together.

Alyssa saw her parents and with a tired smile said, "Mama, Papa, can I play in the gardens tomorrow?"

Dylenn looked at Alezzia who replied, "Of course you can sweetie. I will take you first thing in the morning." Alyssa yawned and returned to playing with her dolls.

Kaia looked at Dylenn and asked, "What did that scout have to say about the Vicar?"

Dylenn just shook his head. Kaia and Bethany looked at each other with depressed expressions.

Alyssa yawned deeply once more. Alezzia knelt beside her and examined Alyssa's wrapped up arm. "Look mama, Mister Benjamin fixed me. He said to get plenty of rest and I will be better really soon."

Alezzia smiled at Alyssa and said, "Well that is good news, but from the looks of things you seem pretty tired."

Alyssa yawned once more as she replied, "No I'm not. I want to play."

Alezzia put her hands under Alyssa's shoulders and picked her up, holding her close to her body. Alyssa held onto her mother and rested her head on Alezzia's shoulder. "Alright sweetie it's time for bed. But guess what?"

"What?" replied Alyssa.

"You and your sisters are going to spend the night with your father and I."

Alyssa didn't reply and Dylenn looked over at her and quietly said to Alezzia, "She is fast asleep. Go ahead and I will bring Kaia and Bethany in a few moments." Alezzia exited the room with Alyssa sleeping on her shoulder.

Kaia and Bethany stood up and wrapped their arms around their father. Kaia asked, "What are we going to do?"

Dylenn looked down at his daughters and said, "I'm going to be honest with you. If the elves launch a full assault on the wall tomorrow we won't be able to stop them. We just don't have enough soldiers anymore."

Kaia replied, "What about Vernon and the Unbroken?"

"What about them?" said Bethany.

Kaia quickly replied, "I don't know, maybe they could do something again. They found me and got me back to the wall. They stopped the battering ram. And...and... Surely they can do something."

Bethany rudely replied, "They are just four people and a wolf, they can't take on the elven army singlehandedly. It would be like a mouse trying to bite off the head of a snake; it just wouldn't work."

Dylenn's forehead wrinkled. "Wait, say that last part again."

"It would be like a mouse trying to bite off the head of a snake," Bethany repeated.

Dylenn kissed his daughters on the head then rushed out the door.

Kaia called after him, "Father what is it?"

Dylenn turned around with a smile on his face and replied, "Go to your mother and tell her I will join her soon. Right now I need to find Izak."

Day Five

38

Leontina hovered over the command table as the morning sunshine peeked through the open tent flap. Alone in the tent, she studied the map as well as the reports of yesterday's skirmish with the Paladins. After several moments of peace and quiet, an elven soldier walked into the tent with a nervous look on her face.

Leontina looked up from the table, "What is it soldier?"

"Prince Domatin is walking this way Imperator. I thought you should know."

Leontina took a deep breath and motioned for the soldier to leave. She grabbed the hilt of her sword and waited. Domatin entered the tent alone. To Leontina's surprise, he seemed to be in quite the good mood.

"It is a wonderful morning wouldn't you agree Leontina?"

Leontina kept her eyes on Domatin as she replied, "It is yes."

Domatin studied Leontina with a gaze of cockiness as he looked from her sword to her eyes. "Oh relax Leontina. Today is a day of celebration. No need to worry yourself sick about me. Not today anyway."

Leontina stood firm with the hilt of her sword in her hand and remained silent. Domatin laughed. "Well perhaps some good news will help you relax."

"And what might that be?" she asked.

Domatin paced around the room as he replied, "I am confident that the digging will be ready within the hour."

"This early? I was expecting it to be ready this afternoon at the earliest," said a surprised Leontina.

A Praetorian walked into the tent as Domatin continued, "These human prisoners worked a lot faster than I anticipated. And the sooner the city falls the sooner we can all go home."

The Praetorian walked up to Domatin and whispered something into his ear; something that surpised him. Domatin nodded and then smiled at an uneasy Leontina who asked, "What is it?"

"Nothing that concerns you my dear. Now if you will excuse me I must go attend to the matter. I leave the assault in your hands. I trust you will not fail—this time."

As Domatin exited the tent along with his Praetorian, Leontina stood baffled. She stepped out of the tent as an officer approached. The elf stood at attention and asked, "What are your orders Imperator?"

Leontina looked toward the wall and replied, "We are taking the wall today. Under no circumstances are any of our soldiers to retreat this day. I don't care if it takes an hour or seven hours, we will fight our way to the Citadel and end the life of the abomination that is the human princess."

Leontina began to walk toward the edge of the encampment facing the wall. The officer followed her, and asked, "How are we going to get past their walls, Imperator? All of our assaults have failed thus far."

Leontina confidently replied, "Prince Domatin has taken care of that problem. The solution will be ready within the hour and I want the army assembled out of sight from the humans as quickly as possible."

"How many of our troops do you want to attack the walls today?" asked the soldier.

Leontina reached the edge of the camp and replied, "All of them."

39

Kassandra yawned as she sat up in her bunk and stretched. She heard the crackling of a fire and looked to see Liam, Konar, and Blaster sitting quietly by the fire. Kassandra reached behind her head to tie her hair back into a ponytail and asked, "Where is Vernon?"

Konar replied, "There was an officers' meeting this morning. It started over an hour ago, so he should be back soon."

Kassandra finished her ponytail and looked over at Liam. She lowered her head remembering with regret what she said last night. She pasted a smile on her face and started to walk over to him but before she could say anything, Vernon stepped into the room.

"Grab your weapons! We are going to the wall. King Dylenn has a plan to defeat the elves. Hurry. I will explain on the way."

Kassandra saw Konar grab his hammer and asked, "Are you feeling well enough today to use that?"

Konar smiled at her and replied, "Well enough."

"What's the plan?" Konar asked.

Vernon trotted toward the wall as he replied, "Today we are going to attack the elves. All of our remaining forces will run out of the eastern gate and rush the elves, catching them off guard. King Dylenn himself is leading the charge."

Kassandra looked toward Liam who was trotting beside her. She stared to say something, anything, to him, but Liam's attention was focused on Vernon.

Liam asked, "What's our part in all of this. Does Izak want us to protect the King?"

"No, that task will be left to the Vicar's Chosen. Our task is to find and kill Imperator Leontina and Prince Domatin. With both of them dead we hope that the elves will lose discipline and scatter."

"Finally," Liam breathed.

They continued toward the eastern inner wall with Vernon and Konar in front followed by Liam, Blaster, and Kassandra. Kassandra got an idea. She cleared her throat and started to sing, "*Only death can keep me from thee, Though the enemy may be near, My love for you shall set me free, I will be waiting for you, Now and Forever, We will be together, Now and Forever.*"

Liam looked over at her with a disgruntled look across his face and said, "Don't start that again."

Kassandra laughed and replied, "Oh come on. You know it's a wonderful song."

"If you say so," Liam replied.

Kassandra took a deep breath and said, "Liam, I am sorry for what I said last night. It was uncalled for, I was just upset about the news with the Vicar."

Liam looked her in her eyes. "If you promise not to sing that song again, we will say that all is forgiven."

"We will see," replied Kassandra with a smile.

They arrived at the back of army. The thousands of remaining human soldiers gathered around the gatehouse waiting for the order to attack.

Vernon turned to his squad and said, "Make your way to the gate. I will join you in a moment."

Kassandra and Konar nodded and began to squeeze their way through the crowd of soldiers to the gate. Liam held back for a second and pulled out his half of the Eacru root from his boot. Vernon smiled and reached into one of the pouches in his belt and pulled his out as well.

Liam saw that Vernon's half was still intact and then put his half back and said, "Just making sure you weren't going to finish it off or anything."

Vernon smiled as he replied, "No, I just need to collect myself." Liam nodded and he and Blaster begin to walk toward the gate.

As more and more soldiers passed by, Vernon took several long deep breaths and he looked up at the clear blue morning sky. He didn't notice that a figure dressed in dark purple robes was standing beside him.

"Do you think my father's plan will work?" Kaia asked.

Vernon jumped slightly, startled by Kaia's appearance, but he smiled when he saw her. The smile didn't leave Vernon's face as he replied, "Yes I do. If we can catch the elves off guard, we have a chance. Now, if you don't mind me asking Princess, why are you not in the Citadel?"

"The elves are here for me. The Vicar isn't going to save us. If I'm going to die, I figured I might as well use my gifts to help take as many of them with me as I can."

Vernon looked around and said, "As long you are close to me, I promise no elf will touch you." Kaia smiled and said, "Please stay safe today Vernon."

Vernon replied, "You as well Prin—, Kaia."

They held each other's gaze for several seconds before Vernon was shocked from his reverie by a sharp thump on the back. Gregory walked in front of them, not recognizing the Princess under the hood.

Gregory laughed and made kissing noises directed toward Vernon. The laughter caught in his throat and Gregory eyes bulged when he finally saw the girl's face. A huge grin spread across his face and he poked Vernon in the chest. "Vernon you sly dog."

Gregory turned to Kaia and winked. "You best take good care of my boy here."

Even under her hood Vernon could see that Kaia was blushing. Vernon said, "Alright Gregory you've had your fun. Let's go to the gate and await the order to attack."

The three of them made their way toward the gate. Gregory said, "Vernon, remember to watch what I do and repeat it. The elves will surely run in terror from me."

Vernon laughed and replied, "The only reason the elves would ever run away from you is if you forgot to take a bath."

Kaia laughed at Vernon's joke. Gregory turned to Vernon and said, "Seriously Vernon, take care of yourself today."

"You do the same," replied Vernon. "I have your back no matter what happens."

Gregory extended his hand to shake Vernon's. Vernon reached for it, then realized too late what was going on as Gregory slapped Vernon across the face. Vernon laughed and shook it off. They kept walking until they reached the gate and joined up with Liam, Konar, Kassandra, and Blaster. Vernon also spotted Zafrinia, Captain Harrison, and Makay.

General Izak and King Dylenn, followed by the two Vicar's Chosen, descended the stairs on the right side of the gatehouse. Dylenn bellowed out, "My friends, it is good to see you here. As many of you know the Vicar will not be joining us after all. His forces were set upon by the elves. I won't lie to you, our situation is dire, but there is hope. No longer will we stand and wait for the elves to come to us. Today we attack!

'When the elves begin to form their ranks, we will storm out of the gate and break through their lines. The plan is simple, we will kill as many of those bastards as we can while The Unbroken fight their way to the elven command and kill their leaders. Without leadership the elves will break and scatter.

'We have all lost people close to us these past few days, but we have also started new friendships—friendships that will last a lifetime. Fight for your friends today! To Victory or Death!"

The Crixarian officers and soldiers cried out, "Victory or Death!"

Dylenn then looked around again and shouted, "Death to Pagans!"

All the Tarium volunteers as well as the Paladins yelled out, "Death to Pagans!"

Dylenn took a deep breath and then raised his fist into the air and yelled out, "Glory to the defenders of Sternz!"

Everyone inside the city raised their fists in the air and let out a glorious shout.

The cries of the eager defenders were soon drowned out by an ever-growing rumble. The defenders fell silent as the rumbling grew louder and the ground beneath them started to shake violently. A section of the wall to the left of the gatehouse crumbled in a cloud of dust as it shattered and fell to the ground.

40

As the dust settled, Dylenn rose to his feet and looked around in shock. Chunks of the wall were scattered everywhere. All the troops that were under the section of the collapse wall were crushed to death or pinned under heavy stones and crying out in pain. Dylenn ran toward the debris and started helping lift rocks off of pinned troops. Soon dozens of human soldiers started to do the same as well. Izak rushed up to Dylenn and Dylenn asked, "How did this happen? I did not see a meteor and it hasn't been long enough for their trebuchets to do enough damage to bring them down."

Captain Harrison joined them and said, "They must have dug under the wall and undermined its structural integrity. Your walls collapsed under their own weight."

The army started to panic. A murmur passed the ranks; "We're all going to die," and "It's over now, the elves have won."

Izak and Harrison moved through the ranks trying to regain control of the rapidly deteriorating situation.

Gregory ran to the top of the rubble pile between the gatehouse and first guard tower. He peered out toward the ridge and saw the elves running toward the wall. He turned and shouted, "Now is as good a time as any! Follow me to victory!"

Gregory let out a yell and ran out toward the elves followed by an ever-growing number of humans from all countries.

As the squad and even Dylenn and Izak made their way toward

the gap, a young boy ran toward King Dylenn yelling at the top of his lungs, "Wait!"

Something about the boy compelled Dylenn to stop. "What is it child?"

"There are two more gaps in the wall, sir. My Mama told me to run as fast as I can to tell you."

"Where? And did you see anything else?"

The young boy looked at everyone and then said, "One was to the left and the other to the right. I also saw that a bigger dust cloud was heading toward the right one sir."

Dylenn took a long breath and told the boy, "Thank you for your courage today. Now go back to your mother and don't come outside until your mother says it's safe."

General Izak said, "Leontina always did favor a heavy attack on the right flank. If we rejoin Gregory's charge we might reach Leontina before the other two groups can figure out was has happened."

Captain Harrison cautioned, "If we fail to kill Leontina and Domatin before the other groups discover what is happening, we will be surrounded and obliterated."

Izak looked to Dylenn, "My King, we need a decision."

Dylenn saw Kaia standing with the Unbroken and said, "We need to separate and try to hold each breach as long as we can. If we can create a funnel, their numbers will work against them. Have the majority of the army follow me to the right breach while a smaller amount stays here and another to the breach on the left."

Izak and Harrison began to relay the orders to everyone around them when Vernon, Kaia and the rest of the Unbroken walked up to Dylenn. Vernon asked, "My King, what are our instructions?"

"I know you may not want to but I need for you all to split up. If all of you are at one spot then that spot may hold but the other two will falter. Vernon, you and Konar are with me and Izak to the breach on the right. Kassandra, I need you to stay here with the shield bearers and cover them the best you can as they hold the elves back. Liam, you and Blaster go with Captain Harrison and Zafrinia to the breach on the left. That breach will have the least amount of soldiers and I need the two best fighters we have there to make up the numbers."

"Where would you like me to go Father?" Asked Kaia.

Dylenn looked at his daughter and said, "Kaia, you have proven time and time again these past few days that you are not just some helpless princess. I trust you to make whatever decision you deem best."

Kaia smiled at her father and said, "Then I will go with you."

Dylenn nodded, then turned to the army assembled behind him and shouted, "The world will know, Sternz did not fall without a fight! Show the elves that it is not just our walls that protected us, but the men and women who fight beside us!" With renewed courage the human defenders yelled one final time before they separated.

King Dylenn led the way to the breach on the right followed by Izak, Vernon, Kaia, and Konar. Half of the remaining human forces followed Dylenn as they ran toward the breach. They neared the breach just as the elves started to run into the city.

"Vernon, I want you and Konar to lead the fight to the top of the rubble and try to hold the elves at the breach," Dylenn ordered. "If we can keep the elves outside of the city, we can hold them." Vernon and Konar nodded in agreement.

When they approached the breach, Izak yelled out, "Weapons ready everyone!" Konar gripped his hammer and Vernon drew his sword. Kaia rubbed her hands and they ignited into flame. The elves turned to face them but the momentum carried by the humans allowed them to slam into the elves. Dylenn and Izak led the push through the Elven numbers as Konar and Vernon started to fight toward the breach. Elves around Vernon and Konar burst into flames as Kaia covered them with fire.

Vernon cut down elf after elf, and Konar crushed them with his hammer. Vernon shouted above the chaos, "Konar! Push them back!"

Konar readied his hammer sideways in front of him and blocked three downward strikes from elves at once. Then with a mighty roar, Konar started to push them back up the rubble. As the elves started to stumble and fall, Vernon and the soldiers following him killed them with sword, spear or even bare hands. Konar continued pushing elves out of his way until he reached the top of the rubble, then he shoved the elves in front of him down into their fellow elves, creating a tumbling avalanche of falling elves.

With a colossal swing Konar knocked four elves to the side as Vernon and the rest of the humans also reached the top. The ensuing battle became one of shoulder to shoulder, and hand to hand, the cramped space left little room to maneuver. Even the dead remained standing from the pressure of all those around them. Kaia stood at the rear of the human forces, ready to shoot a fireball at anyone who broke through.

Kassandra stood atop of the rubble watching as the elves in front of her finished off the soldiers that followed Gregory. In the thick of the fighting Kassandra saw Gregory get knocked unconscious. By now he was dead or a prisoner of war. The elves quickly either killed or rounded up the surrendering humans.

The elven force at the center breach quickly reformed and began to run toward the wall. Kassandra turned and called out, "Shield bearers form up!"

The shield bearers carried their large shields and formed a half circle around the edge of the rubble inside the city using the large chucks of the wall as part of their shield wall. Behind three rows of shield bearers was a horde of infantry ready to engage the elves. Kassandra and the rest of the human archers readied their bows to pick off the elves who were held back by the shield bearers.

The sound of the elven footsteps running toward the breach grew as each second the humans at the center grew more anxious.

As soon as the elven soldiers crested the ridge of the rubble, the human archers began releasing volley after volley of arrows into their midst. Kassandra released her shots quicker than anyone else as her arrows struck home in the chests, heads, and necks of the elven soldiers. The shield bearers braced themselves against the onslaught as the elves impacted the shield wall. The shattering of wood and the shuffling of footsteps were heard as the elves tried to break through the human shields. Arrows hissed all around them. The bodies of the elves began to pile up nearly as high as the rubble.

Kassandra spotted a Praetorian who was communicating with the elven encampment with a pair of banners. Kassandra released an arrow at him, striking the Praetorian in the shoulder. Seemingly unfazed, Praetorian continued his signals. Kassandra released a second arrow, catching him in the back, again producing little noticeable effect. A third arrow pierced the Praetorians throat, and he at last dropped the banners.

Inexplicably, the elves stopped their attack and began hunkering down wherever they could find cover. An eerie silence settled over the battlefield, leaving Kassandra to wonder what was going on. Suddenly Kassandra caught a glimpse of objects in the sky. Her eyes widen as she shouted in warning, "Watch out!"

The warning came too late. Every trebuchet the elves had built launched their payloads toward the center gap. Large rocks slammed into the ground outside of the wall, some impacted the wall itself, and some even fell into the breach. The enormous stones crushed anything in their path, whether human or elf. When the dust settled, Kassandra could see the remnants of the shield bearers. Their limbs shattered, grown men and women weeping in fear, even a man crawling on his stomach while holding his bloody and disconnected leg in his right hand.

As the last of the boulders passed overhead, the elves rushed back over the breach and into the city. With most of the shield bearers dead, wounded, or knocked unconscious, the elves passed through uncontested. Kassandra put her bow down on the ground and drew her daggers. As the human infantry in front of her engaged the elves, she weaved her way toward the conflict and began to fight the elves up close and personal.

Liam paced impatiently at the top of the breach at the left. He look out toward the area between the inner and outer wall, waiting for any sign of the elves.

Harrison walked to the bottom of the rubble and said, "Liam, they will get here when they get here. I would rather have you fight and die beside me than be taken out by a stray arrow."

Liam stopped pacing and took one final gaze out toward the grassland before him. As he walked back down the rubble, Zafrinia had to comment, "A stray arrow to the neck is about as long as he will survive anyway without his friends to watch his back."

Blaster growled at Zafrinia, his ears pointed back and his body low. Harrison turned to Zafrinia and demanded, "That is enough Zafrinia!"

Zafrinia smirked at Liam as he knelt down to pet Blaster. Makay called out, "She is just jealous of you, you beautiful bastard."

Liam laughed. "Why do you call me that, Makay?"

Makay made a scrunched-up face as he shrugged his shoulders and replied, "No idea really. I pretty much just say whatever pops into my head."

"Captain Harrison! Captain Harrison!" yelled out a peasant running toward them.

Harrison turned to the peasant and asked, "Good man, you need to get back to upper Sternz, this is no place for you."

The man looked around and said, "I have an urgent message for you sent by Queen Alezzia."

Zafrinia and Liam walked close to Harrison so they could hear the message. Harrison nodded his head and the peasant continued, "From the towers of the Citadel, she has a better view of the battle and I can confirm her message from what I saw as I made my way here."

Zafrinia, annoyed, shouted, "Well are you going to spit it out or am I going to have to force it out of you?"

Harrison raised a warning finger to Zafrinia and bade the peasant to continue. "Queen Alezzia fears that King Dylenn and General Izak have been fooled. The larger dust trail is a ruse. The main elven force is forming at the center. Queen Alezzia surmised that the elves assumed we would know Imperator Leontina favors a heavy attack to the right flank and set the trap to draw our force away from the real attack, at the center."

Liam whispered, "Kassandra…"

Harrison asked the peasant, "What about here? How big was the dust trail leading to this breach?"

The peasant shook his head side to side and said, "Queen Alezzia said that the trail leading here turned and moved toward the center breach."

Liam turned to Harrison. "This breach must be a decoy. We need to go and aid the center breach!"

Zafrinia butt in and said, "Or it could be another trick. If we leave and the elves attack here they can surround us and defeat us."

Liam ignored Zafrinia as Harrison stood silent, unsure of which course of action to take.

41

Alezzia stood on her balcony dressed in her elegant purple dress, her gaze shifting from breach to breach. Even from her balcony on the top of the hill she could hear the sounds of war, the screams of the dying, the clashing of steel against steel as sword and shields smash into each other. Jaclyn walked onto the balcony and said, "Queen Alezzia, the food and water supplies are ready. You and the princesses should go, before it is too late."

Alezzia remained facing toward the inner wall. "How can I leave when one of my daughters is down there fighting for the rest of us?"

"You know that I will follow any command you give. I would give my life for you and your family, but I must insist that you go now. The men and women down there will fight to their last breath but look at the center breach. It is being taken as we speak," Jaclyn urged.

A knock came at the door and Benjamin entered, dressed in freshly cleaned black robes. Alezzia seemed relieved to see him, "Come in Benjamin. Jaclyn if you would give us a moment of privacy. I will give you my decision soon." Jaclyn hesitated only for a second before giving Benjamin a slight bow and then walked out of the room.

Benjamin walked out onto the balcony beside Alezzia and asked, "How does it look?"

"Not good," replied Alezzia. "The elves just barraged the center breach with their trebuchets and now it is quickly falling."

Benjamin surveyed the breaches and asked, "Do you know where your husband and daughter are?"

Alezzia silently shook her head side to side. Benjamin laughed and said, "Well we can probably guess that they are either at the center or the right. They tend to get in a lot of trouble no matter what they do."

Alezzia continued to look at the conflicts at the inner wall as she said, "Should we go down there and get Kaia?"

Benjamin's eyebrow rose. "You want to go down there and fight?"

"Not unless I have to," she replied.

Benjamin rested his hand on her shoulder, "You know that nothing good would come of that. Kaia can take care of herself and I am sure the soldiers down there would die to keep her safe."

"And what happens when there are no more soldiers left?" asked Alezzia.

"We will get to that if it happens."

"Mama? Mama where are you?" cried Alyssa from the hallway.

Alezzia turned away from the balcony and responded, "I am in here sweetie."

Alyssa ran into the room, jumped into her mother's arms, and squeezed at tight as she could. "Mama, are Papa and Kaia going to be OK?"

Alezzia gently rubbed the back of Alyssa's head and said, "They will be fine my dear. Despite my best efforts, they continue to get into trouble, but they always come back."

Alyssa leaned back and looked her mother in the face. "Bethany said that we are going to leave home soon. Please don't let us leave without Papa and Kaia."

Alezzia smiled at Alyssa and said, "We will wait as long as we can."

Then Benjamin stepped forward and tried to distract the child. "How is your arm today, Alyssa?"

Alyssa turned to Benjamin and showed him her arm, "It's all better, see."

Benjamin smiled as he unwrapped her bandage. All that remained of the assassins' attack were two small scabs where the fangs connected. "You don't need this bandage anymore. You are OK to be your normal, happy self again."

Alezzia put Alyssa back down on the ground and said, "Go find your sister and Jaclyn and tell them that we are staying. Our place is here, where we belong."

42

"Konar! Watch your left!" shouted Vernon.

Konar pivoted to his left and bashed the head of an elf with the hilt of his hammer. He brought the head of the hammer down on another elf while shouting back, "Vernon my friend, this isn't looking too good! We need to regain control and return to the top of the rubble."

Vernon blocked an attack with his shield, then stabbed the elf in the stomach. Vernon looked behind him to check on Kaia who looked drained. Vernon killed another elf and spotted General Izak motioning for Vernon to come to him. Vernon turned to the orc and yelled, "Konar with me!"

Konar head-butted an elf to the ground and shoved his way to Vernon. They grabbed Kaia and made their way to Izak who was standing with Dylenn. The Vicar's Chosen guarded the king, shooting bolt after bolt from their crossbows with deadly effect. Izak and Dylenn, like Vernon and Konar, were covered in blood. Vernon asked, "What is the situation sir?"

Izak replied, "We are barely holding them here but we soon will be overrun. Peasants have been our messengers and they have brought news of the other breaches."

Out of the corner of his eye Konar spotted an elf running toward them. Konar dropped his hammer, and as the elf reached striking distance, reached out and grabbed her by the throat. He crushed her windpipe, then tossed her away and continued in the conversation. "We need to do something fast! Can either of the other breaches send aid?"

Dylenn replied, "Unfortunately no. The breach on the left hasn't had any fighting at all but Captain Harrison feels that it might be another trick."

"Another trick? What was the first trick?" asked Kaia.

Izak responded, "Imperator Leontina must have anticipated that we would assume that she would send the majority of her attack here to the right. When instead it is being focused on the center. It can't hold it much longer; ten minutes at most."

One of the Vicar's Chosen shot his crossbow and then turned and reported in that same emotionless monotone, "King Dylenn, we have used the last of our bolts."

Dylenn nodded. "Well, if I am to die today then I am glad that I will surrounded by friends and family. Let us stand our ground here and now!"

Dylenn let out a battle cry and led them back into the thick of the fighting. The Vicar's Chosen stayed close to Dylenn and intercepted any elves who tried to kill the king, fighting with swords, daggers, and hand to hand. Izak also stayed close to Dylenn and together they both wielded their two-handed swords with deadly purpose, rallying the soldiers around them. Vernon, Konar, and Kaia fought their way closer to the bottom of the rubble.

Six Elven soldiers rushed at Kaia but she shot fire out of both hands and engulfed them in flames. Using so much magic was taking its toll on her, physically, and she leaned over to rest. As Konar finished off two elves he saw another running toward Kaia from behind her. He grabbed his hammer with both hands at the very edge of the hilt and started to spin in a circle. After two complete rotations he released the hammer and sent it hurling through air toward the elf. The hammer smashed against the side of the elf, its momentum flinging him backward several feet away. Kaia stood back up and nodded at Konar. An elf ran down the rubble at Konar screaming like a banshee. The elf swung her sword at Konar, but once again Konar grabbed the elf's wrist and stopped the attack. He held the helpless elf at arm's length while he pulled out his hatchet and buried the blade deep into her skull.

Vernon hurried over to Kaia to help protect her. He blocked attack after attack as the elves become more numerous, and more and more humans fell dead on the battlefield. The pile of rubble could no longer be seen. Dead bodies of humans and elves covered every inch of it.

Vernon looked at Kaia and saw blood running down her face. Kaia saw the panicked look on his face and she reached up to touch her cheek. "My stitches have opened. Nothing serious. Don't worry about me."

Vernon regained his composure just in time to block an elf from stabbing him. Kaia launched a fireball at the elf and hit him in the face. He writhed on the ground, clawing the burning flesh from his skull. Vernon pulled Kaia to her feet. "Go now! We won't last much longer. You have to get your father and escape."

Kaia shot two more balls of flame before replying, "I will not abandon my people, I will not abandon my father, and I will not abandon you—because you have never abandoned me."

At the center breach the human defenders were rapidly being overrun. Kassandra and the rest of the infantry were trying their best to keep the elves from getting to the archers. The archer support was helping but not enough.

Two elves approached Kassandra as she simultaneously threw both her daggers at them. Both daggers struck home. Kassandra picked up a sword to engage another elf. She deflected a thrust, then swirled around and slashed him in the back.

Before she could recover, an elf with a mace swung at her with an uppercut. Kassandra jumped backwards to avoid the blow, but landed on her back. As the elf moved closer to strike down on her,

Kassandra grabbed the body of a dead soldier beside her and pulled it over her. The corpse took the blunt force of the elf's attack, and Kassandra then wrapped her legs around the legs of the elf and pulled him to the ground. The elf landed on his stomach on the tip of a broken spear, impaling him.

Kassandra stood up and caught her breath before moving to retrieve her daggers. She grabbed them just in time to pivot and avoid an attacker and buried a dagger into the side of the elf's face.

She found herself surrounded by a group of six elves. As they moved in to attack, Kassandra spun to her right and extended her leg, sweeping the legs of the nearest elf and sending her crashing to the ground. Then she stabbed the stunned elf in the throat. An Elven spear whirled through the air toward Kassandra but she rolled backward out of the way. She immediately planted her feet and lunged toward the elf and stabbed her in the chest with both daggers. She yanked her daggers free and turned just in time to duck under the attack of the third elf. She bounced back up and slashed, slitting the throat of the elf while throwing her other dagger into the elf running at her from the left. Kassandra didn't see the elf to her right that was carrying a mace scavenged from a dead Paladin. With a loud thud the elf hit Kassandra on the back of the head.

When Kassandra opened her eyes, she was face down flat on the ground. Her ears were ringing and her vision was blurred. She rolled over on her back and could hear muffled laughter above her. She regained focus in her eyes and saw an elf with a mace and another with a spear standing above her. She looked to her right and then left in search of anything she might use as a weapon but saw nothing. The elf with the spear stood over Kassandra. He raised the spear high and brought it down fast. Kassandra closed her eyes and felt blood splatter on her face followed by the clashing of steel.

Kassandra opened her eyes to see the elf holding his throat as blood poured out, and Liam fighting two elves in front of her. Blaster was tearing out the throat of the elf with the mace. Liam slit the throats of the two elves simultaneously with one perfectly timed powerful swing of his left arm. He let out a massive roar, then he reached down, picked up Kassandra's daggers and knelt beside her. Kassandra took the daggers and put them back in their sheaths. She reached up her hand and laid it against Liam's face and asked, "What are you doing here? Shouldn't you be at the breach on the left?"

Liam helped Kassandra to her feet, "There was no sign of the elves attacking at that breach. I think it was a decoy."

Kassandra looked back to where the archers were and saw her bow. She walked toward it with Liam behind her. She picked up her bow and asked, "Well then where are the rest of the soldiers that were there?"

Liam remained silent for several seconds and then Kassandra asked, "Please don't tell me you and Blaster are the only ones who came."

Liam forced a half smile and said, "They thought it could be a trap, but I didn't care if it was or not."

Kassandra looked Liam directly in the eyes and said, "You must have known how bad things were here and that if you came, you might not survive."

A genuine smile crept over Liam's face as he said, "You, Konar, and Vernon are the closest thing to a family that Blaster and I have ever had. And I'll be damned if I let Domatin and those elves take this away from me without a fight."

Liam smiled and declared, "I'll always have your back. Now and Forever."

Kassandra smiled and hugged him. "If this is our time, then so be it. You go and kill as many of them as you can and I will cover you. Don't worry about defending yourself, just kill as many as you can."

Liam nodded and ran toward the breach in the wall. Very few of the infantry were left as Liam ran into the conflict with his swords in his hands and Blaster beside him.

Kassandra reached for a quiver of arrows beside her and wrapped it around her shoulder as she readied herself to cover Liam. Liam took several deep breaths before letting out another loud powerful roar and then ran into the fighting. He slashed left and right as he picked off elves on his way to the rubble. Blaster stayed right beside him and finished off any elf that got knocked to the ground. Liam reached the bottom of the rubble and killed elf after elf as they tried to get past him.

Kassandra aimed her bow and released the arrow into the neck of an elf trying to get behind Liam. Kassandra immediately drew another arrow and shot an elf under the armpit. Kassandra released arrow after arrow covering Liam, refusing to allow any of them to flank him or attack him from behind.

Countless elves fell dead to the ground but the losses of the humans at the center breach grew as well. Kassandra reached for another arrow but discovered none remained. She franticly looked around but all the archers around her were using the last of their arrows as well. Kassandra then looked to find Liam and yelled to him, "Liam! I'm out of arrows!"

Liam turned and looked at Kassandra. The slight distraction gave enough time for an elven soldier to run down the rubble and slash deep into Liam's right arm. Liam cried out in pain before elbowing the elf in the nose followed by a downward strike to the elf's face. Blaster came to Liam's side and pounced on another elf trying to attack Liam.

Kassandra dropped her bow and pulled out her daggers. She turned to all the archers behind her and yelled, "Now is our time! Charge!"

The archers dropped their useless bows, grabbed whatever weapons they could find, and they rushed the breach to give aid. Kassandra fought her way to the bottom of the rubble where Liam had just finished killing an elf. Kassandra asked, "How bad is your arm?"

Liam thrust both his swords into an elf's chest as he replied, "Good enough to kill elves."

Liam, Kassandra, and Blaster continued to fight side by side until only a few dozen human defenders were left at the center of the breach. Elves were already starting to get past them and head to the other two breaches in the wall to finish the siege once and for all. The human defenders at the center breach were surrounded and Liam and Kassandra gave each other one last look. They both let out a roar, but before they could make their final move, an Elven distress arrow screamed high through the air over the battleground, followed by two more screeching arrows in rapid succession. The fighting stopped as both the humans and elves were wondering what was happening.

A Praetorian appeared at the top of the rubble and called out to the elves in the city, "Fall back! Fall back to the encampment immediately. Reform! Reform!"

Confused, the elven warriors nonetheless obeyed the strange order, abandoning the city and ignoring its human defenders. Liam and Kassandra walked to the top of the rubble, curious to find out what could have caused the reversal. At first they could see nothing. Then, past the elven encampment, they saw white banners with gold eagles in the center cresting the ridge.

Liam raised his blood covered fist in the air and shouted in relief at the sight of thousands of Paladins swarming over the hill. For once Kassandra was speechless, tears of relief pouring down her face. Soon as word spread across the city, the relieved shouts could be heard from each of the three breaches as the massive army of Paladins stood on the hill.

Dylenn limped his way up the hill with help from Izak and as he beheld the sight of salvation, tears began to swell in his eyes. He looked to the sky and he quietly prayed, "Thanks be to the One."

Kaia and Vernon were standing beside each other at the top of the rubble holding hands. After several seconds of silence, Vernon turned to Kaia, gently took her face in his hands and kissed her. Before Kaia had a chance to respond, they were interrupted by the distant chant from tens of thousands of Paladins yelling out, "Death to Pagans!"

They looked back to the ridge to see the Paladins charging at the Elven army. The elves tried to form into a defensive line but it was too late. The heavily armored Paladins slammed past the elves in their way. From the broken walls of Sternz, it was clear that the Paladins were obliterating the weary elves.

Dylenn made his way across the rubble to where Kaia stood and as soon as Kaia saw him she rushed over and hugged him. They held each other in silence for several seconds before Kaia said, "The Vicar didn't abandon us after all."

Dylenn smiled at her before turning to Izak, "I would like to speak with Ethan."

Izak nodded his head in agreement and said, "As do I. But first I think it is time we go say hello to the Vicar." Dylenn looked back out toward the fighting and watched the Paladins dealing with the last remnants of the once mighty elven army. Dylenn and Izak wrapped their arms around each other's shoulders and began to walk down the rubble toward the fighting to find and thank the Vicar.

Konar smiled at Vernon and said, "Is it too early in the morning for me to be wanting a drink?"

"After this morning I think everyone could use a drink," Vernon replied.

Konar started walking down the rubble to retrieve his hammer, and said, "Perhaps we should check on Kassandra first."

Vernon turned back to Kaia and asked her if she would like to join them.

Kaia smiled and replied, "I will catch up with you later. I think I should go with my father and make sure he is OK."

Vernon nodded as Kaia walked down the other side of the rubble to join her father and Izak.

At the center breach, Konar and Vernon surveyed the carnage around them. Vernon said, "They really did bear the brunt of it here. I hope Kassandra made it out OK."

They made their way through the corpses and rubble until at

last they saw Liam and Blaster sitting on the rubble in the middle of the breach with Kassandra standing beside them.

"Liam, why are you here?" asked Konar. "Weren't you assigned—"

Liam cut him off. "I got bored. So I came here to help."

Kassandra added, "Just in time too. Although you do need to get your arm and ribs looked at by a doctor."

Liam eyebrows rose. "My ribs?"

Kassandra poked his ribs and he flinched. "Oh yeah. My ribs. No, I'll be fine. I don't like doctors. Besides, I've always taken care of myself."

Kassandra let out a quick puff of air and crossed her arms beneath her breast in a sure sign of annoyance, "Only because you don't trust anyone."

"I trust you."

Kassandra smiled at Liam, then sweetly said, "Stay right here. I'm going to bring a doctor."

Kassandra disappeared on her quest, and Vernon told Liam, "I'm glad you two are OK. From the reports we received it sounded like the center was going to be completely annihilated."

Konar looked around at all the carnage and said, "And by the look of all the bodies I'd say that guess wasn't far off."

Kassandra returned with a needle and some thread in her hands. "Your going to want to bite down on something. This might sting a bit," she said. Blaster yawned and laid his head on Liam's foot.

As Kassandra started stitching, Vernon said, "Konar and I are going to go meet up with King Dylenn and greet the Vicar. Are you three going to join us?"

Kassandra replied, "You go ahead. We'll catch up."

As Konar and Vernon walked away, they heard Kassandra warn Liam, "I only know the basics, so this may hurt more than normal."

43

Kaia caught up with her limping father and Izak as they walked toward a small group of Paladins. Kaia noticed a trail of blood from Dylenn's leg. She slipped her hand into her father's hand and they continued walking together.

Dylenn turned to her and said, "I'm very proud of you Kaia. You proved not just to me but to everyone in Crixaria that you are no longer a little girl, but a strong, beautiful young woman."

Unable to reply to her father's kind words, she gripped his hand tighter and closed her eyes in a vain attempt to keep the tears from flowing.

Izak interrupted. "The Vicar is approaching."

The Vicar was surrounded by four of the Chosen, and armored the same as the Paladins. Instead of their full helmet the Vicar worn a simple white cloth miter.

Dylenn tried to stand up straight, but struggled to maintain a stable footing. The freshly-shaved Vicar called out, "King Dylenn do not worry about formalities. You and everyone in Sternz have been through quite the ordeal these past few days."

Dylenn graciously nodded his head and again put his right arm around Izak for support.

The Vicar continued, "First and foremost I sincerely apologize for being two days late. There was that issue with the horses and then a band of elves that set upon us yesterday."

Izak responded, "We had sent a scout and he came upon the aftermath of the battle. The scout said that besides the bodies he only saw a trail leading back west toward the coast."

"General Izak is it?" asked the Vicar, "Well your scout was not wrong in his report. An elven force of around 50,000 did attack us, but they badly underestimated us. We soundly defeated them. After the battle, I suggested that we fake a retreat and then swing around south and back up to get behind the elves, take them by surprise if we could."

Vernon and Konar approached the group from the open grassland. The Vicar saw them at a distance, but didn't pay them much attention until a second look revealed an orc. "King Dylenn, was that orc loyal to you the entire battle? I thought orcs were all treasonous beasts."

Dylenn beckoned Konar and Vernon to him. He said, "Vicar Matthew, may I introduce you to Konar Qal. I trust him more than most humans. I would trust him to watch over my daughters. He is, after all Unbroken."

"What exactly is an Unbroken?" the Vicar questioned.

Dylenn looked from Konar to Vernon. "The man beside Konar is Vernon Regnier. He is the leader of what all of us in Sternz are calling The Unbroken." Dylenn then spotted Liam, Kassandra, and Blaster approaching in the distance. He pointed to them and said, "Those three in the distance are the rest of the Unbroken. Kassandra Verbeck, Liam, and his wolf Blaster. Time and time again they rose to defend this city."

Vicar Matthew nodded his head toward Vernon and Konar while saying, "Then I commend your valor."

As Liam, Kassandra, and Blaster joined the group, three Paladins walked up behind the Vicar's group dragging an elf behind them with her hands tied together by rope. The Paladin spoke to the Vicar, "Your holiness, this is General Leontina. She was the commanding officer. We have captured her and perhaps 20,000 elves as our prisoners. What would you have us do with them?"

Vicar Matthew turned to Leontina and looked at her for several seconds before turning to King Dylenn. "It is your city and people that have been under attack. This decision is yours."

King Dylenn nodded his head, then studied a disheartened defeated Leontina. He said, "Send them back to their Elven lands."

Izak protested, "Are you sure? The elves have never given back our prisoners, they always execute them or force them into slavery."

"We are not elves, Izak. Perhaps showing them mercy now, one day they will return the favor."

Liam looked at Leontina and demanded, "Where is Domatin?"

Leontina's head flinched as her jaw tightened as she replied, "He left before the battle. I didn't know it at the time but he received news that the Vicar was approaching. That coward ran off without informing me." Liam took a long deep breath as his hands turned to fists and began to shake.

Izak asked Leontina, "What about the prisoners you took when the outer wall fell? Are they alive?"

Leontina looked back toward the remnants of the elven encampment and replied, "Five days ago we had 10,000 prisoners from your troops. Before the walls fell there were about 6,000, and now I would guess about 5,000."

"Why so few?"

Leontina shied away from looking anyone in the eyes as she answered, "Domatin worked them night and day and then probably around a thousand were crushed or trapped in the tunnels when the walls fell."

Dylenn looked back at The Unbroken and said, "Could some of you go and retrieve the elven prisoners inside the city? I fear if I send anyone else those elves might not make it out alive."

Liam quickly replied, "I will go."

Konar added, "So will I."

"Then it is settled!" exclaimed Vicar Matthew. "They will go fetch the elves. In the meantime, I would like to hear about the events of the past few days."

Liam, Konar, and Blaster headed toward the city while Dylenn and the others recounted of the siege to the Vicar.

As Dylenn told the tale, weary Crixarian soldiers began to stumble toward them from the elven encampment, thousands of exhausted, half-starved soldiers walking toward Sternz. Many of them were being carried by the men and women beside them. Through the mass of soldiers, Kaia spotted someone she recognized.

"Captain Tori!" shouted Kaia in surprise and excitement.

Dylenn looked over at Kaia and asked, "You know her?"

Kaia released her father's hand as she replied, "I thought she was dead. When the outer wall fell, she led her soldiers into battle against a larger Elven force to buy time for me to escape."

Kaia ran to Captain Tori hugged her and then helped her back to the city.

Gregory joined the group, much to Vernon's surprise. "I thought you were dead."

Gregory gave him a blank stare and asked, "What happened? The last thing I remember was leading the charge. After that—nothing."

"After you ran out, we learned there were two other breaches. King Dylenn ordered the charge to stop and we separated to deal with the three breaches."

Gregory stared daggers at King Dylenn. "That's twice the Allister's abandoned their troops during this siege. I promise you it will not happen again." Gregory turned to Vernon and said, "I thought you said you would always have my back?"

Vernon put his hand on Gregory's shoulder but before he could say anything, Gregory shrugged it off and walked away toward Sternz. Vernon stood silent for a moment and watched his friend leave.

Liam and Konar reached the top of the rubble and looked at the hundreds of dead bodies being carried away by fellow soldiers. Konar asked Liam, "How bad was the situation here when you arrived?"

"When I got here Kassandra was on her back with two elves standing over her. The elves were overwhelming everyone left and right. I'm honestly surprised we were able to hold out as long as we did."

As they began to walk through the burnt streets of lower Sternz, Konar gave Liam a playful shove and said, "So, did you kiss her after you saved her?"

"No, nothing like that."

"You know that was the perfect time, right?"

Liam raised an eyebrow. "Well excuse me for being more concerned with the hundreds of elves rushing into the city."

Konar patted Liam on the back and said, "I was only joking. Sort of."

They continued through the streets and finally reached a small stone building with four columns in the front. Liam and Konar spotted Ducan and Abby still guarding the door to the prisoners. Abby turned to them and grouched, "You two look awful. Have you thought about taking a bath?"

Konar forced a smile and replied, "Better covered in blood after a hard battle than to be stuck babysitting because I wasn't a good enough fighter to even be considered for combat."

Abby took an aggressive step forward before Ducan stopped her. Ducan turned to Liam and asked, "What is your business here?"

"The King has ordered that the Elven prisoners are to be released without harm. Konar and I are here to make sure that they make it out of the city in one piece," Liam replied.

Ducan opened the door and Abby said, "Good luck with that." Liam stepped inside the door. In the dark room he could barely see the outline of the prisoners and he realized all they could see was the silhouette of him. He cleared his throat and said, "The battle is over. King Dylenn has ordered that all of the prisoners are to be released and are free to return to elven lands. We are here to escort you safely out of the city."

The elves remained in the shadows. Several whispered, "It's a trap," and "they are just going to kill us." Until one elf stood up and walked forward. It was Tauriel, still wrapped in the black fur coat. She walked to Liam and then turned back to her fellow elves and said, "Liam is trustworthy. I will go with him."

Slowly the rest of the elves began to stand up and make their way to the door, squinting at the sudden brightness of the morning sun. Konar noticed the hateful looks the elves were getting from the soldiers they passed. He reached for his hammer and whispered to Liam, "We may have trouble."

Liam readied his swords. "We've had trouble before."

They passed through all of upper Sternz without a problem until they spotted Zafrinia standing at the bridge into Lower Sternz, with 40 Tarium volunteers behind her blocking their way.

Zafrinia challenged them. "Where exactly do you think you are going with those pagans?"

"They are to be released," replied Konar.

Zafrinia shook her head and said, "I don't think so." She grabbed her spear with both hands and pointed the wing shaped tip toward Liam and Konar. The rest of the soldiers behind her drew their weapons and stared at the elves.

As Blaster lowered his body and growled, Konar said to Zafrinia, "Oh, I have waited for this for a long time. I hope Sal is watching."

A voice from behind Zafrinia's troops shouted, "Hold!"

Everyone turned to see Harrison leading a group of 20 Paladins toward them. As Harrison shoved his way through the volunteers, he asked Zafrinia, "What is the meaning of this?"

Zafrinia pointed her spear toward the elves and said, "They are being released? I can't just let them walk out of the city."

Harrison turned to Liam and Konar and asked, "By whose order are the elves to be set free?"

"King Dylenn Allister," Konar replied.

Harrison turned back to Zafrinia and through gritted teeth said, "You fool. You really want to try to start a war with our fellow humans after we just beat the elves as one?" Harrison shouted, "Paladins! Form up around the elven prisoners. We will help escort them safely out of the city."

The Paladins forced their way through the volunteers and took up positions around the elves. Harrison walked past Zafrinia, she said, "You are not in control of me. No one is."

Harrison turned and fixed her with a look of sheer pity. "I know. And that is why you are not a Paladin."

Surrounded by Liam, Konar, Harrison and the Paladins, the Elven prisoners continued on their way without any other altercations. Once beyond the city walls Harrison stopped and said, "I think you will be fine from here. We must stay and help take care of the wounded and give honor to the dead."

Liam and Konar led the elven prisoners to where the King and the Vicar were still outside the city. When they arrived, Leontina saw Tauriel and tried to walk toward her, but her Paladin guard held her fast. Vicar Matthew said, "They have been through much. Allow them a moment."

When the Paladins released her, she ran to Tauriel and with her hands tied, Leontina lifted her arms up and over Tauriel and they embraced.

Leontina whispered, "I had feared the worst."

Tauriel replied, "I am fine, thanks to Liam."

Leontina, too surprised for words, looked at Liam as she lifted her arms back up and over Tauriel. Liam nodded his head and then Leontina turned around to the Vicar and King Dylenn and asked, "Is there anything more you would have of me?"

Dylenn limped toward Leontina with a dagger in his hand and cut the rope that bound her wrists. "You are free to go."

Leontina bowed and said, "Thank you, King Dylenn." She took her place at the head of the group of elves, led them away from Sternz.

Vicar Matthew clapped his hands together once and said, "Now then, I want all of you to go get cleaned up and rested. For tonight all of Sternz will celebrate with a feast unlike any other."

44

The city of Sternz was alive in the night air as everyone from soldier to civilian, from Tarian to Crixarian enjoyed feasting and drinking. Minstrels played their music in the streets as everyone rejoiced in the victory. The throne room overflowed with excited energy and feasting and drinking. The royal table extended directly below the two thrones, and along each of the rows of pillars, to the wall by the entry way. A purple linen cloth trimmed in gold covered every table and held trays laden with meats, fruits, vegetables, breads and sweets.

At the center of the royal table, King Dylenn sat in his chair. Alezzia sat at his right enjoying a glass of fine wine. Bethany sat on the other side of Alezzia and then Jaclyn and Benjamin. To Dylenn's left sat Kaia, Alyssa, Izak, and on the end Vicar Matthew. Everyone was dressed in their finest clothing.

Over the loud conversations from across the room, two people's laughter outweighed everyone else. Dylenn looked over at Vicar Matthew at the end of the table where he and Konar were both laughing hysterically. Vicar Matthew gathered himself before saying, "You know, for an orc you're not so bad!"

Konar slapped the Vicar on his shoulder and replied, "And for a magisterial priest you're not so bad yourself."

Dylenn looked beside Konar to see Vernon with his hand on his face shaking his head at Konar. Beside Vernon, Liam was discreetly trying to keep Blaster from jumping onto the table. Liam whispered, "I've already sneaked you four chicken legs. Now please be calm." Kassandra sat beside Liam giggling. Dylenn smiled at them all.

Vicar Matthew stood up and cleared his throat to draw everyone's attention. As the room quieted, he addressed the gathered crowd.

"Upon being told about the past few days, one word has stuck out every time someone talks about them—Unbroken. The Unbroken showed you good people how to come together despite being drastically different. From Crixaria to Vetin and even the Eacru Wastes, many different cultures have been united and I do not wish for Tarium to be left out."

Kassandra then leaned over and whispered to Liam, "If the Vicar thinks that he can force Zafrinia in, I don't think that will go over very well with Konar."

The Vicar continued, "With that being said I have commissioned that custom armor is to be made for each of you. The finest armorer in all of Tarium will arrive next week and work with each of you to make the best armor possible to suit your needs."

The throne room echoed with clapping as Vernon looked over to Vicar Matthew and said, "Thank you, your holiness."

Vicar Matthew smiled, "It's the least I could do."

Dylenn continued his gaze around the room. From Makay and Ducan, to Zafrinia and Harrison, everyone was enjoying themselves. Dylenn took a quick sip of wine from his silver goblet and stood up.

"My friends, I would be lying to you if I said that these past few days were enjoyable. We have all lost people we know, friends, and family members. But I know that in the future we will look back on these past few days as a time that we not only defeated the elves, but came together as one. Yes, we have all lost people but we also gained new friendships, new *families*, that will last a lifetime. I want to thank all of you for your brave actions in defending not just Sternz, but my family. You all have my undying gratitude."

Vicar Matthew stood up and proclaimed, "As you have all of ours."

"Here here!" yelled several Crixarian officers.

The Vicar continued, "Drink up everyone. Be merry and joyful tonight."

Dylenn sat back down and noticed Alezzia. "I haven't seen you smile like that in a long time."

Alezzia reached over and placed her hand on top of Dylenn's, "Today is a day that will be celebrated for generations to come. Our daughters are safe and a better world is just on the horizon."

Dylenn, unable to lean over and kiss Alezzia due to the distance, gently kissed her hand before turning to Kaia. Dylenn caught Kaia and Vernon exchanging a steady gaze at each other. Dylenn nudged Kaia and with a blush on her face, she said, "You know you can make things quite awkward sometimes?"

"That's what fathers are for," Dylenn replied.

Dylenn then looked over at Vernon and said to Kaia, "Vernon is a fine young man and as long as he will take care of you and make you happy you both have my blessing, although I doubt it matters."

Kaia smiled at her father and replied, "Of course it matters."

Dylenn laughed, "Now if only we could get your sister to hurry up and get married." Kaia and Dylenn share a laugh but were soon interrupted as an argument between a Crixarian officer and a Paladin drowned out everyone else in the room.

The Crixarian officer jolted out of his chair as he slammed his fist on the table and yelled, "That is bullshit!"

A hush fell over the room. Izak stood up and demanded, "What is this about?"

The Crixarian officer turned to Izak and replied, "That Paladin said that the best of Tarium could beat the best of Crixaria in a fight any day, but I say he is wrong."

As Izak was about to reply, the Vicar interrupted, "Now that is something I would like to see! King Dylenn, if it isn't out of place could we perhaps have an exhibition?"

Dylenn looked around the room at all the faces and could tell that both sides wish to see who is right. Dylenn nodded his head and said, "I don't see why not?"

Cheers from the room echoed as Dylenn continued, "Izak, pick a fighter from Crixaria and I will let Vicar Matthew pick his fighter."

Vicar Matthew called to Captain Harrison, "Who is our best Paladin?"

Harrison answered, "If you want the best from Tarium, it won't be a Paladin. Zafrinia may be rash, but she could beat any of my men any day of the week."

Vicar Matthew looked at Zafrinia sitting beside Harrison and said, "Zafrinia, step forward."

As Zafrinia hopped out of her chair with a grin, the Tarium side of the room yelled as they beat their cups on the table. Zafrinia reached down and grabbed her spear and walked between the two tables and stood waiting for her opponent.

Izak turned to Vernon and said, "You are the leader of our best. Who shall face her?"

Vernon stood up and with a confident smile replied, "Liam is our best."

As the Crixarian table yelled and beat their cups faster than the Tarians did, Liam stood up and whispered to Vernon, "You know that I am not from Crixaria, right?"

Vernon replied, "You fought as one of us. That makes you one of us."

Liam nodded then grabbed his swords off the table and walked to meet Zafrinia. As both sides of the room cheered, Zafrinia tossed her spear from side to side and muttered to Liam, "Are you ready for everyone to see you fall?"

Liam forced a smile and replied, "Are you ready to finally learn some humility?"

They faced each other and readied their weapons. An excited hush fell over the room and Dylenn noticed that even the Vicar's Chosen were watching with interest. Dylenn said, "Combatants, remember: we are not barbarians. This contest is not to the death.

Please don't kill each other. The first to force the other to the ground or to disarm the other will be declared the victor." Then he raised his right arm ready to start the contest.

The main doors to the throne room burst open before Dylenn could give the command to begin. Everyone's attention shifted from Liam and Zafrinia to the door where Gregory was entering the room.

"I apologize for the interruption my King, but there is a messenger to see you," Gregory announced.

Dylenn motioned for the messenger to be brought forth and Gregory turned around and whistled out the door. A few seconds later a group of ten Crixarian soldiers escorted an elven mage and two Praetorians, each carrying a small wooden tapped barrel into the throne room.

Many of the officers stood up and readied their weapons but Dylenn said, "Let us hear what they have to say before any rash decisions are made."

The ten Crixarian soldiers stopped at the doorway as the mage and two Praetorians walked across the silent room. Zafrinia and Liam both stepped back to allow the elves to stand before King Dylenn. The Elven mage stopped several feet away from the table and bowed to Dylenn. Dylenn stood up straight. "What is it that you need to discuss with me?"

"I am the selected ambassador of Empress Juliana Ophidian of the Ophidian Dynasty. The Empress as well as the high council of mages has taken note of how far humanity is willing to go to protect one of their own. The high council and Empress Juliana have stated that if Kaia is willing to learn how to control her magic under the tutelage of myself, then we may have peace," the mage replied.

Soft whispers spread across the room. Izak then called out to the mage, "The war with the dwarves must be getting desperate for you elves to agree to ignore someone that challenges your religion."

Captain Harrison then challenged the elves as well, "And for you to be presenting this offer this soon after your loss, your Empress must have sent you in advance to only appear if you lost."

Dylenn raised both hands in the air and motioned for everyone to quiet down. Then he looked around the room from Alezzia to the faces of both Tarians and Crixarians, finally resting his eyes on Kaia. Dylenn smiled as he faced the mage and said, "For 15 long years we have been at war. My youngest daughter Alyssa has never known peace. I think now is a good time for her to find out what that is like." Clapping and excited yells rose to the roof all around the room. Even the Paladins appeared excited at the prospect of peace.

Alezzia wiped her mouth with her dinner cloth and walked over to Dylenn and kissed him on the lips. A surprised Dylenn asked, "What was that for?"

Alezzia smiled and said, "It was for love."

The Elven mage continued, "If it pleases you, we have brought Azara wine, aged for 400 years, in celebration for peace." The mage motioned for the Praetorian on the right to come forward. The Praetorian walked up to Dylenn and Dylenn moved his goblet under the tap. The Praetorian opened the tap and wine flowed into Dylenn's goblet. The Praetorian bowed and stepped back away from the table.

As Dylenn raised his goblet, Izak stood up and protested, "My King it could be poison. Allow me to drink it first so we will know."

Dylenn, still standing with Alezzia beside him, raised his goblet and shouted, "If there truly is to be peace we must start to trust one another." He raised his goblet in the air for a toast, "To peace!" and then drank the wine.

Again celebratory cheers echoed throughout the room. Alezzia returned to her chair as Dylenn sat back down in his. The mage motioned for both Praetorians to take the wine barrels to the royal table. "We brought enough for everyone to enjoy. Just outside the city there are several more barrels."

"Excellent," replied Dylenn. "It is delicious." Then the smile disappeared from his face and he leaned forward and grabbed his stomach. He coughed several times and blood started pouring out of his mouth.

Izak saw this and shouted, "The wine is poisoned!" as he slapped Kaia's goblet away just before she took a drink. Alezzia rushed to Dylenn who was now lying on the floor coughing up more blood.

Liam looked away from Dylenn to see the Elven mage raise his hands. Liam quickly dashed forward and with a mighty downward swing of his swords, he cut off both of the mage's hands. As the mage stood trembling and staring at his missing hands, Liam and Zafrinia engaged the Praetorian on their side. With wine spilled all over the floor Zafrinia and Liam quickly defeated the Praetorians and turned around to see the royal family huddled over Dylenn joined by Vicar Matthew, Izak, Jaclyn, and Benjamin.

One of the Vicar's Chosen used his crossbow to shoot a bolt into the head of the mage. Harrison yelled at him, "You fool! Now we can't question him!"

The room grew silent except for the crying of Bethany, Kaia, and Alyssa, who were kneeling by Dylenn. Small tears fell from Alyssa's face as she asked, "What's wrong Papa? Why are you coughing like that?"

Dylenn reached up and gently touched Alyssa's face, "I love you my little princess."

"Papa?" Alyssa said confused and scared.

Alezzia turned to a teary-eyed Jaclyn and quietly said, "Please take Alyssa to her room."

Jaclyn nodded and walked with Alyssa out of the room. Alyssa's cries grew louder and louder, "Papa! Papa! Let me stay with Papa!"

As tears rolled down her face, Alezzia sat on the floor and put Dylenn's head on her lap.

Bethany sobbed while Kaia laid her head on Dylenn's slow breathing chest, "Please don't go Daddy. I need you."

Dylenn coughed up a little more blood as he looked from both Bethany to Kaia and in a voice that was barely audible, he said, "No father could be prouder of the young women you two have become."

As tears fell from Bethany's face she said, "Don't say stuff like that. You are going to be fine."

Dylenn looked above him into Alezzia's face and smiled as he said, "I love you so much. Try not to spoil the grandchildren too much one day."

Alezzia kissed the top of his head as the life escaped his body. Kaia and Bethany's cries grew louder as Alezzia gently closed Dylenn's eyes. She stood and looked around the room. Most of the Crixarians had tears in their eyes and even a few of the Tarians while the shocked expressions settled across their faces.

Alezzia turned to Benjamin who had moved to the broken boxes of wine on the floor. "What was it?" asked Alezzia.

Benjamin knelt and studied the liquid. He dipped a finger in it, sniffed it, touched it to his tongue and immediately spit it out. "Extract from the tulip of Colubra. Its pedals are so toxic that only after a few seconds after ingestion there is no hope. If I had to guess, their plan was to poison the royal table and then leave to go get the rest of the wine, which probably doesn't exist. They more than likely overdosed the wine, causing King Dylenn to die too soon before they could poison the rest of you."

Izak wiped the tears from his eyes. "My Queen, what are your orders?" As everyone stared at Alezzia, she took a deep breath. There was a cold fire behind her eyes.

"We will take back everything the elves have taken from us. All the way to the elven capitol of Azara and we will burn it to the ground. We go to war."

Acknowledgements

I want to thank Mike Parker and WordCrafts Press for publishing my story, for taking a chance on a new author, and giving me this opportunity.

Thank you to Reuben Lane for his amazing work on the book cover.

Thank you to Aaron Drexler for completing my World of Aclia with a fantastic map.

Thank you to Blake Blackburn for designing the best website an author could ask for.

And most of all, a heartfelt thank you to all my family, close friends, and test readers for supporting me and encouraging me to make this happen.

I thank you all.

About the Author

Luther Salyers has studied battle strategy from his childhood, and he was introduced to the fantasy genre while still in elementary school. His literary encounter with King Arthur and the Knights of the Round Table opened the door to whole new worlds of imagination and adventure.

With his knowledge of history and military strategy—combined with his love of fantastic stories—it was inevitable that Luther's debut series, *The Unbroken*, would be High Fantasy, paying homage to the masters of the genre, such as Tolkien, Lewis, Howard, and Jordan, while creating his own unique, dangerous, and often unpredictable world.

Luther lives in southern Kentucky. When he is not creating new worlds, he enjoys spending time with his playful dog Caesar.

Connect with Luther online at:

http://theunbrokenbooks.com